DELAYING DEATH

Kelley,

If you like novels with high-stakes action, steamy love scenes, and breathtaking prose, I recommend you find a different book. But if you do read this one, I hope you enjoy it!

Joshua Keil

Delaying Death © 2009 by Joshua Keil. All rights reserved. No part of this book may be used or reproduced in any manner whatsoever without written permission from the author except in the case of brief quotations embodied in critical articles and reviews.

This book is a work of fiction. While the political struggle for the EMS contract is based on real events, all other controversies and incidents are products of the author's imagination. All characters appearing in this work are fictitious. Any resemblance to real persons, living or dead, is purely coincidental.

ISBN: 1-44216-788-2

ISBN 13: 978-1-44216-788-9

Cover Photo by Geoff Johnson
Digital Photo Artist: Kate Heller (www.maloneandco.com)
Edited by Dennis Billuni (www.alphaediting.com)

Printed in the United States of America

To Stacie,
My favorite Nebraska co-ed.
Thank you for believing in me.
Thank you for supporting me.
Thank you for marrying me.

DELAYING DEATH

By
Joshua Keil

1.

"Captain O'Malley's daughter?" Carson said from behind the wheel of the speeding ambulance. "Are you sure he wasn't kidding, Eric?"

In the passenger seat, Carson's younger partner, Eric, flipped several switches. Strobe lights lit up the night, and the siren blared into the darkness. "That's what he said," Eric responded, then grabbed the armrest as they sped around a corner.

"Well, what does she look like?"

"I don't know, Carson. When your boss tells you that a girl is coming to work for the company, you don't just ask, 'Is she hot?'"

"*I* would have. And Hank probably would have told me, too."

"I know *you* would have, Carson. Everyone expects that, but I'm not you. We've established that fact many times."

"God!" Carson said, speeding through a red light. "I bet she is hot!"

"You're just fantasizing now. Judging by the looks of Captain O'Malley, I'm pretty sure she's not."

"But what if she is?" Carson said. "Think about it. She must be a rebel. There's no way her dad, a captain in the fire department, would let her work for Eastern Ambulance. And she must be smart. Hank said she's a university student, right? Rebellious, smart . . . Now, if she's only hot, she'd be the full package."

"So, what do you mean by that?" Eric asked before holding his breath as they sped through an empty intersection. "When you say, 'the full package,' do you mean a girl worth marrying?"

"What? Marriage?" Carson said, quickly slowing down checking left and right for oncoming traffic. "You know me, Eric. I wouldn't do that to a girl."

"Oh, God," Eric said, "don't give me that shit again."

"What shit?" Carson said, feigning ignorance.

"Don't start talking about that Angel-of-Death crap again. You're telling me you're not going to marry a girl because you don't want her to be a young widow?"

"Well, you wouldn't want to do that to a girl, would you?" Carson asked.

"No, but c'mon, Carson! I know you've had a few close calls in the war, but thousands of guys did. That doesn't mean you're supposed to die young."

"It's more complicated than that, Eric."

Eric waited for Carson to say more, but he didn't. On this subject, it always seemed like Carson was holding back. Eric didn't know what to make of Carson's off-the-wall theories. Carson Treffer was a competent, respected paramedic—one of Eastern Ambulance's supervisors—but he clung to paranoid, negative ideas, always believing he would not live long. Was it his bad childhood that he rarely talked about? Was it too many years of watching people die in an ambulance? Was it the Army and the war? Carson was morose about life, but competitive, the most caring man in the world, but cynical. After two years as his partner, Eric had learned a lot about him that others didn't know. For one thing, he was much more caring than he admitted to himself. But at the same time, the real Carson Treffer was always more than an arm's length away.

The radio dispatcher repeated the emergency call: "Engine Two, Truck Two, Engine Five, Medic One. Zone twenty-one. Thirty-seven hundred Adams Street on a Code Red."

The units responded each in turn.

"Engine Two clear."

"Truck Two clear."

Carson picked up the microphone. "Medic One clear."

And finally, a familiar voice said, "Engine Five clear."

"Shit!" Carson said. "Mark Rader's on Engine Five tonight. Eric, we can't let them beat us!"

Eric winced as he sensed the adrenaline pumping through Carson's veins.

On the radio, the female dispatcher provided more explanation. "Engine Two, Truck Two, Engine Five, Medic One clear. This is a house fire in Shady Cottonwoods Trailer Court. The family is reported to be out of the building."

Eric, deeply troubled by Carson's last statement, said, "It doesn't matter if they beat us on one call, Carson, even if it is Mark Rader!"

"Eric, they'll use anything against us! And none of the firefighters is worse than Rader!"

"I'm just sayin' they're closer than us, and it doesn't matter if they beat us on one call! And if they do, they're not going to 'use that against us.'"

"Eric, you're completely underestimating the fire department; they'll use anything to make us look bad. I know what I'm doin'! Engine Five is almost as far away as we are."

"Oh, God," Eric said when Carson floored the accelerator, "just don't kill us on the way!"

The ambulance swung left onto Adams Street. As they passed a streetlight, its beams momentarily lit up Carson's face. He was about thirty, with short blonde hair and chiseled good looks. His tanned face and five o'clock shadow made him look rugged and distant. Taller than Eric by a few inches, he had a trim, muscular body along with a personal confidence and a swagger that attracted some and repulsed others. Although eight years older, Carson was much too reckless for Eric's tastes. But Eric supposed that was natural for a man who didn't believe he would live long. Despite their conflicting personalities, they were great partners, and good friends.

"God!" Carson said, "for as often as we come here, you'd think half the people in Nebraska lived in this trailer court."

"I know. I wonder whose trailer's burning. Maybe it's Betsy's and she'll claim she needs narcotics to put out the flames."

Carson laughed.

In the darkness of the cab, Eric Wright pulled the penlight from his holster and checked the bulb. The glow illuminated the alert eyes and likable face of a man in his early twenties—a face that most girls described as cute rather than handsome. He wasn't a boy, but he felt like one next to the older medics at the Eastern Ambulance Company. Once they got to know him, however, they realized he was mature beyond his years. That's how he landed this job in the first place.

Eric reholstered the penlight and braced himself on the center console while Carson swung the ambulance onto Forty-eighth Street, the tires squealing around the corner. Then another thought struck him. "Or it could be that Adam kid with cerebral palsy," he said. "His family lives down here, too, don't they? If it *is* his trailer, I hope his mom moves closer to the hospital. If we're gonna transport him every other week, it might as well be a short trip."

"Yeah, but for his sake, I hope it's not," said Carson.

"I was only joking."

"I know."

Carson approached the trailer court gently pressing the brake pedal. Eric gazed at what he saw. The trailer court was difficult to find, especially in the dark with most of it buried in the cottonwood trees that gave it its name. But tonight the trees glowed red in the firelight. Smoke billowed out of the tiny forest that was "Shady Cottonwoods," and Eric felt as though they were descending into the crater of a volcano.

Carson spoke into the mike with an air of satisfaction, "Dispatch, Medic One on location." He had beaten not only Engine Five, but Engine Two and Truck Two as well, and it was now on the record as such. Only a police cruiser was just arriving.

"Clear, Medic One," the dispatcher replied.

"They must've been asleep," Carson said.

"Must have," Eric said, barely wanting to concede that Carson had been right. In the distance, though, Eric already saw the lights of an approaching fire engine.

People stood outside, some of them still dressed, others in robes. The emergency lights combined with the red glow of the fire to create a panoply of light under the trees.

"I think that *is* Adam's trailer," Carson said. "God, I hope everyone's out."

The trailer was in danger of being entirely lost. Flames in the back half poured from the windows and roof. In minutes it would be gone. A policeman approached a woman and two small children ahead of Carson and Eric. Carson parked the ambulance on the side to leave room for the fire engines that were not far behind. Since he wasn't a paramedic, but only an EMT, Eric knew his role was to collect the bags while Carson took charge. He was tired. It was three o'clock in the morning, and the night was only getting worse.

"Is everyone out of the building?" Carson yelled.

"God, I hope so," the policeman said, approaching the family.

The fire engine, whose lights Eric had seen in the distance, now arrived. Mark Rader, the Engine Five paramedic, slammed his door and ran toward the family. Firefighters jumped from all sides like paratroopers landing.

Carson ran to the woman and her children, donning rubber gloves. He recognized them. Adam's brother and sister stood next to their mom, but Carson didn't see Adam anywhere.

"Is everyone out of the building?" Carson asked the woman.

"Yeah," the mother replied. She looked shabby, as did the two children standing beside her.

"Where's Adam?" Carson asked.

"He's with his dad," she said. She was jumpy. Her hand trembled as it smoothed out the lines in her cheeks. Carson was relieved. His chest muscles relaxed and he took a deep breath.

"You guys breathe any smoke?" Mark Rader asked.

"What?" she said. Her voice was raspy from years of cigarette abuse. "Oh, just a little bit, maybe," she said. Mark indicated for her to open her mouth. He peered inside with a flashlight.

As Carson and Mark spoke with the mother, Engine Two and Truck Two arrived. They sprang into action as quickly as the others. Eric came alongside Carson with two medical bags and placed them on the ground. Carson examined the children.

"That's good," he said. "You sure everyone's okay?"

The mother's eyes darted at him then looked down at her feet and hands, turning them for examination. "Yeah, I'm fine."

He was perturbed. "How 'bout the kids?"

"Oh, yeah, they're fine," she said, dismissing them with a wave. "They're practically indestructible."

After making a cursory examination of all three patients, Carson asked, "Where did you say Adam was?"

"Adam?" she said, looking more nervous. "Let's see, what's today?"

"What do you mean, what's today?" Carson asked. "Today's Wednesday."

"You mean . . . today's Wednesday because it's after midnight?" the woman asked.

"No, I mean, it *was* Wednesday. Now it's Thursday, August twenty-seventh."

"So, it's Thursday now?" She paused and looked at Carson out of the corner of her eye.

"Ma'am," Carson demanded, "where's Adam?"

By now, two streams of water poured down on the trailer with several hundred pounds of pressure. The Engine Two Captain directed a third team of men into position.

Carson grabbed the woman's elbow. Her mood became suddenly frantic. "Oh my God! Adam! He must still be inside. I think he was here tonight! I thought this was Thursday and . . . and I'm just so tired and . . ."

Carson released her elbow and yelled to the Engine Two captain. "Marty! Marty! We have somebody still inside! Eight-year-old boy in a wheelchair!"

Marty's eyes widened behind his mask. "Got it!" he yelled.

Marty ran up to the forward hose, yelling instructions into the firefighters' helmets. Immediately, the men on the hose made their way to the front of the trailer, which had not yet succumbed to the flames. They cooled the path ahead of them with a wide spray, and disappeared inside.

Carson and Mark Rader waited with the family. At Carson's prompting, Eric retrieved the cot from the ambulance. They had responded to many fires on standby but rarely used the cot.

In less than a minute, the firefighters appeared at the door. Hurrying toward Carson and Eric, they carried the blackened body of a young boy in their arms. Carson barged past Mark Rader with the cot.

"Okay!" he yelled, "lay him down!"

Carson's heart sunk when saw the boy. It took only a second to estimate that 80 percent of his body was scorched, his hair and eyebrows mostly gone. Eric cut off the boy's burnt shorts, the only clothing he had on. Carson turned him on his side to examine his back, which was relatively unscathed except for several large bedsores on his thin little body.

Carson felt for a pulse. At the same time, he lowered his ear to Adam's mouth and watched his chest for breathing. He looked up at Eric.

"I've got nothing, Eric! Let's go!"

Eric handed Carson a bag-valve-mask which he placed on Adam's mouth and began pumping.

Carson looked at Rader. "Mark, we're gonna get goin' on this.

Are you comin'?"

"Yeah, I'm comin'."

Carson turned to the paramedic from Engine Two. "Joe, we need you, too! We need somebody on CPR."

"Sure thing," Joe said.

Eric lifted the foot-end of the cot as Carson slid with it into the ambulance. Mark and Joe climbed in after him. Eric slammed the doors and asked Adam's mother if she would ride with them.

"I . . . I don't think so," she said, shouldering a bag she had been carrying. "I should probably stay with these two."

Eric nodded, not wasting any time.

"Do you think he'll make it?" she asked.

"I don't know, ma'am," he said, walking away. "I know he's in good hands, though. We'll do our best."

"But isn't he dead already?" she asked through exaggerated sobs.

As he ran to the door, Eric yelled. "I can't say, ma'am. We'll do our best! He's in the hands of the best paramedic in the city."

Carson yelled up, "Eric, we're going to Saint E's. Turn and burn."

"Gotcha!"

Eric placed the ambulance in gear and backed out. He spoke into the microphone, "Dispatch, Medic One."

"Go ahead, Medic One."

"Medic One en route Saint Elizabeth's, Code Three, ALS."

"Clear, Medic One," said the ever-present, calm voice of the dispatcher.

In the back, Carson and the others struggled to revive the boy.

"Okay, Rader, let's get an airway established," Carson barked. "Hand me the kit from the bottom cabinet."

"Here."

"See if you can get an IV going, Mark. Joe, get on those compressions!"

Carson assembled the laryngoscope that he would use to open Adam's throat.

"Watch the bumps, Eric!" he yelled through the small opening to the cab.

"All right!" Eric said. Eric hogged the middle of the road to find the smooth center.

Carson inserted the lighted laryngoscope into Adam's mouth.

"Huh!"

"What?" Rader asked.

"He doesn't look too bad in here," Carson said. With the tube in place, Carson pumped oxygen directly into his lungs.

"Mark, you got that IV?" Carson asked.

"Yeah," Rader said.

"Okay, open it up. Let's get it flowin'."

"I know what I'm doing, Carson."

Carson looked up at Rader to say he couldn't deal with any bullshit from the firefighters right now, but Rader refused to look back at him.

"C'mon, Adam," Carson said. "Stay with us!"

"I don't know, Carson," Rader said. "It doesn't look good."

"C'mon, Adam! Eric, how much longer?"

"Just a few minutes! Are you gonna call the hospital or am I?"

"I will!" Carson said, reaching for his handheld radio.

Within minutes, the ambulance arrived at Saint Elizabeth's. A doctor and several nurses worked quickly. As they did, Carson outlined everything he knew of Adam's medical state. However, all his efforts up to that point proved fruitless.

Eric immediately went to work cleaning the ambulance in case another call came in. As he removed the sheets from the cot, a television van pulled up. A reporter jumped out and started asking him questions. "Are you the ambulance that just came from Shady Cottonwoods Trailer Court?" she asked, jabbing a microphone toward Eric.

Eric threw the linen into a used hamper by the ER door. "Yes," he said.

They turned on a camera. "How's the boy doing?"

Eric realized the reporter had been listening attentively to her Police and Fire radio. "I'm not exactly sure. You'll probably have to talk to the doctor about his condition."

"Is he dead?"

"Again, I can't say. I'm just the driver." Even though in reality Carson hardly ever let him drive, Eric used that excuse a lot. "You'll have to talk to the doctor or one of the paramedics."

At that moment, Carson emerged from the ER doors looking disheveled and exhausted. The reporter noticed him before he had a chance to sneak away. "Are you the paramedic from the trailer fire?" she asked.

He momentarily shielded his eyes from the bright lights of the camera. "Yes," he said.

"What can you tell me about the boy's condition?"

"He didn't make it," Carson said.

"Did he die en route?"

He took a deep breath and ran his fingers through his hair. "No. Unfortunately, he was in cardiac arrest before he was removed from the trailer. We found him burned in his bed."

"Were there any attempts to rescue the boy from the fire?"

"Yes, when the fire department arrived, they extricated him from the building."

"So, the fire department arrived after you?"

"Yeah, Engine Five was there in less than a minute, though, and Truck Two and Engine Two arrived a few minutes later."

"How long did it take before the boy was removed?"

"Oh, just a few minutes, I guess. A crew from Engine Two got him out probably five minutes after we got there."

"So Engine Five didn't go in right away?"

Mark Rader, who had slipped unnoticed out the ER doors, stepped alongside Carson. The reporters recognized him by his uniform.

"Unfortunately not," Mark said. "We didn't know the boy was in the house at the time."

The reporter was shocked. "Someone was in the burning building, and there were no attempts to rescue him for several minutes?"

Rader was defensive. "Believe me, we would've rescued him right away if we'd been given good information by Eastern Ambulance."

Carson's face contorted in disgust. The reporter asked Mark to explain.

"When we got there, Eastern Ambulance had already been questioning the family about who was inside. I trusted they would have informed us if anyone was still in the building. I guess that was a mistake on my part."

Carson stared at Rader in utter disbelief while Mark continued.

"It wasn't till several minutes into the call that Eastern notified us there was potentially a boy inside."

Carson interjected. "What are you talking about, Mark? You were right there!"

"I wasn't there the whole time."

"You were standing right next to me when I talked to the mother!"

"What did the mother tell you?" the reporter asked.

"I asked her if there was anyone still in the building. She distinctly said 'no.'"

"So, you're telling me that even though her own son was in the building, she told you everyone was out?"

"That's exactly what I'm saying," Carson said, "and Mark Rader was right there when she said it. Mark, I know you heard that as well as I did."

Rader looked at the garage floor, then up at the camera again. The reporter jabbed her microphone under his chin. This was potentially the hottest story she'd had all week. Mark looked her dead in the eyes. "Actually, no. I didn't hear anything like that."

The reporter was confused. Carson's face twisted in greater displeasure. "What do you mean, Mark? You were right there!" Carson said. "I asked her, 'Is there anyone still in the building?' She looked me in the eyes, and said no. I know you heard that!"

Rader shrugged his shoulders. "What can I say, Carson? I didn't."

Rader turned to the reporter. "I wish I had listened to my better judgment and asked her myself. Perhaps there would have been enough time to do something."

"I *did* ask her that!" Carson yelled in Mark's face. "And you heard it just as well as I did!"

Mark brushed Carson off. "Carson, let's not get overly dramatic about this. I understand; we all forget what we're doing sometimes when the pressure's on. It was partly my responsibility. As the firefighter on-scene, I should have been the one asking the questions."

Carson glowered at Mark. He wanted to say more but didn't. He faced the camera one more time. "I'm sorry, folks" he said, looking almost apathetic. "All I can say is that a real nice kid died tonight, and if I could have done something about it, I would have. His name was Adam. The truth is that I *did* ask if there were people inside, and I got a straight answer right away. Why she said what she did, I don't know. And how my fire department friend here can forget that, I don't know either."

Carson looked at the ground and shook his head. "Could we have saved him if we had known earlier? I highly doubt it. I think he died well before we got there, and it was only the difference of a few minutes anyway. Maybe we'll find out from the autopsy. If not, it's just a question that will haunt us, I guess. I know it will haunt me."

This spawned more questions in the mind of the reporter.

"Mr. Treffer, why did the mother tell you that no one was in the trailer? Mr. Treffer, was the boy alive when he came out?"

Carson brushed the questions aside. "I'm sorry, ma'am. I can't take anymore questions tonight. You'll have to talk to the police." He turned and walked back to the ambulance where Eric had been listening. Carson climbed into the passenger seat, which was unusual for him.

"Can you believe that crap, Eric?" he said as they drove away. "Can you believe Mark Rader would stoop to that level?"

"No," Eric replied, "I can't. That's taking politics to a whole new level."

Carson didn't reply.

Eric added, "I guess you were right."

Carson opened his eyes and looked at Eric. "Oh, yeah? About what?"

"I *was* completely underestimating the fire department."

Carson closed his eyes again and massaged his temples. "Get used to it. I have a feeling this is only going to get worse."

2.

A little more than twenty-four hours later, at 7:00 A.M., Eric reported to work for another shift. He climbed the stairs to the crew quarters at Eastern Ambulance's Station One. There he found Carson, with two girls.

"Eric, this is Lauren," Carson said, indicating an attractive blonde who leaned toward Carson from her armchair. "She's an EMT student at the community college."

"Oh, are you a ride-along?"

"No, not yet," Carson said, answering for her. "I just brought her in this morning to show her the ambulance and the station."

Given the fact there were two girls there, Eric realized he shouldn't ask more questions. "Oh, I see."

Carson added, "And of course, you know Stephanie."

"Yeah, hi," Eric said. Stephanie was a nurse in the emergency room at Lincoln General. In her view, she and Carson were seeing each other, and from her seat next to Carson, she looked more than a little displeased at Lauren's presence.

"You headin' to work?" Eric asked Stephanie.

"No, I worked last night. I just came by for a visit." It was her third visit in two weeks.

Eric tried to act pleasant. "We've got enough people here for a party."

"Yeah," Stephanie said with a cynical smile, "almost."

The phone by the armchair rang. Eric grabbed it to extract himself from the conversation. After a short talk, he hung up and turned to Carson.

"Carson, Hank wants to see us downstairs."

"About what?"

Eric rolled his eyes. "He didn't say, Carson, but I'm guessing it has to do with the call yesterday and the fact that your face was all over the TV."

The new girl, Lauren, looked over at Carson with surprise. Carson glanced at her before he asked Eric, "So they put all that on TV?"

Eric was impatient with Carson's theatrics. "Yes."

"What's that all about?" Lauren asked, her eyes wide with wonder.

Carson acted embarrassed, but Eric wasn't fooled.

"Oh, just more shit from the fire department. This guy, Mark Rader, basically accused me of lying on TV."

"About what?"

"About whether we knew if there was still a person inside a burning building."

Her eyes grew even wider. "Was there?"

Carson started to speak, but paused in apparent pain. Eric couldn't tell if this was more gamesmanship or not. "Yeah," Carson said and looked out the window.

Lauren looked as if she was going to ask another question, then glanced at Eric and decided against it. Based on the expressions on their faces, the answer to the question was obvious.

Both Lauren and Stephanie made excuses to leave and walked partway out with Carson and Eric. After leaving the guys, the two women separated without saying a word. Eric and Carson climbed down the stairs to the basement.

Hank Jenkins was the Associate Director of Operations at Eastern Ambulance, the man who ran the company on a day-to-day basis. He was a short, thin man in his mid-fifties who carried authority disproportionate to his size. His office was in the basement of the three-story headquarters that also served as Station One. He could have had an upstairs office with the rest of management, but he liked to be down here, near the garage and the company dispatch center so he could keep a close eye on business.

Hank's office contained several bookshelves full of numbered folders, each corresponding to an ambulance or "car." Hank still called the van-type ambulances cars from the days when Eastern Ambulance operated hearse-like Cadillacs, and the word stuck.

Pictures of wrecked ambulances adorned an entire wall. Eric wondered if they were meant to keep the ambulance drivers sober-minded. Scattered among the wrecked ambulances was other paraphernalia—pictures and patches from EMS providers around the country. Most noticeable of all, however, was the collection of model ambulances that populated a whole bookshelf in the corner of the office. Hank had been in EMS since its inception, and many of the older toys reminded him of what it was like in the beginning.

Rounding the corner to his office, Eric and Carson found that Hank was not alone. Another young kid, probably about Eric's age, sat in civilian clothes in one of the chairs facing Hank's desk. At least Eric *thought* he was about his age, maybe he was younger—he had a boyish face. This boy and Hank were in conversation when Carson barged right in.

"Hank, I've got to tell you that woman *did* tell me no one was in the building."

Hank sat with his fingertips pressed gently together in front of his face. He turned his attention away from the kid and toward Carson.

"I know, Carson," Hank said without changing his demeanor. "I believe you."

"She said everyone was out of the trailer, and Rader was right there when she said it!"

"You don't think I figured as much, Carson?" Hank said and motioned for them to sit down. "We can talk about this in a minute. If you hadn't noticed, I'm in the middle of a conversation."

"Sorry," Carson said, turning to acknowledge the kid.

Hank introduced them. "Brent, this is Carson Treffer, one of our paramedic supervisors, and this is Eric Wright, one of our EMT-Intermediates. They're on the 'D' team. Guys, this is Brent Cunningham. We just hired him as an EMT-Basic."

Brent stood to face them, and Eric noticed he had an unruly cowlick that stood out from his otherwise perfectly parted brown hair. He also had slightly large front teeth that reminded Eric of Dennis the Menace. They shook hands.

"Pleased to meet you," Brent said with a farmboy accent.

"Likewise."

Eric sat in the chair next to Brent while Carson chose to stand in his favorite spot next to Hank's desk. As Carson propped one of his legs up on a chair, his plain, black cowboy boots became apparent.

Brent asked, "You wear cowboy boots in uniform?"

Carson's chin rested in his hand, and his elbow rested on his knee. He looked down at the new kid through the bottom of his eyes. "I wear them in and out of uniform."

"Why?"

"Because I don't waste time lacing them up."

"Oh," Brent said, feeling scolded. "I guess that does make sense."

"You guys sit tight a minute," Hank continued, "and let me finish briefing Brent."

Before Hank could speak, Brent asked, "Am I gonna be havin' run-ins with the fire department like that?"

"You mean like Carson?"

Brent nodded his head.

"You shouldn't," Hank said. "You don't run into them very often on a transfer car. We only work with Lancaster County on emergencies."

"Is Eastern's relationship with the fire department that bad?" Brent asked.

"No, it gets blown out of proportion," Hank said. "We used to get along with the fire department real fine, Brent. Actually, when Max Dougherty started this company twenty-five years ago, we had no problems with them at all. Not till about six years ago. That was when Lou Killion got hired as the deputy chief and O'Malley became the fire union president. That's when they and a few others started talking about taking over the ambulance service."

At the mention of O'Malley's name, Carson remembered something he wanted to ask. "Oh, speaking of Captain O'Malley," he said with a questioning tone, "Eric tells me that you hired his daughter to work for us?"

Hank looked a little annoyed at the interruption. "Yes, that's true Carson. She's a Basic as well, and will start in a few weeks."

"Holy shit!" Carson said slowly. "I can't believe it. Is she hot?"

Now Hank was really annoyed. He turned to look at Carson. "What does it matter if she's hot, Carson? She's a pre-med student at the university and she wants some medical experience. She'll be working one of the transfer cars and that's all you need to know."

Carson stood there with a whimsical look, trying to read Hank's face, then said. "Yep, she's hot. I told you so, Eric."

Eric shook his head and didn't get a chance to speak before Hank cut in. "Now I didn't say that Carson. You'll meet her in a few weeks and you can form your own judgment." He turned back to Brent. "Now . . . where was I?"

"You were talking about O'Malley and Killion wanting to take over the ambulance service," Brent said, though he seemed more interested in the previous conversation.

Hank leaned forward and rested his pointy elbows on the desk. "That's right. You see, about eight years ago the County created a new position—Deputy Fire Chief—and they hired a head-hunting organization to find a guy with a lot of expertise probably to make up for Chief Winkenwerder's lack of it. They found this guy, Lou Killion, from some Long Island department with a Master's Degree in management and a lot of fire and EMS experience. The fact that they hired a guy with EMS experience shows that they may have been planning for the future way back then, if you know what I mean. Well, he really took charge and made the department his own. Winkenwerder is almost just a figurehead now. Killion and Captain O'Malley are good friends and they're the ones pushing for the EMS contract."

"Why do they even want it?" Brent asked.

"You see, Brent, it's kind of a pride thing for firefighters. I think it's tough when firefighters in Lincoln talk to other departments like Omaha, and they have to admit that they answer to a private company in their own city. I'm sure you learned all about this in your EMT class—how a lot of fire departments in the country are runnin' out of things to do since there aren't that many fires anymore. With all of the building codes and alarm systems, the amount of real fires in most cities has declined about fifty percent. So, that's another factor, I guess. It's hard to keep justifying your budget when you're runnin' outta work."

"Yeah, we talked about that some in class," Brent said.

"But I have to say, I think it's probably more of a pride thing. One thing you'll learn before long is that there is no shortage of ego in emergency services. Ain't that right, Carson?"

Carson raised his eyebrows and bobbed his head, taking the jab without rancor. Brent replied, "Oh, you don't have to tell me about fire departments. Remember, I've been a volunteer on Saline County

Fire and Rescue for two years. My dad's the chief. I'm not new to this stuff."

Hank laughed. "That's right, I forgot. I can see we don't need to explain pride to this guy, huh Carson?"

"Nope, he'll fit right in," Carson said, only half listening. He slapped Brent on the back as he went out for coffee.

"And don't forget," Brent said. "I didn't just take an EMT course. I'm close to having my Fire Science degree."

"Well, then you know how the fire department feels, I guess. Everyone wants to rule their own turf." Hank leaned back, put his hands behind his head, and thought a moment. "But there's probably things going on here we don't know, too," he said. "Who knows what the County might have told Killion when they hired him. Maybe there's some sort of understanding there that it's his job to eventually get the contract. Who knows? All I know is that ever since they hired him this issue keeps rearing its ugly head over and over."

Carson returned from the nearby kitchenette and leaned against the doorjamb. "Have I got a treat for you guys!" His words dripped with sarcasm. "I almost forgot. I picked up a little gift for you down at the Lincoln General ER the other day. Hank, you can use it as a teaching aid."

Carson lifted a maroon coffee mug.

"It's a gift the fire department handed to the staff in the hospitals a few months ago. Stephanie told me about it and gave me one."

"Well, that's awfully nice of the fire department," Hank smirked and reached for the mug. "Let's see what it says. Oh, that's nice. Happy EMS week . . . Lancaster County Fire Department . . . New decade . . . New hope."

"Man," Hank continued, "they're really goin' for it this time."

"What do you mean, 'this time?'" Brent asked.

"Well, about six years ago, we first started to learn that the department was gunning for the EMS contract. O'Malley became union president. Deputy Chief Killion had only been in the job for a few years and he turned out to be real anti-Eastern. We knew that he and a few others felt that way, but that wasn't much of a threat to us since these guys were in the minority. Besides, Chief Winkenwerder has never had any ambitions about taking over EMS. It's questionable whether they'd ever actually get the contract without the Chief's buy-in."

"Yeah right," Carson said, "Winkenwerder lets Killion pretty much run the whole department. Winkenwerder is so old; I think he's just biding his time until he can collect a pension check."

"Is that true?" Brent asked.

"Well, Carson's partly right. Chief Winkenwerder is not near as involved as his deputy. And it's true that Killion is in line to be chief someday, but Winkenwerder is the chief now and that's what counts."

"So, what did they do six years ago?"

"Lou Killion decided it was time the fire department got more involved in medical calls. At the time, all the firefighters were BLS— Basic Life Support. But Killion, and probably O'Malley, decided that they wanted to train some paramedics. They claimed that the Advanced Life Support role was necessary since the fire department was already responding to all medical calls. Not to mention the Union was really pushing for the ALS role too, because it would mean a pay raise for the paramedics."

"And that's what happened?" Brent asked.

"Yeah, that's what happened," Hank continued. "That's basically the situation we have today. The fire department is the 'Quick Response Team' as they always have been, only now they have a Fire/Paramedic onboard every engine instead of an EMT-Basic like they used to. When Eastern medics arrive, though, we immediately assume full control of patient care. This great compromise, Brent, is the system we've been working under for the past four or five years."

"But now the firefighters want more?"

"Exactly. We supported the compromise because we wanted to put an end to the whole debate; we thought everyone would be happy."

"We were wrong," Carson said between sips of coffee from his fire department mug.

"Yes, we were," Hank continued. "I've come to learn that they won't stop until they have it all. That's obvious now. During the last election, the Fire Union campaigned heavily for Commissioner McDaniels and for County Councilman Moscatelli. They raised somewhere around $15,000 for Moscatelli's campaign. Obviously, he was reelected for the fourth time and with help from three new board members, he is now Chairman of the Board. Last May, the night of the election, Commissioner McDaniels and Chairman Moscatelli threw a victory celebration at the Fire Union Hall."

"Yeah, I heard about that."

"Since the election, the commissioner has been quite clear about where he wants to take Emergency Medical Services. This time, the county wants the whole EMS contract."

"So," Brent asked, "even though the fire chief isn't too interested, the people below him and the people above him want the contract."

"Yeah, that sums it. Winkenwerder is stuck in the middle, and Killion must have some sort of pull with the county."

"Or the other way around," Eric added. "The county may have pull with Killion."

"True," Hank said.

"What do they have to do to get it?"

Hank took a deep sigh and leaned closer to Brent. "We have to rebid our contract every five years, you see, and it expires December 31. We're usually the only bidders, but this time the fire department is putting in a bid too. They're due in a week. Two weeks after that, on September 17, the county council is going to hold a public hearing and then vote on it. We're all gonna be there to make our case."

"What do you think Eastern's chances of winning are?" Brent asked.

"I'd say they're pretty good. We're not just gonna roll over and let this happen. We've got some big guns to pull out at the county board meeting, and we even have options after that. There's a whole lot of hoops the commissioner and the firefighters have to jump through in order to take this business from us. And as you can see, this isn't a new issue."

Hank looked again at Carson's coffee mug, which was now sitting on the desk. He picked it up and read it again. "Lancaster County Fire Department . . . New decade . . . New hope . . ." He placed it back on the desk and added, "But really, it's the same old shit."

No one laughed.

"Now, gentlemen," Hank said, "Brent is gonna be riding with the two of you for a while to get acquainted with the system. Take good care of him and don't teach him any bad habits . . . *Carson!*"

"What? I'm so sure!"

"Now, what is it you came barging in here about?"

"It's about yesterday."

"No surprise there."

"I think we should go talk to the fire department," Carson said. "We can't have that kind of shit goin' on out there. It was totally unprofessional!"

"I agree, Carson. We need to leave the politics out of patient care. Let me talk to them first. I'll try to schedule a meeting for us with Chief Winkenwerder and Rader, and we can talk about it then."

Carson looked surprised that he got his wish so easily. "All right, just let me know when and where."

Hank took a sip of his own coffee, then said, "Question for you, Carson."

"Yeah?"

"What is the deal with the mom?"

Carson rubbed the bridge of his nose and didn't answer right away. "I don't know," he said. "I don't know."

"What did they find out about the kid?"

"Adam?"

"Yeah, Adam."

"I don't know that either. I'm thinking about going over to St. E's to find out."

"Sounds like a good idea. Why don't you take Brent with you before you get busy."

Carson nodded.

"Is that all you wanted, Carson?"

"Yeah, I guess so. I just really think we need to confront these guys, otherwise they're just gonna keep having their way with us."

"I know. I'll see what I can do."

Before Carson walked out the door, he turned. "Oh, just one more thing. I was wondering if you've thought more about putting CD players in the ambulances?"

"No!" Hank said, "and don't ask me again. Those ambulances are not your personal toys. They're work vehicles!"

Carson did not look surprised. "Got it. Just thought I'd ask."

Hank shook his head. "Now get outta here and let me know what you find out."

Carson fired up the diesel engine. Brent climbed in the back, and Eric sat in the passenger seat. It was a sunny day, yet not too hot for August. Eric tried to read the paper, but Brent kept asking questions about what different buttons were for, so he gave up, folded the paper, and talked with him. Carson remained silent, nursing his coffee. Eric thought it was funny to see Carson drinking from his new mug: "New decade . . . New hope . . ." Carson had no hope about anything, let alone the fire department.

They parked the van outside the Saint Elizabeth's Emergency Department. Inside, Carson proceeded directly to the administrative wing, followed by the other two. He found the office marked, "Jim Homestead, Chief Executive Officer," and marched into the secretary's waiting area.

"Hi, Carson," the secretary said, pleasantly surprised. Her name was Jenny. She was young and relatively good-looking, with great eyes. Eric knew that Carson had dated her at one point, but she was looking for a long-term relationship and Carson would have none of it. It didn't fit in with his mantra of living every day like it was your last. It wasn't just a mantra, though; he really did think every day was his last.

"You didn't tell me you were going to bless me with your presence today," Jenny said.

"Oh, I'm just stoppin' by to talk to Jim."

"Oh," she said, her voice dripping with sarcasm, "I thought you might have realized the worst mistake of your life and were coming to beg forgiveness?"

"Jenny, when you're ready to stop talking about the next fifty years and ready to start living life one night at a time, give me a call."

"Likewise, Carson, when you're ready to grow up, give me a call," she said nonchalantly. "So, you wanna see the boss?" She was confident and sexy, and even Eric thought she was too good for Carson.

If Carson smarted at her comment, Eric couldn't tell. "Yes, I do."

"He's in there with some doctor, but I don't think it's too important."

Jenny phoned in, "Sir, Carson Treffer is here with some other EMTs to see you."

"I'll be right out," a voice from the speaker answered.

Eric didn't appreciate the way she said "some other EMTs." He should have stayed back in the truck, he thought. He didn't know Jim Homestead like Carson did. But it was too late now, and Jim appeared at the door.

"Carson!" Jim said in a booming voice. He was a big, thick man. "What the hell, ole' buddy? I was just talking about you a few minutes ago."

He took Carson's hand and slapped him on the back. Carson didn't appreciate it. "Lloyd, this is the guy I was telling you about—my personal golf tutor. Lloyd Rickers, this is Carson Treffer."

The doctor shook Carson's hand. "Pleased to meet you, Carson. Jim was telling me about your golf skills. Where did you learn to play?"

"Mainly in high school."

"Oh yeah? Where?"

"Oh, a little town out in Western Nebraska you probably never heard of."

"Western Nebraska," the doctor said. "Now that's about the middle of nowhere, huh? How did you manage to escape?"

"The Army took me around the world for a while," Carson said.

"Oh, yeah?" Dr. Rickers said. "Iraq?"

"Afghanistan and other places," Carson said before changing the subject. He turned toward the CEO. "Jim, I came over to see if you knew anything more about the boy we brought in here yesterday?"

"Sure, Carson. You mean the dead boy in the burn center?"

Only Eric could tell Carson was slightly annoyed by Jim's blunt words.

"Yeah, Adam Turner."

"Yeah, let me see. I don't have the file on me, of course, but the police and press are all over this one." He scratched his head. "The medical examiner took the body for autopsy yesterday."

"Did he? I figured he probably would. Did he find anything significant?"

"They're still waiting on some toxicology reports, but it sounds like the boy didn't die from the fire. There was no burning or smoke damage in his respiratory system."

"I noticed that."

"His carbon monoxide levels were normal – way too low, they tell me, for someone to have died from smoke inhalation. He was significantly malnourished, with some muscle damage from that, and . . . what else? He had some bedsores. I guess he had muscular dystrophy or something?"

"Cerebral palsy," Carson said.

"Yeah, that's what it was," Jim said, pointing at Carson. "The doctor said it looks like he died of pneumonia. I think that's what he said, anyway."

"Pneumonia? Are you kidding me? How long had he been dead?" Carson asked.

"Sorry Carson, I don't know. You'll probably get all the details from the paper. Real sad case, though."

Jim changed the subject. "So, Carson, we gonna tee-up on Wednesday?"

Carson looked up at him with a sick look. "Golfing?"

"Of course I'm talking about golfing. What else? Dr. Rickers is going to go with us while he's in town."

"Uh, geez, Jim, I'm not sure that I can. Eric and I work on Wednesday."

"Come on, Carson," Jim said. He put his hand on Carson's shoulder and winked. "You owe me."

"I know I do," Carson said, obviously dejected.

"I've been working on that swing you taught me, but I don't know where to go from here." He made a fake swing through the air. "So, I'll see you around eight on Wednesday?"

"I don't think I'm going to be able to make it this time, Jim. We'll get together soon, though. Maybe this weekend or something."

"All right, Carson, but don't forget . . . you owe me. You owe me for a few times."

"I know. We'll get around to it."

Carson said good-bye to Jenny. She pretended not to care. The three made their way back to the ambulance, which was refreshingly warm after the frigid air conditioning in Homestead's office.

"That's too bad about Adam," Eric said.

"Yeah it is," Carson said. "I can't believe it."

"How weird is that—that he was dead before the fire? Do you think Jim just got confused or something?"

"No, that's what I suspected he'd say."

"Really?"

"Yeah, I noticed that night that there was no burning in his trachea; he hadn't been breathing at all during the fire."

"What do you think happened?"

"I don't know, Eric. I'm pretty sure we're gonna find out, though. This call's not gonna go away. And the craziest thing is that Mark Rader is using it to make us look like bad guys."

"That's fu—," Eric stopped, trying to remember his resolution to swear less. "That's screwed up," he said instead. "Well, at least now we know there was nothing we could've done."

"Unless we had done something sooner."

"What do you mean?"

"Like, we could have had him taken away from the mother or something."

"You mean, weeks ago?"

"Yeah."

"You think we could have?"

"I don't know. Probably not, but if that's what really happened, somebody should have."

"Yeah, that's for sure."

Brent butted in. "Can I ask you a question, Carson?"

"Sure."

"If you don't want to go golfing with that guy, why didn't you just say 'no?'"

"Because I owe him a few favors."

"For what?"

Carson paused before starting the engine. "For asking favors for other people," he said. "It's not a big deal." Brent looked at him with a questioning look, but Carson said nothing more.

3.

"I think it's about time for a campus cruise," Carson said later that day. He had been reading an article in the paper, but slapped the folded paper on his knee in disgust. It was only a small article about the fire and Adam's death along with the coroner's statement that Adam had been dead long before the fire started. Eric had already read it, and so had Brent, who was sitting in the back of the ambulance.

Eric knew that when Carson suggested a campus cruise, he wanted a distraction. "Sounds good to me," he said. Besides, business was slow, and it was a cool, late-summer day. In fact, it was one of the first days that felt like autumn, and Eric wanted to appreciate the summer while it was still around.

"What's a campus cruise?" Brent asked, sticking his head in the cab from the back of the ambulance.

Carson looked over at Eric before answering. "Uh, I thought that was pretty obvious, Brent. It's a cruise . . . through campus."

"I figured as much, smart-ass. What do you do there?"

"Nothing, just cruise through campus," Carson said, placing the paper on the table. "You know, to check out the scenery."

Carson took the long way around to take more time, and they approached campus from Vine Street. The closer they got to the university, the more the football stadium grew ahead of them. They made their way past the small, older homes, the homes they worked in, day in and day out, the decrepit, hot homes where people got sick more frequently than usual. They reached the university, and Carson turned left onto Sixteenth.

Now the scene changed. Taking advantage of the cool day, young people in sweatshirts and tennis shoes threw footballs in front of fraternity mansions. Many more drove their convertible Mustangs and Jeeps—so many, in fact, that it took several minutes to drive a few blocks. The traffic was not a nuisance, however; it facilitated the slow driving necessary for their purpose. Down the sidewalks strolled the coeds, textbooks embraced in their arms, leaves swirling at their feet, tight blue jeans swaying as they walked. They talked and laughed, and turned and smiled at Carson and Eric as they drove by. They liked the attention, or men impressed by them, or maybe they just smiled at everyone.

It was a strange ritual, but it had healing, amnesiac qualities. In the past few days they had checked on Mrs. Blakely, the diabetic double-amputee, who lived alone and regularly called 911 to relieve the intense loneliness. They flew to nursing homes twelve times to treat the lonely and diseased. Some of them thought they were dying, others were dying, and two of them were dead on arrival. They treated the old, alcoholic Indian named Spirit Dog, passed out in an alley one time and sprawled out in the park another. They found Mr. Krueger sitting again in his own excrement in his wheelchair where he had been for several days, before his wife finally called the ambulance because her husband looked "like he was about to die." And of course, there was Adam.

None of that stuff happened here. People weren't sick and people didn't die. The people were nice to look at here. Today, there were more students out than usual. Work on homecoming floats had begun. Nebraska would be playing Kansas State at Homecoming, and beaten-down Wildcats were already taking shape on the manicured lawns of the dormitories, fraternities, and sororities.

Eric remembered going to school here. It wasn't much fun at the time, but now he looked back on it differently. He didn't like to admit it, even to himself, but he wondered what stupid idea ever made him leave. Only two years ago, he had been one of these people. Now he was a spectator. He had quit after two semesters to pursue the EMT thing, and because he was tired of the homework. But now he wondered if he could ever go back.

As the ambulance made its circuit around the streets, beautiful coeds swarmed all around. In front of the Neihardt Dorm, one particularly nice girl walked with a group. The ambulance slowed. Carson and Eric finally lost their ability to stare discreetly while they watched her and her friends walk ahead of them. From their vantage point, all they could see was long, wavy, red hair and blue jeans that outlined curves, and that was enough.

"Ho-ly shit!" Carson said, shaking his head like the girl was committing a crime.

Brent leaned forward to look as well. "Let me see!"

"Get back there, you idiot," Carson said and pressed back on Brent's cowlick. "We're trying not to look like a bunch of desperadoes. If you wanna look, look out the back windows when we pass."

Unfortunately, Carson could drive only so slow. As they passed the girls, the redhead turned and smiled as if on cue. She *was* pretty. Much to the crew's surprise, however, she then waved at them. Not just a "wave-and-maybe-they'll-go-away" gesture, but more of a "hello" wave. Maybe she was just teasing them. Carson briefly stepped on the brakes before realizing he shouldn't stop traffic. This action resulted in a stop-and-start jerk that looked foolish. The girl laughed as they pulled away. Her friends got a kick out of it too.

"Nice maneuver, Jeff Gordon," Eric said. "Now that we've completely freaked them out."

"Do we know her?" Carson asked.

"Well, if we did, she's going to deny it now."

"She acted like she knew us, I thought. Did you know her in college?"

"No. If I did, do you think I'd be here? She looks like she's probably a freshman."

"Really? She looked older to me," Carson said, peering into his side mirror.

"You're just trying to ease your conscience."

Carson gave up trying to see her again and focused on the road ahead.

"Maybe she did know you, Carson," Eric said facetiously. "Maybe she's your long lost *daughter*!"

"Very funny, Eric, but that *is* a good point." He pretended to look in the mirror again. "It *did* look like she needed a sugar daddy."

"Oh God," Eric said, rolling his eyes. "Then you've got a problem; you have no money."

"Yeah, but I can make up for that with my looks."

"Whatever!"

They both chuckled but deep inside were depressed to return to their day-to-day lives. Carson refused to let go, though, and thought about her for the rest of the day.

Much later, in the early morning hours, Eric awoke suddenly to Carson's voice coming from the other room. They had been sleeping at the station.

"Let's go! Let's go, he's not breathing!" Carson yelled.

Damn! Eric thought, I was so tired I didn't even hear the tones! He bolted up in bed, his uniform still on, and began to lace his boots. This was the worst of times. Eric had been lost in a dream but couldn't remember what it was about. He was back in college, he remembered, and oh yeah, he was walking with the beautiful redhead in front of Neihardt. It didn't matter now. It was time to work. He had been jolted from deep sleep to nervous anticipation in a matter of seconds. At least, he told himself, he had finally gotten to the point where he could sleep soundly at the station.

"Let's go, let's go!" Carson yelled. Eric saw Brent slowly getting up and didn't feel so bad; Brent clearly hadn't heard the tones either.

Carson seemed agitated, and Eric noticed the paramedic hadn't taken his utility belt and holster. Eric grabbed it for him. He and Brent ran down the stairs to the garage. Carson waited in the cab.

"Let's go!" he yelled. "Those bastards blew him up!"

Carson wasn't making sense, but whatever it was sounded bad. Eric jumped in the passenger seat, with Brent in the back. Carson stared out the windshield and waited for the garage door to open.

Eric grabbed the mike from its clip. "Medic One, clear," he said.

It took the dispatcher a few seconds longer than normal. "Go ahead, Medic One."

Now Eric was really confused; the dispatcher wasn't supposed to say that. "Medic One is clear. Could you repeat the call?"

Again, several seconds passed. Eric was just too damned tired to put anything together. "Medic One, there is no call at this time."

Eric looked over at Carson, who was staring glassy-eyed out the windshield.

"Dispatch, Medic One. I apologize . . . our mistake," Eric replied.

When she responded, Eric heard amusement in her voice. "No

problem, Medic One. You can go back to bed now."

No one said anything for some time. Eric leaned his head against the window and rubbed his aching temples. He hated the feeling of being too tired to move or think but feeling on edge with his heart thumping in his chest. This wasn't the first time he had seen Carson in an agitated dream state.

"I must've been dreaming, I guess," Carson said.

"You think?" Eric said sarcastically. "What were you dreaming? You looked crazy mad!"

Eric's eyes were closed, but he heard Carson slump his head against the headrest.

"Adam, I think."

"Adam?"

"I think so."

"You said something about some bastards blowing him up."

Carson looked over at Eric in surprise. "I said that?" He swallowed. "I think I thought the kid was blown up by an I.E.D."

"A what?"

"An improvised explosive device. You know, it was a dream. I was just mixin' things up in my head. You know the way dreams are."

Eric didn't know what to say. He and Carson didn't talk about Army matters; he learned to avoid it early on. He was actually surprised, however, at how much the call with Adam had affected Carson.

"Carson, I hope you don't worry about Adam. There was nothing we could have done for him."

"Yeah, but I should've never trusted his mom. My gut was telling me to ask about him right away, but I didn't."

"It doesn't matter. He was already dead."

"I know that, but that's not my point. I knew not to trust her."

"What do you mean?"

"His mom! She didn't care about Adam. She was always feeding us lies. The second she told me no one was in the trailer I should have known she was lying again."

"Carson, you're being totally unrealistic. Even if he was still alive, you couldn't have gone in there. The place was on fire!"

"You're missing my point, Eric. She's been lying to us all along.

Those times when I asked her if he was eating enough, if he was getting his medications, and all that. She was just telling me what I wanted to hear, and I knew it all along."

"Then why didn't you say something?"

"Thank you! That's exactly what I'm saying, Eric!" Carson clenched his fist as he emphasized this. "That's my point. I should have said something about it to the authorities."

Eric realized he'd made a blunder. "Carson, I didn't mean that you should've said something. What I meant was that if you really felt that way, then you *would've* said something. See what I mean?"

"Yeah, but when I think about her that night, and the look she gave me when she said that, it was the same look she always gave me. I should've seen through it before."

"Yeah, but I didn't either."

"But you're not the paramedic, Eric." Carson squeezed the bridge of his nose. "I noticed the last time we were there that he was getting too thin."

"He's always been thin."

"He was thinner and just looked hollow inside."

"Are you saying that you should've known that he was being neglected or something?"

Carson turned away and gazed out the window.

"No, I'm saying that I *did* know."

Eric thought about it a moment, then shook his head. "I disagree, Carson. I don't think there was anything you could've seen there."

"You're wrong, Eric. There were things, and I saw them."

"What? That he had gotten thinner?" Eric grew frustrated. "He had cerebral palsy, Carson! He was a sick, dying boy! Of course he didn't look good!"

"But I knew she wasn't taking care of him. I knew she didn't even *like* him. I could hear it in her sappy words. And I could . . ." Carson swallowed, "I could see it in Adam's eyes every time, like he wanted to be rescued from his home."

Eric had worked with Carson for fourteen months and had never seen him so shaken up.

"Eric, it was like he never wanted us to leave."

Eric thought about the times he had seen Adam, and now he was being drawn in, like one alcoholic being asked to drink with another.

He remembered a time when Adam grasped Eric's arm as he made his way to leave. Eric had to remove Adam's hand in order to go. "Now, don't bother them, Adam," his mom had said. "They're busy." The emotional pull Eric felt that day returned, but this time it was much sadder.

"Carson," Eric said, feeling ashamed because it sounded more like a whimper.

"Yeah?"

"Did you ever see bedsores or anything like that?"

"Well, his skin never looked too good."

"But were there real bedsores?"

"Not really."

"Yeah, I never saw any either." He paused for a moment, then realized what he was doing. "Listen to us. Now you've got me looking for ways to make myself feel guilty. If bedsores or anything else were an issue, the ER would have noticed it."

"That's true," Carson admitted.

"You're reading *way* too much into this, Carson. I guarantee that no one would find you, or me, or anyone at fault for Adam's death. He died in a fire!"

Eric realized his last statement wasn't quite true, but it was too late.

"No, he didn't," Carson said. "He died of neglect."

"But that's not your fault, Carson."

"I could've prevented it."

Eric leaned his head against the side window, looking off toward the garage wall. He stopped rubbing his temples because it no longer helped. "I still disagree," he said, knowing in part that he had to do it out of principal. "I see your point, but we had no grounds that would have removed a boy from his home."

"You might be right," Carson said, "but maybe if we looked for it, we could have found some."

Eric simply shook his head. He was too tired to do this anymore.

Carson pushed the button on the garage door opener, and they watched the door reach for the ground with a metallic whine.

"There's no use us talking about this now," Carson said, "especially at this time of night. I'm sorry I woke you up."

"No problem."

Carson opened the door and exited the ambulance. Eric took a deep breath before doing the same. As he did, the back door of the ambulance slammed, startling Eric. Between the time, the fatigue, and the confusion, they had forgotten that Brent was even there.

4.

"Man, this is an old ambulance!" Brent said on the next shift. It was the middle of the afternoon, and they were just leaving a fast-food parking lot when the engine momentarily choked accelerating into traffic. Carson was in a hurry. He preferred eating at the station in front of the TV, but the city was getting busy.

"You're not kiddin'!" Carson said. He looked down at the squared-off, old-fashioned gauges and the archaic emergency switches bolted to the dash. It didn't look like an ambulance; it looked like a van with ambulance equipment awkwardly placed inside. "E22 is the oldest ambulance we have."

"Is it reliable?"

"Mmm . . . yeah, for the most part. It's got over 200,000 miles, so you have to expect it's not perfect. But it gets the job done, and it's only temporary."

"What do you mean?"

Carson nodded his head. "We're only in this old thing until our mechanic, Joe, gets the Aluminum Falcon up and running."

"What's the Aluminum Falcon?" Brent asked. While Carson drove, Eric and Brent started to eat their food.

"E60, the fastest ambulance we've got. It's not the newest, which makes it better, because the newest ones at Medic Two and Medic Four aren't as nice. They're not allowed to have armrests for one thing, and they're a little heavier. The Aluminum Falcon is our primary ambulance, but it's taking forever for Joe to fix it."

Eric interjected, "I think you, of all people, shouldn't be complaining about E60 being wrecked. Maybe when we get it back, you'll appreciate it and not drive so fast."

"Eric, it wasn't my fault. That guy pulled out right in front of us."

"I know, but if you weren't driving so fast, maybe you could have avoided him. I thought that after that pipe almost came through the windshield, you'd have learned your lesson. That scared the crap out of me."

Carson didn't say anything for a moment as he thought about that day, and how close he had come to dying. "You don't understand, Eric. I couldn't have avoided that. The truck came after me."

"Oh, here we go again," Eric said, rolling his eyes.

"Eric, I know you don't believe it, but it's true."

Brent asked, "What are you guys talking about?"

Eric looked over at Carson to see if he minded him talking about this. Carson didn't say anything, so Eric took free rein. "Carson thinks he's fated to die."

Brent had a quizzical look on his face. "Are you being serious?" he asked.

"Eric's exaggerating," Carson said, pulling away from a stoplight. "I've just had a lot of close calls, you know, and it makes you wonder sometimes."

"Like what?"

Carson grimaced, like he didn't feel comfortable talking about it. "Well, for one thing, I got real sick as a boy and almost died, and then just things like that wreck in the Falcon."

That didn't sound too convincing to Brent. "Hmm, interesting," was all he said. Eric turned toward Brent and circled his finger around his ear.

Carson laughed. "And yes, I'm a little bit crazy, too."

"Only a little?" Eric asked.

Carson turned to him. "You're right. I'm totally nuts."

Eric shook his head; he never understood why Carson always blamed everything and everyone but himself for that collision. "I will agree that you're lucky to be alive after that wreck. I just think you have to admit you had something to do with it."

"Maybe."

Before Eric could convince Carson to take responsibility, the dispatcher's voice sounded. "Medic One, dispatch."

"Shit," Carson said, and picked up the microphone. "I knew we didn't have enough time." He responded with their location. "Medic One's at Forty-eighth and Vine."

"Medic One, could you proceed to Forty-eighth and 'O' to post?"

"So much for getting to the station," Carson said.

Brent asked, "Where are we going?"

"To a parking lot in the middle of town. The city is 'Status One' right now; there's only one ambulance available, and that's us."

"Man, I guess we don't have to worry about getting bored today," Eric said.

They were silent for several seconds while Carson looked for a place to turn around. Then Brent said, "Well, we may be busy, but the calls we're going on are boring ones."

"What do you mean?" Eric asked.

"We haven't done any car accidents or fires or anything."

Carson and Eric pondered Brent's statement while Carson turned the ambulance. Getting back up to speed, Carson said, "Maybe what you think a paramedic does is not really the case, Brent."

"What do you mean by that?"

Carson, who somehow managed to eat, drive, and talk at the same time, said, "You see, Brent, there are two types of calls we go on. There are what we call legit calls and non-legit calls. The kind of calls you're thinking about—where you rush into danger and save the hurting, innocent people—those are legit calls. But they hardly ever happen."

"I see that."

"When you think about it, the kind of calls you're thinking about, the legit calls, are calls you see in movies."

"The kind of stuff Superman would do," Eric joked.

"I think I'm more of a Batman guy," Carson said rather seriously.

"Really? Batman? He doesn't really swoop in and save people in the daylight."

Brent found this mental foray into superheroes absurd, but it continued.

"Yeah," Carson said, "I think I'm more of nighttime guy, you know. I've got that dark side."

"I guess I could see that," Eric said, eating a french fry like they were having a completely normal conversation.

"Batman knows you have to be bad to bad people sometimes."

"Hmm, that's a good point."

"Anyway," Brent interjected, "you were talking about legit calls."

"Oh yeah, legit calls," Carson said. "Legit calls are the little kid who has been hit by a car or fell out of a tree. His parents are telling him, 'Hang in there, Johnny, the paramedics will be here soon, and they'll make you feel better.'"

With mock enthusiasm, Eric sang, "Here Carson Comes to Save the Day!"

"I told you," Carson said, "I'm *not* Superman!" Then he added, "I do have a Superman shirt under this uniform, though, to bust out whenever I need it."

Brent furrowed his eyebrows. "You do?"

"No," Carson said, wondering if Brent really believed it. Brent felt stupid for asking, and Carson added, "But I do have a pair of Superman underwear."

Brent could never tell when Carson and Eric were joking, but he was sure this was a joke. "I'm so sure," he said.

Eric said, "No, he really does," with a tinge of humor in his voice.

Brent got tired of these games quickly. "Whatever, guys. I'm not that stupid."

"No," Carson said, "I really do. They're not mine, though. A girl left them at my house, and I still have them. I'm just hoping she'll come back to get them someday."

Eric tossed his head back and laughed. Carson laughed along with him and shook his head, relishing some experience from the past.

"Okay, we're getting *way* off subject here," Carson said, trying to control his amusement. "What I'm *trying* to say is that we don't do those Superman calls too much."

"We do at Saline County Fire and Rescue."

Eric raised his eyebrows as if to say, *Well, aren't we high and mighty?*

Carson said, "You know, Brent? While we're on the subject, you do strike me as the kind of guy who probably *at least* has Superman pajamas."

Eric broke into a slow laugh that caused his head to bend forward and his shoulders to jerk while he tried to suppress it. Carson's statement pegged Brent for what he was.

Brent was not amused. "You know what I mean. I'm just saying most of our calls are real emergencies."

Carson realized he shouldn't jerk the poor kid around any longer. "Well, yeah, I guess it is more like that on a rural squad, but it's not so much like that in town."

"Why not?"

"We spend all our time running the *same* people to the *same* hospitals for the *same* reasons."

"Like we're doing today?"

"Yeah. We clean the homeless people off the streets and give Dextrose to the same diabetic who's passed out at Wal-Mart again."

Eric, who had finally gotten over his amusement, added, "Or we run addicts in at three in the morning."

"Yeah, and we put Band-Aids on families who have beaten each other up for the tenth time."

"And a lot of attempted suicides too," Eric said.

"Okay, okay, I get your point," Brent broke in. "You're depressing me even more."

"That's reality," Carson said.

"They should get someone else to do that stuff," Brent said. "That's not what EMS is for. They should get social workers to run around in a van, or some private company."

Eric turned and looked at him. "We *are* a private company, Brent. And we *are* in a van."

"Yeah," Brent said, groping for words. "I mean . . . a different company, I guess."

"That's pretty much what we are, though," Carson said. "We *are* social workers. We just occasionally do EMS."

"But that's not what we're supposed to do," Brent said. "We're not here to counsel people. Our job is to save people's lives."

"What do you mean? We still do that," Carson said. "What do you think we did today with that lady in the nursing home? She was about to go into cardiac arrest when we got there, but she's still with us."

"But didn't you guys say you did the same thing for her a few weeks ago? Who knows if she even wanted to be revived when she doesn't even talk. She's so old!"

"He's got a point, Carson," Eric said. "You know, in cases like that, we're not really saving her life, we're just putting off her death."

Carson had nothing to say as he pulled the ambulance into the parking lot where they would post. Eric continued, "We do that for a lot of those patients, you know, especially in the nursing homes. I once heard someone say—maybe it was in college—that with all of our modern advances in medicine, we've gotten good at adding *years to life*, but bad at adding *life to years*."

Carson's head bobbed slightly while he and Brent processed Eric's statement.

"Think about Evelyn Bower," Eric said. "Do you remember her?" Carson nodded and shifted into Park. He reached over for the rest of his food.

Eric turned back to Brent. "She was an old woman who used to walk to the grocery store almost every day. We used to see her a lot. We once had to treat her when she fell down and cut her knee. She told us about all her grandchildren while we were looking at her leg—even pulled out pictures right in the middle of the call. Well, she had a heart attack one day. Carson and I showed up, found her in cardiac arrest, and worked her for a long time. By the time we got to the hospital, we had brought her back, but her brain was almost dead. Now she's a vegetable. She lives in a nursing home and can't walk or feed herself. She can move and look at you, but she can't make any meaningful words."

"That's sad," Brent said.

"Shoot!" Carson said, slamming his palm on the steering wheel.

"What?"

"We should have visited her today when we were at Lancaster Manor."

Eric shook his head. "You're right . . . but I don't feel like she even knows us when we're there."

"But that doesn't mean we're not getting through to her on some level."

Carson stared out the window for a moment and thought about Eric's arguments. He'd heard them in various forms before, and as always, he found himself wanting to refute them. Unfortunately, Carson never had a complete answer.

"So, do you think that's what we're doing out here, Eric?" he asked. "Do you think all we're doing is adding years to life, but not life to years, or however you said it?"

Eric was depressed, and he was honest. "Yeah, sometimes I think so. Not on every call, of course. Not the legit calls. But a lot of the time I think so."

Carson said, "I like to think that we do both. We add years *and* life. Don't you think we ever make a difference in anyone's lives?"

"Well, of course we do on the legit calls, when we save someone's life. I mean in those cases where it really means they have their life back."

"And the other times?"

"I don't know."

Carson, who had stopped eating, looked out his window again, like he was looking at the treetops for something. "You see," he said, "we have a real problem with this line of work."

"What's that?"

"We don't ever spend enough time with people. We swoop in, talk to them for a few minutes, if they can even talk, and then turn them over to someone else as soon as possible. You know, when you really stop to think about it, we don't really do much at all. Only once in a great while do we actually *heal* someone. We don't heal them; the doctors and nurses in the hospitals do that. We just keep them going until we get them to someone who can really help."

"Yeah, I guess I never really looked at it that way," Eric said.

"And even putting the sickness issue aside for a second, think about what we do for people's lives. We don't spend enough time with anybody to make a meaningful difference. I don't even think they remember our names. Why would they? We're taught to be the 60-second EMT and everything. The only people who really have a chance at making a difference in people's lives are the doctors and nurses who spend weeks with them and listen to their stories. The Boy Scout leaders, teachers, and coaches, even the police have way more interaction with people than we do. You know when people grow up and they say, 'You know, so-and-so really made a difference in my life. Just when I was hitting hard times Dr. So-and-so, or my coach, or my pastor steered me in the right direction.' They remember them. They never forget that person or their name."

Eric nodded as Brent sat and listened.

"They don't do that for us. And it's no wonder. First of all, who remembers someone they met during a traumatic experience for just a few minutes? And second, how often is someone's life better off after they met the paramedics than before? Not very often. If they don't end up a vegetable like Mrs. Bower, then they're usually maimed or hurt in some way. And if anyone helps them through that, it's not us. We're like caught in the middle. We don't get to see them before there's a problem, and we don't get to see them after."

"That's true, I guess," said Eric. "I don't know what else we can do though." Then he added facetiously, "Maybe you're in the wrong line of work. Maybe you're really a social worker at heart."

Carson laughed, somewhat relieved that Eric brought some levity to the situation. "Maybe you're right," he said, "but I can't really see myself doing that either. Maybe I need to come up with something new, something that would really make a difference."

"Like what?"

"Maybe Brent was onto something when he said 'social workers in vans.' Maybe I'll start my own company. Just some guys goin' around in a van, spreadin' the love, providing preventive medicine to those who need it, passing out antibiotics, looking for neglected children, visiting the lonely." He smiled at the other two to make sure they knew he was joking.

Eric asked, "What would you call it?"

"Hmm, that's a good question. How 'bout Treffer's City Repair Service?"

"Mmm, I don't think that really gets to the heart of the matter. You don't want people to think you do plumbing. How about Treffer's *Society* Repair Service?"

"Yeah, that's good. Treffer's Society Repair. We do it all, from broken marriages to broken bones. Give us a call. What do you think, Brent?"

"I think I'll stick to being a fireman . . . or a medic."

"Suit yourself, Brent. But don't come beggin' to me when this thing takes off."

Carson looked like he was going to say more but stopped when he looked in his side-mirror. "Oh, geez," he moaned, "looks like we've got company."

Eric looked in the mirror. A red fire engine approached on Eric's side. It was Engine Five.

Carson said, "I wonder what made them come out of their cave?"

As the truck pulled alongside, Eric rolled down his window. The driver was Manny Alvarez, seated next to his mentor, Mark Rader. Behind them was Nathan Tompkins, the Engine Five captain. Nathan had worked with Carson for years and was a friendly man who wanted only to fight fires and not Eastern Ambulance.

Manny rolled his window down and cut the motor since it was so much louder than E22's. "Things busy enough for you guys?"

Though Eric was closer, Carson answered, "Nope, it's never busy enough, Manny. What are you guys up to?"

Alvarez jerked his thumb over his shoulder, "Oh, we stopped at the supermarket to grab a few things for dinner. We thought we'd have spaghetti tonight. How 'bout you guys?"

"Well, you know how it goes on an ambulance; our lives are devoid of luxuries. We grabbed the 'Eastern Special'—fast food."

Rader had been sitting quietly looking out his own window. "That's why you guys should put more ambulances on the street. Then you would have more time, and the city wouldn't go Status One like this all the time. But I guess corporations just like to keep their costs to a minimum, don't they?"

Carson's hand tightened on the steering wheel. "Leave it to you, Mark, to ruin a cordial conversation. But if you must get into it, that's how we pass cheap prices to the patient. And I think we've got more than enough time. Don't you, Eric?"

"Oh yeah, we're already staffing four ambulances when the contract only requires three. Any more and we wouldn't have any work to do."

"Say, Mark," Carson said, "has Dave Conrad contacted you guys about a meeting?"

"For what?"

"We need to talk about what happened the other night," Carson said in a stern voice.

"What's there to talk about?"

"What's there to talk about?" Carson said, beginning to lose the restraint in his voice. "How about you telling the reporter you didn't hear the mom say everyone was out of the building!"

Rader looked at Carson with the beginnings of a smirk. "Again, what's there to talk about?"

Carson leaned over the center console, almost into Eric's space as he grew more agitated. "Rader, that is the shittiest thing I have *ever* seen you do, and if you pull any more stunts like that, we're going to take it to the papers and the county council and whoever else will listen. If they find out about stunts like that, you guys will never get the contract."

"You're assuming they would believe you over me, Carson. Nobody was there to witness what she said."

"Okay, guys," Nathan said from the back, "that's enough." Mark looked forward again. Carson sat upright in his own seat. "Let's not get into this again," Nathan continued. "Carson's right, Mark. Perhaps we need to sit down and talk about this before it gets outta hand. Carson, if you guys give us a call, I'm sure we can find the time."

Carson appreciated Nathan, one of the only reasonable people on the fire department. "Well," Rader said, "we'll see what the bosses have to say about that."

Eric noticed an almost imperceptible expression on Nathan's face. Nathan stared at the back of Mark Rader's head with shock and helpless resignation.

Carson debated in his mind how to respond to Mark's comment, but the radio tones sounded, followed by the dispatcher's voice. "Medic One, Engine One. Detox Center, 1401 South Sixth Street on seizure-like activity."

Carson cursed the interruption. After a brief pause, he picked up the mike. "Medic One clear."

Rader spoke up. "The Detox Center? Whoa, you guys got a long ways to go, but don't worry, it won't take Engine One long to get there."

"I know where it is, Mark!" Carson said. "But I'm surprised you could hear that considering all the hearing problems you've been having lately."

Before any of the firefighters had a chance to respond, Carson backed the ambulance away and drove off with the emergency lights beaming.

5.

Mark Rader was right; Engine One had them beat by a mile. Actually, it was more like two and a half miles. Fire Station One was downtown, near the Detoxification Center. Eastern Station One was even closer, but that didn't help when the ambulance itself was posted at a central location miles away. They had a long way to go, and it took six minutes.

The Detox Center was in a rundown public building under an overpass. Its purpose was to rehabilitate substance abusers, or at least those with no money. It lay just outside the developed downtown area in a much older industrial zone. The center was staffed by two older women who were paid very little but did their job because they had a heart for the displaced, homeless population that filled their beds.

Carson and Eric unloaded the cot and equipment and swiftly made their way inside, followed by Brent, who carried the remaining bags. The Center's halls were long and windy, but the cold concrete floors had been traversed many times by Eastern medics. There was no one at the door. Carson and Eric knew where to go, and they wound their way back into the large, cavernous room lined with small bunks.

In the adjoining room that served as an office, there was a small group of firemen talking to one of the Center's workers. They had obviously been in conversation for some time.

In the large room, several bunks held patrons, many of whom were Native Americans. Some lay beneath the charcoal-gray blankets, apparently asleep. Others sat on their bunks facing west toward the action at the end of the room and toward the sun that streamed in through a window on that side. They sat with blankets over their heads and shoulders, some of them oblivious to the scene, the conversations, or their surroundings. Instead, they gazed out the window toward the sinking sun, their faces showing no sign of emotion. Sometime back in their lives, or in their lineage, a great disconnect occurred. The world had moved without them, but the sun still set every evening. Life was punctuated by the next drink or the next ambulance.

When Carson made his way into the room, cot in tow, some of the stoic men livened a bit, and turned away from their steady gaze. "Carson," one of the men said, smiling in his direction.

Carson nodded at him. "James, how's it goin'?"

"Not too bad, man."

In the back corner bunk, the one near the window, a man lay on his side surrounded by a firefighter and the other Detox worker. Medic One made their way toward them. The man on the cot was Samuel Spirit Dog, a familiar face. He lay, barely conscious, in his worn blue jeans wet with urine. By the bed, his brown, beaded Western boots sat side-by-side, the leather tops flopping to the floor.

The Detox worker sitting next to him on the bunk was Mary. She placed her hand on Spirit Dog's shoulder. "Carson, he's really bad," the elderly woman said. "He's been having the shakes all over, and he hasn't eaten since he's been here."

"How long has that been, Mary?" Carson asked.

Before Mary could answer, the main group of firemen and Gladys, the only other daytime Detox worker, emerged from the office. The group that comprised the Alpha shift on Engine One was a disturbing lot. The Captain was Mike O'Malley, the president of the Firefighter Union. A firefighter for nearly thirty years, he'd risen through the ranks to Union President, a position of great power outside of the internal department chain of command. A tall, muscular man with a ruddy complexion, he hated Eastern Ambulance with a passion and hated Carson most.

The Paramedic onboard Engine One was Sheila Olson. She, too, had been a Lincoln firefighter for many years, though not nearly as long as O'Malley. Jeff Petrolak, another crewmember, was a middle-aged, squat, bald man who had worked on the department since he was old enough to work. He had achieved a spot on the engine with the "Boss" (as O'Malley was known) through seniority, and because he was one of O'Malley's few good friends. There was only one person on the crew that Eric and Carson liked. Tyrone was a tall, burly man who had not been a member of the fire department more than a few years. He was on Engine One because they needed some youthful energy to round out the crew.

As this was a medical call, and Sheila was the Paramedic, she initiated the conversation with Carson.

"As you can see, Carson, it's Samuel Spirit Dog again. It looks like ol' Samuel's been having a few drinks, just like he did last week and the week before that." As a downtown medic, Sheila knew most of the city's drunks by name.

"Carson, I don't know about you guys," she continued, "but we feel it's not necessary to take Spirit Dog to the hospital by ambulance. He's having some bad alcohol withdrawals and may or may not need to be seen by a doctor, but we were just explaining to Gladys that we don't feel it's necessary to involve EMS in this."

Gladys, who was now standing behind Sheila, said, "I'm sorry, Carson. We just didn't know. It's just that we were worried about him, and we have no way of transporting him. We thought a doctor should look at him."

Carson stopped her. "No, Gladys, we know you can't do that. It's no problem; you did the right thing."

This obviously perturbed the firefighters. Eric couldn't believe how quickly Carson could rile them without even trying.

O'Malley was the first to reply. "Actually, Carson, they probably *can* do this themselves. They *do* have a car." O'Malley had a vein that ran diagonally down his forehead when he grew agitated. It was prominent now in the perpendicular light of the setting sun.

"What's the problem, O'Malley?" Carson retorted. "You're not the one who has to transport him."

"No, but we *are* the ones who are supposed to be out there for car accidents and fires, and we can't be doing that when we we're down here in Detox all the time, can we, Treffer!"

Eric, who had been trying to stay out of the conversation, now spoke. "This is part of your job too, O'Malley."

"Stay outta this, kid," Petrolak said.

"Shut up, Petrolak."

Carson, who was sitting down on the opposite side of the bunk now stood. He was mad, but he clenched his fists and suppressed his emotions. "Okay, guys, I would love to sit around and discuss this, but the sooner we get Spirit Dog down to Lincoln General, the sooner we'll be done. And yes, we are taking him down there, because he does need to see a doctor, and because these ladies cannot lift him, carry him to their car, and take him down there by themselves!"

As Carson turned his attention toward the patient the emergency tones went off on the handheld radios. "Engine Three, status Red, Seventeenth and 'O' on an injury-accident."

Seventeenth and "O" was in both Engine One and Medic One's districts, but they were obviously occupied. "Status Red" indicated that all four ambulances were currently busy. Engine Three, the next closest unit, would have to treat the patient on-scene and wait for one of the ambulances to come back in-service.

O'Malley relished the situation. "You know, Carson, that's just what I'm talking about. This sounds serious, and we're stuck here babysitting instead. If you were smart, you'd go in-service so those people in the car wouldn't have to wait."

Over the radio, Engine Three cleared, and the dispatcher replied, "Engine Three, Status Red, Seventeenth and 'O' on a car-bicycle collision. Patient on the Southeast corner with bystanders."

"Engine Three clear," a voice said over the radio.

Everyone in the room heard the report and wondered if Carson would change his mind. Brent broke the silence, "Oh man, it sounds like they've got a crowd out there! How long will it be before they get an ambulance?"

No one answered, so he looked over at Eric. "I don't know," Eric said.

Carson tended Spirit Dog. As he felt for his pulse and tried speaking to him, he pretended not to hear O'Malley's suggestion.

"Samuel!" he shouted, "can you hear me?"

Carson tried to gauge the severity of Spirit Dog's condition. He rubbed his breastbone to elicit a response but got nothing. Brent, who was seated next to Carson and Sheila, looked over at him and said, "You know, Carson, we're not saving a life here."

Carson looked over at Eric for just a second, then stood up and momentarily gazed out the window. The edge of the sun was just beginning to dip under the horizon, but in that position it filled this cold, concrete room with a warm glow. Carson turned around and saw the other patrons staring back at him, as well as the firefighters. "You know, O'Malley, I don't think we can leave him here. We're gonna take him in. Eric, get the cot."

Eric walked away from the group toward the cot. At Carson's last statement, two of the firefighters left the crowd as well. As they stepped away from the group, Petrolak rolled his eyes in disgust and said, "This is so ridiculous."

O'Malley, right next to Eric, added just loud enough for all to hear, "That's what happens when you've got a fuck-up medic like him."

Carson pursed his lips in the middle of taking Samuel's blood pressure. Eric braced inside, fearing Carson would retaliate.

"You ready, Eric?" Carson said with deliberate coolness.

Eric lowered the cot to match the height of the bunk. "Yeah," he said.

Carson straddled the bunk at Spirit Dog's head, while Sheila stood at the foot. They lifted his shoulders and knees, and placed him on the cot.

"Carson," O'Malley said, "we're gonna split to get this other call."

Carson fastened a seatbelt around Spirit Dog, stood upright, and looked O'Malley in the face. "By now, Engine Three will get there before you guys do. We need you here so we can four-point the cot down the steps."

O'Malley took a step toward Carson. "I don't answer to you, Treffer. Last time I checked, you don't pay my salary, and you're not the fire chief. I didn't work twenty-six years in this county to answer to some punk-kid paramedic. I've already made the decision that Engine One is going to the other call."

The young firefighter, Tyrone, spoke up, "Hey, boss, I could stay here with these guys and help them out with the cot . . . that is, if you don't need me."

O'Malley turned to look at him.

"I mean," Tyrone continued, "just 'cause they need four men to get down the stairs."

O'Malley glowered at Tyrone, like he was an Army private mounting an insurrection. "All right, Tyrone. We'll pick you up at the hospital later."

Over the radio came a man's voice, "Dispatch, Medic Four is in-service at Bryan Memorial, we'll take that call at Seventeenth and 'O.'"

"Clear, Medic Four," the dispatcher replied.

The firemen quickly gathered their bags and equipment while the "Boss" picked up his handheld radio. "Dispatch, Engine One is in-service at Detox. We'll respond to the call at Seventeenth and 'O' as well." O'Malley made his way toward the door, and motioned for the other firefighters to follow.

"Clear, Engine One." The familiar, faceless voice emanated at once from the many radios in the room.

Shortly thereafter, Engine One left with lights and sirens blazing. Eric, Carson, Brent and Tyrone loaded Spirit Dog into the ambulance. He was having more delirium tremens and was still unresponsive.

"I'm so pissed!" said Carson. "There is no way Sheila should have suggested this guy go by POV." Carson used the official term for "personally owned vehicle." "I'm not the 'fuck-up' medic here—she is."

"Well," Tyrone said, "that's what happens when you keep someone on the payroll to shut them up."

"Yeah," Carson said, "that's terrible."

It was Carson's turn to tend the patient, so he climbed in the back with Tyrone while Eric drove. They used neither lights nor sirens since Spirit Dog was in bad shape, but not on the verge of immediate death.

Usually, Brent would ride in back as well, but when asked he replied, "No, that's okay, this one's kinda boring." Carson wanted to say something, but didn't.

"Man, that was stupid back there," Brent said to Eric in the cab.

"You're not kidding. I thought we were gonna get in a fistfight. Those guys were being such assholes to the Detox workers."

"Yeah, I thought so too, but that's not what I'm talking about. I mean, here Carson was just complaining about not getting any good calls, and then he decides to do this taxi ride instead of going to the pedestrian accident."

Eric looked over at Brent with incredulity.

Brent continued, "I mean, I don't think there's time for this kind of stuff in the city."

"No, Brent, he did it because it's still a medical call! You better watch what you say. You're beginning to sound like one of the firefighters."

Brent looked angry, like he was going to say something, but changed his mind and kept his mouth shut the rest of the trip.

6.

Two days later, Carson, Eric, and Brent stood around the gas pump as it churned and clicked, filling up the large tank on E22. As they did, they heard another loud diesel engine pull up alongside them. It was a huge, truck-type ambulance, painted red with the gold words "Lancaster County Fire Department" emblazoned across the square box. It made Eastern's white, van-type ambulance appear small and unimposing. The driver door opened, and Mike O'Malley stepped out, his white teeth showing through a smile he couldn't hide.

"Hey, guys," he said, "how's it goin'?"

Mark Rader appeared from the passenger's side. It was their day off, but there they were, the Union President and Vice-president testing out potential equipment.

Carson responded in a strained and obviously curious voice. "What the hell is this, O'Malley?"

O'Malley turned to look at the ambulance he'd just exited. It struck Eric as ironic that Mike O'Malley and Carson Treffer looked like two friendly neighbors standing side-by-side admiring a new pool in the backyard. The feeling wouldn't last.

"Oh, it's a new ambulance we're trying out. We're looking at ones from a few different companies, seeing what we like—what works for us."

Carson's face turned into a perplexed, troubled look. "Don't you think that's a little premature?"

Mark Rader exited from the passenger door and joined the others, his arms folded across his chest in a look of triumph.

"Premature?" O'Malley said. "Are you kiddin' me, Carson. It's the beginning of September. If we win the contract, we have to start providing emergency transport in less than four months. The way you guys keep stringing this thing out, we can't afford to sit around and let it all get thrown on us at the last minute."

Eric and Carson both knew that O'Malley was right. Still, they were caught off guard and greatly disheartened by the sight of a fire department ambulance. It was at that moment that a change occurred in Eric's mind. He felt it right away. It was the sudden realization that this wasn't just a paper game or a war of words. The fire department was trying—no, more than that—the fire department was actually *planning* to take their jobs from them very soon.

Neither Carson nor Eric had anything to say. O'Malley saw it in their eyes. Rader stood alongside the box with his hand on the red paint as if he were a used car dealer trying to make a sale.

"So, what do you guys think?" he said.

Carson stammered, "It's . . . it's nice." Then he tried to be more gracious. "It's quite impressive really."

"Yeah," O'Malley said, "the company is letting us borrow it for six months with the option to buy. They call it their Medical Attack Vehicle—the M.A.V."

O'Malley noticed Eric's eyebrows move in opposite directions and added, "I know the name's kinda cheesy, but that's what they call it. It's an appropriate name, though. It's got everything you need to treat several patients at once."

"You wanna see inside?" Mark Rader asked, knowing the interior was the clincher. Eric almost expected him to say, "You and the wife are gonna love the amenities inside."

Carson did want to see the inside merely out of a paramedic's curiosity but didn't because of O'Malley and Rader. The former urge was more powerful, however. Besides, saying no would make him look childish. "Yeah, let me finish up here," he said with his hand on the nozzle.

"Say," O'Malley said, "you know you're not supposed to fill up your tank with the engine running. That's a serious fire hazard."

Eric wondered if O'Malley could fine them for something like that.

Carson turned and looked at his old ambulance. "Oh . . . yeah, I know we're technically not supposed to do that . . ." Carson looked up at O'Malley. Rader stepped alongside the Boss like he really was going to fine them. "But we usually have to keep the engine runnin' all the time 'cause sometimes it doesn't start reliably." Carson's words were choppy and stilted.

"Seriously?" Rader said, his voice dripping with disdain.

"Well, to be honest, it probably wouldn't be a problem right now. It's been running all day, and it's plenty warm right now. It's just like that when it's cold."

O'Malley raised an eyebrow, and Mark shook his head noticeably, letting out a small, "Humph," as he turned away in disgust.

When the tank was full, Carson replaced the gas nozzle. The entire group walked around to the back of the big red beast. They climbed inside, where there was easily room for all of them. O'Malley stood at the back door. It was cavernous. Was there an opposite feeling to claustrophobia, Eric wondered. If so, he was feeling it now.

Rader pointed out all the amenities as he sat in the cockpit-like jump seat at the head of the cot.

"As you can see, if you need to, you can actually stand on the other side of the patient too, in case you need better access to the right side."

Carson and Eric only nodded their heads in a mixed feeling of genuine interest and suppressed humiliation. Brent, on the other hand, "oohed" and "aahed" with wide-eyed wonder. O'Malley enjoyed all three expressions. After the brief tour, they exited and returned to the space between the two ambulances, and for the first time it dawned on Eric that O'Malley didn't need gas—the fire department had its own gas—they had stopped only to show off their new vehicle to their least favorite ambulance crew.

"Carson," O'Malley said, "don't get me wrong. You guys have decent enough ambulances to get the job done . . ." He turned and looked at E22 with its engine still running. "Well, let me take that back. You have ambulances that barely get the job done."

"You can't judge us by this ambulance, O'Malley; you know that. This is only temporary. E60 and the others are top-of-the-line Type II's."

"Okay, Carson, but you have to admit that they pale in comparison to an ambulance like this."

Carson was cornered. "What can I say, O'Malley, it's pretty nice. It certainly does have some advantages to it." Carson tried to stop babbling. "One thing I will say, though, is I wonder how well it would fit in between cars and down narrow alleys?"

"Oh, c'mon, Carson. You know those are rare circumstances."

"I don't know," Carson said slowly. "It's amazing how many times a few extra inches would mean getting stuck at a busy intersection."

O'Malley was getting mad now. "Believe me, Carson, this thing would go wherever it needs to go, and the extra engine gets it there quickly. Unlike your vans, it doesn't get pushed all over the interstate by the wind; at ninety-five miles per hour, this thing holds the interstate like a train on rails."

Carson nodded his head in affirmation and growing defeat. "That's true; these aren't the best vehicles on the interstate."

"Plus," O'Malley added, "you've got twice as much space inside, and it has a GPS tracking computer in the cab. Did I show you that?" O'Malley grabbed the door handle and pointed inside. "Do you wanna see it? It's pretty impressive."

Carson waved his hand and said, "No, that's okay. I'm sure it's pretty nice."

"It's also got more storage, a built-in respirator, and of course, traffic-signal pre-emption."

When O'Malley finished, Carson was silent for a few seconds, then said, "What can I say, O'Malley? It's certainly the nicest ambulance I've ever seen. Is that what you want me to say?"

"I don't want you to say anything. I just thought you might enjoy it."

"Hmm."

O'Malley sensed the resignation in Carson's voice. There was no denying that the mere sight of the ambulance had affected him.

O'Malley opened his door like he was getting ready to leave but wasn't finished. "Who knows, maybe some of your Eastern buddies will be working in one of these soon."

Carson was mad now. "Yeah, I don't see that happening, O'Malley." Then he touched his finger to his bottom lip. "Say, Mike, that reminds me of a rumor I heard recently. I heard that you have a daughter who might be working with us soon."

The fire captain's eyes narrowed. "She was thinking about it," he said. "But she's changed her mind. It'll never happen. I promise you that." He climbed inside and started the engine, then rolled down the window to say, "I'm glad you like fire department's ambulance,

Carson. You have to admit—it certainly has all the bells and whistles a man could ask for."

Happy to get the last word in, O'Malley drove away. When Carson and Eric returned to E22, it felt more archaic than usual.

———

That afternoon, Eric, Brent, and Carson sat in Station One trying to fill up dead time before an important company meeting that night. There was no denying that Carson and Eric felt morose after their run-in with O'Malley and his "Medical Attack Vehicle." Eric read a book, and Carson flipped through TV stations. After seeing O'Malley again, Brent recalled the scene at the Detox Center and remembered something he had been wanting to ask.

"What did Tyrone mean when he was talking about Sheila and said, 'keep someone on the payroll just to shut them up?'"

Eric looked over at Carson with a telling look.

"You've got a lot to learn about the fire department, Brent," Carson said as he flipped through the channels. "Don't you read the *Cowboy*?"

"The what?"

"The *Lincoln Cowboy*. It's an alternative online newspaper."

"No, I've never even heard of it."

"You've never heard of it? We've got to introduce you to this; it's important stuff." Carson turned off the TV, thankful for the distraction, and climbed out of his seat.

Carson took Brent into one of the bedrooms where the computer was located. Eric remained on the couch reading his novel.

"If you want to be fully informed about everything that's going on in our city and county governments, Brent, you've got to read the *Cowboy*."

"Don't listen to him, Brent," Eric yelled from the other room. "Unless you believe all the crap in the tabloids, you're not going to get anything useful off that Web site."

"Never mind him. He only believes what he wants to believe. Here it is." Carson had pulled up the Web site at lincolncowboy.com. "You see, this guy, Harvey, is the editor of the paper."

"He's the *everything* of the paper!" Eric yelled again.

"Would you just shut up for a second! If you're gonna take part in this conversation, then come in here. Otherwise, be quiet and read your dumb book!"

"All right! Calm down," Eric said, putting the book down to join them.

The home page was up. *The Lincoln Cowboy*, it ran. "Standing against corruption in local government."

Carson continued. "Harvey runs a pool hall and does this on the side. Now, let's see . . ."

"He does what?" Brent asked.

"He runs a pool hall. He's the owner and bartender. It's kind of a hole-in-the-wall joint."

"So this is like a hobby?"

"I guess you could call it that."

"Why doesn't he sell the paper?"

"I think he wants to someday, but it has to catch on, I guess. I don't know, ask him."

"What does he report on?"

"What *doesn't* he report on?" Eric interjected.

"Hold on, I'll show you," Carson said as he clicked through the pages. "This is an older article, but it talks about what Tyrone was talking about."

"County Deputy Fire Chief Suspected of Sexual Assault," the headline ran.

"Deputy Fire Chief Lou Killion is currently the darling of Commissioner McDaniels' administration; however, everyone seems to have forgotten the troubled history he has had with the fire department.

"In February, 1997, Firefighter Sheila Olson filed a complaint with the County's Equal Opportunity Office alleging that Deputy Killion had sexually assaulted her. According to Olson, Killion grabbed and fondled her when they were alone at Fire Station Nine. He then tried to remove her clothes and attempted to have sex with her. She warned him that she would scream for help if he didn't stop and eventually persuaded him to back down. Ms. Olson claimed at

the time that she had been bruised on her wrists during the altercation with Killion.

"Within weeks, Ms. Olson withdrew her complaint, citing the fact that enough action had been taken in the case, and that it had gotten blown out of proportion. The commissioner's office encouraged her to pursue action if she felt it was necessary, but she declined."

"Wow, that's crazy," Brent said with a skeptical look. "Do you think it's true?"

"Yeah, probably," Carson said. "But it's kind of a he-said, she-said thing. I'm pretty sure Killion did something, but she even said herself that it got blown outta proportion."

"What do you think, Eric?"

"I guess I wouldn't be too surprised if it was true. But I agree with Carson, it's a he-said, she-said thing."

"Does it say anything else?" Brent asked.

"Not about that incident," Carson said, "but there's more about Killion. Check this one out."

"Deputy Fire Chief in Ugly Divorce," it ran.

"Not reported in the mainstream media is the divorce being filed by Lynda Killion against her husband, Lou Killion, deputy fire chief of the Lancaster County Fire Department. Mrs. Killion filed in Seward County in an effort to keep the divorce low profile. In papers filed, Mrs. Killion reports incidents of abuse, citing three instances in the last year in which Deputy Chief Killion allegedly choked her and threatened violence to himself if she ever left him.

"According to a source close to the deputy chief, Mrs. Killion has removed herself from the home. Their two children stay with their father, however. If the allegations prove to be true, it will not be the first case in which Deputy Chief Killion was accused of violence (click here for further details), and this paper would not be surprised. We contacted Commissioner McDaniels' office to inquire what action the county is taking in the case. The commissioner's press secretary says no action is being taken at this time, citing the fact that the allegations concern the deputy's personal life, and that he continues to perform exceptionally well in his role as deputy chief. Jack Winkenwerder, chief of the Lancaster County Fire Department, had *no comment on the case. Stay logged onto the Lincoln Cowboy for updates as they come."*

"I don't know about this," Brent said. "This guy just seems to be digging up trash on the fire department. They're right; divorce is someone's personal life."

"Yeah, but who 'threatens violence to themselves' if someone is going to leave them?" Carson said. "The guy has some issues, and he might not be in the right state of mind to be in a position of power."

"I guess that's a good point," Brent said. "I wonder who this source close to the deputy chief is?"

"Yeah, that's what we were wondering. It could be any number of people. It could be Tyrone or Marty or Sheila, or anyone as far as we can tell."

"What else do they have?" Brent asked, still peering over Carson's shoulder.

"There's a whole section of stuff about the fire department and us," Carson said, clicking on the link: "Click here for related articles."

This brought up a page entitled, "AMBULANCE ISSUE." Brent saw about a dozen articles, two of which were now colored purple: "Deputy Fire Chief Suspected of Abuse," and "Deputy Fire Chief in Ugly Divorce."

The most recent headline was emblazoned across the top: "Deceased Child's Mother Arrested; Social Worker Under Investigation."

"Oh my God," Carson said, squinting his eyes to focus on the screen. He clicked the link.

"This morning, police officials reported that Barbara Turner, 32, was arrested on suspicion of child neglect in connection with the death of her eight-year-old son, Adam Turner. Adam, who suffered from cerebral palsy and was bound to a wheelchair, was found on the morning of August 27 when emergency personnel responded to a fire at his residence.

"Upon arrival, EMS and fire personnel found Mrs. Turner with two other children outside the burning trailer. There is some contention between Eastern Ambulance and Lancaster County Fire personnel as to whether or not Mrs. Turner stated that no one

remained in the building. Eastern Ambulance paramedic, Carson Treffer, claimed she had reported that no one was left inside, but fire personnel could not corroborate his statement. Later, Mrs. Turner also denied making such claims.

"Soon after containing the fire, emergency personnel did learn that Adam was inside. Firefighters retrieved him from the building but found him severely burned and unconscious. Attempts to revive him both en route to and in the hospital proved unsuccessful.

"An autopsy later confirmed Adam's death was not a result of the fire. Carbon monoxide levels in his blood were less than one percent. Officials at the medical examiner's office stated that a person who has died from smoke inhalation typically has carbon monoxide levels of thirty percent or higher. Furthermore, there were no signs of burns or smoke inhalation in the child's trachea or lungs, indicating that he was not breathing at the time of the fire. The cause of death was identified as complications from pneumonia. It was also discovered that the child had not been given his anti-seizure medications. His body was emaciated, showed signs of malnourishment, and had several bed sores.

"Fire officials continue to investigate the cause of the fire but have ruled out accidental ignition from a fan in the room. Evidence indicates that the fire started in Adam's room, which he shared with an older sibling.

"The findings of the autopsy prompted police to arrest Mrs. Turner on the charge of neglect of a dependent. An investigation has been launched by Child Protective Services into the actions of HomeCare social worker, Thomas Murray. As Adam's caseworker, Mr. Murray was charged with ensuring the safety and health of the boy, and it is now being determined whether he was negligent in his duties. Stay logged onto the Lincoln Cowboy for more details as they become apparent."

"Oh, man!" Brent said. "I can't believe they arrested her. Do you think she let him die on purpose?"

"I have no idea," Carson said. He stared at the monitor with the mouse in his hand.

Eric said, "You see, Carson. There are plenty of other people who saw Adam enough to see if he was neglected."

"Yeah," was all Carson could say.

"Don't start second-guessing yourself again. We hadn't even seen him before that for a month. The kid we found that night was *not* the kid we saw all those other times. Carson, you've got to lighten up on yourself."

"You're right, Eric. I know you're right. I just wish I could've prevented it, and there's a part of me that still thinks I should've somehow. One thing's for sure, though."

"What's that?"

"As this story heats up, it's that much more important that we get in and talk to the fire department. I don't want any of us to get dragged into this blame game, and the way it reads now, it sounds like I'm trying to cover up something. I wonder if it's in the real newspaper, yet."

"I hope Hank and Dave are working on that meeting," Eric said.

"They'd better be," said Carson, "or I'm gonna have to do it myself."

7.

Dave Conrad, the General Manager, had scheduled a company-wide meeting that night. These meetings were regular events during which certain ambulance runs were picked out for educational purposes, but they had grown in scope and included plans, strategies, and issues surrounding the possible loss of the contract. There was also rumors of an important announcement.

Station One had a large room on the second story that was used for CPR classes and was simply known as the Classroom. Since they were working on Medic One that night, Carson, Eric, and Brent only had to walk down the hall to attend the meeting. Most of the others had the day off and wore civilian clothes. The only disadvantage to being on duty was leaving the meeting when the tones went off. Sometimes it happened, sometimes it didn't.

As he walked into the room, Eric saw that it was filling up quickly. The room held three rows of tables facing the dry-erase boards on a long wall. Carson sat in the second row on the far side of the room talking to an older woman who was not overweight, but somewhat short and stocky. It was Leslie Hunter, one of Eastern's more senior Medics, having worked with the company for more than fifteen years. Those fifteen years had passed, though, and no one had bothered to tell Leslie. She took pains every morning to prepare her hair with an odd assortment of heat and chemicals to create the perfectly out-of-style look she adopted sometime in late high school.

Leslie was slightly older than Carson, but the cumulative amount of time she put under tanning bed lights gave her skin an unbelievably dark hue and a leathery coarseness that would have fooled any carnival guesser. Her older appearance once caused Carson to call her "Mama." She mistook it for a sign of respect, and the name stuck.

Eric made his way to an open seat near them and could tell the gossiping had already started. The love for bad news about the fire department had become an almost universal obsession, and Leslie was especially good at it.

"Are you serious?" Carson said to her as Eric approached.

"Yeah, I heard about it from somebody who works downtown."

Eric knew he had missed something, and he asked what it was. Leslie repeated her story, and Carson kicked back in his chair, put his cowboy boots up on the table, and folded his arms in disgust.

"I know a girl who works for the county in the Department of Buildings and Safety who says that the Commissioner's been replacing some of them with firefighters."

"Is that wrong?" Eric asked, not knowing anything about the Department of Buildings and Safety.

"Well, yeah! That office is generally run by architects and engineers, people who know a lot about buildings. Jamie said that one engineer got fired last year for too many tardies, and the next thing they knew there was a retired firefighter working there. I guess he had a back injury and couldn't work as a fireman anymore."

Eric was interested but thought the story sounded groundless and typical.

"That totally sounds like the Union pulling a few strings," Tim, another senior medic, said in his gruff, smoker's voice.

"I know; that's what Jamie thinks. That was last year, but a few weeks ago, they hired Inspector Stanley to *run* the department after the last guy resigned."

She paused a few seconds as if the words were profound and needed time to sink in. But seeing something between skepticism and ambivalence on Eric's face, she said, "Don't you get it, Eric?"

"No," he said with one eyebrow raised. "What's wrong with Inspector Stanley getting hired in a department that does inspections?"

She didn't appreciate his sarcasm. "First of all, Eric, *maybe* Inspector Stanley would know enough to work in the department, but not *run* the department! And besides, I don't think he knows that much about engineering and architecture. He was a fire inspector. And second, Jamie doesn't even know why the first guy even resigned, but she knows he wasn't happy with the new 'selection procedures.'"

Leslie said the last two words making quotation marks with her fingers, then crossed her arms as if her words were shocking. Carson now had his fingers locked on top of his head. He looked over at Eric as if to say, "See what I've always told you."

"That's crazy," was the only thing Eric could think to say. However, as usual, he thought they were making a big deal out of nothing.

By now, the room was nearly full. Though the meeting was officially mandatory, it didn't have that feel. People poured into the classroom, accompanied by a great deal of harassing, back-slapping, and talking. Some of the more senior medics, like Leslie, were supervisors of one of Eastern's four teams. The four teams were organized around four scheduled shifts. Leslie was supervisor of her partner, Tim, the middle-aged man with terrible smoker's voice, and several others on the A-team. Carson was supervisor of the D-team. He called them the Delta Force, after the elite Army unit.

Each team had eight medics. Plus, there were several more EMTs that worked the "transfer cars," the Basic Life Support ambulances that moved stable patients from hospital to hospital or nursing home to physician office, which was Eric's job in the past and was now the job Brent was slated to do after his ride time. But the ensemble of about forty-five front-line medics comprised only half of Eastern's employees. Eastern also had an internal dispatch center, a billing office that contracted with hospitals and doctors' offices, and a small cadre of administrators like Dave and Hank and several others. All told, nearly ninety jobs were on the line.

The room reached capacity, and many had to stand at the back. Attendance had improved since the meetings had become less about education and more about survival.

Dave Conrad, the company president and a rather plain-looking man, began the meeting by getting everyone to hush. "I'm glad everyone could make it tonight," he said. "I didn't know you guys liked donuts so much, but if it works, it works."

Dave was certainly not a comedian, and it was evident when no one laughed.

"We have several things to go over tonight. First, we need to take care of some announcements and a few matters of business. Then I just want to open things up for discussion, because I know everyone has a lot on their minds. Lastly, we have a new member of the team who we will introduce."

Carson looked over at Eric to indicate mutual anticipation.

"First I want to thank everyone for their hard work. I know that the call volume has been increasing, and a lot of our crews are really being pushed hard, but you guys are still doing a great job. It doesn't seem like it sometimes, but I know the city really appreciates your work and the quality of service you deliver. We get a lot of letters or calls to say thank you from people whose lives we've touched, and I always try to pass those on to those who were involved.

"Also, I want to point out that it looks like we're on track for having more code-saves this year than ever before. Many of you have participated in at least one code-save this year, and one medic, Carson Treffer, already has five. That's five people whose hearts had stopped but are still with us today because of Carson's hard work. I think that deserves a round of applause for Carson, for his partner, Eric Wright, for Leslie Hunter, who has three, and for all of you that have made at least one 'code-save' this year."

As he clapped, Eric leaned over to Carson, who looked somewhat uncomfortable when Dave singled him out, and said, "Good job, man. I hear that means a lot more money for you."

"No kiddin?" Carson replied with mock enthusiasm. "Will that push me above the poverty level?"

"Probably not."

Dave continued, "I know that if Max Dougherty were still alive today, he would be proud of what Eastern Ambulance has become. We have not only made a fine name for ourselves here in Eastern Nebraska but have done so in Grand Island and our other Central operations as well. That is solely a result of our great employees."

He continued for several minutes about Eastern employees and the great tradition of the company, and all the other mandatory things that managers have to talk about. Then he introduced Susan Bledsoe, Eastern's Quality Improvement Coordinator who reviewed two ambulance calls. One was, she said, "just a unique situation," and the other was a "learning opportunity." They were typical and yielded only moderate debate. People didn't care about that stuff anymore.

Then Dave said he had a call he wanted to talk about. It was Eric and Carson's call with Adam Turner. "It's on everyone's minds," he said, "and we may as well discuss it." He briefly related the story and informed those who didn't know about Adam Turner's death, and about Mark Rader's comments to the media.

"Talking with Carson, management has decided to schedule a

meeting with Chief Winkenwerder, Deputy Chief Killion, and Mark Rader. We need to talk about Rader's actions and give them a strong message that we need to play together as a team. We've contacted the chief several times, and he said he was working on a time to meet with us. So far, our schedules have conflicted too much, but we'll get to that soon, I'm sure."

Several people booed out loud.

"They're not gonna meet with us," Tim growled from his seat.

"Well," Dave said, holding his palm out toward the crowd, "I wouldn't count that out just yet. They said they plan on it; we just need to wait for a time when it fits into everyone's schedules."

The next ten or fifteen minutes dissolved into a free-for-all with people making comments like, "Isn't there some way we can get the people of the city to know about this stuff?" Or, "If the fire department is like this now, how much worse would they be if they won the contract?" Again, same ole comments, Eric thought. People vented. Some tried to come up with real ideas. Others just discredited Deputy Chief Killion, Captain O'Malley, and "all the rest of 'em."

Finally, Carson spoke up, "Why don't we just go over there?"

"Carson," Dave replied, "you know we can't do that. You can't just walk into somebody's office and demand to speak with them. That's too aggressive."

"But they're being aggressive."

"I know, Carson. We'll work on scheduling a meeting, but if they don't cooperate, we've done all that we can do."

"Which isn't much," Carson said under his breath. He was displeased, but in reality, deep down he had always known that there would not be a meeting, and he resigned himself to that now.

Usually, a meeting like this would drag on, but not tonight. Dave had to stop the complaint session early, because as he had promised there was one more item to take care of.

"As all of you know," he said once he got their attention, "we have become a little short-staffed in recent months. We've lost a few people to the fire department, and others have moved on to other parts of the country. Also, we promoted some of our EMTs to the 911 trucks. As such, we've been short on people to work the transfer cars.

Well, we've just hired two new EMT-Basics to fill those positions. By now, I'm sure you've all met Brent Cunningham."

Dave pointed at Brent, sitting in the third row. "He is a registered Basic, and is in the process of getting his Associate's Degree in Firefighting Science at the community college. He is a volunteer firefighter and EMT at Saline County Fire and Rescue, and has been riding with Carson and Eric for his orientation." Dave elicited a short applause from the group by clapping his hands.

"Recently we hired another Basic. I'm going to ask Hank to come up here to introduce her."

Hank had been standing near the side of the room but now walked toward the front—folding his thin, leathery arms in front of his chest. "Well, as Dave said, we just hired another EMT-Basic. She just received her registry from Southeastern Community College and has come to us for experience. She's fresh out of school."

Hank extended his hand toward the back of the room. Eric and all the others turned. It took only seconds for Eric to realize that it was the girl who had waved to them on campus that day.

"Oh—my—God," Carson said quietly through clenched teeth.

"I guess that's why she waved at us," Eric said under his breath. "It's O'Malley's daughter."

She looked almost too young to work on an ambulance, Eric thought. But then again, people often thought the same about him. She had reddish-brown hair and green eyes that smiled all on their own. She was even prettier than she appeared the other day. She stood with her hands in her back pockets and blushed while Hank continued his introduction.

"She's also a full-time student at the University of Nebraska and will be working with us mainly on evenings and weekends, but also on weekdays when she doesn't have classes. Everyone, I want you to meet out newest employee, Katie O'Malley."

O'Malley? Immediately, Katie's demeanor revealed a subtle change. She was scanning the crowd to gauge impact.

"And," Hank continued, "we may as well answer the question that's on your mind. She has a great deal of exposure to EMS and fire issues because her dad is a firefighter here in Lincoln whom you all probably know."

"Oh—my—God!" Carson said again, biting one of the fingers in his closed fist.

To say her father was a firefighter here in Lincoln was certainly an understatement. Captain O'Malley! Hank was trying hard to dissipate that issue as soon as possible, Eric thought, but it wouldn't go away. Even Hank had to know that.

"Soon," Hank continued, "Katie will be doing some orientation with various crews. We haven't determined which ones yet."

Carson leaned over. "Shit, we already have Brent as a tag-along." But his words were loud enough for those around to hear, including Brent.

Eric winced in frustration at the thought that they already had a ride-along, then turned to the back of the room again. He could tell Katie was uncomfortable with everyone facing her. It was like being the daughter of a celebrity, he thought, an infamous one. So he turned to the front of the room to save her the pressure of at least one set of eyes.

Obviously, Hank shared Eric's thoughts. "Okay everyone, give the poor girl some breathing room," he said waving his hands toward the front of the room, "but as you do, join me in welcoming her to the team."

Hank clapped and everyone followed suit.

Dave took over again and droned on about the status of the company. Eric couldn't pay attention. Carson had been right—she was hot, and had to be bold, even rebellious. Otherwise, she wouldn't have chosen to work at Eastern. She looked like so many of those beautiful sorority girls he'd seen on campus. Yet, what kind of sorority girl leaves the confines of campus to become an EMT for a company her dad loathes? There was no way in hell that O'Malley approved of this.

The meeting ended only slightly late. Carson and Eric got up and moved toward Hank and Katie, but just as soon as Dave concluded the meeting, Hank and Katie ducked out the door. Eric figured they had more business to take care of. Most likely, though, Hank was just trying to shield Katie from too many uncomfortable questions early on. Eastern Ambulance had good people working for them, but they weren't necessarily a tactful bunch. Eric understood, and as difficult as it was, he decided not to follow.

Carson, however, was gone. He was a flirt of high repute. That was certainly Carson's biggest weakness. His vices never bothered Eric much (other than his fast driving), but as Eric watched Carson dive out the door, he realized his friend's vices bothered him now.

8.

Eric was tempted to leaf through the newspaper as he drove but didn't, knowing it was an obvious traffic hazard. How many times had he seen people make the same mistake and end up paying for it with a trip to the hospital? Instead, he waited until he was safely inside the parking garage at Station One.

Though he was heading to Station One, he was not on his way to work. Eastern Ambulance was having a picture taken for a public relations ad in the paper. The county council vote was in little more than a week, and administration was ramping up the effort to win.

Eric would have been far less enthused about going to work on his day off were it not for his newest coworker. It was one of the reasons he came early. The other reason was that he and Carson wanted to have a talk with Hank, which was, after all, a related issue.

He parked his car in the small lot located under half of the building (the smallest "parking garage" Eric had ever seen) and opened the paper. Sure enough, in the Local section there was an article about the ambulance situation. As he read it, Eric heard Carson coming up the road in his old pickup.

Eric finished the article and got out of his car to wait for Carson, who swung his pickup into an open spot. He opened his door, and a Coke can fell on the pavement.

"Shit!" Carson said. He picked up the can and threw it back into the truck before slamming the door.

"You know, Carson," Eric said, "there's a trash can right here."

"Hmm . . ." he said, looking to see if it was worth going back to the truck to get it. Apparently, it wasn't. He shrugged his shoulders and continued toward Eric.

"Anything good in the paper?" Carson asked.

"Yeah, something about the social worker."

"Let me guess—fired?"

Eric nodded. "You already read it?"

Carson folded his arms and stared down the road. "No, but that's what I thought would happen after reading that article in the *Cowboy*."

Eric said, "He hadn't made a visit to Adam in over three weeks. Prior to that, his reports show Adam was doing 'normal.' They say that those last two weeks were the critical ones, though."

"We hadn't seen him in five weeks," Carson said.

"Yeah, that sounds about right."

"No, it was five weeks. I looked it up on my last run report."

"Oh, yeah? Anything stand out?"

"No, just another seizure. Mom wanted him to go to the hospital. The usual."

"I remember."

"Yeah, and I did note that we looked at his back and legs for seizure injuries."

"And no sign of bedsores?"

"No, and he was doing fine post-seizure, but we took him in anyway. I'm glad we took him in. That really covers us."

"What do you think she wanted?" Eric asked. "For somebody to keep him at the hospital or something?"

"That's possible. Maybe she thought they'd determine he was too sick to be left with her, and that Child Protective Services would keep him or something. Maybe she was trying to raise enough flags to have him actually taken from her."

"Who knows?" Eric sighed as the two of them made their way inside. "Maybe she was crying out for help in her own strange way?"

—

"Aren't you guys early?" Hank asked. "The picture's not till one."

"Yeah, we know," Carson replied. "We just wanted to talk to you about something first."

"Uh-oh, I don't like the sound of that," Hank said, scratching his nose.

Carson and Eric plopped down in two chairs in front of Hank's desk. It was nice to be here in street clothes for a change, and not to worry about the tones going off.

"No," Carson continued, "it's nothing bad, really. It's just that

Eric and I don't think the whole thing with Brent is working out. We're not really seeing eye-to-eye on things, and I just think it might be better for him to rotate onto some other truck."

"You guys wouldn't have any ulterior motives would you? Like, another trainee?" Hank asked.

"Well, yeah, there might be that too," Carson said in a matter-of-fact tone that only he could pull off, "but that's beside the point. He's really just starting to get on our nerves."

"Well, Carson, I don't think you have to worry about that anymore," Hank said as he leaned back in his chair. "Brent quit."

"What?"

"Yeah, he quit yesterday."

"Oh my gosh!" Eric said. He felt inexplicably guilty.

"Why?"

"You'll never guess."

"Were Carson and I not accommodating him enough?"

"Hmm, I don't know, you tell me," Hank said.

Carson said, "We were always super friendly to him! And we always let him in on whatever calls he wanted. That's the problem; he was only half-interested most the time!"

"Oh, okay," Hank said. "You guys were just making me think I should ask. No, he quit because he actually got hired by the fire department."

"Are you serious?" Eric asked.

"Yep."

Carson looked over at the wall like he was thinking. "That's what he always wanted, wasn't it?"

"Probably so," Hank said. "He was in school to get his Fire Science degree, ya know."

"He just came here as a stepping stone to get to the fire department," Carson said indignantly.

"But there's nothing wrong with that," Hank said, leaning forward again. "You've gotta do what you've gotta do, ya know. I just can't seem to get our transfer car staff up to a hundred percent."

"He didn't even give two weeks?"

"No, he said he had to start today. And since he wasn't really working yet, he asked if I thought that was a problem. Of course it wasn't; better get him off the payroll now while he's not contributing anything. The problem is that we're short again for the long haul. I bet he didn't think he'd get hired so soon."

"So, is he just a basic firefighter?" Eric asked.

"I guess so. But as you know, all the new firefighters have to be certified EMTs now."

"That makes sense," Carson said. "I don't think he ever was that interested in the EMS side."

"Yeah, I don't know. Maybe he still wants to be a Fire-Medic someday."

"Man, that was a waste of our resources," said Eric. "He never even finished training."

"That happens sometimes. On a brighter note, I don't think our newest Basic will do the same thing. She seems to be doing this because she really likes medicine. I think she wants to be a doc."

"Yeah, but what about her dad?" Carson asked, cutting straight to the chase.

"I asked her in the interview if it was going to be a problem for her family. She said she was living on her own now, and that she was an adult. That was good enough for me and Dave."

"So, have you decided who she's going to be doing her ride-alongs with?" Eric asked.

"No, I actually have to talk to her more about that. I was thinking about Leslie, but it will depend on her schedule and whether she has any preferences or not. Don't worry, guys. I can see that you're worn out by ride-alongs; I won't burden you with another one."

Carson shook his head. Only Hank laughed.

"Don't worry," Carson said, "she'll want us."

A man popped his head in the office door and tapped on the door jamb. "Hank Jenkins?" he asked, looking toward Hank's desk. He was an older man with a gray Fu Manchu moustache, a camera in his hands, and bags slung over his shoulders.

"Yeah, that's me," Hank said. He stood and extended his hand.

"I'm Charlie Overstreet . . . from the paper."

"Yeah, thanks for coming, Charlie. This is Eric and Carson. They're two of our medics on the D-team."

"Pleased to meet you guys," the reporter said, shaking hands. "You guys gonna be in the picture today?"

Carson started to speak but was interrupted by Hank. "Yeah,

they'll be there."

"Great, how many people do you expect, Hank?"

"I'm hoping just about everybody." Hank began shutting down his computer. "So that should be at least seventy or eighty. They'll be strollin' in soon, but some of them will probably be late."

"Yeah, I already saw a group of twenty or thirty up there," Charlie said with evident enthusiasm. "Now, I know you call the shots, but I'd like to go out in front of the building and check it out."

"Let's do it." Hank waved his guest back to the door.

"I'm just gonna change into uniform first," Carson said.

"I'll be down in a second," Eric said. "My uniform's upstairs."

Eric went up to the crew quarters in a hurry. He opened the second bedroom door and stopped in his tracks. Katie stood with her back to him in a new Eastern Uniform looking into the mirror. She fiddled with her shirt buttons and appeared to have just finished dressing.

"Oh," Eric stammered with his hand still on the doorknob.

Her reflection in the mirror looked up at him in surprise.

"I'm sorry," he continued. "I mean . . . I should have knocked."

Eric could see why Katie was messing with her shirt. While it fit everywhere else, it was too tight around her bust. Eric started to close the door in front of him.

Her reflection now revealed a quirky, forlorn smile.

"No, don't worry," she said. "I guess I should have made sure the door was locked. But I'm done. It's just that the shirt's a little too small."

She was turning red now. Eric guessed she had been messing with it for several minutes. She had gotten it buttoned, but it looked like the buttons might burst.

"Oh?" he said. He wondered if he shouldn't have stared at her chest. "Doesn't Hank have any more shirts?"

"No . . . I mean, yeah, but they're up at the warehouse. He just brought this uniform down for me for the picture. I have to get fitted for my real uniform tomorrow."

"The pants fit nice," Eric said, then realized that came out wrong too. "I mean—"

She smiled. "Thanks. But they're a little loose around my seat."

"What size is it?" he asked.

"The shirt or my seat?"

Eric chuckled. "The shirt."

She returned the chuckle. "It's a Small, which is what I asked for," she said, somewhat exasperated as she dropped her arms and looked at herself in the mirror, "but it's just too tight."

She stopped speaking when she looked up and saw Eric staring at her chest again. He noticed and averted his eyes.

"I can see that," he said. "Well, I have a Medium you could probably wear for now." He made his way over to his bag in the corner.

He moved to the other side of her, and she turned to look at him.

"Really?" she said. "That would be so great."

"But it's not clean. As long as you don't mind that."

"No, that's fine!" Eric handed the shirt to her. "As long as it's not totally disgusting."

"You'll have to be the judge of that."

"You weren't planning on wearing it, right?"

"No. I should have another one in here." Eric searched through the bag, but after a few seconds, he realized he didn't.

"Okay," he said slowly, "I guess I took that one home to wash it."

"Oh, here, nevermind." Katie handed the shirt back to him.

"No, you can wear it. I could probably wear the Small."

"You think?" She looked him up and down.

"Yeah, it shouldn't be a problem. I have to get the mediums taken in at the waist anyway."

"Are you sure?"

"No, but we could at least try it."

"If it doesn't work, we won't do it."

"Okay. Just hand it out to me when you're done," he said and closed the door.

Eric stepped into the hallway and waited for her. Man, I can't believe you stared at her like that, he told himself, leaning against the wall. He thought about the way he could see her skin through the buttonholes. Apparently she hadn't thought to bring an undershirt either.

The door opened a crack. She poked her head and bare shoulder out, one hand holding the Medium in front of her body, and the other handing him the Small.

She must have seen the tense look in his face but misinterpreted it.

"You don't have to do this if you don't want to," she said.

"No, it's not that," he said, a forced smile on his face. "This will be fine."

She started back into the room, then stuck her head out again.

"I'm Katie, by the way," she said. She extended her bare arm toward him and couldn't help but smile at the circumstances.

"I'm Eric." He took her hand and shook it. It nestled small and confident in his, and begged to be pulled toward him. He let it go.

"Nice to meet you." She disappeared into the bedroom.

Eric stepped into the darkly lit common space to change into the spare shirt. Unfortunately, it was too small; he knew it would be. The shoulders were tight, and the sleeves were short. He was lucky to fit into it at all, and he knew he looked like an absolute idiot.

Katie came out and Eric dreaded being seen in it.

"Eric?"

"I'm in here."

She came around the corner. Eric could see that the new shirt fit, but didn't fit well, as it was now baggy everywhere else. Her eyes adjusted to the darker light in the room, and then she laughed.

"Thanks," he said.

"I'm sorry, that's terrible of me to laugh."

"No, it's okay."

"Here, I'll just change back," she said. "I don't need to be in the picture anyway."

"No, I'm fine. I'll only be wearing it a few minutes. It's not that bad."

"Are you sure that's gonna look okay?"

Eric didn't like the sound of that, but let it go. "Yeah, I'm sure."

"Did you say you get your shirts tailored?"

"Yeah, I hate for them to be baggy around the waist. I think they make all of them for fat people."

"Well, looking at most of the people around here," she said, "I'd say that was pretty appropriate."

He laughed, and she smiled at the fact that she made him laugh.

"I think that's what I'm gonna have to do," she said, "get Mediums and have them taken in."

"You know, they make women's shirts, too. You won't have to try to fit into these. I'm pretty sure Hank has plenty up at the warehouse, but he's not always thinking about the details."

"Oh, that's nice to know now!" she said, trying to act mad.

Eric looked at his own shirt on her again. "Yeah, you definitely need a woman's shirt."

"What the hell?" Carson said when Eric came into the garage.

Eric grumbled, "Katie's shirt was too small, so we switched for the picture."

Carson doubled over, laughing. Tim and a few others did the same.

When Carson had composed himself somewhat, he put his hand on Eric's shoulder and said, "I'm sorry, I'm sorry."

Then he doubled over laughing again. "I'm sorry, I can't help it. Though I can't help but say I'm a little jealous."

His eyes were now scanning the crowd for Katie. He saw her not too far away talking to Hank and Leslie.

"Wow, she just keeps getting better, doesn't she!"

"Tell me about it," Eric said as he rotated his arms backward like chicken wings in the shirt. "You should have seen her in this."

"Oh, I can imagine. God bless her!"

"All right folks," Charlie, the photographer, yelled from atop a ladder. He had positioned the crowd of nearly seventy people in front of two ambulances parked nose to nose.

"Let's try to bring it together!" he said. "That's it!"

He tested the shot through the lens.

Eric and Carson made their way in but tried to distance themselves a little bit.

"Lookin' good! Can we get Dave and Hank to move more toward the center in the back there?" the cameraman yelled.

Eric made a little room for them and saw that Katie was now standing very close on his left.

"All right, that's good!" the man yelled from his perch. He snapped off a few pictures.

"Now, can I get Hank and Dave to come to the front? And

everyone else, I need you to squeeze in a little tighter! Good! Perfect!"

Eric looked over at Katie, who now stood right next to him now. She saw him and pulled the collar of the shirt she was wearing up to her nose and smelled it. "Nice cologne," she said with a grin.

Eric's heart skipped a beat as he looked up at the camera just in time for a new round of pictures. "Everyone smile!"

The photographer took several shots. "All right! That's a wrap! These are gonna look great!"

9.

After the last picture was snapped, Dave clapped his hands a few times and yelled, "All right, can I get everyone's attention! If you have time, we're all gonna go across the street to P.O. Pears for lunch and a few drinks. Join us if you can."

Eric leaned over to Katie. "Are you going?" he asked.

"Hmm, I don't think so."

Carson joined them. "Hey, you guys goin' over to P. O. Pears?"

Of course, Carson knew that Eric was going; he didn't really care about that.

Katie answered again. "No, I don't think so."

"Oh, come on! Why not?"

"Well, first of all, I'm not twenty-one—"

"How old are you?" Eric asked.

"Nineteen."

"Nineteen!" Carson said. "That's close enough."

"Are you kiddin' me?" Katie said, laughing at the proposition. "I'm not gonna break the law!"

"Oh, one of those types, huh," Carson said. "You're almost twenty-one, anyway."

"I'm so sure!" Katie retorted. "Hank and those guys know how old I am."

"Hank!" Carson yelled, much to Katie's dismay. "Hank! Katie's thinking about not joining us at P.O. Pears."

"What?" Hank said. "Now, Katie, you don't want to make a bad impression on your new boss, do you? Come on; you don't have to stay long."

"But I'm—"

Carson interrupted, "See, I told you."

"Carson's right, you should. I'll see you guys over there."

Hank walked away with the others who were already forming a herd to cross the street.

"See," Carson said, "he's probably even forgotten your age

already. You don't need to worry about it."

"Let me go change, and I'll think about it," she said.

"Do more than think about it, Katie," Carson said. "We'll make sure you don't get caught."

She cocked her head sideways and looked at him with a displeased look. He only laughed. Eric and Katie went upstairs to change, while Carson waited for them in the garage.

"Eric?" Katie said as they climbed the stairs.

"Yeah?"

"Thank you so much for switching shirts with me. That was very nice."

"Don't mention it."

After a pause she asked, "Do you think it's okay for me to be doing this?"

"Doing what?"

"Going to the bar?"

Eric laughed. "Absolutely. It's not a bar; it's a restaurant. Carson was just making it sound bad. You don't have to be twenty-one to go there."

"Really?" she said, scrunching her nose in embarrassment. "Why didn't Carson say that?"

"Yeah," Eric said. "Carson just likes to sound like he's getting you to do bad things." Eric added with a chuckle, "They might card you if you try to order something off the kids menu, though. That's strictly for kids."

Katie laughed—at the joke, and at herself. She then put on a serious face. "I don't know, Eric. I *do* look pretty young; I might be able to get away with a kids meal."

"As long as they look at you from the neck up," Eric said.

Katie blushed, and pursed her lips. It didn't take long for Eric to learn that this was what she did when she wanted you to think she was mad.

"Now, don't try sipping outta my beer when you're over there," Eric said. "That *is* against the law, and I don't want to get thrown in jail for contributing to the delinquency of a minor."

"All right," she said, "we'll save that for some other time."

Eric wondered if she meant sharing a beer, or contributing to her delinquency in general.

"How old are you, Eric?"

"Twenty-two."

"Oh, I thought you were closer to my age."

"Oh, thanks! It's only three years. I'm not an old man."

"No, I didn't mean that. Besides, older guys are nice; they're more mature. I generally don't like guys my age."

Eric looked at her. He felt the whole conversation was very promising.

Unfortunately, the process of changing out of their uniforms was less eventful than changing into them. Within minutes, Eric went downstairs to meet Carson, and Katie followed shortly thereafter.

"All right," Carson said, "let's go."

P. O. Pears had become the Eastern Ambulance hangout by virtue of its proximity. It was only two hundred feet away. It was quicker to walk there than to drive down the ambulance road, under the overpass and around the block due to the one-way roads and the fact that the city didn't allow the station to put a drive onto Eighth Street. P.O. Pears was decorated with movie memorabilia and had a clean, smokeless ambience. Eric, Katie, and Carson found that half of the Eastern employees had walked over for lunch or a quick drink.

"After you," Carson said, gently placing his hand on Katie's back to usher her in. Tim motioned them over to a booth where they all sat down.

"Carson," Katie said as she sat down, "I can't believe you made me think I was doing something that would get me in trouble."

"I'm just preparing you for the future," Carson replied, raising the corner of his mouth in a wicked grin.

Tim joined the conversation. "I imagine *this* is something that would get you in trouble," he said in his gravelly voice.

"Two of whatever's on tap and a Coke," Carson said to the waitress. She cast a skeptical glance over at Katie, then looked back at Carson.

"She's okay, Laurie. She's with us," he said, smiling.

Laurie smiled back. "That's what I'm worried about, Carson." She laughed, and turned to leave.

Carson looked not at all embarrassed.

"I'm sorry, I don't know you," Katie said, extending her hand to Tim. "I'm Katie."

"Tim. Pleased to meet you."

"I'm sorry, I didn't quite hear what you said?" she asked.

"Well, I didn't mean much by it. I was just sayin' that I imagine you would get in trouble for being here with us—from your parents, I mean."

Leave it to Tim to hold no punches.

"That's a good point, I guess." Katie fumbled with her napkin. "Yeah, my dad wouldn't be too happy."

Since they were already on the subject, Carson decided to plow ahead, even if the question was obvious. "Why not?"

"Well, you know who my dad is, right?"

"He's the Engine One captain and the Fire Union President."

"Well, that pretty much answers the question, then, doesn't it." she said.

Laurie returned with the drinks. Carson, who sat across from Katie, took his mug in his fist and pried deeper. "I can't even believe he let you work here."

"He didn't. He's very controlling. I did it anyway."

"I know he is," Eric said. "I can't imagine what it would be like to live with him."

"Yeah, it sucked. I don't live with him anymore. I moved into my own apartment."

"So you don't live on campus?" Carson asked.

"No, I can't move into my sorority until I'm a sophomore, and I didn't want to do the whole dorm thing."

"Oh."

"You're dad's not gonna send some death squad after us is he?" Tim asked.

"I hope not," she said, grinning.

Eric chuckled. "That doesn't sound too encouraging."

Katie laughed too. "I didn't mean for it to sound like that. I just meant that I hope I don't make things worse for you guys by working here."

"I wouldn't worry about it," Eric said. "Carson makes it worse for us every day."

They all laughed, except Carson who had heard similar jokes a hundred times.

"Why *did* you come to work here?" Carson asked.

"For a lot of reasons, I guess."

Carson looked at her as if he meant for her to continue.

"Well, for one—and I hope this doesn't sound bad—but I think it would look good on an application to medical school."

Eric shook his head in affirmation, as if he had the knowledge of the admissions boards.

"Two, it sounds cool and exciting. I really think I'll enjoy it. And I could really use the money, because my dad cut me down to just paying for tuition after I got my apartment."

"I'm gathering he didn't want you to live off campus," Carson said.

"No, and when I did, he stopped paying for housing."

"Why don't you move into a dorm then?" Eric asked.

"Because that's what he wants me to do." She smiled.

The other three raised their eyebrows.

"Whoa," Eric said, "is it worth it?"

Katie took a drink of her Coke, set the glass down, and looked Eric in the eyes. "I guess I'll find out. My dad thinks I'll experience the 'real world' and come home crying."

Carson continued with Eric's train of thought.

"Yeah, but still . . . it's tough to pass up free room and board."

"Not when your dad controls your whole life." She paused, realizing she had spoken too freely again. These men were, after all, nearly complete strangers, even if one of them had seen her bare shoulder.

But it was too late, and Carson drove through the door she had opened. "What do you mean, he controls your whole life?"

Katie pursed her lips, and toyed with the napkin under her Coke. "For one thing, he tried telling me what I should major in. I wanted to major in Sociology, but he said I should major in Biology. I told him that I still wanted to go to medical school, but that I didn't have to major in Biology to do it. I told him I could get into medical school just as easily with a degree in Sociology."

Eric nodded again like a university dean. "Yeah, I think you were right about that. But he wouldn't buy into it, huh?"

"No!" Katie said, her voice rising in intensity. "He told me that when I was older I would see he was right."

"No, you're totally right about that whole major thing," Eric said, causing Carson to glance over at him with an annoyed look.

Katie slapped the edge of her napkin back down on the table. "I *know* I am," she said, sounding as if she didn't need Eric's opinion. So Eric decided that it was a good time to take a drink. She toned down and continued a little quieter. "He told me to listen to him about all kinds of things, and that I would thank him for it later."

"Like what?" Carson asked.

Katie took a deep breath. "He didn't let me date anyone unless he approved of them, and he didn't approve of anybody. He never let me go to parties, or get a job, because he said it would hurt my grades!"

"Well, he might be right about that," Eric said.

"Hey, professor!" Carson said, "would you just shut up and let her talk! God!"

"Sorry, I was just sayin' . . ."

Katie looked at Eric like she felt sorry for him. "Yeah, but that's not the point. The point is that I can decide for myself! He wouldn't even let me buy the clothes I wanted. And I'm not just talking about high school!"

She was on a roll and no one tried to stop her. "I'm in college now, and he still won't let me wear a bikini. In *college!* I bought one, and he found out about it and wouldn't let me outta the house until I changed into a one-piece. Can you believe that? I'm nineteen years old, and my dad wouldn't let me outta the house!"

She stopped to take a drink of her Coke, realizing she had divulged too much again. The guys stayed quiet as they watched her take a big gulp, hypnotized for a few short seconds.

Carson reeled in his thoughts and tried to put some sentences together. "That doesn't surprise me about your dad at all," he said. "He tries controlling everybody."

"He controls you too?" Katie asked, feeling a new bond between her and these medics, a bond that she had suspected would be there.

Carson replied in a cold tone, "No, I didn't say he *does* control us. I said he *tries*."

"Hmm," she said before taking a small sip from her glass, "You're probably the only person in the world he doesn't control."

Carson looked at her and said, "No, I think we can squarely put you in that category too."

"Okay, well I'll give you something," the source said over the telephone. "I'm working on another story."

The owner/reporter of the *Lincoln Cowboy*, Harvey Miller, was talking to Sheila again for more fire department information. He called her often, hungry for more dirt.

"It's an ongoing problem," she continued, "but I'm looking into it more and I'm trying to get pictures to back it up."

Harvey's eyes lit up. "Pictures would be great. Can you tell me what it is?"

"No, not yet. It's not *huge*, but it's bad. And I promise it puts the fire department in a bad light."

"Okay," he said.

"But I'll tell you more about it when I've got some proof. I don't want you spreading rumors."

"All right. Just send me a message as soon as you can."

"Okay, but it might be a while. I'm just gonna lay low for a bit."

"Why? Do you feel that's necessary?"

"I don't know. I just feel I should."

"You don't think they would ever be violent, do you?"

"No, but they'd find a way to ruin my career this time, and they'd definitely try to ruin yours."

"You don't think they already are?" Harvey said.

"What do you mean?"

"I've received e-mail from them."

"You have?"

"Yeah, I'm pretty sure it's from them anyway. You know, the usual stuff like 'you'd better not throw stones when you live in a glass house.'"

"You'd better be careful," she said, speaking to him for the first time like a person, rather than a business associate.

"Nah, I don't put much stock in it. Only cowards attach no names to their e-mails."

"Well, I think you should be more worried."

"I appreciate your sympathy. But they'd never do anything to me, because they know I'd rat them out."

"All right," she said. "If you say so."

"I know what I'm doin'."

"Okay, I'll talk to you again when I can."

"I'll be waiting," he said before he hung up the phone. A minute later, he returned to the bar to help his wife serve drinks.

10.

"All right, you two yahoos!" Hank said as he stepped outside the garage door a few days later. Carson and Eric were doing the morning ambulance inspection outdoors with E22 running. They had a hard time starting it that morning and didn't want to turn it off. They looked up from their work.

"I don't know how you guys lucked out, but Katie said she wanted to ride along with you."

Carson pretended to be casual while he rummaged through the Airway Bag. "I don't think luck has anything to do with it, Hank," he said. "If you wanna be the best, you've gotta learn from the best."

Hank ignored him. "I didn't think it was a good idea to have her ride on the downtown truck because of possible run-ins with her father, but she wanted to start here. Maybe she just wants to get it over with."

"You mean today?" Eric asked as he closed the hood of the van.

"Yeah, she'll be in around noon." Hank shook his finger at both of them. "Now, you guys take care of her and watch the jokes and the language! She's a fellow employee, and you'll respect her as such!"

Carson looked put-off by the insinuations and raised both hands in the air. "Back off, Hank! What are you talking about? I know how to be a gentleman."

"Oh, really? Did Eric give you remedial instruction or something?" Eric smiled gloatingly at Carson.

Before returning to the building, Hank added, "And don't forget to get E22 up to the garage today for a new battery?"

"It needs a helluva lot more than that!" Carson yelled, but it was too late for him to hear. He and Eric continued with the checklist.

Only minutes after Hank left, the overhead tones went off, followed by the dispatcher's voice: "Medic One, Engine Five, Twenty-Seventh and Vine on an injury-accident."

"Engine Five clear," the radio buzzed back. It was Mark Rader's voice.

Carson looked up from the bag, his face alert and intent. "Let's go, Eric!"

Eric quickly screwed the cap back on the tire nozzle, and ran to the back of the ambulance to see if Carson needed help putting things back together.

Hank reappeared in the doorway. "Carson, I don't want you confronting Rader on this call, you hear me!"

Carson ran for the driver's door, and Hank yelled after him. "Calls are not the time or place to talk about our issues!"

Carson didn't stop to answer. Instead, he jumped into his seat, flipped the engine off high idle, and grabbed the microphone.

"Medic One clear."

The dispatcher responded, "Clear Medic One, Engine Five. Twenty-Seventh and Vine on a two-car collision. Occupants in the vehicles."

Carson, who was already out on the road with lights and sirens, tried to make his response but didn't beat Rader's voice.

"Engine Five is on-scene," Rader said with the sound of sirens in the background.

"Shoot!" Carson said before he keyed the mike. "Medic One is clear and en route."

Carson drove like a madman, Eric thought. He didn't stop at the red lights; he only slowed. Eric knew it was technically illegal; he should at least stop for a moment to confirm that the intersection was clear.

Three minutes later, Medic One approached the scene of the accident. Two cars sat corner to corner in the middle of the intersection, their front fenders badly damaged. A third car had struck one of the first two from behind but didn't show serious damage. Crowds mingled on the sidewalks. A middle-aged man, apparently the driver from one of the vehicles, stood talking to Manny Alvarez from Engine Five. As a new firefighter, Brent was there with him.

"Oh, great," Carson said, parking the ambulance. "The last bunch of people that Brent needs to learn from is Engine Five. Eric, you wanna see what's goin' on over there?"

"No problem." Eric grabbed a bag and half-jogged in that direction, feeling how awkward it was to have Brent there in a firefighter's uniform.

At the same time, Carson walked toward an older woman who sat in the driver's seat of a damaged vehicle, her legs out the side and her head in her hands. Mark Rader was talking to her, palpating the back of her neck when Carson approached.

"Watcha got, Mark," Carson asked in a steady, demanding voice.

Rader didn't answer but continued his questioning.

"How does this feel here?"

"I don't know," she said through sobs. "I don't feel anything's wrong exactly."

"Do you feel like your head got whiplashed during the impact?" Rader asked.

"No . . . I don't know. Maybe."

"Would you like to go to the hospital to get checked out?" Carson butted in.

"No, I don't think so."

She sobbed a few times. "You're from Eastern. You're the paramedic, aren't you?"

"Yes, ma'am. This firefighter is a Paramedic too," Carson said, not even looking at Rader.

"No, I want to talk to you," she said.

Rader stopped palpating her neck and stood. Carson approached her.

"What seems to be the problem?" he asked, squatting to bring his face down to her level.

"I . . . I don't know. It just happened so quick. I hope I didn't hurt my neck."

"Do you feel any pain?"

"No, but I've heard about so many people hurting their necks in accidents like this. Do you think it's possible I could've hurt it?" She looked Carson in the eyes and tried to gain control over her tears.

"Well, that's true," he said. "Some people may have some injuries that they can't detect right away. Even though you don't feel any pain or discomfort right now, that doesn't mean you may not want to get it checked out. Are you sure that you have no other injuries?"

Carson glanced inside her vehicle, quickly checking the windshield for "starring" and the interior for damage that would indicate the impact of her body. He saw nothing to cause alarm. He held his hand out to Rader, who was holding a list of the woman's vital signs. Mark handed it to him reservedly, and Carson glanced over them.

"Yeah, I'm sure," the woman said.

"Were you wearing your seat belt?"

"Yes, I was."

"You didn't hit your chest or anything . . . or hurt your wrists on the steering wheel?"

She wiggled her wrists a little and felt her breastbone. "No, they seem to be fine. I really don't think I'm hurt. I'm just kind of scared, you know."

"How about your neck?"

She rubbed the back of her neck, then turned her head side-to-side. "No, it's fine, really. I don't feel anything."

"Well, I tell you what. I think just to be safe, you might want to get checked out at the hospital. We will be more than happy to take you in the ambulance if you want. I don't think you have any serious conditions that you need to worry about right now, but you might want to do it just to be sure."

"Okay, I'll do that, but I don't think I need to go in the ambulance. My husband is already on his way. He can take me to the hospital, can't he?"

"Absolutely. As long as you're comfortable with that, I am. We'll be around until he gets here, and if you change your mind or feel any new pain, just let me know. Meanwhile, I'm gonna go check on the others."

She took his hand and looked him in the eyes. "Thank you so much."

"No problem," he said. "That's what we're here for."

"All right, ma'am, that takes care of that," Rader said. "I'm sorry Eastern Ambulance was late getting here. I know you were really concerned about that for a while."

"No, that's okay," the woman said, looking a little embarrassed. "I was just overreacting. I was just shaken up at first." Carson cast an angry glance at Mark.

Carson walked away from her toward some of the others. Rader followed by his side. When they were out of earshot, Carson spoke.

"Why the hell did you have to say that, Mark?"

"Hey!" Mark responded, "don't start with me. It took you five minutes to get here! She was worried!"

"Five minutes is well within parameters, Mark!" Carson stopped to face him. "I am so tired of the shit you're pulling, especially on-scene, in front of patients and reporters! If you have any problems with me, then deal with me—alone! Don't air it out in public!"

Carson turned and walked again. Rader peeled off in the direction of his fire engine. Carson approached Eric, who was just finishing a blood pressure on the driver of the other car. Eric indicated that everything was okay.

"Good," Carson said.

"How's Rader?" Eric asked.

"He's pullin' the usual crap. I'm gonna go talk to him."

Carson looked around the scene one last time. Tow trucks had already arrived to remove the cars, and the older lady's husband arrived and was talking to his wife. Rader and the other firefighters were putting their gear away. Carson approached them at a brisk pace.

"Rader!" he shouted, but not too loud for bystanders to hear. "Did you understand what I was saying back there?"

"I don't know what you're talking about, Carson," he said in a nonchalant tone.

"You know the kinda stuff I'm talking about—telling the reporter that you didn't hear Adam's mom and that shit you just pulled back there about us being late!"

Rader would not look Carson in the eyes and instead reached down to stow more gear.

"Carson, I don't know what you expect me to do. Do you want me to lie for your sake?" He finished whatever it was he was working on, stood up, and looked Carson in the face. "You don't expect me to make this easy for you, do you, Carson? I'm not in this for you. I'm in this for the patient. My conscience won't let me overlook your mistakes!"

Carson's eyes narrowed, and he looked like he wanted to say something, but an awareness of the people around him held him back. He turned and walked away.

Eric, who had been standing nearby, walked with Carson. Carson pondered Mark's comment about being 'in it for the patient' and thought about saying more, but he was so furious he knew he had to keep his jaw clenched. It would all be for nothing anyway. Eric followed Carson's lead and walked along the shoulder of the road with him.

The firefighters had returned to their truck and were leaving the scene. As they turned around, the front corner of the truck swung dangerously close to Eric and Carson. They were forced to step off the shoulder into the ditch to make way for the oncoming fire engine. In the process, Carson's boots, which didn't have a lot of tread, slid on the grass. He almost did a face-plant before he caught himself with one hand in the mud.

Just after passing them, the fire engine slowed almost to a stop.

"Hey, Carson," Manny Alvarez yelled. "Maybe you should get yourself some real boots! I can't believe Eastern lets you wear those."

Carson, still picking himself up, said nothing. Rader leaned out his window.

"No, there is something I want to say to you, Carson . . . really," he said, with as much sarcasm as he could muster. "I heard about your idea for the city. You know—Treffer's Society Repair Service. I just wanted to know if you were still taking applications. It sounds really sweet."

Nathan Tompkins leaned forward, yelled something at Mark, and indicated for Manny to drive away. Manny laughed, and they left the two Medics on the side of the road. For a brief moment, Carson saw Brent's face inside. As soon as he made eye contact with Carson, he turned away.

Carson, breathing deeply and purposefully, wiped the dirt from his hands. He and Eric watched them pull away.

"Let me guess," Eric said, "you're going to count that as one of your close encounters with death."

"That's not fuckin' funny, Eric."

"Sorry, I was just trying to lighten the situation."

"Maybe I should have let them hit me," Carson said.

"What, are you suicidal now? Are you serious!"

"Yeah, I should have let them hit me," he said unapologetically.

"Are you totally losing it, Carson?"

"Well if they did, maybe people would see what they're really like!"

Carson wiped the remaining mud from his hands. As they walked back to E22, Eric said, "Throwing yourself in front of a fire engine is not gonna solve our problems, Carson."

"I'm beginning to think our problems are not going to be solved by anyone else. You're right that I can't throw myself in front of a fire engine, but before all is said and done, I think I'm gonna have to take matters into my own hands."

11.

After gassing up, Carson and Eric were back at the station. To their delight, they found Katie waiting for them in the crew quarters.

"Hey, guys!" she said, closing a textbook she'd been reading. She had on a new uniform, tailored by the looks of it.

"Ready for your big day?" Carson asked, his mood picking up quickly.

She got up from the recliner and stretched. "I'm ready."

Katie reached down and touched the various pockets in her shirt and pants as she indicated her gear. "I've got my BLS Quick Reference book, a blank notepad, my penlight, my clothes-shears, and a pen."

Eric and Carson chuckled.

"You've got more than I do," Eric said.

"Oh," she added, "and a medium *woman's* shirt."

"You can wear whatever kind of shirt you want around here," Carson said. "Even if they're too tight. We don't care."

"Thanks, Carson," she said with a wry smile on her face. "You're very thoughtful."

"Don't mention it."

"And guess what else I brought?" Katie went over to the table and picked up a newspaper. "Just in time for Monday's county council vote, it's the Eastern Ambulance ad!"

She opened the paper, revealing the full-page picture they had taken a week prior. The top read: "The Eastern Ambulance Team. Proud to serve Lincoln for 35 Years," and across the bottom: "Proud to serve for the next 35 years."

In the middle, the cluster of Eastern employees waved up at the camera. Carson took the paper from Katie's hands. He peered closer and broke into laughter.

"Oh, geez," Eric said, guessing what he was laughing at.

"I'm sorry, Eric, I can't help it. That shirt's a classic look for you! Why the hell were you smiling so big?"

Katie snatched the paper from Carson's hands. "Laugh all you want, Carson. I didn't see you offering to act chivalrously."

He controlled his laughter somewhat. "No, you're right. That was a nice gesture on Eric's part. Thanks for showing us the ad, but I have to say that I don't have a lot of faith in it."

"I think it's nice."

"It's nice, but do you think 'nice' will sway the board members?"

"I don't know. Maybe."

"Cute newspaper ads aren't going to affect them, Katie. There are higher, political forces at work here. Anyway, I don't feel like getting into all that. Let's talk about today. I'm glad you chose to ride with us."

"Thanks," she said. "I'm glad you're willing to host me."

"Don't hesitate to ask questions. We'll try to get you involved in good stuff early on but don't get stressed. You can hang back and watch or get as involved—" The emergency tones sounded again. Over the pulse of the tones, Carson grabbed his utility belt and yelled, "I guess you're not gonna have to wait! Let's go!"

The dispatcher called out the units and the address. "Engine One, Truck One, Engine Two, Air One, Medic One. Two-Eight-One South Fourteenth Street on a house fire."

Carson looked up at Katie. "Engine One? Wow. You ready for this?"

"Let's go," she said. Katie got in the jump seat behind the cab where Brent used to sit. Eric took the radio, and Carson drove.

At the scene, Carson, Eric, and Katie saw the smoke billowing from the windows of a run-down Colonial-style home. Carson pulled the ambulance into a spot beside one of the fire engines. Firemen were already dragging lines and hooking up to a hydrant at the corner.

Carson put the ambulance in Park but left the emergency lights on. "All right, Katie, your first call should be pretty uneventful, at least from a medical standpoint. I don't know what to say about your dad. All we need to do is make sure there are no patients. If not, we just sit back, enjoy the show, and hope no one gets hurt."

"And try to avoid your dad," Eric added, knowing that his comment carried so much more weight today.

Though none of them had talked about it, all three had made the mental calculations en route as to which firefighters would be on this call. Eric was glad they would not be seeing Rader again, but Engine One was certainly not a welcome alternative. Seeing O'Malley for the first time with his daughter was going to be awkward at best. They saw O'Malley standing in front of the house pointing directions at several other firemen.

Eric and Carson exited the ambulance, but Eric had to open the side door for Katie; she wasn't good at opening it from the inside yet.

"You getting out?" he asked.

"Yeah," she said in a flat voice, though Eric could detect the slightest hint of reluctance.

Carson was already on his way toward O'Malley. Eric stood near the front of the ambulance, as did Katie.

She asked, "Don't we need to go over there with Carson?"

"No, if he needs us, he'll signal us, and we'll bring the bags and stuff." He looked over at her. "But you're more than welcome to go over there if you want."

She glanced hesitantly toward Carson and her father. O'Malley had turned and saw Carson's approach. He also saw his daughter standing by the ambulance in an Eastern Uniform. He knew this day was coming, but it bothered him more than even he had expected. The appearance of Carson *and* Katie made him very displeased.

"Umm," Katie finally said in answer to Eric's question, "I'll just wait here for now."

Eric was simultaneously anxious and enthralled by the situation. Just when he thought it wasn't possible, he discovered that his job had become immensely more interesting. "All right," he said.

Carson approached O'Malley and asked, "Got any patients, O'Malley? I mean people-type, of course; I know you don't have the other kind."

O'Malley turned away from Carson before answering. "No, you can go back to your ambulance."

Carson's brow furrowed, and he crossed his arms. He didn't move. O'Malley yelled more instructions to a fireman who was up on the roof with an axe. He and Carson surveyed the scene in silence for more than a minute. Fire hoses bore down on the building and appeared to be working, for there was very little smoke left.

After a short silence, Carson spoke again, "Your daughter started working with us today." It was so matter-of-fact, it sounded like a voice a man would use to say to his neighbor, "I see you got a new car in the driveway."

Again, O'Malley did not turn to face him, but glared at the building. Out of the corner of his eye, Carson could see the anger in O'Malley's entire demeanor, and he knew he had him going.

"It looks like she'll be doing some ride-alongs with me and Eric for a while."

"No she won't," he said.

"Excuse me?" Carson said.

"She won't be working with you very long."

"Don't tell me you're gonna make her quit, O'Malley. I think she really enjoys this line of work. In fact, I don't think you could make her quit even if you wanted to; she seems like a pretty spirited girl."

O'Malley's face grew redder with every sentence, but he didn't respond.

"Seriously, Mike, (O'Malley hated it when Carson called him by his first name) what makes you think she's not gonna work here long?"

"You just don't get it, do you, Treffer? It's pretty simple. I'm not gonna make her quit; I don't have to. I'll just see to it that her employer goes away."

Carson was taken off-guard. "How can you know that, O'Malley? The vote's not till Monday. It could go either way." Carson only partially believed this, but he wanted to hear O'Malley's response.

"Maybe you are as naïve as you look," O'Malley said before yelling another instruction to the man on the roof.

Carson stood in silence for a moment. He was now angrier than O'Malley, and that bothered him even more.

"That's interesting," he said. "If that's the case, and you really *have* bought off the politicians already, then we've only got a few months left. That still gives us three-and-a-half months of quality time with Katie. We've gotta make sure she gets all the life experience she can get."

O'Malley turned and looked at Carson like he was going to kill him.

"I mean, for med school and all," Carson added.

O'Malley marched straight past Carson toward Katie and Eric.

"Katie!" he yelled.

Katie took a step toward her father. To Eric, she did not look at all intimidated.

"Katie!" he said again as he drew closer. "This is enough! You've made your point! Now I want you outta that uniform! You don't have time for this nonsense! You don't have time for a job! This phase of yours has gone way too far!"

"Daddy," she responded, quite composed, "I'm not doing this because of you. I'm doing this for me. This is what *I* want."

O'Malley's face was a blend of anger and exasperation. He was nonplussed, a state strangely at odds with the quiet serenity on his daughter's face.

"Then we'll just have to talk about this later," he said, his voice quivering with tension. "You've taken this too far, Katie. You hear me! You've taken this too far! The last thing I wanted to see was you working with these two." He jerked a thumb toward Carson and Eric. "Now, I want all of you outta here. I don't want to see *any* of you right now!"

Carson shrugged his shoulders, and Eric opened the side door for Katie. Before she got in, she turned to speak to her father again.

"Dad," she said in a firm voice, "you're gonna be seeing me a lot with these guys, and you'd better just get used it . . . for your own sake and mine."

O'Malley clenched his teeth and made every effort not to look at Carson or Eric. He couldn't stand to see his daughter crawl into that ambulance with those two. When Eric closed the side door, and Katie was out of earshot, O'Malley turned to walk away but was interrupted by Carson's voice.

"O'Malley," Carson said, standing on the step between the cab and the door. O'Malley turned to look at him. "I don't know how you think you can control the county council," he said with a victorious smile on his face, "when you can't even control your own daughter."

If O'Malley had had a brick nearby, he would have tossed it through the ambulance windshield. Instead, he stewed in anger. "I have more control over her than you know. And I have much more control over your life than you know. Don't make me end your career, Treffer! I'll see to it that you never work in this town again. She's a sweet girl, a family girl, much too classy for trash like you."

Carson resented O'Malley's underestimation of him even more than the threats. For every jab that one of them threw, the other came back with something more spiteful, and Carson would not be outdone.

"She is a sweet girl," Carson said. "And you have to admit, she's kind of like your Medical Attack Vehicle—she has all the bells and whistles a man could ask for."

O'Malley's face grew disturbingly redder, and he started walking toward the ambulance. Carson ducked into the ambulance before things got uglier, but as he drove away, he knew it was too late. As usual, his mouth had gotten the best of him. Now O'Malley would do anything to make Carson's life miserable.

—

That night, O'Malley and Rader met with the deputy chief in his office at Fire Station One. It was located three rooms back from the fire engine bay. A metal door with a large pane of glass opened from the garage into a dimly lit hallway lined with coat hooks. On the right side of the hall, a door opened to a firefighters' lounge, which had an open view of the garage through a large window. Past that was the secretary's office, and finally, at the end of the dark hallway was the door marked: "Lou Killion, Deputy Fire Chief."

Lou Killion leaned back in his oversized leather chair with his hands clasped behind his head. He was not red and muscular like O'Malley; he was pale, only slightly taller than average with a thick, stocky build. His head was completely bald, shaven clean every day. The smooth dome of his head fell straight down to the back of his neck, which creased into several large folds of skin over his collar. He had two steely gray eyes and a flat nose, and a face that was always shaven as clean as his head. The only interruption to this generally featureless landscape was the cigarette that often jutted from the corner of his mouth. He listened to O'Malley relate the events of the afternoon. Throughout his talk, O'Malley grew angrier and angrier, but the deputy chief (a title often abbreviated to "chief" by those who worked for him) maintained his stoic demeanor, the only disturbance being the occasional, almost imperceptible, tick in his right eye.

After listening to the complaints of his two closest subordinates,

Deputy Killion sighed, scratching the smooth skin on his head. "He certainly is a wild card," he muttered, the slightest hint of his Long Island accent cropping up in the word "certainly." "Hard to predict," he added. He worked hard at losing his accent, which branded him as an outsider to many Lincolnites, but had not quite perfected the famous accentless speech of a Nebraskan.

Both O'Malley and Rader nodded, waiting.

"Mark," he continued, "you say he clenched his fists when you guys were talkin'?"

"Yeah, he was this close to swinging at me," he said, holding his thumb and forefinger an inch apart.

"That's what I figured. And that's what I mean when I say he's a wild card, a loose cannon. He could go off at any moment, and so much the better. I say, let him act that way. Keep doin' what you're doin'. One of these days he's gonna snap, and he's gonna swing at you. And when he does, the press will be all over it."

"You think he'd really do that?" O'Malley asked.

"Yeah, I do. He's already close, and if we keep puttin' the pressure on him, he'll snap."

"But what if I snap first?" O'Malley said before he was interrupted by a knock at the door. The deputy glanced at O'Malley with a knowing look. "That must be Tompkins," he said.

O'Malley pursed his lips, wishing they could have finished their conversation.

"Hey, Mark," Killion said, "I've got to talk to Nathan about a personal issue. If you don't mind excusing us, that would be great."

Mark looked a little shocked that he would have to leave a meeting.

"Really, it's personal, Mark. Nothin' to do with the department."

After a second's pause, Mark said, "No problem," and got up to leave.

"When you get outside, send him in?" Killion said.

Nathan Tompkins appeared in the open doorway. Immediately, he sensed a cool reception. O'Malley, who remained in his seat, was the only one to acknowledge Nathan's presence with a nod. The deputy chief reached over, extinguished his cigarette in an ashtray, and waved Nathan over.

Nathan walked in and sat down.

"Do you know what this is about?" Killion asked.

"If it's about what I said to Mark today when he goaded Carson Treffer, then let me explain my side—"

"No, that's not it," the deputy interrupted.

Nathan was genuinely shocked. "Oh," he said, growing more concerned, "in that case, I really don't know what this is about."

"It's about keeping personal things personal, Nate," the deputy chief said. "Do you know what I mean?"

"No, not really."

"What I mean to say, Nate, is that things that happen in a family are personal matters. They're personal affairs, you see. Everybody has rough patches in their family, and they do their best to work through those issues, together as a family."

The deputy looked up at Nathan, whose face remained impassive. Killion continued. "As you know, Nate, my wife and I are having some problems at home." Now there was the slightest hint of understanding in Nate's eyes, but Killion went on.

"They're big problems, but they're not insurmountable problems. She's somehow come up with the idea that we are headed for a divorce. Now, honestly . . ." the deputy chief looked Nathan in the eyes at this point, "I don't know where she's getting ideas like this, but they seem a little extreme. I'm doing everything I can to keep this marriage together."

Nathan couldn't just sit and listen anymore. "Now look, Chief, if this is about my wife just being a friend to Lynda, then—"

"She's doing more than being a friend, Nate," Killion said in harsh, clipped words. "She's helping her. She's assisting her. For Christ's sake, Nathan, she's *driving* her down to her lawyer to file for divorce and custody of our kids!"

Nathan tried to maintain his composure. "Like I said, Chief, she's just being a friend."

"That's more than being a friend, Nathan, and you know it! She's providing more than assistance; she's providing encouragement! And frankly, I don't need that now when I'm doin' what any man would do to keep his family together."

"Chief," Nathan said in a serious tone that was almost angry, "I cannot tell my wife what she can and cannot do with her friends. And frankly, I don't think you can use your position like this to ask me to do that."

"You're accusing *me* of interference!" the deputy chief said, leaning across his desk. "You and your wife are the ones who are interfering."

O'Malley, who had been quiet throughout the conversation spoke now. "Lou, Lou, take it easy. Nathan," he said in a fatherly, sympathetic voice, "the chief is not trying to tell you how to handle your family, just like he doesn't want you to tell him how to handle his. That's the whole point, you see. Things can get ugly when people get involved in other people's affairs. I know your wife is Lynda's friend—so is my wife—but that doesn't mean she's going out of her way to help her along with this divorce. You know how women are. Once they get another woman to encourage them, they sometimes do things they wouldn't necessarily do on their own."

O'Malley paused, hoping his insight would register with Nathan, but judging by Nathan's indignant expression, it wasn't. Killion, who was trying hard to let his friend fight his battle for him, lit another cigarette.

"Not only that, Nate, but it just plain looks bad. Right now, Lou and the fire department are under a lot of scrutiny, and the last thing we need is for something like this to bring unwanted attention. It's also very stressful on friendships. Family difficulties can get ugly, and they have a tendency to tear friendships apart. The way I look at it is Lou and Lynda have their own issues to work out, but if my wife or your wife gets involved, it can tear all of us apart, *and* make it even more difficult for Lou and Lynda to patch things up. Besides, it just puts Lou in an awkward position when he knows you might be exposed to only Lynda's side of the story. That just makes it hard to work professionally, and it's not good for the department."

Nathan, who had been in absolute disbelief throughout the majority of the conversation, finally saw a little merit in O'Malley's last statement. Already, his wife's dealings with Lynda had eroded his confidence in the deputy chief. "I guess that last point's true," was all he could bring himself to say. Besides, he knew he would have to make some conciliatory remarks to be able to leave on amicable terms.

"There, you see what I'm saying," O'Malley said. "Lynda is a big girl and can take care of herself. She *has* her own car. We're obviously not telling you what to do; we can't do that. All I'm saying is that it just looks real bad. Even if there's no real harm being done, imagine what it looks like to the papers, to the public, and especially to the guys in the department. It looks like we have internal dissension, and that compromises our ability to do our jobs. People can't start questioning authority when you work in life and death situations like we do."

Nathan was still angry but intellectually agreed with that point, at least on a superficial level. "I agree with that. I want you to know, though, that I in no way have ever intended to undermine the department."

The deputy chief broke in again, proud of the arguments his friend had made. "We know that, Nate, and I don't want you to take this personally." His hand trembled slightly as he brought the cigarette to his mouth.

"I won't," he said, "but what are you suggesting I do?"

Killion took a few puffs before replying. "I can't tell you what to do, Nate, because if I did, then *I'd* be interfering with your life. I obviously don't want that. I just want all of us to keep our home lives separate from our work lives. And as O'Malley said, once we all start getting mixed up with each other's family lives, it's going to hurt us all."

"All right," Nathan said. "I can't promise anything, but I'll at least talk to my wife. But she's a strong woman, and she'll do whatever she thinks best. All I can promise is that I won't get involved, and I won't take sides."

"Good, I'm glad to hear that," said the deputy chief. "Try to make her see how it hurts the department. Then maybe she'll think differently about things."

12.

The seventeenth of September arrived. Nearly all of the Eastern Ambulance employees made an effort to attend the county board meeting. They came in twos and threes, many wearing their uniforms. Eastern hoped that bodies in force and faces attached to the issues would sway the minds of the board members.

Carson and Eric arrived fifteen minutes early to get good seats. It was apparent that the right side of the room had been taken by the firefighters, many of whom wore red T-shirts and sweatshirts with their union emblem. On the left side sat the Eastern employees, as well as their various physicians, accountants, and other supporters.

Carson chose a spot midway up the room, right behind the row containing Leslie, Tim, and several others. Unlike Leslie and Tim, Eric and Carson were wearing civilian clothes, though Eric had his blue Eastern sweatshirt on. The two left a seat between them, and there was no mistaking who it was intended for. She was not there yet, and they were not certain she was coming. Her father sat across the aisle in the front row next to Chief Winkenwerder and Deputy Chief Killion. Left arm on chair, O'Malley's round red face occasionally turned to scan the crowds, taking in who was and was not present. Mark Rader sat next to him, doing the same. While O'Malley scanned the firefighter side of the room, Rader scanned the Eastern side.

Eric eventually did the same for the right side of the room, trying not to look too intent. Brent was there. He sat toward the back where the firefighter crowd mixed with the general public. Eric briefly made eye contact with him before Brent shifted his eyes forward again. Eric felt sorry that he was sitting alone, and wanted to ask him to sit with them, but he knew it couldn't happen.

Rader got up and made his way down the center aisle. He shook hands with various firefighters, made a few remarks to each, and patted them on the backs. He asked John Watkins how his wife was doing, pointed at Sam Miller when he saw him, and teased John

Bradford about fitting in the small seats. Rader was a politician through and through, Eric thought.

Rader found Brent in the back and let go of John's arm. "Brent, what are you doing back there? Get up here." He motioned for him, smiling the whole time. Mark was loud enough that he now had the attention of most everybody on the left side of the room. "Here, you guys scoot down and open up a seat for Brent," he said to some firefighters.

Brent, a little embarrassed, stumbled over a few people and made his way to a seat near the aisle. The firefighters who had to make way for Brent didn't seem too happy when they turned to see who he was. But he wore the same red T-shirt that many of them wore, and they figured he must be the new "transfer."

"Glad you could make it, Brent," Rader said, loud enough to be heard over the din of the crowd. "I'm glad you decided to join our team. If you need anything at all, you just come to me. I think you'll see tonight that you made a good career move."

At that last comment, many of those on the left side of the room groaned or made some retort or another. Not a few of them wanted to stand up and challenge him on his comment, or worse. But Carson did nothing, so the rest of them did little more than cast dirty stares in Rader's direction.

Eric looked over at Carson, who was not even turning his attention toward the scene. Instead, Carson rubbed his chin and looked over his shoulder toward the door. His face relaxed, and he stood up. Eric saw Katie standing just inside the door against the wall, where many of the crowd now gathered. She wasn't in uniform, but the fact that she was there was enough.

Carson waved at Katie, indicating the open seat between him and Eric. "Katie," he said rather loud.

"Don't, Carson," Eric said through clenched teeth.

"Don't what?"

"You know what I'm talking about. Don't make a scene."

"I'm not going to. I'm just getting her attention." Carson's face was contorted in disgust at Eric's comment, and Eric wished he hadn't said anything. Maybe, he thought, his own tension made him misjudge his friend.

Carson didn't need to say anything. The scene spoke for itself.

Katie O'Malley, the daughter of Captain Mike O'Malley, made her way through the crowd, up the center aisle, right in front of Rader, and into the left side. Once there, she was welcomed by Leslie, Tim, Eric, and, of course, Carson. As they took their seats, Carson gave Rader a steely glare, who returned in kind, brushed his black hair over to the side with his hand and made his way to his seat in the front row.

Many heads turned, not just because she was Captain O'Malley's daughter. Strangers turned their heads as well because, as Eric had already learned, that's what happened when Katie walked into a room. She squeezed her way into Carson and Eric's aisle, bracing herself by placing her hands on the row ahead. She inched her way in front of Eric, causing his heart to skip a beat. She sat down and smiled a hello at him.

The seven board members began the meeting with absolutely no fanfare, even though every seat in the house was taken, television cameras stood on tripods, and the two sides of the room looked like sports teams preparing to do battle on the field. The board members played it cool as they went through the usual rules of order and covered the topics of necessity.

Eric wondered if county business was always this mundane. There was a proposition on expanding the asphalt on Clark Lane three additional blocks. One old Lincoln man stood up to read a prepared statement opposing the expansion. The residents on that street could not, he maintained, pay the appropriate taxes needed to cover the asphalt. The county council voted for it anyway.

Sam Moscatelli, the current chair of the Lancaster County Council, sat in the center of the semicircular table. The mid-thirties Moscatelli pushed business along. He had the support of the three other members of his party and was a known friend of the firefighters. No one owed more of their success to the diligent campaigning of the fire union than did Moscatelli.

"Finally, concerning the Request for Proposal for the EMS contract," he said, "we will begin with the public hearing."

"Is there anyone here who would like to speak on the subject?"

What a stupid question, Eric thought. There were at least a half-dozen people with canned speeches sitting in the front row.

Everyone stirred. People talked, deliberated, and looked around to see who would move first. Dave Conrad spoke with the cadre of business-suited individuals up front, then stood.

"Yes, Mr. Chairman. I have a few things I would like to say, but I'll quickly relinquish the floor to others who also have a lot to present."

Moscatelli looked bored. "Go ahead."

Conrad cleared his throat. "I'm sure most of you know who I am. My name is Dave Conrad. I'm the Director of Eastern Ambulance. I am here to represent eighty-seven dedicated employees who are doing an excellent job providing EMS services to Lancaster County and the city of Lincoln."

Dave then went on to cover the history of Eastern Ambulance, the services they provided, and finished by briefly outlining what he called an "exemplary" record. He concluded by saying, "As people so often say, 'If it ain't broke, don't fix it.' For thirty-five years we have provided exemplary service, and we will continue to do so for the next thirty-five years."

Eastern employees clapped as he finished. They weren't necessarily impressed, but they were satisfied.

The next speaker was a bit of a conundrum, however. Chief Jack Winkenwerder stood to address the board. Often quiet and relegated to the sidelines, this man, the chief of the Lancaster County Fire Department for more than twelve years, had a lot of influence on this process, but his opinions were virtually unknown.

"Mr. Chairman, I would like to speak," the elderly man said. He was tall and dignified with glasses, gray hair, and a dark moustache. He must have been in his fifties, Eric thought.

"The floor is yours," Moscatelli replied.

"Mr. Chairman, I want to be one of the very first people to say thank you to Eastern Ambulance for doing what they have for so many years. We have enjoyed working with them throughout that time. I personally have developed a friendly relationship with them after serving alongside them for so many years."

Everyone in the room was quiet. Even the Eastern crowd respected the fire chief and really believed his kind words.

"However, Mr. Chairman, I'm sure you know what I know, and what the citizens of this county know. And that is that it is time for a change in Lancaster County's EMS system. Three years ago, when you, Mr. Chairman, ran on a platform to improve the EMS service, the citizens of Lancaster County responded overwhelmingly by electing you to represent our fine county. Now I and my team of talented firefighters are working hard to make that campaign promise a reality. I bear no ill will toward Eastern Ambulance or any of its employees, but I think the time when private companies ran the EMS service has come to an end. The evolution of the EMS profession makes these changes more of an inevitability than anything. If chosen for the contract, Mr. Chairman, we will likely even hire many of Eastern's medics who are willing to be part of the L.C.F.D. team. We have a strong business plan that we would like to present. It has been prepared under the leadership of our talented deputy chief, Lou Killion, and will be presented by him. Thank you."

At that, the fire chief turned to his deputy. Immediately, Lou Killion stood to be recognized, his pale dome of a head not reaching as high as the chief's thick silver locks.

"Go ahead, Deputy Chief Killion," Moscatelli said. Winkenwerder resumed his seat.

Killion started by reiterating many of the chief's points, saying nice things about Eastern that sounded not near as convincing as they did coming from the chief. Then he got to the core of the matter.

"Mr. Chairman, the chief just mentioned that the citizens overwhelmingly voted for you on a platform of EMS change. Now, there are many reasons for this. First, the people know that while Eastern has been doing their job, they haven't necessarily been doing an outstanding job. Right now, the Eastern standard is to respond to ninety percent of all calls in eight minutes or less. The fire department responds to ninety percent of all calls in *four* minutes or less. Time and time again, citizens calling 911 have seen the fire engine arrive first to give them care in their times of need. We are faster."

Nearly everyone in the room could detect Deputy Chief Killion's Long Island accent, especially when he said the word, "faster," nearly leaving the "r" off the end of the word. This simply highlighted what many in the city already felt about him—that he was an outsider, hired by the county to do their dirty work. Eric wondered if he ever would be accepted as the chief someday. Though he clearly had expertise, power, and influence, he wondered if the firefighters really thought of him as one of their own. He stood in juxtaposition to the home-grown

Chief Winkenwerder.

"Second," Killion continued, "while many Eastern employees are dedicated and competent workers, their company is not able to provide the competitive wages needed to attract long-term, dedicated professionals. In fact, many Eastern employees are making little more than minimum wage."

Eric felt a twinge at that comment. That, at least, was true, especially of the EMT's on the transfer cars.

"As might be expected, Eastern loses a good number of their more seasoned employees to other jobs, because they can't sustain them economically. Except for a few individuals, this sadly leaves Eastern's workforce very young and somewhat inexperienced. Furthermore, to make up for the difference, Eastern employees often work long hours, sometimes more than eighty in a week.

"Now, you may ask yourselves why Eastern employees get so little. You're saying to yourselves, isn't the fire department claiming that they can provide the same service cheaper? Yes, we are. That is my third point. Let me explain how we can do that.

"Eastern Ambulance is, as we all know, a private company. And as we also know, the purpose of a private company is to make money. Eastern has several owners throughout the city who have grown wealthy off the profits of Eastern Ambulance. The fire department, on the other hand, is of course not-for-profit. We would only charge enough to cover our own expenses.

"Also, Eastern Ambulance and the county dole out large amounts of money to the Medical Oversight Agency. This board oversees both Eastern and the fire department and requires a large staff, including two doctors to review all charts. County law requires that the county split the cost with Eastern to maintain the service.

"Our plan, however, streamlines this function by doing away with the M.O.A. The fire department plan includes funds for us to hire our own medical oversight physician and put him on staff. This scheme works for hundreds of fire departments across the country.

"Finally, the fire department will be able to provide cheaper service due to the efficiencies of scale held by the department in conjunction with the city. We have access to cheaper gas contracts, as well as being able to utilize county legal services, pension plans, and the list goes on. We will do all of this by billing patients much the same as Eastern does, albeit at a lesser rate. We will *not*, let me stress, will *not* use any tax dollars to provide EMS services to Lancaster County or to the city of Lincoln.

"I would like to conclude by succinctly stating the fire department's plan. First, we currently respond and will continue to respond more rapidly to emergencies than does Eastern Ambulance. We will be *faster*." He held up his thumb on the word "faster."

"Second, we are able to employ and retain dedicated, educated, long-term professionals whose knowledge and skills will only improve with time. Our service will be *better*." He held up two fingers now, focusing his speech on the board members.

"Third, lack of the profit-motive, and economies of scale will enable us to do it *cheaper*."

The third finger joined the other two, before they all closed and opened again, one by one. "Faster. Better. Cheaper. *That* is the fire department's plan. *That* is what the citizens of Lincoln want and what they deserve. And *that* is what the Lancaster County Fire Department will give them if you vote for our EMS plan tonight. Please consider it carefully, board members. Thank you, Mr. Chairman."

Deputy Chief Lou Killion took his seat amidst applause from the red side of the room. It was a very effective tactic but for the fact that the words he emphasized, "Faster, Better, Cheaper," also emphasized his foreignness. Eric wished that would matter, but knew they would need much more. The rebuttals began.

13.

The next person to stand and speak was Mr. Harry Jensen, C.P.A. "Hello, everyone." He wiped the spit from the corners of his mouth. "I have been asked to come here by Mr. Dave Conrad and the administrative staff at Eastern Ambulance representing my accounting firm of Jensen, Taft, and Geoffries.

"My firm was asked to look at the financial outlook of the Lancaster County Fire Department's business plan should they come into possession of the EMS contract. We have been provided data from Eastern Ambulance concerning the number of calls per month they performed in this past year, and with these numbers, we performed a full financial analysis of the proposal.

"We have determined that based on the fire department's proposed reimbursement rates for both BLS and ALS calls, they will encounter a budgetary shortfall in the first year of $435,000."

Deputy Chief Killion smirked and raised both his arms, palms up. Mr. Jensen did not look in his direction. "We found that the fire department's estimation of the number of calls that they will make is overly generous."

Killion interjected, "We used the numbers provided to us by the county!"

"Sit down!" some citizen yelled from the back. "You had your chance!"

"No!" Killion said as he stood and turned to face the jeering crowd. "We have been directly accused, and I feel that it would only be fair for me to be able to address this attack."

Moscatelli didn't say a word. Neither did the chief. It was becoming apparent that he made his compulsory remarks to back the county's plan, but that he would likely go no further.

Killion continued. "Mr. Jensen is accusing of us of exaggerating the numbers, of trying to paint a rosy outlook. That is simply not true. The county keeps detailed accounts of all EMS calls performed. I don't know what numbers Eastern gave Mr. Jensen here, but they are not the right ones. Based on our proposed rate of $625 for an ALS call, and $350 for a BLS call, the fire department will finish easily in the black."

Mr. Jensen worked up some courage. "I have to disagree, sir. The numbers I used were based on the actual number of transports performed by Eastern, and I think you used the total number of EMS calls that the dispatch center received. That may sound the same, but you know better than I that not every EMS call results in a billable transport. You have overestimated your revenues by over $400,000."

Killion's steely blue eyes glowered at Jensen, and perspiration drops appeared on his bald head as he groped for words. Instead, Captain O'Malley stood up next to the deputy chief and addressed the crowd. "I'll tell you why there is a discrepancy. There is a discrepancy in the number of transports Eastern Ambulance makes in relation to the number of calls they receive. They are missing out on hundreds of transports a year."

Councilmember Rick DeLong, the unofficial leader of the opposition party now asked, "What do you mean, Mr. O'Malley, 'missing out on calls?'"

"What I mean to say," he said in a cool voice, "is that too often Eastern medics do not transport patients when they should. They are too quick to tell the patient to take their own car to the hospital!"

The crowd made a collected hodge-podge of responses. Some of the firefighters shook their heads slowly and groaned as if their Union President had just thrust a deadly blow.

Eastern supporters yelled, "Gimme a break!" or "That's not true!" Eric would probably have yelled something, too, if Katie had not been seated next to him. Carson was silent.

DeLong raised an eyebrow and turned toward Dave Conrad in the front row. Dave was consulting with some of the doctors seated near him, then stood to speak.

"That's not true, Mr. Chairman," he said, not loud enough for those in the back to hear. Firefighters laughed and some jeered. Conrad turned to talk more with his strategy team.

O'Malley seized the moment. "It *is* true Mr. Chairman! Eastern employees are often choosing not to transport patients, even when many of them are sick or in a serious condition."

"Why would that be so?" Councilmember DeLong asked.

"There could be many reasons," O'Malley said. "For one, they're probably too busy to perform all of them. Two, they simply have a different philosophy. And three, their medics may not be performing medical care when they should."

This last comment elicited an uproar from the blue side of the room.

"Is this true, Mr. Conrad?" Moscatelli asked.

"No, it's not true, Mr. Chairman."

"You don't ever send patients to the hospital in their own cars?"

"No! I mean . . . well, yes, sometimes we do." More noise from the crowd. "I mean . . . sometimes that's the best thing to do."

Again, firefighters laughed and jeered. "I find this quite disconcerting," Chairman Moscatelli said.

"I'm sure there's an explanation," said DeLong.

"There *is* an explanation." The forceful voice that spoke silenced the crowd somewhat. It was Carson. All eyes turned toward him. "There is *definitely* an explanation. Is it so crazy to think that not every person who calls 911 needs an ambulance?"

After one statement, what seemed like a troublesome proposition only seconds ago was now quite understandable. Carson looked each of the board members in the face before answering his own question. "Of course not."

"We are trained, knowledgeable medics. We have been taught how to assess the seriousness of a patient's condition and determine the urgency. In fact, while we respond with lights and sirens to every call, only a small proportion of those patients are ever transported to the hospital that way. That's just not medically necessary. In the same vein, it is often not necessary to transport someone in an ambulance at all.

"So why not do it anyway, like the chief suggests?" Carson said, asking himself the question. "Well, I'll tell you why not. As we all know, an ambulance ride is not cheap. For many patients it's a huge expense. Of course, we will always transport a patient when they want it, but often we explain to them that it's not medically necessary. I did this very thing just yesterday, and it was the right thing to do. That way, the patient is not out five hundred bucks for nothin'. Also, a lot of people flat-out don't want to go with the ambulance, and if they don't need it, I don't do it."

Before sitting down, he finished with one last thought. "We're not gonna transport every cut, scrape, and cold to the hospital just to milk the patients for money. I know the fire department, though, and I'm sure that's what they're planning to do. But there's no way they're even gonna come close to transporting every single person that calls 911!"

Some Eastern people clapped and cheered before Moscatelli hammered his gavel.

As Carson sat down, Katie turned and smiled at him. Carson had stood up to her dad, and she was impressed. Without fully realizing the reason herself, it made her very attracted to him.

Councilmember DeLong spoke, always the clever politician. "Thank you for clarifying this issue for us, Carson. I see now why Eastern has such a policy, and I stand by it wholeheartedly. I also see why there is some confusion as to the number of transports the fire department plans to make. It's suddenly all very clear."

Commissioner Moscatelli responded. "I don't see the fire department numbers as being unreasonable. I would imagine it's fair to plan the number of transports based on what you think is the appropriate course of action."

"But what if the fire department is unable to make the transports they're planning on?" DeLong replied. "What then? Are the taxpayers going to have to fund this expedition by the fire department?"

Moscatelli deferred the question to the deputy chief. "Deputy Chief Killion?"

"You don't need to worry about that, Councilmember," Killion said, without directly looking at DeLong. "We've put together a sound business plan."

"I understand that, Mr. Killion," DeLong said, addressing him directly, "but what if you find it really *isn't* medically necessary to transport as many people as you plan? What if—"

"I'm telling you, Councilmember," the deputy interrupted, "we don't have to worry about that. Our people will be able to make enough transports. I'm confident of that."

"But I *am* worrying about it, Mr. Killion. Let me make my question clear. What will happen if the fire department does not bring in the revenue they expect to generate, as Mr. Jensen has proposed?"

"Our business plan is based on numbers provided to us by the county and is a very conservative estimate."

The left side of the room now laughed.

"Perhaps I am not expressing myself clearly, Deputy Chief. Your business plan numbers aside, I want to know where the money would come from in case the fire department falls short. Perhaps something unforeseen comes along. From the beginning you have promised not to use a penny of taxpayer money for EMS services. Would you raise the rates you charge patients? How do I know that if you win the contract, you are not going to turn around and raise rates to the level of Eastern's or higher? Or maybe that is your plan? And also, how do I know that you're not going to make the taxpayers pay for your mistakes?"

The deputy chief's response was short. "Because I said so."

Jeers and boos emanated from the crowd. DeLong threw his hands in the air in exasperation. "Oh, okay, that's all I needed to know, Deputy," he said sarcastically. "You should have used the real numbers, from the *real* number of transports made by Eastern."

"That's your opinion," Killion replied, "and you're not an accountant."

"But Mr. Jensen is!" DeLong replied. The room clamored with conversation.

Moscatelli beat his gavel. "Quiet . . . quiet please," he said in an amazingly restrained voice. He still looked bored.

Once he accomplished his goal, he spoke. "Do you have any more questions, Councilmember DeLong?"

"No, but I would like to say that I am *certainly* glad that Mr. O'Malley brought up the whole issue of the difference in philosophies, which was so clearly explained by Carson Treffer. Clearly, the fire department has not done their homework, and as such they cannot be awarded the contract with all these loose ends hanging in the air."

"Very well, then. Let's continue with the hearing."

The next hour contained many more witnesses and concerned citizens than most people cared to hear from. Over half were there for Eastern. Dr. Denson spoke on behalf of the medical society. She vouched for Eastern's standard of care, as well as the professional job they had performed. She also added that the medical society would support any entity that continued to adhere to those standards and remained accountable to the medical community via the M.O.A. She assailed the fire department's plan to operate with their own medical oversight, pointing out that a physician who drew a paycheck from the fire department could not truly be an unbiased quality check.

At least one doctor disagreed. He was the man identified as the probable hire for that job. As the appointed future medical advisor to the fire department, he did not agree that the M.O.A. was necessary. He reiterated that most fire departments around the country operated with the same model that the Lancaster County Fire Department proposed.

Finally, toward the end of the night, some of Eastern's own medics got up to read prepared statements. Leslie's was perhaps the most moving. She informed the board of how many years she had worked for Eastern, making a point that not all of the company's employees were new. She then proceeded to say how much she loved caring for the citizens of Lincoln.

"I have dedicated many years to this city, not for the pay or for the social prestige, but because I love it, and because that is my job. We at Eastern do everything we can, every call, every day for this city. We believe in the fine job we have done, and we look forward to the fine job we will do in the future. My only request is that you allow us to continue to do that job."

It was a bit melodramatic, Eric thought, but by that time of the night, about everything in the meeting had become so. Finally, there was no one else who wished to speak. Moscatelli was clearly relieved. It was getting very late, and he wanted to get on with the vote.

It was looking positive, Eric thought. Clearly, the debate had gone in Eastern's favor. The accountant was able to bring the fire department's plan into question. Killion, and to some extent, O'Malley had made fools of themselves. The respected medical community had done as much as possible without being too partisan. And most of the good speakers at the end supported Eastern.

Moscatelli spoke quietly to some of the other members. They were obviously wrestling among themselves. Moscatelli uncovered the microphone as if he were about to speak, then covered it again, and talked more with the members of his own party. He glanced at

Deputy Chief Killion, who merely buried his furrowed chin in his hand and leaned on the armrest of his chair. Even Chief Winkenwerder looked apprehensive. Finally, Moscatelli spoke.

"We thank everyone for their input tonight. I know that my fellow board members and I have been deliberating on this issue for some time, taking the time to read each of the proposals carefully.

"We had hoped to be able to bring this issue to some sort of closure relatively soon, but many issues were brought up tonight that require answers. It is for this reason, therefore, that I would like to move that the bidders be given three more weeks to re-work their plans and tie up some of the issues raised tonight. It will also give us more time to weigh the issues carefully."

The crowd sat hushed in disbelief. It was the most unexpected and anticlimactic outcome Eric could have guessed at. For most everyone in the room, it was a bitter pill to swallow.

Councilmember Martinez seconded Moscatelli's motion.

"Any discussion?"

"Yes, Mr. Chairman," DeLong said. "I don't feel we need any more time to discuss the issue at hand."

"Very well, Mr. DeLong. Any more discussion?"

"I agree with Councilmember DeLong," another member said. "We've had enough time to go over this issue. I say we vote tonight."

"Okay, thank you, Councilmember Brown. Any other discussion?"

No one had anything else to say.

"No? Then it's time to vote on the motion to postpone any decision on the ambulance issue for three weeks, to the first Friday of October. All in favor?"

All but DeLong and Brown raised their hands.

"The ayes have it. We will put this matter to rest until three weeks from today. In the interim, we will discuss the matter amongst ourselves, seeking any further information we deem necessary. Thank you all for participating in the open forum and thank you for coming."

He pounded his gavel. It was over for now.

Eastern employees slowly got out of their seats and made their way to the exits.

Eric looked over at Katie. "So what do you think of that?" he said, not knowing what else to say.

"I think they didn't want to vote tonight, because they didn't want to look like fools."

"I agree."

Carson sat a while longer. His elbow rested on the armrest, with his hand holding his chin and a single index finger pressed up against his temple. Eric figured he didn't want to talk right now. He and Katie joined the crowd that slowly herded out of the chamber.

As they entered the lobby, someone came up behind them and grabbed Katie by the elbow. It was her father.

"Katie," he said in a stern voice, "let's go home. We need to talk."

"Let go of me, Dad." She gently removed her elbow from his grasp and spoke quietly to prevent making a scene.

"Honey," he said with only a veneer of sincerity, "I think it's time we go home now. Your mother and I need to have a talk with you."

Eric stood beside Katie without moving.

"Do you need a ride home, Katie?" Eric asked, trying to think of the best course of action.

O'Malley turned with great force and pointed his finger in Eric's face. "You stay outta this, boy! This is family business, and you sure as hell had better stay outta this. You will *not* be giving my daughter rides in your car *anywhere* at this time a' night!"

"That's her decision."

O'Malley pursed his lips and turned away from Eric, trying hard to ignore him. "Katie," O'Malley said, "just come home for a little while. Your mother and I want to talk to you."

Katie was keen not to make a scene and resigned herself to leave. She looked at Eric to let him know it was all right.

"All right, Dad! We can talk . . . briefly, but I need to get to bed." She spoke to Eric again to show her dad she wasn't entirely submissive. "I'll see you later, Eric."

"Are you sure that's what you want to do?" Eric asked.

"Yeah," she said, looking him in the eyes, "don't worry about it."

Katie and her dad turned and walked through the remaining crowd. O'Malley cast a threatening look toward Eric one last time. As they walked away, Eric could hear O'Malley still talking to his daughter. "How could you humiliate me like this in front of the chief?" His voice was lost in the crowd.

A little later, Eric shuffled in the same direction, feeling angry, confused, and frustrated. He felt like he should have done something, but then again didn't know if there was anything he needed to do. He just knew he wanted to hit the man square in the jaw, but at the same time he didn't, because he was Katie's dad. He definitely knew he would have no qualms about doing the same to Chairman Moscatelli or Deputy Chief Killion.

The only consolation Eric had was that he didn't have to go home and fume. He went to P.O. Pears with the others.

Eric sat with Carson in a corner of the bar with a beer in his hand. Hordes of Eastern people mingled throughout the place, all venting their frustrations. Eric related to Carson what had transpired with Captain O'Malley. Carson listened intently. He had already been stewing before Eric arrived and boiled over now.

"She can do whatever the hell she wants," he said. "She's nineteen years old. He's got the worse case of not-letting-go I've ever heard of."

Carson looked down at his beer and tapped the sides with his fingers. "Maybe I need to kiss his daughter on his front doorstep; it might be therapeutic for him. Painful at first, but therapeutic."

He chuckled, lifted his glass, and took a few gulps. Eric was too put off to say anything. He thumbed the handle of his mug and stared at Carson.

"Can you imagine the look on his face," Carson continued, "seeing his little girl with me? He'd be so disgusted with her that he'd have to let her go."

"You make me sick, Carson," Eric said, literally losing his thirst.

Carson looked up at Eric and scrunched the side of his face in disgust. "Lighten up, Eric. God! You can be so frickin' . . ." he paused, looking for the word, "so frickin' touchy sometimes! Ever since we met Katie, you've been all clenched up. What is this? Are you jealous?"

"Of course!" Eric said, letting his voice rise. "I guess if you want to put it that way. I don't want to picture you with Katie!"

"I was only joking, Eric!"

"And I really don't think you being with her in front of her dad would benefit to anyone. The only thing that would accomplish is to start a war, and that's the last thing we need."

"We're already in a war, Eric."

Based on the angry look on Carson's face, Eric wondered exactly who Carson was referring to.

14.

Three days later, at nearly five o'clock in the morning, Carson and Eric slept in the crew quarters at Station One when someone gently knocked on the door jamb near both of their rooms.

"Eric?" Katie whispered. "Carson? Are you guys awake?"

Eric heard her somewhere in the back of his mind, but it didn't fully register since it blended so well with his dreams.

"Carson," she said a little louder. Finally, Carson, who looked like he'd been tossing and turning all night, threw back the wool blanket that covered his face. His eyes squinted as he tried to make Katie out in the bright hallway.

"Katie?" he said. "What are you doing here?"

It was ungodly early, and their shift was due to end in a few hours. Katie wore a newly pressed uniform, a stark contrast to the wrinkled ones that Carson and Eric had worn and slept in for the previous twenty-one hours.

"Look what I brought," Katie exclaimed, a bag in one hand and a cupholder in the other. "Donuts and coffee." She felt guilty about waking them and wondered if this was a good idea.

Carson pushed back the rest of the blanket while Eric realized he wasn't dreaming, sat up, and placed his feet on the floor. He yawned and stretched.

"Good morning," Katie said.

"Good morning," Eric returned. "Are you insane? What are you doing here?"

"I hadn't seen you guys in a few days, and I thought I could squeeze in a few hours of ride-time before your shift change."

Carson and Eric followed Katie to the common space, drawn by the smell of warm donuts, hot coffee, and recently shampooed hair. Her long tresses were one of her most beautiful features, Eric realized. She set the food on the table and the guys gravitated toward it.

"I really appreciate this," Carson said, "but you're probably not gonna get a lot of value out of two hours."

"I know. I mainly wanted to say hi and to get you this as a way of saying thank you for having me as a ride-along."

Eric warmed his hands around a hot cup of coffee. "Wow," he said, "I didn't know if I'd see you back here after that incident with your dad the other night."

"Yeah, well . . . I'm here," she said, opening the box of donuts.

"What did he say?"

"I went home, and he and my mom talked to me about how I didn't need to do this to get back at my dad, and stuff like that. They wanted me to move back home and said that if I did, they'd make sure I didn't have to work. You know how it is."

By this time, Eric and Carson had learned that if they just kept quiet, she would keep talking.

"I told them that I wasn't doing any of this because of him. I was doing it because it's what I wanted, and that I was happy living on my own. My dad was mad, and my mom was crying, but what else could I do. We stayed up talking till about one in the morning, then I just had to leave.

"Oh, yeah," Katie added, looking up at Carson, "my dad also told me to watch out for Carson, and that you said something about me 'having all the bells and whistles a man could ask for?'"

Carson choked on his donut and covered his mouth so it wouldn't fly onto the table. He looked up at Katie as he tried to recover. She stood there with her lips pursed and eyebrows raised, waiting for an answer, but somehow, she didn't look mad.

"Well, the only reason I said that was because . . ." He stopped and took a drink of coffee. Katie placed her hands on her hips, but she looked almost like she was smiling. "Was because your dad was threatening me, and he had made a comment like that to me about an ambulance before, trying to make me feel bad, and—"

"And?" she said.

"And . . . I know it was wrong, and I regretted it right away, but your dad just makes me so mad sometimes, and I have a tendency to shoot off at the mouth. I'm sorry. I admit it was totally inappropriate."

"Thank you," she said with a smile and turned to get her own coffee. She bent over with her back to him.

Without making a sound, Carson leaned over and mouthed to Eric,

"But it's totally true."

Eric raised his eyebrows in agreement and changed the subject.

"I'm glad it turned out okay," Eric said. "Or kinda okay, I guess. I felt bad that night, because I didn't know if I should've done something."

Katie looked genuinely moved. "Oh, Eric, that's nice. I know you would've helped if I needed it." She took her first small sip from her Styrofoam cup. "But it's my dad. He seems really terrible sometimes, but he really has a soft heart inside."

Katie saw the disbelief in both their faces and laughed. "No, I'm serious, guys. He may not have a soft heart toward you, but he does toward me. That's part of his problem."

"Okay," Eric said. "I won't worry about it then."

"Good, don't worry. If I ever feel like I really need your help, I'll ask you for it; you won't have to wonder."

"All right," Eric said.

"That goes for me, too," Carson said.

"All right, Carson. I appreciate you guys supporting me."

"We have to," Eric said between bites. "The last guy quit on us."

She laughed.

Carson finished his second donut. "Well," he said, brushing the crumbs from his hands, "there's one thing we can do to occupy your time here."

Katie looked at him, expecting an off-color joke. "You'll be pleased to learn that we're getting out of E22."

"Really?" Katie said. "That is good news!"

"Yeah, we have to go up to the shop to switch it out with E35. Joe's done with its overhaul, and he's going to work on E22 a bit while it's just used for stand-bys."

Eric wiped his hands with a napkin. "You can be our honorary escort as we lay E22 to rest—or, at least put it on the shelf for stand-bys. I wish we could lay it to rest for good."

"I'm honored," she said. "I'm ready whenever you are."

—

"Hey," Sheila's voice said over the telephone, "I've got something for you."

"Yeah?" was all Harvey said in reply.

"You know that story I told you about before? The one that I said I was working on?"

"Yeah?"

"Well, here it is," she said. "Deputy Chief Killion is turning a blind eye to guys at the station who drink on duty."

"On duty?"

"Yeah. I don't mean anyone's getting drunk off their ass, but some of them sure as hell drink a few beers at work, usually at the end of a shift."

"Oh, that's good stuff," the amateur newspaperman said. "And you know for sure that Lou Killion knows about this?"

"I think so."

"Does *he* ever drink?"

"No, but I know he's seen others doing it."

"What about O'Malley? Does he know about it?"

"Yeah, I'm tellin' you, everyone knows about it. It's just that that's the way it's always been. Kinda hush-hush, but it's accepted. Doesn't happen too often."

"Is there an official policy on it?"

"Of course! No drinking on duty and no coming to work drunk. But guys still have beers sometimes when they're on duty. The guys at Station Five made pasta a week ago, and there was a six-pack there. We stopped by with O'Malley, and he didn't say anything to them."

"Did you say anything?"

"Why would I say something if O'Malley didn't?"

"I don't know. I was just asking. So, do you have any sort of proof? You were saying something about pictures earlier?"

"That's what I would like to have, but I don't know how."

"Hmm . . . pictures would be perfect. We could release them just before the next county board meeting. Without a picture, they're just gonna deny it. Then they'll put the kibosh on the drinking altogether, and we wouldn't have anything."

"You got any ideas?"

"You don't think you could take a picture?"

"What?" the woman said. "Are you crazy? There's no way—"

"Okay, I guess you're right. That's too risky."

"Besides, as soon as they saw the picture on your website, they'd probably know it was me. That's suicide! I'm already lucky to still have a job."

"You got any better ideas?" Harvey asked.

"Actually, you might think this is kinda crazy too, but I was thinking that you should come and see it yourself? Just say that you were comin' to do an interview or something, and show up right in the middle of dinner or something."

"What good would that do?"

"You could say you saw it with your own eyes, and you wouldn't have to rely on an 'unnamed source.'"

"I don't think so," Harvey said. In a sarcastic voice, he added, "Hey, guys, I'm here. Oh, what's that, a beer?" He switched back to a normal tone. "You see what I'm saying?"

"Yeah, you're right. Stupid idea."

There was a moment of silence as the two thought it over. Then Harvey asked, "Are they ever in a position where I can take pictures from outside?"

"Hmm, I guess that could work. You mean, like through the windows or something?"

"Yeah. The windows are usually open aren't they?"

"Oh, I've got a better idea," Sheila said. "A lot of times we eat in the garage, when we're having a barbeque or something. Usually, the garage door is open. That would be easy!"

"That could work," Harvey said, slowly thinking it through in his head. "What I'll do is try to find some place to set up across the street. Which station should I focus on?"

"There's some dumpsters and bushes by the soup kitchen across from Station One."

"All right, all right, that could work," he said. "The only thing I need you to do is let me know when it's gonna happen. Is that a problem?"

"I don't think so." There was mild trepidation in her voice. "But what should I say? Because I'll have to be there, and I really don't want them to hear me. I need like a password or something."

"No, just text me. You got my cell number, right?"

"Yeah."

"Good. When it happens, put in 9-1-1 and then the time that you think it's gonna happen, and I'll set up right across from Station One."

"All right. 9-1-1 and then the time. Got it!"

Twenty minutes later, the three who comprised the new Medic One parked their ambulance in front of Eastern's mechanic shop and warehouse. All of the garage doors were closed, so they entered through the office door. Three ambulances of similar design but differing age and quality sat inside, all in various states of repair. One older model appeared to be missing an entire engine. The Aluminum Falcon stood in the middle looking brand new with a fresh paint job, but she had no nose. Instead, a radiator stood in plain view without the surrounding fenders, hood, and bumpers that would make her complete. As they walked by, Carson slid his hand gently over her taillights and backdoors, feeling the new paint, longing for the day she would be done. He felt it was close.

On the far end of the garage sat the third ambulance, E35, the ambulance that would now become Medic One until E60 was complete. It looked tired next to E60, but it was a step up from E22. A loud humming sound emanated from her other side where Joe was doing some last minute work. As the crew rounded the corner they saw Joe using an industrial-strength heat gun to melt a worn-out decal from the side. He didn't notice their presence due to the noise. They watched for a few seconds as the heat blast from the gun shriveled the plastic decal until it peeled easily from the paint.

Carson got Joe's attention by saying, "Does Leslie know you borrowed her hair dryer, because I don't want her coming in on a bad hair day."

Joe laughed hard and said, "Carson, you say some ballsy things sometimes. I just might have to tell her you said that." Eric and Katie couldn't help but laugh even though it made Katie feel guilty.

"Yeah, I'd appreciate it if you didn't," Carson said. "I've got enough problems right now."

"It might cost ya."

"Yeah, whatever. So, let me guess, you're not quite ready for us yet."

"Hold yer horses, Carson. This will only take me fifteen minutes, and she'll be ready. I couldn't finish until you got here anyway; I need one of you to help me hold the new decal while I burn it on."

"All right, you always have some excuse. Eric, can you help Joe while Katie and I start gettin' the bags out of the Ghetto Sled?"

"Sure."

Eric held the corner of the large Shield of Life as Carson and Katie headed back to the door.

Outside, the sun was rising over the city. Carson opened the doors of the ambulance and unlocked the narcotics cabinet. Katie opened the back doors and sat on the bench to load some supplies into the BLS bag, but she paused to feel the warmth of the sun beaming into the cabin.

She looked out and sighed. "You know, Carson . . ."

"What's that?"

"I'm so glad I decided to work here. I haven't done much yet, but I've met some great people, and I can tell that this was the right move. I actually love this job, and I haven't even really started yet."

Carson was pleased she felt that way. He smiled at her. "I'm glad to hear that. And for the record, I'm glad you came here too."

"I'm so glad I decided to get out from under my dad's thumb," she said. "I feel so free, so liberated."

"Yeah," Carson said, "I'm sure that's nice." He paused and looked down at the vials he was counting then added, "I'm sorry if this bursts your bubble or anything, but I have to say something."

She opened her eyes and turned from the sun to look at him. "What's that?"

"Your dad still controls you more than you know."

Katie looked at him and laughed. "What are you talking about, Carson?" She shook her head, and went back to work in the BLS bag. "You say the craziest things sometimes."

"You know what I mean. You moved out of the house because he controlled you, and he wouldn't let you do any of the things you wanted to do, but you still don't do them."

"Yes I do," she said with more curiosity than certainty.

"You do?"

"Yeah. I go home whenever I want. I date whomever I want. I live on my own, and I'm still working here! I'd say that's living pretty independently."

"But that's what I mean," he said, locking the narcotics sheet in the box. "You don't stay out late. You don't date . . . I mean, you don't as far as I know."

Katie never really talked about dating, and Eric and Carson had been curious for obvious reasons.

"Okay, I guess you're right about that," Katie admitted.

"I mean, you're not dating anyone, are you?"

She looked at him sideways. "No, not outside sorority functions. At least, not at the moment," she said. "Why do you ask?"

"I'm just curious," he said. "And you don't stay out late at night, do you?"

She frowned a little, beginning to understand his point. "No."

"Why not?"

"I don't know." She seemed as genuinely intrigued as Carson now. "The point is that I could do those things if I wanted to, but I guess I just don't have the time with school and work and everything."

"Maybe you need to take the time," Carson said.

"What are you suggesting, Carson?"

"I'm suggesting that you go out and have some fun. You probably don't do any of those things because in the back of your mind, your dad still controls you."

Katie slung a few bags over her shoulder, and Carson grabbed the rest as they exited the van.

"Maybe that's a good point," she said. "I don't really know. I guess if I have to be totally honest, I am a little scared of what he thinks. Maybe he made me think that doing all that stuff was bad or something."

"What do you mean?"

"I still don't want to do the things that he and my mom taught me were wrong. And that's really bad of me! I'm an adult now, and I don't even live with him anymore. I'm still trying to be such a good little girl."

"There's nothing wrong with being a good girl," Carson said, holding the door open for her. "In fact, the world needs more of them."

"Oh, I know. That's not what I'm saying, but you can't be perfect all the time." She thought for another moment, and said, "Okay, so we need to go out tonight while we have a night off. What's something fun we could do?"

Eric came around the corner of the ambulance wiping his hands.

"You guys going out tonight?"

"No, *we're* going out tonight," Katie said, "all three of us, and whoever else wants to come."

Joe, who was now in his office, stuck his head out and yelled, "I've got fresh coffee in here if anybody wants some!"

"Thanks," Carson yelled, "maybe in a minute."

Eric couldn't think about coffee; he felt like a load of bricks just dropped on him. "I can't; I have to work tonight."

"Tonight?" Katie said, "But you're just getting off this morning?"

"Yeah, I volunteered to do the standby at the racetrack with Tim tonight."

"Are you serious, Eric?" she said looking legitimately disappointed. "That sucks."

"Yeah. Believe me, I wouldn't have signed up for it if I'd known we'd be doing something."

"Can't you get someone else to work that shift?"

"Are you kiddin' me? Everyone hates that standby, and now it's last-minute."

"We can try, though," Carson said.

"You think?" Eric asked.

"No, not really."

"Yeah, I didn't think so either." Eric forced himself to be polite. "But if it doesn't work out, definitely don't hold back because of me. We'll just do something some other time. What do you guys think you'll do, anyway?"

"That's a good question," Katie said, looking over at Carson. "Do you still want to do something?"

"Yeah, well . . . it's up to you."

Carson did a darn good job sounding casual, Eric thought, but then again, Eric was doing the same.

"Okay . . . what?" Katie asked.

"I don't know. I'll think about it."

Carson and Katie started unloading their bags into the proper compartments in E35.

"I'll go grab the cot," Eric said. "Is there anything else we still need?"

"Yeah, grab a few more cannulas and the clipboard."

"All right. I'll be back."

"Thanks."

Moments later, Carson said, "I think I've got an idea."

She looked up with intrigue. "What?"

"When it gets dark tonight, why don't you and I go to this park I know outside of town and go swimming in the lake?"

"Isn't it closed after dark?"

"Yeah, but that's the point. You always said your dad wouldn't let you go out after dark or anything. You never break the rules. Isn't that what you wanted?"

"I guess," she answered reluctantly. "But . . . won't we get in trouble for that?"

"Only if we get caught."

She smiled. "Maybe. Let me think about it."

"All right, you can think about it, but not too much or you won't do it. It'll be fun. And just so you know, this is your chance to wear whatever kind of swimsuit you want."

Katie blushed. "Oh, whatever! You're such a player! I'll wear whatever I feel like wearing. But right now the only thing I'm gonna do is exercise my freedom to go get some coffee. You want some?"

"Sure. And think about it. I promise you, you'll have tons of fun and you won't regret anything."

At the coffee machine in Joe's office, Katie noticed her heart beating slightly faster. She couldn't believe herself. She was thinking about going out with Carson Treffer, the man her father hated most. She would be swimming in a lake after dark, when it was closed to the public, and he was suggesting she do it in her never-used bikini. Well, she definitely wasn't going to do that! Anyway, that would be too cold, she told herself.

She made her way back to Carson, who was making a mental check, looking through all the compartments. Eric had not yet arrived. As she handed Carson one of the three cups she had in her hands, she said, "Okay, Carson, let's do it. I probably shouldn't, but that's also the reason why I should."

Through the office window, she saw Eric head toward the coffee machine not knowing Katie had already got him a cup. She looked down. "Are you gonna tell Eric?"

"I was just wondering about that," he said. "I don't want him to feel too left out while he's sitting at the racetrack tonight. Maybe we should just tell him we're meeting up tonight and that we'll decide what we're gonna do later."

Katie looked down at the concrete, holding two warm coffees in front of her, one of them wasted. "Yeah, you're probably right. I don't want him to think he's missing too much."

15.

Fourteen hours later, Eric was back in E22. That's the way it always was with this job, he thought—another ambulance, another place. Sometimes, when he closed his eyes at night he saw dashboards under his eyelids. Sometimes it was a modern, blue dashboard, like E60's, but increasingly it was a nondescript, black dashboard from a 1994 Ford van like this.

He had gone to his apartment during the middle of the day, but he didn't sleep much. There were bills to pay and groceries to buy. Even when he did lie down, he couldn't sleep well. He closed his eyes and felt his heart beating fast. He couldn't relax. Light streamed in through the window. The phone rang once, and he shot through the roof. It was a telemarketer, so he hung up. After that, his heart beat faster, and when he closed his eyes he saw dashboards again and little blinking lights.

Now he was sitting in front of a real dashboard. Through the windshield, mini "outlaw cars" zoomed by on a dirt track. Mud flung up from their tires onto the windshield of the ambulance. Two-stroke exhaust fumes permeated the air, and the cars were so loud that Eric and Tim stuck tissue in their ears. No wonder everyone hates this standby, Eric thought.

Tim had been droning on about his divorce. It was getting nastier—typical divorce stuff. Typical EMS divorce stuff, Eric thought. Always gone, not enough money, always worn out, didn't want to do anything else. Tim's wife had wanted to get on with her life, and now she was. Meanwhile, Tim grew increasingly bitter. Thank God for the ear plugs.

Eric had to think of something else, so he thought of Katie. His mind wouldn't let him think of anything else anyway. He thought of the way she looked at him when she said all three of them were going out. That sounded fun—that is, if Carson weren't going. But that's what she was doing now, only with Carson, and not him.

Tim's voiced droned on through the tissue paper, and Eric let his mind wander further. What if he had stayed in school and met Katie at the University? He wondered if they would have hit it off. He would go to class during the day, study in between, and hang out with Katie at night.

What would they do? He'd probably hang out at her apartment a lot. Maybe they'd both study. He could picture that like it was real—Katie in sweatpants and a T-shirt, sitting Indian-style over a book. He would be laid out with head in hand trying to concentrate on his studies. They would get distracted and start talking about other things. What would they talk about?

Eric knew she was smart. He pictured them talking about politics. Health policy, maybe. Was the Consolidated Omnibus Reconciliation Act of 1986 a good idea for society? He was sure she would have an opinion on that. After all, she was studying to be a doctor.

He would probably go pre-med too, and they would have classes together. They would probably be studying the same book, he thought, and they would quiz each other. "Okay, recite for me the Krebs cycle." He pictured her biting her lower lip, as she so often did, and counting it out on her fingers.

She seemed like a girl who would make a lot of flash cards. He wouldn't have any, so she would quiz him off hers. He probably wouldn't be able to concentrate. It would be a terrible environment for studying. "Eric, pay attention!" she would say, laughing.

"I'm sorry, what was the question?"

"The question is . . . oh, never mind. Come over here, you daydreamer. If we're not really studying, we may as well put the time to good use."

On the other side of the city, the real Katie pulled her car into a small gravel parking lot at the lake. It was already dark. In the distance, the lights of Lincoln cast a haze in the sky. She could feel her heart beating beneath the baggy Cornhusker sweatshirt that covered her bikini top. She felt the smooth curve of the gas pedal beneath her bare foot. She had accidentally packed her flip-flops in the bag with her towel, and never took the time to get them out. She was glad; it was a novel feeling driving a car without shoes.

Her headlights lit up the trees when she swung the car around, the beams resting on Carson's pickup. He's already here, she thought. My dad would kill me if he knew I was here, but he would kill Carson first.

She grabbed her bag, walked across the gravel, which hurt her feet, but her jeans were long enough to provide some protection for her heels. She looked and saw that Carson wasn't in his truck.

"Carson?" she called softly. There was no answer. The darkness was intense, but she made her way to the grass. It was cool and offered some relief. She felt the blades between her toes as she shuffled her feet toward the lake. It was probably messing up her jeans, but she dismissed the thought more easily than she normally would have. They were old jeans anyway.

The wind made a rustling sound through the trees, then subsided. In the momentary silence, she heard movement in the water.

"Carson?" she said a little louder.

"I'm in the water," he called back. "I was beginning to think you weren't comin'."

She walked down the bank to the water's edge. There, at the edge of the trees, she could see somewhat better. Carson was swimming, silhouetted by the moonlight behind him.

"Well . . . I'm here," she said.

Her heart beat rapidly again. Was she scared? Maybe it was the thought of swimming in a dark lake; she couldn't tell. Were there fish in there?. She didn't ask; she didn't want to sound like a wimpy girl.

"Are you a good swimmer?" he asked from the water.

"Yeah," she said. "Why? Is it deep?"

"It gets deep, but it slopes gently at first. If you decide you don't want to do this, you don't have to, you know."

"You think I'm scared or something?" she said in a defiant tone.

Carson, who had stopped swimming and was now standing in chest-deep water, said, "No, I was just saying that you don't have to."

Carson could see her perfectly as she stood on the bank. With the moon behind him, she could see only a black silhouette, but he saw her fully illuminated in the moonlight. He stood and watched, skimming his hands back and forth underwater.

She glanced both ways to make sure no one else was swimming at that time of the night. "Get ready, 'cause I'm coming in," she said, mimicking enthusiasm. She reached down with both hands and pulled up her sweatshirt. The breeze rushed through the trees again and blew across her bare midriff. She felt a chill.

"Don't say anything," she said.

"Don't worry. It's dark; I can't see much," Carson lied, watching her undress on the bank.

She unzipped her jeans. They were tight and had to be wiggled down until they crumpled to the ground. She folded them and placed them next to her sweatshirt. She looked up and scrunched her shoulders to her ears when she looked over the water.

"Is it cold?" she asked.

"Mmm, a little at first, but not bad once you get used to it."

Truthfully, Carson was feeling a little cool. He shivered for the first time since he'd entered the water.

Katie waded into the water slowly. Mud squished between her toes. She thought about how dirty her feet were getting, then realized the water would wash it all away.

"Where are you?" she said. "I can barely see you."

"Over here."

"Okay. Wow, it's not too bad!" she said, her voice quavering.

Carson made sure he swam away from her. He didn't want her to feel threatened. "Am I close to the drop-off?" she asked.

He turned again to look. She was hip-deep, her fingertips just testing the surface. In the full moonlight her body curved and arced. She was not much taller than average, and not too skinny. Though she had a small waist, she was full and proportioned. Carson thought he had never seen a more beautiful woman. She looked up at him and smiled, masking her trepidation.

"Yeah, it's close. You should probably start swimming from there."

She felt naked in the cold evening air. It was a feeling she had never had before. Looking out over the water, trying hard not think about fish, she braced herself and dove in.

Resurfacing, she pulled her hair back with one hand, treading water with the other.

"You look like you're enjoying this," he said.

"I am!" she said, her voice trembling quite a bit now.

"Good. I'm glad. You need to loosen up." She was smiling ear to ear, and he added, "Isn't this better than studying?"

"Definitely! It's *definitely* better than studying. I waste too much of my life." She floated onto her back with a few short strokes. "It's colder than I thought, though."

"Yeah, there are definitely cold spots where it's deep."

With a few more swishes of her hands and two quick scissor-kicks, she was gliding backward into a warm spot. She felt the water permeate her hair, the individual strands floating around her shoulders. For several minutes, she lost herself and nearly forgot Carson was there.

After having swum farther out into the lake and returning, she felt uncomfortable and didn't know what to do next. Perhaps even more mystifying, she didn't know what Carson intended.

He didn't seem to care though; he swam around, paying no attention to her. So she swam too, alternating strokes. Occasionally, he disappeared underwater, not resurfacing for many seconds. She hoped he wouldn't come up and embrace her. She didn't think she was ready for that but didn't know.

Each time, however, he resurfaced far away and continued to swim as if she were not there. It took all of Carson's will to give that appearance. When he inadvertently got within three feet of her, the blood rushed from his face, and he felt weak.

Soon, she grew more comfortable. She was glad it was dark and that Carson wasn't able to see her. Then she thought about Eric. He most certainly would be jealous if he knew about this. She wondered about that a moment, then realized Carson was swimming toward the shore. When he reached the shallow area, he waded through the water.

"Where are you going?" she called.

"I'm done," he said.

"You're done already?"

"Yeah, I've been in there a lot longer than you."

"Yeah, I guess that's true. I'm kinda tired too, I guess."

Katie, having now switched places with Carson, saw how well he had seen her undressing, and she felt her face grow warm. She saw his back lit by the moonlight. As he reached the shallows, his backside and legs came out of the water. They were bare.

She gasped and covered her mouth. She felt hot in the cold water.

"Carson!" she yelled. He began to turn. "No, don't turn around!"

He stopped and chuckled. "What?"

"What do you mean, 'what'? You're naked!"

"I realize that. You didn't have to look." He made his way onto the shore, into the shadows, and started dressing.

Katie didn't know what to say.

"Don't you have swimming trunks?"

"I might; I haven't checked in a while."

"Why not? You enjoy swimming naked?"

"Yeah, why is that so surprising? Anyway, why bother with swimming trunks when you always swim in the dark?"

She shook her head and chuckled to herself. Everything Carson did surprised her, but then it always made sense at the same time.

"Okay," she sighed. "I guess I'm done too. I don't want to be alone out here with the fish."

She approached the shallows and found her feet. Carson was fully dressed, though still dripping with water.

"Oh my God! I can't believe we . . ." She didn't finish her thought.

"We what?"

"Nothing. I just can't believe you would do that."

"Why not? Sometimes, it's the best way to unwind."

He thrust his wet hands into his wet jeans and stood waiting for Katie to dress.

"I mean," he continued, "it's the best thing I can do to clear my mind. Usually, when I'm out there I never once think about Eastern Ambulance or the Lancaster County Fire Department or the people I see when I'm out there. I get away from it all here."

"Did it work tonight?"

He watched her step onto the bank and realized why her father was so worried about her wearing a bikini. "Not so much."

She could read it in his face. "Because of me? I'm sorry."

"No, it's not you." He watched her trying to pull her tight jeans over her swimsuit and added, "Well, maybe it's a little bit you."

"Stop watching me! Turn around!"

She continued with her jeans, but he didn't turn around. Instead, he kept talking. "Do you know. . . ?"

She stood there, still dripping. The breeze made her shiver. He looked warm in his old flannel shirt, with his hands in his pockets.

"What?" she said, covering her body with her sweatshirt.

"I hope this doesn't sound cliché, but you are truly one of the most beautiful women I have ever seen."

She felt more uncomfortable, but very grateful. No one had ever said that to her so sincerely before, and she didn't know what to say.

"You don't have to say anything," he said, reading her mind. "I just wanted you to know that. I guess I'll head back toward the cars and let you finish."

"No," she said, surprised to hear herself say it, "It's pretty out here. You don't have to leave." She quickly put her sweatshirt back on and pulled her long hair out from the back. "We haven't talked all night. We can enjoy the scenery for a while, can't we?"

"If that's what you want."

She placed her towel on the grass near the edge of the bank, sat down, and hugged her knees to her chest. Carson sat next to her. He was strangely uncomfortable with the situation. Was it the age thing? That hadn't stopped him before. No, it was the "talking" that made him uneasy.

"Okay," he said, "what would you like to talk about?"

"Well, I don't know. I feel like you know so much about me because I'm always talking, and I don't know anything about you—like, literally, almost nothing. You know who I am, what I do, and all about my family. You know my family almost better than I do, and I don't even know if you have a family."

He knew "talking" would lead to this. He should have suggested something else.

"Hmm . . . well, I guess I don't talk about my family much, do I."

"Why not?"

"Well, because both my parents are dead."

Katie felt a rip in her heart. If she had known, she wouldn't have asked. "I'm sorry, Carson, I didn't know."

"That's okay."

"Do you mind if I ask what happened?"

Carson looked up at the moon and drew a deep breath. His face grew sullen. "I grew up on a farm, and my dad died in a farming accident when I was young. My mother died of congestive heart failure several years after that."

"I'm sorry."

He tried to look at her, but could only do so for a second. "Yeah, that's life, I guess."

"But it's a shame when it happens so young."

"I know." He picked up a nearby stick and began drawing lines at the edge of the grass. "It's really sad because my dad was the last person who deserved to die. He always cared about everyone else more than himself."

"It sounds like you had a really great dad."

"Yeah, he was always doing things for other people. I think I resented it some as a kid. We once took in a poor family to live with us for a while. I was mad because I had to share a room. We were pretty poor too, you know. But my dad always gave and gave and gave. I remember one time when my dad heard that a family in the church didn't have anything for Christmas, he made us give some of our presents to them before we opened them. I was so mad at first."

"But it was very nice."

"I know. I realized that later. But it's hard for a six-year-old to understand that. All the kids in that family drew up cards for us. My dad was so proud of those homemade cards. He placed them on the piano and said that was the best Christmas present any of us got that year. Then he started to keep a collection of cards that we got from people like that. They were on the piano, the wall, on our refrigerator—like Thank You cards from other farmers when we helped them buck hay and stuff like that.

"That's awesome," Katie said. "At least it sounds like he lived a great life."

Carson's eyebrows furrowed in pain again. "Yeah," he said, "but the craziest part of all is that I don't think my dad was meant to die so young."

"What do you mean?" Katie asked. She was cold and felt herself leaning imperceptibly closer to Carson until her shoulder and hip pressed against his.

"Wow," he said, letting the stick drop motionless for a second, "I wasn't really thinking I would get into all this."

"I'm sorry; I'm not trying to pry. I just wondered what you meant by that."

"I don't talk to too many people about this. Eric thinks I'm crazy."

Her face turned toward his, riveted by the mystery that was Carson Treffer. "I won't think you're crazy, Carson. You can tell me whatever you want."

After a few seconds of internal debate, a subconscious dam broke within Carson's mind, a dam held tightly shut when he wasn't dreaming. He traveled a hundred miles away, back to the Plains and his boyhood home.

"When I was eight years old, I had a bad case of influenza that led to pneumonia. I ended up in the hospital for several weeks, far away from our farm, ya know. I remember how bad my dad felt when the doctor said it could have been prevented with a simple vaccine, but that it was too late now. I passed in and out of consciousness so much of the time. I feel like I lived in that little hospital for a year. I remember my parents crying over me, and the doctor saying it didn't look good. There were always people coming in and out of the room—the pastor coming to pray for me, nurses, and sometimes just someone standing in the corner in the dark. I don't know who it was."

Carson looked down at the ground and bit his lower lip as his eyes grew glassy. "But what I remember most is my dad coming to visit me at night and praying for me all alone. He had big, calloused hands, and he held one of my hands in both of his when he prayed. I was too weak to move. I remember him praying, asking God to let me live, and that no parent should outlive their child. The craziest thing—and this is just like my dad—is that he asked over and over if God would take his life instead of mine. 'I offer my life to you, God,' he would say. 'I've lived a good life and you can take it from me now. Just let my son live. Let him grow and live longer than me and his mother, so she can see him grow up to be a man. When he gets older, he can take care of her in my place.'"

Katie was captivated. Her eyes welled up and one tear escaped down the side of her face. Carson's cheeks were no longer dry, and he wouldn't look at her.

"Carson," she said, "your father sounds like he was a wonderful man, and a wonderful father."

He shook his head.

"What happened when you recovered?"

"The fever broke one morning . . . at some point I don't

remember. I don't remember several days, actually. I just started getting better, and when I was strong enough, my father picked me up and cried against my chest. I didn't understand so much back then. One day, my father carried me to his truck, and he and my mom took me home."

"Thank God for that," Katie said. She so desperately wanted to hear more, to hear what happened to his father, but he wouldn't volunteer anything. She wanted to be sensitive. "How old were you when he died?"

"Twelve."

She understood how a young child might connect the two events. It was a terrible burden to bear. "Carson," she said, "I don't want you to think I'm belittling your loss, but I think I know what you feel. You feel like God let your dad die in your place."

He looked up at the stars and tossed his head side to side like he didn't really believe it.

"I just want to say that your dad died four years after you were sick—in an accident. His death had nothing to do with you. The only thing the story tells me is that your dad loved you very much."

Carson tried to relax, to change his mood. He folded his hands behind his head and lay down.

"That's what my mother always told me. But there's more to it than that. I started to believe that, but I've had too many close calls since then, and I don't know what I believe anymore."

Katie turned to lie on her side, propping her head on an elbow. He finally looked at her, at her moist eyes, and the curly tresses that fell around her face. He turned to face her, wondering if her youth, her vibrance, her beauty could be an antidote for the pain—an elixir for the death that stalked him. He reached over and placed his hand on her waist, just in that spot before it rose sharply to her hip. She held his forearm in her palm, her eyes wide with wonder and speculation. She shivered as the night grew colder, and he felt her body tremble. They had no blanket, only a wet towel that barely covered the hard roots below them.

"It's cold out here," Carson said.

"I'm freezing," she said.

"Do you wanna go to my truck? I'll turn the heater on."

"That would be nice."

The move was a terrible intrusion on the moment, but he wasn't eighteen years old; he knew it was necessary. They got up from the cold ground and the wet towel, and walked toward his truck.

"Carson," Katie said, taking his hand in hers, "I want to say thank you for bringing me out here tonight."

"Are you having a good time?"

"Definitely, but I don't think I should come out here anymore." Carson looked disheartened. She added, "It's just that I don't want to disrupt your routine."

"What!" he said, stopping to look at her. "You have to come out here again. You need this more than I do. It seems like you're relaxing and enjoying something for once."

"You're right, I am."

Katie looked over at Carson's pickup. It looked inviting and scary at the same time. Carson saw the hesitation in her face. "What's wrong?"

Katie was a breath away from saying "nothing," then stopped herself and looked at Carson.

"Carson," she said, "all of this is pretty new for me, and sometimes I'm not sure I even know what I'm doin', or what *we're* doing. I don't want the night to end so quickly, but I don't think . . ." She spoke hesitantly, searching for words. "I don't think I feel comfortable going to your truck tonight. I mean, a part of me wants to . . . I really mean that. I would like to talk more, but I know what might happen if I do that, and a big part of me is not ready to move that fast."

Carson didn't answer with apologies or vague attempts to explain his motives. He simply said, "I don't want you to feel uncomfortable."

Saying that had the reverse effect, making her feel almost comfortable again. "Thank you. I appreciate that . . . a lot. I want to come out here with you again sometime since you don't mind, but I need to take it slow. Maybe next time I'll try swimming your way first."

He chuckled and asked, "That's taking it slow?"

"It is compared to going to your truck," she said with a wry smile.

"I guess you've got a point," he said, and he couldn't help but laugh at her, and a little bit at himself. "I'll be waiting until next time, then."

She took one of his hands in both of hers and pressed it firmly. "Thanks, Carson. And thank you for sharing with me about your family. That meant a lot to me. I hope you think about what I said, and I hope we can talk about it more sometime." She gently kissed his lips, turned, and walked toward her car. She wanted to leave on a happier note, though. Halfway there, she turned and looked at him again. Walking backwards, she pushed a strand of wet hair behind an ear, and said, "Besides, I don't know if you're ready for all the bells and whistles." She smiled and turned away.

Carson stood and watched her go. There was a time when he wouldn't have let her go so easily. Every chemical in his brain told him to keep her near, but the man inside him let her go. He watched her taillights until they were out of sight. He stood alone in the darkness, frustrated, cursing the cold night. It ended so quickly, but he understood her, and he was not entirely dissatisfied. After a minute to himself, he stepped into his truck and left.

—

The last race had ended, and the people in the stands began to clear.

"Maybe we should wait a little longer before we leave," Eric said.

Tim had his hand on the ignition. "Why?"

"Because there's still a lot of people around, and—"

"And what?"

"You know what! It's just really embarrassing trying to start this thing in front of people."

"Oh, gimme a break, Eric," Tim said and turned the key. The engine whirred sporadically for several seconds without starting. Tim gave it a rest.

"You see!" Eric said. "*That's* what I'm talking about! This is a freakin' ambulance! It's not supposed to sound like Carson's pickup!"

"Chill out! You're so wound up tonight."

"I'm so wound up every night, Tim! Don't you know me?"

Tim turned the key again. He let the engine whir even longer this time, but it didn't even start to chug. A woman walked by Tim's window with her kids. She turned and stared at the ambulance with a perplexed look.

Eric buried his forehead in his hand. "This is exactly why we're not supposed to turn E22 off."

"Eric!" Tim said, beating his hand on the steering wheel. "We have to turn it off when we're at the racetrack! We can't let it run for three hours! We'd run outta gas!"

"Thank God we don't have an emergency right now. Just wait a few seconds; we don't want it to get flooded."

"It probably already is," Tim said, finally removing his hand from the key.

Luckily, most of the small crowd had cleared by now. Eric didn't want to look at any of the passersby. Why could he not make management understand that this thing was a moving billboard for the company, and as such, somebody had to do something about it. Every time Joe took it into the garage for a tune-up, it was better for a few days but returned to its normal, pathetic state in no time.

"All right. Try it now," Eric said, "but don't give it any gas."

Tim complied, resulting in a few more seconds of whirring. Then the engine chugged to life, albeit with a good deal of smoke. Eric jerked his head back to the headrest like he had just survived a scary movie.

"I tell you what, Tim. This stupid ambulance is going to be the death of us."

16.

Early the next morning, Deputy Chief Killion lounged in his office with Captain O'Malley and Mark Rader. Outside, daylight was just starting to brighten the city, but there were no windows in the deputy's office, or in his secretary's, for that matter. Only by peering through his glass door, down the long, dim hallway, through the door at its end, past the fire engines to the open garage doors could Lou Killion see what was happening outside. Deep in the cinderblocks, he relied on the fluorescent bulbs above and a small desk lamp to illuminate the newspaper in his hands.

"This is perfect," he said, tapping his cigarette into the ashtray.

Captain O'Malley sat facing his boss with his hands on his knees.

"I thought so. It's a little weak because it's only 'alleged,' but it's still going to meet its intended purpose."

"I agree," the deputy chief said.

Then he turned to Mark Rader. "Good job, Mark. Good job. It's important that people learn stuff like this. As we learned the other night, we've been focusing too much on the county council and have neglected the people in the city. It's time we start focusing on what the average Joe on the street thinks, and this . . . this is a very good start."

It was awkward seeing Carson in the morning, but Eric acted as normal as possible.

"How was the racetrack?" Carson asked as they sauntered from their vehicles toward Station One.

"Sucky, like usual. How 'bout you? You guys do anything last night?" Eric asked as if he hadn't been dying to know the answer to that question all night.

"Yeah, we went down to the lake for a swim."

Eric said nothing for a second, then realized he shouldn't pause.

"At the lake?" Thoughts swirled through Eric's mind, but he tried to think of something calm to say. "Wasn't it closed?"

Carson chuckled. "Why does everyone ask that? Yes, it was closed, but you can't exactly lock it up."

They kept walking. Eric thought about swimming at the lake with Katie, and immediately he realized that not calling in sick last night was one of the dumbest things he'd ever done.

"That sounds like fun," he said indifferently.

Carson played it down as well.

"Mmm, I guess it was pretty fun." He shrugged his shoulders. "We were probably only there for half an hour or so."

Eric was relieved but didn't let it show. "Oh yeah? Why so short?"

"Well, it was pretty cold, and there's only so much swimming you can do. I thought it would be a good way for Katie to let her hair down."

It was on Eric's mind, so he decided to ask it. "I bet she looked amazing, huh?"

"Yeah," Carson said, nodding.

They both thought about that for a moment before Eric asked, "You guys didn't go out after that?"

"No, she said she'd had enough fun for one night. I guess she's breaking in slowly."

Eric didn't know if he liked the sound of that. It sounded like Carson was breaking in a colt (which, knowing Carson's stories, was probably something he had actually done). But one thing Eric did know—breaking her in slowly sounded better than breaking her in fast, at least until he had his own chance.

They walked inside where they met Leslie coming off her twenty-four. She was in the garage, restocking IV tubing into the Airway Bag.

"What's up, Big Mama?" Carson asked, tossing more tubing to her.

"Long day," she said, "followed by a long night."

She looked haggard. Apparently, she didn't have the time to put on all her makeup either, and Eric thought she actually looked better for it.

"You guys goin' to the company meeting at Station One today?"

"Yeah, if we can. You?"

"Yeah, if I can get some sleep."

She stopped rummaging through the bag and looked up at Carson. "You see this morning's paper, Carson?"

"No. Why?"

She frowned, got up from the bench, and went over to the table. She picked up the morning newspaper. "It's got an article about you in it."

Carson stood for a second, looked her in the eyes, took the paper and unfurled it. Eric came close by to read over Carson's shoulder.

A sidebar headline ran, *"Paramedic Suspected Abuse, Didn't Report."* Carson's brow furrowed as he and Eric read the article to themselves.

"The Lincoln Tribune has learned that Eastern Ambulance paramedic, Carson Treffer, had long suspected that eight-year-old Adam Turner was being neglected by his family. Turner suffered from cerebral palsy and was confined to a wheelchair. His body was found August 27 by firefighters while attempting to contain a fire in Turner's Shady Cottonwoods mobile home.

"Mr. Treffer was one of the paramedics on-scene who first believed Adam's condition was a result of the fire. Physicians later determined that Adam had been dead for over twenty-four hours before the incident. The autopsy revealed that Adam was significantly malnourished, had several bed sores, and had not been given his anti-seizure medications. He ultimately died from pneumonia, which had been undiagnosed.

"Adam's mother, Shirley Turner, is awaiting trial. Thomas Murray of Lincoln, the social worker assigned to Adam's case, has since been terminated for failure to carefully monitor the boy's condition. Nebraska law requires that social workers, paramedics, and other rescue workers report findings of child abuse to Child Protective Services immediately. A former employee at Eastern Ambulance, who asked that his name not be released, reports that the Eastern Ambulance supervisor had expressed to him and others that he had long suspected child neglect in the case but had not reported it to authorities.

"We contacted Child Protective Services who maintain that Mr.

Treffer had not filed any reports prior to Adam's death, but that he had called them after the incident and relayed his fears. No report was filed with hospital staff or the Medical Oversight Agency. However, the M.O.A. said they will look into the case and determine whether there was any wrongdoing on the part of Mr. Treffer.

"Lancaster County Deputy Fire Chief Lou Killion was asked about standard procedures for reporting child abuse. 'Obviously there are gray areas when there is some suspicion in your mind,' he said. 'What I tell my guys is that when in doubt, at least talk to a coworker about it, and usually we'll report it just to be safe. What troubles me about Adam Turner's situation is that Mr. Treffer had apparently not talked to anyone about it, and his phone call to Child Protective Services after the fact is an indication that he should have known what to do.' Mr. Treffer was not available for comment."

"That bastard!" Carson said, looking up from the paper. "I can't believe . . ." Carson was speechless with anger. "I never said I long suspected child abuse."

Eric thought for a moment and looked up at Carson. "It was Brent, huh?"

Carson didn't respond.

Eric continued. "Rader or Killion probably grilled him about everything he heard when he worked with us. That's obviously where they got that 'Society Repair' comment from the other day. He told them about that night we were talking about Adam, and I bet they ate it up."

"This is the most blatant manipulation of the press I've ever seen!" Carson said and slapped the paper in his palm.

"Did you call Child Protective Services?" Leslie asked.

Carson stopped ranting for a moment and looked up at Leslie.

"Yeah," he said, "I wanted them to know what I knew about the mom." He squeezed the newspaper in his hands. "I thought they might be able to use it in their investigations."

"What exactly did you tell them?" Leslie asked. "Did you say that you suspected child abuse?"

Carson leaned back against the ambulance, hooking the heel of his cowboy boot on the tire.

"I don't know what I said exactly. I told them the way she acted, and how I thought she never really loved the boy, never showed much concern for him."

Eric interjected. "That's not unusual. We deal with that all the time."

"That's true."

"That *is* true," Leslie said, "but it sounds bad to C.P.S. and to the public."

"I know that sounds bad, Les, but I was just trying to help. The way she treated him should tell us something about what happened that night. I feel I could've done more if I had at least thought about it."

"Exactly, Carson!" she said. "That's *exactly* what's going on here. Did you say something like that to them?" She didn't give him a chance to answer. "You feel you 'should've known,' but you *didn't*. But to them—and the way the department is making it sound—you *did* know, and you didn't do anything about it. That's not the way it was! You told me yourself that you hadn't seen Adam for months. You never saw anything. You never had anything to report. You can't report hunches! And now the department is manipulating the public."

"I know," he said.

"They've found the perfect thing to break you up, confuse you, and make you second-guess yourself. Who cares if Brent said this about you? Who cares? The M.O.A. will ask a few questions, but once they talk to you, they won't find anything wrong."

"Because if you're in trouble," Eric said, "then so am I, and so is everyone at the hospital. If there was evidence of neglect, then we *all* should have seen it."

"But you're not the Paramedic," Carson said.

"Stop doing that, Carson," Leslie said. "What you should be focusing on is the fire department." She pointed out the garage door toward downtown. "They're the ones who've got problems! Quit beating yourself up about this and let them know how you feel. They're trying to make you feel responsible for things you're not responsible for! Weren't they on those calls with Adam, too?"

Carson looked up at her and nodded his head in affirmation. It was such a good point he didn't have to say it.

"Maybe . . ." Leslie said, "maybe they should be writing an article about themselves. Call it 'Fire Medics Examined Boy Many Times; Didn't Report Abuse.'"

"I know, I know, Les. I know all that, but do you think everyone who reads this article is gonna understand that? No. They're gonna see this, and it's going to bring our competence into question. Even if the M.O.A. looks into this, and they find that I did nothing wrong, just the fact that there was an investigation with all kinds of bad press is going to sway people's minds."

"Yeah, so, what's your point?"

"They've scored a small victory, at my expense."

"So, what are you gonna do about it? Go write up some bogus story about them?"

"No, but we just can't sit idly by while they snipe at us like this."

"You have any ideas?" she asked.

"No, but I need to let them know that they can't run roughshod over us, that they can't just push us around. I'm just gonna have to go talk to them."

"You'd better talk to Hank and Dave about that first."

"I'm going to."

—

"Of course I saw the article," Hank said in his office just minutes before the meeting. He was speaking to Carson. Katie was there as well. "I think it's ridiculous. How could they even print crap like that without talking to you? Did they even call you?"

"I don't know; I haven't been home much."

"Carson, you need to check your messages more often."

"I know," he said, "but it's too late now. What's gonna come of this?"

"I don't know yet. Dr. Windholz will probably determine whether the M.O.A. wants to make an issue of it. They might have to do it just for procedure's sake."

"I'm going to talk to the deputy chief," Carson said bluntly.

"Here we go again." Hank, who had been resting his elbows on his desk, leaned back and placed his arms on the elbow rests. "Carson, let's not overreact here."

"I'm not overreacting, Hank. All I want to do is tell him that I don't appreciate their underhanded tactics. We need to let them know we won't tolerate it."

"Carson, I tell you what. Why don't you let me or Dave place a call to Chief Winkenwerder to express our concern over this."

Carson looked as though he were going to say something but stopped. Then he added, "How 'bout this? You can do that, and I can write a letter to the editor explaining everything I said about Adam so they can see where I was coming from."

"No, you might just incriminate yourself. I'll talk to our lawyer, and to Dave, and Dr. Windholz. We'll see what we need to do. Carson, let us handle this."

"Are you sure, Hank? I really feel like I need to respond in some way. This isn't just the company's reputation; this is my name on the line."

"I know, Carson, but we've got to let the professionals help us work through this. We don't want to turn this into some sort of pseudo-war with County Fire. I'll figure out what we need to do, and I'll let you know."

Hank could see the frustration in Carson's face. "Don't worry, Carson, we're gonna respond to the fire department. That's what this meeting's about. Now, you guys get upstairs, and I'll be up in just a second."

Carson and Katie walked into the hallway. Katie spoke first.

"I kind of thought the letter to the editor was a good idea," she said.

"So did I," Carson replied, "but Hank likes to play it cautiously, I guess."

Katie stared at the ground as they made their way up the steps. She felt somehow guilty, trying to guess how big her father's role was in this. She guessed it was a major one, though, and she felt like she had to make it up to Carson.

—

"All right, folks!" Dave Conrad said in an effort to get everyone to quiet down. "All right, we've got a lot to talk about, so let's not waste any time."

People shuffled around the room and found seats. Many people had gathered around Carson to discuss the newspaper article. They rehashed the same arguments he went over with Leslie earlier. In fact, Leslie was there to rehash them herself. All told, the article did nothing but further anger and embitter the Eastern Ambulance staff. Dave Conrad overheard some of their rumblings. He knew he could do little about the article and was pleased he was able to make the announcement he was about to make.

"I know you've all been waiting for this meeting," he said. "We've told you about plans that we've had brewing, and we want to bounce those off you tonight. A lot of fuss has been made in the papers and in the county council meeting about Eastern Ambulance not arriving on time."

A few people in the crowd made booing noises.

"I know, I know. That's simply not the case. Now, as always, our average response time to the patient is well within the parameters of the contract, which are the national standard in cities across the country. But that's not how people see it. At least, that's not how the fire department wants them to see it. They see fire engines arriving first more than half the time, and they think that means the fire department ambulances would be faster. They don't know that there are three times as many fire engines in this city, and that the fire department doesn't plan on having any more ambulances than we do."

Someone yelled out, "Then why don't we just tell them that?"

"We *have* told them that," Dave replied. "We wrote an editorial to the paper a month ago explaining that very thing."

"I don't think many people got the message," the same voice—Tim's—yelled again.

"You're probably right, Tim. People are convinced that the fire department can provide faster service than Eastern Ambulance, and we can't seem to shake them of that.

"But that leads me to why we're here tonight. I sat down with Hank, Susan, and the Board, and we've devised a way to improve our service. If the fire department wants 'faster,' then we'll give them faster. If the fire department thinks we underpay, then we'll pay more. If the fire department claims our people are overworked, then we'll give them shorter shifts. And if some people think we're just gonna roll over and let the fire department take our jobs, then they've got another thing comin'."

Wow! Eric thought, where was this Dave when they needed him at the county council meeting? At least this Dave made an attempt to rouse people.

"We want to introduce you to something we call the Millennium Plan."

Dave continued. "Here's how it works. First of all, before people get too confused, I want to clarify that we obviously don't have the money to significantly raise everyone's salaries. That's not what I'm talking about here. What I am talking about is paying you the same, maybe a little more, but with less hours. What we want to do is have everyone work shorter shifts, but to get paid more per hour. This will be better for you, and it will help with recruitment and retention.

"Right now, everyone works twenty-four-hour shifts. What we're proposing is to change to twelve-hour shifts. We'll still have the four teams, but they may be shaken up a bit. There will be two day teams and two night teams, and everyone will work every other day. Everyone will have at least one day off every weekend. And the key thing is that everyone's shifts will only be twelve hours long."

"Can we do that?" Leslie asked.

"Yes, almost. We may need just one or two more people to make it work. We'll have the same amount of people working the same number of ambulances. They'll just be working a very different schedule."

"So, what about the money?"

"Well, at its simplest, the Millennium Plan means that over the course of a year, you will make approximately the same wage because you'll have a lot less overtime, but you will be working fewer hours for that wage. While the yearly salary does not change that much, the hourly wage increases significantly, and that's what looks good when you're advertising for jobs."

Some people in the crowd nodded their heads, obviously wanting to hear more.

"We found that at certain transition times, we were unnecessarily overmanned. In addition to the increase in the hourly rate, I am pleased to announce that management is giving everyone an overall salary raise of three percent."

People in the crowd started to mumble to each other.

"I know that's not a lot, but we haven't been able to give a good raise over the past few years as we've tried bringing our ambulance fleet up to snuff. We're pretty much through with that. Joe is up at the garage right now working hard on E60. We got it back from the body shop, and he's putting the finishing touches on her. It should be ready later today."

"So how does this make us faster?" Leslie asked.

"Oh, I'm digressing," Dave said with obvious enthusiasm. "*This* is how it makes us faster. The way things are now, we are basing out of our stations. We have to do that because we work twenty-four-hour shifts. Obviously, you have to sleep when you can. But with a twelve-hour shift, there's no need to sleep. That's the same as working a twelve-hour shift in an ICU or on a hospital ward. In a twelve-hour shift, you're awake, you're alert, and you're there just to do your job. That is what will allow us to be faster. Now we're basing out of our stations, but in the Millennium Plan, we're gonna start street-basing."

Carson, who had been coolly listening to the whole speech, finally had his curiosity roused. "Street-basing?" he asked.

"Street-basing," Dave continued. "It means no more messing around in the stations, watching TV, browsing the internet—you know what I mean. We'll be out there on the streets, ready for our next call, ready to jump on the call before the fire department is even off their couches."

Carson's eyes widened ever so slightly, and he nodded his head as he mulled it over. "When do we start?" he asked.

"We think we can start next week if we put our minds to it. We have a preliminary template put together based on our current teams. Some people will just have to pick up some overtime hours until we get more people."

"When will we be able to get back into E60?" Carson asked.

"Tomorrow, I think. That shouldn't be a problem, as long as Joe says it's ready."

Carson looked over at Eric, who smiled back with a pleased look.

"So," Dave continued, "E60 aside, what do you guys think of the plan?"

People throughout the room nodded their heads in general approval.

"How 'bout questions?" Dave asked.

Many hands went into the air. Dave fielded questions about everything from federal taxes to scheduling, and by the end of the meeting, most people were onboard. People talked behind the scenes, jostling for positions on the night or day shifts.

"Folks," Dave said, "I know we can make this thing work. We're going to transition as soon as possible—I hope before the next county council vote. Maybe this is something we should have done a long time ago, but sometimes it takes hardship to shake up an organization. The point is, we're doing it now, and it's going to make us better and faster. That's going to be a lot better for our patients, *and* it's going to take some steam out of Deputy Chief Killion's arguments."

Everyone liked the sound of that.

17.

That night, Katie left her apartment to have dinner with her parents. She met with them for a family meal once a week, but her schedule had prevented that lately.

"How's school, honey?" her mom, Margaret, asked as she poured gravy over Katie's potatoes. Katie would have poured it herself, but her mother had always done it this way, and Katie couldn't get her to change.

"It's going well."

"Good, I'm glad to hear that," Margaret, who was still holding the gravy, pushed her glasses onto the bridge of her nose with the back of her wrist. "Your grades are doing well?"

"Yes, Mom, my grades are fine."

"That's good. I was just wondering because you have so much going on with that new job and you going out more at nights."

"What do you mean, 'going out more at nights?'"

Her mom began fidgeting with the top button of her blouse, a habit Katie remembered her always having. "I ran into Jenny the other day at the supermarket, and I told her that I hadn't talked to you much recently. She said you had been going out at night with some of your work friends."

Katie's father walked through the French doors as Katie answered her mother. "I haven't been going out that much, Mom."

"I'm glad to hear that, Katie," Mike O'Malley said.

"You know," he said, taking the bowl from his wife, "I'm glad you came over tonight. I want to put the bad times we've had behind us."

"Dad! There's nothing we have to put behind us. Let's just forget about it, and it won't be a problem."

He waited as if he expected her to say more, but she didn't.

"I worry about you, Katie. I'm afraid you're taking on too much at once."

"I'm not, Dad."

"I know you don't think you are, honey, but sometimes you don't realize it until it's too late."

"I know, but I'm managing well and keeping my grades up."

"That's good, honey, but that's not all I'm worried about."

"Oh geez, Dad," she groaned, "I thought we were putting all this behind us?"

"We are, honey. That doesn't mean I'm not gonna take an active interest in your life. We need to talk about these things."

"What things?"

"Well, for one thing, we don't like you going out after dark like you do."

"Dad, I'm in college! Everyone goes out after dark!"

"That's not true, Katie, and you know it!"

"Yes it is, Dad."

"Katie, I've given you a lot of leeway lately. You know how bad it is for me, and how much it bothers us that you're working for that company now."

Katie just stared at him, forcing him to make a point.

"I'm just saying I'm letting you make your own decisions in life no matter how much I disagree with them."

"And . . .?"

"And that's just it. I don't want you going out with those guys alone after dark."

Katie knew that it took a lot of guts for her father just to come out and say "those guys," and his concern almost touched her heart, but not quite.

"Dad, I'm not doing anything wrong."

"I know, honey." He reached over and placed his palm on her hand. She thought about how only a week before, he had grabbed her elbow. "I know you're a good girl, and I trust you." He smiled, then turned his attention to his food. "I just don't trust those boys."

"Dad, there's nothing wrong with them."

"Honey, if you heard half the stories I've heard, you'd know better."

Katie *did* want to know more about that, but she was too proud to ask. Besides, it would make her look naïve and that's the last thing she wanted.

"Katie, a guy I know said he saw you going outta town the other night, down toward the lake."

"What?"

"That's what he said. Is that true?"

She hesitated. "I . . . yes, I went down to the lake, but I didn't do anything! Do you have people watching me or something?"

"No, honey, he just happened to see you." O'Malley paused with a piece of roast beef halfway to his mouth, looked at it, and replaced it on his plate. "So it's true, then?"

"Yes, Dad! I already said that it was, but nothing happened!"

He pushed the roast beef around the gravy on this plate. "Well, your word does make me feel a little better. Who did you go with?"

"Dad, stop worrying about me."

"I can't, Katie. Were you there with a man?"

"Yes, but all I did was go swimming. I promise there was absolutely nothing else."

O'Malley put his fork down and looked like he was going to get sick. Katie could tell he wanted to ask who it was, but he was too afraid to ask.

"Just do something for me, Katie."

Again, she didn't answer.

"I've been letting you do whatever the hell you want. I let you move out and get your own apartment. I'll let you do what you want with school. I'll even look over the fact that you've chosen to go work for that company."

"If what?"

"Just let me finish, honey. Just promise me you won't go out with any of your friends from Eastern."

"Dad, I already have."

He clenched his jaw and took a deep breath.

"Then promise me you won't go out with them in the future."

"Do you mean dating them, Dad? Is that what you mean?"

"Yes, and more than that. I would just rather you stay away from them. If you have to see them at work, that's one thing. You remember how you told me that day to get used to seeing you with them at work?"

"Yes."

"Well, I'll make a deal with you. I'll get used to your job, at least for the next few months while they're still around, but it would break my heart if you got involved romantically with one of those guys."

"Dad, you're being ridiculous!"

"That's all I'm asking from you, Katie. Your mother and I have given you and *are* giving you so much. We only want what's best for you. We just ask this one thing."

Katie rolled the peas around on her plate, then looked up and saw both her mother and father looking at her with that ever-present concern in their eyes.

"Dad," she said, "I'm not dating any of them, but they are my friends, and I want to be able to hang out with them as friends."

O'Malley sighed. "Okay, Katie, I can see that you want to have your way. How about we arrive at a different compromise?"

"Why do I feel like we're in negotiations? What do you mean?"

"How about saying that you can see them and hang out as much as you want, but can you at least promise that you won't hang out with them alone after dark?"

She rolled her eyes and looked at her mother who gently nodded her head to say those were her wishes too. Katie was used to her dad setting the law, but already tonight and in the past few weeks, he had backed down a lot. She realized that that was part of her growing power as an adult, but she also realized that since her dad had conceded so much, she could ask for no more and still be on good terms with him.

"Okay," Katie said, "as long as you know that I may hang out with several of them after dark, then I promise I won't go out with just one."

O'Malley sighed in relief. "And that means no more going down to the lake at night," he said sternly, stopping short of pointing his fork at her.

"Yes, Dad."

"Not even by yourself."

"What?"

"It's dangerous, Katie. You don't know what kind of riffraff might be down there, and what would happen if you got hurt and no one was there to help. Plus, it's supposed to be closed at sunset."

"Okay, okay," she said, speaking with mock, robotic tones. "I promise I will not go down to the lake even by myself because it's dangerous . . . and closed!"

"You know that your mother and I only want what's best for you."

"You already said that."

He was looking at her again and reached for her hand. She pulled it away and took her fork.

He sighed and stood up, making his way to the cabinet. "I was going to wait to do this until after dinner, but now's as good a time as any." Katie could tell he had lost his appetite.

He pulled a small white box off the shelf and handed it to her.

"What's this?" she said.

"It's just something your mother and I want to give you."

"What's the occasion?"

"No occasion. We miss you, and when we saw it, we just wanted to get it for you."

Katie opened the box and found a velvet jewelry box. Inside was a necklace. It had six small diamonds—one in the center surrounded by five others in the shape of a flower. It was pretty, but Katie thought it looked juvenile.

"Go ahead," her mother said, "try it on."

Katie removed it from the box and clasped it around her neck.

"What do you think?" her dad asked.

"It's . . . very nice," she lied, literally at a loss for words. "Thank you."

"Do you like it?"

"Yeah, Dad . . . it's nice. I hope it didn't cost too much."

"Aw, don't worry about that; I just like making you happy. It looks good on you."

"Thanks," she said touching it with her hand as it lay upon her chest.

"Katie?"

"Yes, Dad."

"I'm sure glad we had this talk tonight. As your father, I worry about you, but having a daughter like you makes up for all the worrying I've ever done."

She quickly forced the corners of her mouth into a smile and began eating to avoid any more serious conversation.

The next morning, Sheila lounged with the rest of the Engine One crew and the Truck One crew at their station. They had only one call all day and an uneventful one at that, so they watched TV and listened to the dispatch speaker on the wall. The Eastern ambulances had plenty of work to do, but it was always in another fire station's district.

Perhaps it was the heat. For mid-September, it had grown unusually sultry in the past few days. The residents of Lincoln sat and sweltered or confined themselves to the air conditioning. The Engine One crew did the same but were getting antsy. If some old fool would just insist on jogging, they'd have a patient and have something to do. And of course, there would be someone like that somewhere, but most likely in someone else's district. It was just that kind of day.

O'Malley threw the TV remote down on the coffee table.

"I can't stand this anymore!" he exclaimed. "There's nothin' on!"

"I thought that 'Ten Best Beaches of Florida' thing was pretty good," Tyrone said.

"Watch whatever the hell you want, Tyrone." O'Malley said. He had treated Tyrone differently since the day he offered to help Carson at the Detox Center. O'Malley stood up and paced over to the window. "I'm tired of being cooped up in here."

Phil Johnson, a bodybuilder type from Truck One, said, "We're thinking about washing the truck later when it cools down a bit."

"What the hell for?" O'Malley asked. "You guys haven't taken that thing out since the last time you washed it?"

"It gets dusty in the garage. Maybe your engine could use a wash too."

O'Malley thrust his hands in his pockets as he gazed out the window. "I don't know, Johnson. Maybe."

O'Malley jingled the change in his pockets, as most of the men and the one woman in the room focused on him.

"What's the matter with you, boss?" Tyrone asked without turning his eyes from the TV, "Somethin' gnawin' at you?"

O'Malley furiously jingled his change three more times before he turned away from the window. "I just can't stand the thought of Katie being out there with those two fuck-offs."

The room was silent. O'Malley opened the fridge to see if anything interested him. There was nothing.

The only other senior guy in the room spoke. It was Jon Carver, the Truck One captain. "Is she out there with them right now, Mike?"

"I don't know if she's working right now, Jon. Hell, I don't know her schedule anymore, but I hear Treffer's voice on the radio, and she's been assigned to him."

"He probably requested her," Phil Johnson said before realizing his mistake.

O'Malley's jaw stiffened. "I don't doubt that, Phil. Thanks."

"Well, maybe it's time you put your foot down, Mike," Carver said.

"It's not that simple, Jon. She's hard to control. I've already pushed her too far, I think." He leaned against the kitchen counter. "Maybe if I hadn't pushed her, she wouldn't be workin' with them at all. That girl's too much like her damn mother!"

"Too much like you, I think," Carver said.

O'Malley didn't laugh. He merely looked at Carver out of the corner of his eye before he took a drink of water. When he finished, he said, "She'll be grown up soon, and I just hate to see her make terrible decisions so early on."

"She's already grown up, Mike."

O'Malley put the glass inside the sink, placed his hands on either side, and hung his head between hunched shoulders.

"Not yet, Jon. She's not quite grown up yet. She'll come to the light soon. I won't let her embarrass herself too long. That's just my responsibility as a parent . . . as a good parent, ya know. I don't want to see her make a mistake with either of those boys that she'll regret later. They have no future."

"She's a good girl, Mike. She'll soon fizzle out, and she'll quit. She can't keep up with work and school at the same time. It's just a phase."

"Oh, believe me, Jon, I've told her that a hundred times."

Jon went up to O'Malley and placed his hand on his back. "Stop worrying about this. It's bad for your health." He turned around and faced the group. "Here's what we'll do. This afternoon we'll wash the trucks, and then we'll have a barbeque. Once the sun starts goin' down, it'll be perfect weather to open the garage doors, let the trucks dry, and cook some bratwurst. How does that sound?"

Some of the guys nodded their heads, which is how most firemen show enthusiasm when they're around each other. O'Malley turned from the sink and leaned back on the counter.

"All right, Jon. Let's have a barbeque. I'll go back to see if will want to stick around too. I think he wants to try to see his wife tonight, but we'll invite him at least."

After that, most of the firemen in the room went back to watching TV or doing whatever they were doing until it was time to wash the trucks. Sheila got up and made her way to the restroom. She sat on the toilet seat without raising the lid and pulled out her cell phone. She dialed a number and entered, "911 700."

18.

Carson picked up the phone in the crew quarters at Station One. "Hello."

"Carson Treffer?" the voice asked.

"Yeah, who's this?"

"This is Harvey Miller. I'm a reporter."

"I know who you are."

"You do? Good. So, you're familiar with my website?"

"Yeah. I've read it quite a few times actually. It's good to see somebody tell the truth about our county government. What's up?"

"I've been following the ambulance issue, you know, and I read that article in the *Tribune* about you and that boy saying you had suspected abuse. You know the one I'm talking about, right?"

"Yeah."

"Well, I was wondering if you had any comment on that?"

"It paints the wrong picture."

"What do you mean?"

Carson wondered where this part-time reporter was going with this. "Are you writing an article about this or something?"

"I'm not sure yet. I'm just fact-gathering at the moment, but I might. Do you mind?"

"No, not at all."

Carson rubbed his eyes and made an effort to think.

"Good," Harvey said. "So what were you saying? You said it paints the wrong picture?"

"What I mean is, it makes it sound like I knew about some sort of abuse or something, and that I was supposed to report that."

"And you didn't?"

"No. I mean, I could tell the boy didn't have the wholesome family life you think kids should have, but I never saw anything that screamed out 'abuse.' What that article is referring to is a comment I made in front of an EMT who now works for the fire department."

"He's the 'former employee' they alluded to."

"Yeah."

"Who is it?"

"Brent Cunningham."

"What did you say to him?"

"Oh, I was just saying stuff like I should have known and that I wished I had picked up on the signs and everything. He must have reported to someone in the department, and they took it out of context."

"Or they purposefully *put* it out of context."

"Yeah, that's more like it," Carson agreed.

"Have you done something that would make them mad at you?"

"Well," Carson sighed, "that's a loaded question." Then he chuckled. "But nothing specific really."

"What do you mean?"

"I just mean that we really don't get along—the fire department and I."

Harvey started to speak, but Carson cut him off when he had another thought. "I mean . . . let me reword that. There are some people in the fire department that I get along with just fine, in fact, quite a few of them. But there's a small minority that I don't. It just so happens that they're also the small minority who are in the positions of power."

"I see. You're talking about Chief Killion, Captain O'Malley, and people like that."

"Exactly. And Mark Rader."

"But you don't think they've singled you out for some reason? They're just trying to attack Eastern, and this is one way of doing it?"

"Yes and no. I think it's that I'm a supervisor, I tell them what I think, and I don't care who they are. When you stand up to them, they come after you, I guess."

"You did a good job standing up to them at the county council meeting."

"You were there?" Carson asked.

"Yeah, and I'm just saying that that was an excellent point you made about why you don't transport everyone to the hospital."

"Somebody needed to say it, and no one else would."

"Yeah," Harvey said after giving it some thought. "I imagine you're not just some random Eastern medic that they've picked out. I imagine you're on their hit list."

"Their 'hit list?'" Carson thought about all the conflicts he'd had with the fire department and the comments he'd made to O'Malley about Katie. "Yeah, I'd definitely say I've made their hit list. That's not in question. The question is whether anyone else has."

"Well, I definitely am."

"Oh, really? How's that?"

"My reporting on this issue hasn't exactly made me a popular person with the Lancaster County Fire Department."

"I would imagine, but do you know that for sure?"

"Yeah, I've gotten some pretty nasty e-mails."

"Really?" Carson said, growing more intrigued. "What do they say?"

"Oh, things like 'if you're gonna throw stones, you better not live in a glass house,' and stuff like that."

"*Really!*" Carson said again. "Have you done something about this? Maybe you should complain to the county or something."

"I've thought about that, but I can't really pin it on them. The e-mails aren't signed. Obviously, I'm pretty sure I know who they're coming from. I mean, I'm pretty sure they're not from some concerned citizen."

"Yeah," Carson said with a laugh, "that doesn't sound like an ordinary concern."

"Another one I got said, 'You'd better be careful, because you live in a dangerous part of town.' You know, stuff like that."

Carson paused. He was genuinely bowled over by this information and didn't really know how much he could trust this muckraker.

"If someone is really threatening you like that, I'd like to know who the hell it is. Most of the firefighters wouldn't do that, but I guess I wouldn't put it past a few of them—those same ones I was talking about earlier?"

"Like the deputy chief?"

"Yeah," Carson said, "or one of his lackeys like Mark Rader or Manny Alvarez or Phil Johnson or somebody. Definitely not the fire chief, though."

"What about Mike O'Malley?"

Carson had to think about that one for a while. "No, I don't think so. He's definitely not one of the good guys, but I don't think he's as ruthless as Killion, or as childish as the others."

"So you just think it's just childish gestures?" Harvey asked. It was funny that Carson could almost detect some concern in his voice now.

"Yeah, it's definitely childish."

"That's what I thought," he said, sounding a little relieved. "I really don't think they mean anything by it? They're just bluffs . . . just threats. They want to intimidate me, but they never back it up. I've been doing this kind of stuff about the government for ten years now. People try to intimidate you. That's just what they do."

"Yeah, I think you're right. But still, if I were you, I'd maybe report it to the police."

"I can't. I can't because I don't know who's e-mailing me. I've got a reputation for just diggin' up trash, you know, and I don't know if they'd take me seriously. It'd just be hearsay. That's the thing about my line of work. You can't publish anything until you can back it up with evidence. I'm working on something right now actually—working on some good evidence tonight, I think."

"Against the fire department?" Carson asked.

"Yeah."

"Do you need any help?"

"No, I've got it covered. Why do you ask?"

"Well, like you said, I'm on their hit list. If they're attacking me, I might as well fight back."

Carson could almost hear Harvey laughing again. "I like your attitude. Maybe we can fight them together, but I don't need any help tonight. I could definitely use you to keep your eyes and ears open. You're out there in the field with them everyday. I could definitely use you as a source."

"All right. Done deal. So, what's your story about? Maybe I can help you with information."

"Mmm . . . I really don't want to say yet. It's not *huge*, but it'll be good if I can pull it off. Just some pictures of them at work mainly."

"I don't get it."

"If everything goes right, you'll see soon enough. It's just some stuff the people of Lincoln wouldn't like to see."

"You'd better be careful. If you start diggin' up some big stuff, you're not just talking about losing a contract, you're talking about people losing their jobs and their pensions and everything that goes with that."

"Yeah, I know how important that is. I have a wife and kids too."

"People will fight when you threaten that stuff. Does your wife know about all this?"

"Not much."

"Does she know about the e-mails?"

"No, I don't want to needlessly scare her. If she heard about that, she'd probably make me quit. I'm playing it cool. I'm not gonna push anything too hard."

"All right," Carson said, "just let me know if you need anything."

"I will." There was a pause before Harvey continued. "I'm sure I'll be talking to you again."

"Call me anytime and stay outta trouble."

"I'll do the best I can," Harvey said.

Carson hung up the phone and went to the other crew bedroom to find Eric. "You'll never guess who I just talked to," he said.

"So you guys wanna get into E60?" the mechanic, Joe, asked Carson and Eric later that night. "What, E35's not good enough for you?" They had been bugging Joe all day, calling and asking when it would be ready. He told them to come to the shop around five. They gave him a few extra minutes, but he still wasn't ready.

"What's the rush?" he asked.

"We need a much faster ambulance," Carson said, "and a more comfortable one."

Joe rolled his eyes as they followed him to the side garage. "What the hell for?" he asked.

"Have you heard of the Millennium Plan?"

"The what?"

"Yeah, I know, it sounds kind of corny. It's basically the plan management came up with to make us compete with the fire department. We're gonna go to twelve-hour shifts and move to street-basing."

Joe fumbled his greasy hands through small greasy boxes on a shelf. "What do you mean?"

"It means we're not gonna hang out at the station anymore. We're gonna stick to the streets the whole shift so we can respond quicker."

"So, you're starting the plan tonight?"

"No, not officially until next week, but Eric and I are gonna start street-basing tonight."

Joe found the light bulb he was looking for. "You guys are real pieces of work! You mean to tell me that you plan on staying up all day and all night just to shave a few seconds off your response times? You're gonna kill yourselves . . . or die of boredom."

"Eric," Carson said, "show him the entertainment."

Eric pulled a small portable DVD player out of the cab of E35.

"What the hell is that for?" Joe asked.

"It's entertainment," Eric said. "We're gonna need something to help us stay awake. We've got a twelve-volt plug for it and everything."

"Oh my God! Do Dave and Hank know about this?"

"No," said Carson, "and they probably don't need to."

"Do they even know you're street-posting tonight?"

"You mean street-basing. And no, we're just getting a head start."

"What's this have to do with E60?"

"You're missing the whole point. We've got to have a more comfortable truck, one that will make this plan a little easier for us. We need the Aluminum Falcon back."

Joe walked between the old ambulances toward the garage where he had recently moved E60. "I've gotta replace one more light bulb and check everything out before I sign her over."

"We appreciate this, Joe," Eric said.

The side garage was Joe's special garage. The rest of the warehouse was more like a large hangar for several vans. This was the garage where Joe did most of his serious work. Large, wheeled tool chests stood around the sides, and small black parts crowded the shelves around the outer walls.

On a board behind one of the workstations, Joe hung a calendar from an ambulance manufacturer featuring several of their top-of-the-line products. However, Joe must have found it lacking, because he had cut-and-pasted bikini models onto the pictures as though they were leaning over hot rods. Around this calendar he hung pictures of real hot rods, with pictures of not-so-real girls already on them.

It was good to see E60 again, Eric thought. He forgot how modern she looked. Her lines were rounded, not squared like the older models. The body workers at Ford had done an amazing job fixing the wreck. Eric was hard-pressed to remember the mangled front end he had seen only months before.

Joe climbed into the cab and turned the key. It fired without effort, a stark contrast to E22. He turned on all the emergency lights, one at a time.

"Now you guys remember," he yelled, "don't start all these at once. It's bad on the electrical system."

"We know," Carson yelled back over the loud diesel engine. "You've told us a hundred times."

Joe stepped out, leaving the engine and lights running. The garage door was closed, and the room quickly filled with exhaust smoke. The strobe lights and light bar sprayed beams through the smoke. Eric could barely see the bikini-clad girls on the walls, and with the ambulance lights, the room was beginning to look like a disco.

"What are you doing?" Eric yelled.

"What does it look like I'm doing? I'm changing the light bulb!"

The front headlights were alternating high beams side-to-side as Joe put one foot on top of the tire, and the other in the crack of the open door. Climbing to the roof, he unscrewed a few sections and removed the cover on the light bar.

"I talked to a buddy of mine who said he saw you guys on a call!" Joe said.

"Oh, yeah?" Carson asked. "When was that?"

"Oh, a few days ago. It was an accident downtown at Tenth and 'P'."

"Yeah, that was probably us."

"Were you guys late or something?"

Eric didn't know how Joe could stand the fumes. It was getting so thick that he could hardly breathe. Both his and Carson's eyes welled up with tears, but Joe appeared unaffected.

"No," Carson said indignantly. "What do you mean?"

"He said the fire department arrived on the scene right away, but they had to wait for Eastern Ambulance."

Carson pressed his forehead into his palm. He was so tired of explaining this. "Of course they did! There are only three or four emergency ambulances in the city at any one time! All cities have more fire engines than ambulances."

"Yeah, well, maybe you should have been there to explain that to him. He said maybe it would be better if the fire department ran the ambulances since they get there quicker."

"Oh my God! If I hear that one more time . . .! That's what *this* is about, Joe. We're gonna change that starting tonight!"

"What are you talking about, Carson?" Eric said, obviously perturbed. "We've already explained it to them a hundred times. What else can we do to tell people why we get there later?"

"You're missing the whole point, Eric," Carson said without taking his eyes from the beaming, clouded ambulance. "It's simple—they're just not gonna beat us anymore."

The garage clouded unbearably now. A thick, white fog nearly obscured Joe atop the ambulance. The only things that showed clearly were the dozens of flashing lights that pierced the cloud like bursts of red and white lightning. Eric closed his eyes for a second. Tears streamed down his cheeks. Eric thought, "Oh my God! Carson is going to kill us."

"All right! That's it." Joe climbed back down. "You guys should be good to go."

"Thank God!" Eric said. "Can we open up the friggin' door. I can't stand it in here any longer."

Joe looked confused for a second, then laughed. "Yeah, no problem. Just hurry. I don't want to let all the air conditioning out." He pushed a button on the wall.

"You're insane," Eric said.

"You got any paper, Joe?" Carson asked.

"Paper? What do you mean?"

"Blank paper . . . to write on?"

"Yeah," he shrugged, "there's some in my office, in the printer. "What for?"

"I'll show you in a minute. Eric, can you pull the truck out? I'll be right out."

Eric climbed into the cab. One of the niceties that made E60 special in his eyes was the fact that unlike the newest models (of which Eastern had two, at Medic Two and Medic Four), it still had armrests. Clean, supportive seats and armrests. That was the beauty of E60. Carson was right—it was the best of the old and new.

Outside, Eric rolled down the windows and turned the vent on "HI." It was nice to be sitting in his old truck again. A gentle breeze blew from the vents around Eric, clearing out the stench of the smoke. The van felt streamlined and slick, and the engine hummed with hard, gently pounding pistons.

A minute later, Carson came out of Joe's office with a few pieces of paper.

"Hey, Carson," Eric said.

"Yeah?"

"I'd like to start driving more often if I could?"

"Yeah, sure, maybe a little later on. One thing's for sure, you and I are gonna have to take our driving to the next level. We're gonna be right there with the fire engines."

"No problem."

"No fuckin' way!" Joe said, overhearing their conversation. "You need to take your driving *down* a notch! That's what got her in here in the first place!"

"No, Joe," Carson retorted, "that was a careless person pulling out in front of us. That couldn't be avoided. When I say we're gonna take our driving up a notch that also means were gonna to do it more skillfully. We're gonna be awake and alert and more serious about our jobs."

Joe shook his head, not believing a word Carson said. He was already planning in his mind how long it would be before he had to change the brakes on that ambulance, and he walked away in disgust.

Eric took his spot on the passenger's side and found a place for the portable DVD. Carson grabbed the aluminum clipboard from its upright slot between the seats, folded the paper in half, and placed it on the clipboard. He took out a pen and began to draw a small fire engine in the upper left-hand corner.

"What are you doing?" Eric asked.

"I'm creating a tally sheet."

"For what?"

"Every time we beat a fire engine or match it, we're gonna mark it on this sheet."

"Isn't that going a little far," Eric said. Then he teased, "Are you going to use it for evidence or something?"

Carson ignored Eric's mocking attitude. "No, it's just for us. It's to make sure we never slip back into the routine of taking a backseat to those guys. From here on out, we have to stay focused."

Carson finished the drawing and took two rubber bands out of his pocket. He placed the paper on the top side of his sun visor and secured it with the rubber bands. He flipped the visor up, then down again and stared at it briefly. It was quite a testing process for a piece of paper, Eric thought. When Carson was satisfied, he flipped the visor back up and said, "All right, let's get our stuff and get outta here."

———

Several blocks away, the men at Fire Station One prepared their barbeque. They had already washed Engine One and Truck One, both of which now sat gleaming in the driveway. Jon Carver wheeled the grill outside the garage door and lit the coals. An hour earlier, some of the guys had gone for groceries. The temperature started to cool with the setting of the sun, and as smoke from the briquettes filtered into the garage, the men's spirits began to rise.

Across the street, Harvey Miller set up camp. He had parked his car several blocks away and walked to the soup kitchen. There was a crowd there, mostly old men. They either waited in line for their food or mingled outside. Homeless people have the same social repertoire as everyone else, talking and bartering goods. Harvey mostly ignored them. Instead, he carried his bag to the corner of the parking lot, which had a tree, a few bushes, and a dumpster. He squatted in the middle of all three.

He unzipped his camera bag, and one of the shabby, homeless men came up to him. "What are you doing?" the man asked in a friendly voice.

Harvey was immediately conscious that the man was clearly visible from across the street. He became short with the man. "Nothin'," he said. "I'm just doing some work over here. Please leave me alone."

"That's cool, man, that's cool. What kinda work you doin'?"

"I'm a writer."

"Awesome, man! I'm a writer myself. I write about stuff people don't think about. They don't think about those trees, you know. They don't think about the beautiful spirit that a tree has. Writing can show them that."

"Sir!" Harvey said. "I can't talk right now. It's very important that you leave me alone! Could you step away, please?"

"Oh, you're one of them," the man replied.

"I don't know what you mean."

"I mean one of those yuppie guys who won't talk to a guy like me because you like to judge people! I'm just a fellow writer, brother. All right, asshole, I don't want to talk to you either! I'm done with you."

The man stomped off toward the kitchen. Harvey had not quite planned to be here at dinnertime, and it was clearly interfering with his plans. Instead he decided to squeeze a little farther in behind the dumpster. It was not just the firemen he had to worry about, but the small homeless mob as well.

19.

Medic One was almost ready to go. Carson asked Eric questions that sounded like a takeoff checklist.
"Airway bag?"
"Check."
"ALS bag?"
"Check."
"Narcotics."
"Locked."
"Engine oil?"
"Normal."
"Tire pressure?"
"I put four pounds in the left rear."
"Rudder?"
"We don't have one."
"Just makin' sure you're paying attention. Turbocharger?"
"Spinning up."
"Portable DVD player?"
"Check."
"Oxygen?"
"Twenty-two hundred pounds."
"Busty, red-headed college student?"
"At class tonight."
"Damn!" Carson slapped the steering wheel. "How do they expect us to do our jobs without the right equipment?"
Eric shook his head, pretending to be mad at management.
"Tally sheet?"
"Check, but with a lot of white space."
"Don't be so negative. This is our first night. IV fluid?"
"Twelve bags in the rig."
"Tubing?"
"Check."
"Catheters?"

"Check."
"Splints?"
"Check."
"Anything else we need to worry about?"
"Nope."
"All right, let's lock and load."

Carson put the transmission lever into "Drive" and pulled away from the garage. "Where should we post tonight?" he asked.

"I don't know," Eric said. "Just drive downtown for now. We've been lucky we haven't had any calls while we've been up at the garage."

"You're right. I want our first call on the tally sheet to be a win. But I need some driving music."

Eric reached for the radio's power button.

"No," Carson said, "that's not what I'm talking about."

Eric looked confused as Carson pulled the portable DVD player out of the console, plugged it into the cigarette lighter, and placed it on the dash.

"If Hank won't put CD players in the ambulances, we'll just have to put 'em in ourselves. This isn't just for DVDs."

Carson pushed "Play" on the machine, and one of his old rock CDs blared loud and strong.

———

In the middle of preparing the bratwurst, one of the guys pulled a six-pack out of a brown paper bag. It was almost clockwork, Sheila thought. The fireman, Jeff Petrolak, completely oblivious to any wrongdoing, pulled the cans out of the plastic and passed them around.

"Johnson," he yelled out, "you want one?"

"Yeah," Phil Johnson yelled back and caught it in midair.

"O'Malley?"

"No thanks, Jeff. Hey, you guys make sure you stay in the garage with those. I don't want anyone outside with it, got it!"

"No problem."

Sheila was not even offered a beer. Petrolak knew she would say no.

"What's the occasion?" a new voice asked. It was the deputy chief.

"Hey, Chief," Jeff said. "No special occasion. Since when do we need an excuse for a barbeque?"

Lou Killion patted his friend on the back. "Since never, Jeff. I was just wondering if I missed something. It's good for you guys to unwind. I'm thinking, though, that after the county council vote, you guys can barbecue every day of the week for all I care. We just have to be mindful of how people perceive us until then."

"Are you saying we shouldn't do this?"

"No, no, it's fine. One beer only, of course."

"If anything," Petrolak continued, jerking his thumb toward O'Malley, "the boss needs to unwind."

"Is that true, Mike?" Killion asked his long-time friend.

"I was just restless today," O'Malley said. "Bored and restless." O'Malley noticed the deputy's eyes shift to something across the street. "Something goin' on, Chief?"

Killion stared again for a few seconds. "No, just looks like some of the usual soup kitchen crowd yelling at each other again. They'd better not make us go over there."

Deputy Chief Killion stared across the semi-darkened street for a second more. "Anyway, this is good. In fact, I'm glad you guys thought of it. We could all stand to unwind a little. O'Malley, you guys don't mind if I stick around a while, do you?"

"I was just comin' back there to ask you. No dinner at home, I guess?"

Killion grabbed a Coke and took a seat at the indoor picnic table with the others. "No, Lynda's visiting her parents for a few days with the kids. I've got nothin' but time."

Everyone in the room understood the deputy's statement. They knew his wife was divorcing him, and that they were separated, but they didn't talk about it.

"Good!" O'Malley said. "With all that's been going on lately, we've all—"

O'Malley's thoughts were interrupted by the overhead speakers. "Engine One, Medic One. Nineteenth and 'P' on a suicide attempt."

"Shit!" O'Malley said, setting down his Coke. "Don't stop the party on account of us. Just a few blocks away—shouldn't be a big deal."

The men and woman on Engine One—O'Malley, Petrolak, Tyrone, and Sheila—put down their food and drinks with the efficiency trained into every fireman. Trucks did not respond to medical calls, and their friends on the truck company just watched. They slid into their gear and ran toward their freshly cleaned fire engine. Doing so, they heard Carson's voice clearly on the radio overhead.

"Medic One, clear and en route."

"What the hell?" O'Malley said. "He's got a jump on us!"

Then they heard a siren, but the sound did not come from the speaker. It came from the street. All the firefighters stopped and looked. It was Medic One passing right in front of their station. As they passed at high speed, Carson switched the siren from "wail" to "phaser" and back to "wail." They were out of sight in a flash.

"That motherfucker!" O'Malley yelled. He and his crew ran to their rig.

———

Carson and Eric arrived on-scene a few minutes later. It had grown quite dark as they carefully negotiated the gravel parking lot and heard the sound of Engine One moaning in the distance. They grabbed their bags.

"Well, Eric," Carson said, "there's one Fire Engine for the tally sheet. Don't let me forget to mark that."

"I'm sure you won't forget," Eric said with sarcasm. Yet, Eric found himself relishing the thought a little bit.

"Apartment Eight, right?" Carson asked, knocking on the door without waiting for an answer.

"Yep."

An apparently healthy man appeared at the door.

"You call 911?" Carson asked.

"Yeah," he said without emotion.

"Where's the patient?"

"He's right here."

"What?"

"I'm the patient."

"All right, sir. Can we come in?"

"Can't we just go to the hospital?"

"Well, we need to look at you first. You told the dispatch center that you tried to kill yourself?"

"Yeah."

"What did you do?"

"What do you care?"

"Sir!" Carson said, "I need to know, so I can determine what we need to do for you."

The man grew immediately angry. "Oh, the goddamned ambulance driver thinks he's a doctor now?"

Carson was only mildly shocked at such behavior anymore. The man was apparently high on something.

The Engine One crew came up the stairs behind them. Eric took over the questioning to start the conversation anew. "Sir, we're here to help you. There's no need to antagonize us. If you've done something to make yourself sick, we need to know about it."

"You know what?" the man said. "Never mind, I'll drive myself to the hospital."

"Whatcha got, Carson?" Sheila asked.

"The patient isn't being real cooperative, and now he says we should never mind, because he's going to drive himself to the hospital."

Sheila walked past Carson toward the man. As she did so, she whispered to Carson, "Let's see if a woman's touch can help." Carson nodded with skepticism.

"Sir, are you willing to talk to me?" she said.

"About what?"

"About what happened. What happened to you?"

"I took a bunch of pills." Sheila looked over at Carson.

"When?"

"Last night."

"How many pills did you take?"

"The whole bottle."

"What were they?"

"Aspirin."

"Okay. How many were in the bottle?"

"I don't know."

"Are you feeling sick?"

"I feel okay for now."

"Can we take your blood pressure?"

"What the fuck!" the man said. "Now you're some kind of doctor, too?"

Carson looked at Sheila and gave her a false sympathetic smile.

The patient continued, "No, you *can't* take my blood pressure. Just take me to the goddamned hospital!"

The police were on-scene now. After a few minutes of wrangling, Sheila convinced the man they would take him if they let him take his blood pressure in the ambulance. Carson was happy to take him to the ER for the mere satisfaction of knowing the man would have a tube shoved down his throat. The man agreed to go only if Sheila was his medic. She reported this to O'Malley so the Engine would pick her up at the hospital.

The short drive to the hospital was accompanied by more raucous, uncooperative behavior. Sheila managed to get a blood pressure, while Carson sat in the jump seat filling out the call sheet. There wasn't much to report. The ER would have to sort out what was in this man's blood. He was stable, and that's all he had to worry about. He tried asking a few more questions, to which the man told Carson to "shut up."

In the ER, Carson, found an open spot at the nurses' station to finish charting the call while Sheila gave a turnover report to the ER nurse. Engine One waited for Sheila outside. Carson listened to the man yell and discredit the ER nurses now. He was beginning to find it humorous. Carson was interrupted in his musings by Jim Homestead, the hospital CEO, who had just come through the door.

"Carson," he said in his loud, booming voice, "how the heck are ya?"

"Jim," Carson said, looking a little preoccupied, "I'm glad to see you; I want to talk to you about this patient we just brought in." He pointed toward Bay Four.

"Oh God, Carson!" Jim said before he could finish. "Don't even ask! You already owe me two golf lessons that I haven't collected on."

"You don't even know what I'm gonna ask," Carson said, slightly put off again.

"Oh, c'mon, Carson, it's always the same. Let me guess."

"Okay," Carson said, folding his arms and leaning back in his chair, "let's hear it."

In sarcastic tones, the hospital CEO said, "It's a *real* sob story. You've got a patient in there that you know—you *just know* is too poor to pay his or her hospital bill, and you know the hospital is not gonna be able to collect on it anyway. You've seen their house and you've talked to the dad, and you think it would be best if I just wrote this one off. Well, I hate to tell ya, Carson, but I've plain run outta charity money this year." Then he added with a touch of amusement, "And you're not too good at meeting your end of the bargain, either."

Carson looked unmoved. "Well, that was a good guess, Jim, but that's not what I was gonna ask."

Jim was genuinely surprised. "Oh really, what was it?"

"I've got a guy in there who's a real asshole, and I want you to bill the hell outta him."

Jim was speechless for a moment. "What happened to Mr. Nice Guy?"

Carson hurriedly placed his signature on the chart and tore off a copy for the hospital record. "Mr. Nice Guy is tired of 'nice' getting him nowhere."

He folded the piece of paper and placed it in Jim's hand. He motioned to Eric, and the two walked out the door.

As they stood in the parking garage, Eric called Dispatch on the radio. "Dispatch, Medic One, Engine One back in service."

"Clear, Medic One," the dispatcher replied. "Medic One, Engine One in-service. Stand by, we may have another call coming in for you."

The three medics picked up their bags, and made their way toward their vehicles where O'Malley and the rest of Sheila's crew waited.

Carson was now in a humorous mood. "Sheila, why did you have to start playing doctor with that man?"

"Funny, Carson. What did you guys do to make him clam up?"

"I don't know." Carson thought for a second then said with a completely serious face, "For some reason, when Eric started putting on his gloves, he told the man to bend over."

Sheila tried not to laugh but couldn't help it. "What were you thinking, Eric?"

Eric also tried not to laugh, because he never wanted to encourage Carson, but somehow he always did. "I don't know. I just . . ."

Eric continued to speak as Carson noticed O'Malley talking on his cell phone.

"What's that," O'Malley said with his back to them. "All right." He paused. "All right, we'll be right there."

He turned around and looked a little surprised to see the three medics standing so close.

Carson, who had been eyeing him suspiciously, said in a cool voice, "O'Malley, what's goin' on?"

O'Malley completely ignored Carson and asked Sheila. "You guys done here?"

"Yeah, that guy was loony-tunes," she said.

"Good, let's get back to—"

He was interrupted by the emergency tones, followed by the dispatcher's voice. "Medic One, Engine One, Truck One, Eighteenth and 'R' on a head injury."

"Eighteenth and 'R'?" Eric said in surprise. "Maybe you guys' barbeque exploded at the station or something."

"Medic One clear," Carson said into his portable radio and hurried to the ambulance.

"Engine One clear," O'Malley said into his own radio.

The dispatcher repeated, "Medic One, Engine One, Truck One. Eighteenth and 'R' at the soup kitchen. Patient received a blunt trauma wound to the head and is unconscious."

"Engine One clear."

"Medic One clear."

"Truck One clear." The last voice was Deputy Chief Killion's. "We're right across the street, and are walking over now. You can put us on-scene."

The dispatcher continued: "Clear Truck One. All units, this is Eighteenth and 'R' on a man down with a blunt head injury. Several bystanders are on the scene. LPD advises standby for scene security. Patient identified as a middle-aged white man in a blue T-shirt near the dumpster by the soup kitchen."

Carson slowed for a second, and glanced over at O'Malley with an inquisitive expression. O'Malley's face was tense, but relaxed when he saw Carson looking at him.

O'Malley began walking faster toward his Engine. Carson hurriedly picked up his bags without taking his eyes off O'Malley and made his way even more quickly to the ambulance. Eric, not quite understanding what was going on, followed suit.

They climbed into the ambulance. "Hold on tight, Eric!" Carson said, starting the engine.

"What's goin' on, Carson?"

"I'm not sure, but it makes me think of something."

Carson hurtled the ambulance out of the garage. The Fire Engine was parked in the street and Carson zoomed right around it.

"You're acting a little more schizo than normal, Carson." Eric clutched his armrest. "What's goin' on?"

"You know that conversation I told you about with Harvey Miller?"

"Yeah."

"Well, he mentioned something about taking pictures of the fire department. If you were gonna take pictures of the fire department, where would you set up?"

"At the soup kitchen?"

"Exactly."

Carson wound the ambulance around the corners leading out of St. Elizabeth's, and the turbo-diesel pulled with all the torque it had. Not far behind them, the motor on the fire engine blared loud, spewing black smoke, doing it's utmost to keep up with the brightly colored van in front of it. But it was impossible. Sirens whined. Eric and Carson watched Engine One's blinking lights fade in the mirrors as they continued to accelerate.

The ambulance propelled them up the street once they hit the main drag. Cars fell behind rapidly. Carson maneuvered the van around cars like cones on test track. He drove with a delicate balance of speed and control. Still, Eric yearned for less speed and more control. O'Malley and the Engine fell farther behind. That was the beauty of E60.

Within minutes, they rounded the corner onto Eighteenth Street. The soup kitchen had attracted a large crowd of people out front. The open bay doors of Fire Station One glowed behind the crowd, seemingly watching the activity. Carson finally let the diesel unwind, pulling as close as he could to the nexus of people. Without speaking, he jumped out of the vehicle and donned his rubber gloves. Eric radioed on-scene and retrieved the bags from the back.

More police arrived. Several firemen stood around a man who had obviously regained consciousness and lay on the pavement. There was a bright red stain on the bandage they had placed on his head. Many homeless men crowded around. Kneeling at the patient's head was Samuel Spirit Dog.

"What's the patient's name?" Carson asked as he approached the firefighters.

"Harvey," Chief Killion said. "Harvey Miller." The deputy chief looked at Carson to see if that name meant anything to him. It did. Carson's face distorted with alarm. He suddenly felt unsafe.

Carson tried to piece together what had happened as he knelt at Harvey's side.

"Harvey, can you hear me?"

"Yes," a low voice murmured, the same voice Carson heard on the phone earlier that morning.

Carson turned to Spirit Dog. "What happened here, Samuel?"

"I don't know, Carson. I heard some of the guys talking, saying there was a man bleeding in the parking lot, so I came outside, and sure enough, there was this man bleeding."

Chief Killion jumped in. "Apparently, one of the locals hit him over the head. There's a small laceration and a hematoma starting to form."

"Can I look at it?" Carson asked.

Killion looked put off as Carson unwound a little piece of the bandage they had just applied. O'Malley and the men on Engine One arrived. "You can look at it if you want to," the deputy chief said, "but it's just what I told you."

"No exposed bone, no cavitation, no depressions?"

"No, just a laceration and a small hematoma."

A policeman in the back was taking notes.

"Who did this, Samuel?" Carson asked.

"I don't know, Carson. Some of the guys were around him. They were talking about his money and stuff, saying he was an asshole and stuff."

Again, Killion interjected, speaking both to Carson and the

policemen as he pointed at Spirit Dog. "When we arrived, this man was crouched over him. There was no one else around."

Samuel's eyes widened in fear, and he turned toward Carson. "Carson, I didn't do anything. The guys were out here and asking whether this man had money and stuff. I told them all to get away. I told them to leave him alone. Honest, Carson, that's exactly how it happened. I didn't do anything."

The deputy chief looked at Spirit Dog with obvious skepticism.

"I know, Samuel," Carson said. "I know you didn't do it."

"I'm only saying what we saw," Killion said, directing his comment to the police officer. "I'm not directly accusing anyone."

Carson looked up at the deputy chief with an expression of anger and hatred that made the man blanch. He knew then that Carson Treffer was going to be an issue, an issue that was not going away.

Carson turned his attention back to the patient. "Harvey, what day is it?"

"Wednesday?"

"How many fingers am I holding up?"

He stared for a few seconds. "Three."

"Good. We need to get you to the hospital, okay?"

"Okay."

Carson proceeded to give orders as the group of men placed Harvey in a C-collar and a spine-board. They loaded him onto the cot. As Carson tightened one of the buckles across Harvey's chest, he glanced up in time to see O'Malley look at Killion. The chief made eye contact with him and quickly turned away.

"Do you want me to ride with you, Carson?" Sheila asked.

"No, Sheila," Carson said, "I don't think so."

"I'd *really* like to go," she said under her breath.

Carson made eye contact long enough to see she was desperately asking. "Okay."

Eric placed the end of the cot in the ambulance and lifted it as Carson slammed the cot's wheels up. The two slid the cot forward in one unified motion.

"O'Malley," Sheila yelled out, "I'm riding with them."

"All right," he said, looking a little puzzled.

Sheila and Carson climbed inside. "Eric, Lincoln General. Code One."

"Got it." He closed the doors.

Inside, Carson dimmed the lights because Harvey was covering his eyes with his hand.

"How ya feeling, Harvey?"

"It hurts."

"Sheila, can you get a blood pressure?"

"Sure." Sheila fumbled through her own medical bag.

"On a scale of one-to-ten, how bad does it hurt?" Carson continued.

"Four . . . or five."

Carson was writing on the clipboard as Eric pulled away.

"Do you feel pain anywhere else?"

"No, I'm fine. Just my head, I think."

"Good. Harvey, you know who I am, right?"

"Yeah, Carson Treffer."

"So, what the hell happened back there?"

"I don't know."

"You have no idea?"

"I really don't remember."

"What were you doing there?"

"You know that scoop I was talking about?"

Carson looked at Sheila in case Harvey hadn't noticed that a firefighter was there.

"She's okay," Harvey said. "She gave me the scoop."

Sheila looked at Carson with pleading eyes. "Don't tell anyone, Carson."

"Oh crap, guys. I don't want to hear this."

"Where's my camera?" Harvey asked.

Carson picked it up. "Here it is."

"Does it still have its memory card?"

Carson looked and found the flap for the card. He opened it. "No, it's gone."

"Well, I didn't get the pictures, I guess."

"What were you taking pictures of?"

"The firemen and their barbeque. Some of them were drinking beer."

"Oh my God!" Carson exclaimed. "You mean to tell me that you went through all this for a few pictures of firemen drinking beer?"

Sheila leaned forward from the bench and said, "I'm sorry, Harvey."

"Sheila, what happened to me?" he tried to speak despite the C-collar pressed beneath his chin.

"I don't know. I was out on a call with Carson."

"That's right . . . that's right. I remember you leaving now."

Carson took a more somber tone. "Did *they* do this to you?"

Harvey pressed his hands against his temples. "I don't know."

"You can't remember at all?"

"I don't know! I'm trying to think."

"Well, who else would it be?"

Harvey thought harder. "It could have been one of those homeless guys."

"Not Spirit Dog! He wouldn't hurt a thing."

"No, not him. There was another guy I pissed off earlier."

"How?"

"I just told him to go away . . . to leave me alone. He called me a yuppie and cussed at me."

Carson looked skeptical. "But do you think he would have done this?"

"I don't know."

"It had to be the department. Who else would take your memory card?"

Carson leaned his back against the wall and rubbed his forehead. "Oh my God!" he said. "Harvey, I told you to be careful! You were doing stuff that could have cost people their jobs . . . and their retirements and everything!"

"You were right."

"You're gonna have to press charges."

"Press charges? Against who?"

"I don't know, Harvey! Maybe you at least have enough evidence for a case. You were attacked!"

Harvey thought for a moment and gently touched the bandage wrapping his head. "I don't know, Carson! I don't even know who to press charges against. Maybe I should just leave this whole thing alone for a while. What do you think, Sheila?"

"I don't know. We've got to figure out what happened first . . . if we can. Because if one of the firefighters did this, then we definitely have to do something. They've gotten way outta hand."

Carson said, "This *has* gotten way out of hand. I don't know what to do. I'm afraid . . ." He paused, his countenance emanating anger in every vein and muscle. His eyes moistened with emotion.

"Afraid of what, Carson?"

"I'm afraid of how I'm going to react if no one does anything about this shit. Someone is gonna have to put a stop to this. And if no one else does, I'm not gonna be able to hold it in much longer."

20.

"I still can't believe that's what happened," Eric said to Carson in the cab of E60 six days later. "How sure are you that it was the fire department?"

"I'm 90 percent sure. He was taking pictures of them, trying to discredit them, and one of them probably saw him. It's not very far from here to there." Carson pointed at the Fire Station. Since beginning the Millennium Plan, he and Eric had posted outside Station One the last three shifts, and since the incident with Harvey, there had been no ramifications, no conclusions by the police, and little press coverage. But Carson wanted to make a point that *he* knew what happened, and that he was watching.

So they posted there all night between calls, right in front of the soup kitchen. Every time they had a call, whether a fire engine from Station One was dispatched or not, Carson flipped the siren on just to wake them up. They'd had three calls since ten o'clock that night that didn't involve Engine One, so O'Malley was disturbed from his sleep at least six times. Four of those times, they beat whatever fire engine was there, bringing the tallies up to twenty-three. They stayed awake most of the night, sometimes watching a DVD. Only in the late-morning hours did they start to snooze in the cab, but they awoke with the bright, morning sun. E60 had everything but full window shades.

"What if we told the police what Harvey was doing?" Eric asked. They had talked a lot about Harvey's situation during those three nights and thought about it alone during the three nights they had off, but they had reached no conclusions. The only pretty certain piece of evidence was the missing memory card from the camera, but that proved nothing.

"What do you think that would do?" Carson said. "That's conclusive of nothing. *They* would probably know what happened, but they couldn't exactly put it in their reports. If no one saw who did it, and Harvey didn't see them either, then he was just 'attacked by unknown assailants.' End of report."

"Have you decided on who you think did it?"

"No, I still can't decide. I honestly can't picture any of them being that violent. I guess maybe Petrolak or Johnson."

"Do you think Deputy Chief Killion was involved?"

"I think he at least knew about it. He was acting kinda weird, and it sure seemed like he was really trying to pin it on Spirit Dog."

Carson started the ambulance's engine.

"Johnson seems like the most likely one to me," Eric said.

Carson bit the corner of his lip and cocked his head. "Could be, I guess. Yeah, could be."

"Do we need gas?" Eric asked.

"No, we're at three-quarters. Leslie and Tim can get it. Let's head back."

As Carson pulled away from their vigil at Fire Station One, he changed the subject. "I like working the night shift, but one thing that really sucks is that Katie doesn't ride with us much anymore."

"I know. She had Biology class last night," Eric said.

"Oh yeah? When did she say that?"

Eric wished he hadn't mentioned it. "Sunday afternoon."

"You talked to her on Sunday?"

"Yeah, just briefly on the phone."

"Oh yeah?" Carson waited for Eric to volunteer more, but he didn't. "What did you guys talk about?"

Eric didn't want to get into all this. "I asked if she wanted to go out to dinner or something Sunday night."

"Did she?"

Eric pursed his lips. "Yeah, but she couldn't because she had a study group that night for a Biology exam she had last night."

Carson yawned, then laughed. "That's ironic."

"What is?"

"That biology is what caused you to call her, and biology is what kept you from seeing her."

Eric felt his jaw stiffen as he stared out the windshield. "Biology is not what caused me to call her."

"Whatever."

Eric became angry, which wasn't so hard early in the morning. "Carson, sometimes you have such a one-track mind!"

"*I* have a one-track mind!? Don't be so hypocritical, Eric! The first thing you asked me after I went swimming with her is what she looked like in a swimsuit!"

Eric was speechless for only a second. "That's not exactly the same."

"It's not?"

"I'm just saying that I see Katie as a lot more than a pretty face and a great body. I actually like her as a person."

Eric realized too late how bad that sounded.

"What do you think *I* think, Eric? I don't think of her as just a nice body either. If you want to date her exclusively, that's fine. All you have to do is say it, and I'll back off."

Carson turned the ambulance in the drive to back it into Eastern Station One, waiting for the garage door to creep open.

"What do you mean, 'do I want you to back off'?"

"You know what I'm saying, Eric."

"What, are you planning on hooking up with her or something?"

"Yeah, is that such a difficult concept to grasp? She's obviously a girl who makes a guy think about stuff like that?"

Carson brought the ambulance to a stop in the garage. Hank and Dave were there talking with Leslie and Tim before their shift. Carson cut the engine. Before they opened their doors, Eric said, "When you say you want to hookup with her, are you just saying you want to tag her, like some sort of trophy . . . because she's Captain O'Malley's daughter?"

Carson, who had already started to open his door, slammed it shut again and pointed at Eric. "Eric, don't *ever* accuse me of something like that again. That's not all she is to me!"

Eric didn't respond at first, but as they both exited the vehicle, he said under his breath, "No, that's just part of it." Carson slammed his door in anger; Eric closed his quietly in regret. He looked up to see if the others had noticed their conversation.

The other four had been standing in the back of the garage when Eric and Carson pulled in but were now stirring. Dave walked toward the ambulance, followed by the others. They were staring neither at Eric nor Carson, but at the ambulance itself.

The object of their attention was a line of bright red spray paint that covered the Eastern Ambulance decals and the Shield of Life.

For twenty seconds, no one said anything. Leslie and Tim gawked at the graffiti while Hank pondered how much it would cost to fix it. Dave asked, "Is there anything else?"

Carson stood in his place, eyeing the line with an ice-cold expression. At Dave's prompting, Eric circled the ambulance looking for more graffiti.

"No, that's it," he said.

"Who did this?" Dave said.

"I don't know," Eric said, not wanting to state what was foremost on his mind.

"This will take a week to undo. We'll have to buy new decals. Did you guys leave the ambulance anywhere?"

"No, we were in it the whole time, except while we were in the hospital, of course."

"You mean to tell me that someone wrote on the side of our ambulance with you guys sitting in it?"

"I guess," Eric said slowly, at a loss for any other excuse. "They couldn't exactly do it while it was parked in the hospital bay." Well, after further thought, he couldn't rule that out either. Carson still said nothing.

"Where were you guys?"

"Parked in front of the soup kitchen," Eric said.

"The soup kitchen?! That's a real nice part of town to place an expensive piece of equipment."

"It wasn't the soup kitchen," Carson said quietly.

"What?" Dave asked.

"It wasn't the soup kitchen people who did this. They're not gangsters; they're homeless people."

"I know what you're thinking, Carson," Dave said, "but you don't know that for sure. Don't start throwing accusations around that you can't back up. Because that's a pretty serious accusation," he said, pointing at the ambulance.

"I know. That's why I'm gonna go find out." Carson walked back to the door of the ambulance.

"Carson, stop! Don't be reckless," Dave said. "The fire department would not do this! You're making things up now."

"You're right, Dave, a fire department may not have done this, but a fire*man* might have. We parked in sight of their station all night! We woke them up six times in the middle of the night! We beat them four times last night because we were street-basing, and we were posting on *their* street, within short walking distance of their front door!"

"What do you mean you woke them up? Please don't tell me you've been antagonizing them!"

"Hey, we were just street-basing in a central location, and the siren's gonna wake somebody up no matter where we are."

"Don't get smart with me, Carson. You know what I'm saying. If what you're telling me is true, then *you* brought this upon us!"

"I think Carson's probably right," Hank said.

Dave looked over at Hank, giving more weight to his opinion than he did to Carson's. "Do you really think so, Hank? Do you think the fire department would act worse than the soup kitchen patrons?"

"I can't rule it out, but that doesn't negate the question of why Medic One was posting there all night." He looked over at Carson. "And why they were waking the Fire Captain up with their sirens. That's inexcusable."

Carson ignored the comment. "We need to go talk to them. I'm going over there."

"Carson!" Dave said, "you can't do that!"

"We need to talk to them, Dave! Whatever happened to that meeting you were supposed to schedule between us and Rader and the chief?"

"They keep postponing it."

Carson's jaw stiffened, and he looked away from Dave at the ambulance again. "And they're just gonna keep postponing it until they have our jobs! Don't you see that, Dave? We have to be more aggressive!"

Dave ignored Carson. "What do you think, Hank? Do we need to file a complaint with the county?"

"I don't know if we can. We don't have any sort of proof."

"Oh my God!" Carson said. "I'm getting so tired of people talking about 'proof.' We're never gonna have it unless we go and get it! That's why we need to just confront them. I'm going into their garage, and I'm looking for a can of red spray-paint. And if anyone asks me to stop, I'll tell them I'm a county taxpayer, and as such, a part-owner of that garage."

"Carson, don't be ridiculous! You can't go over there and just look through their stuff. They're not gonna let you do that."

"It would be even better if they tried to stop me!"

Dave grew worried because he knew Carson was serious. "Carson! We are not going over there with our knuckles and six-shooters to look through their stuff and fight any of them that get in our way! That's not the way the world works anymore."

"It isn't?" Carson said slowly. "That's what they did to Harvey Miller!"

"This isn't the Wild West, Carson! If you go over there, your job with Eastern Ambulance will be terminated!"

Carson stared back, his body wired for action, then said, "Dave, if we do nothing, all of our jobs will be terminated anyway."

"What you're suggesting is not going to help any of that. Don't you understand that, Carson?"

"I used to understand, but I'm understanding less all the time. Don't you see those guys are running over us, and we just roll over and take it again and again? Don't you see what they're doing here? They know what they want! They want what we have, and they're willing to use threats, blackmail, and even *force* to get it, and we just keep taking it from them! Until we fight back, we're just gonna get rolled over again and again, just like Harvey Miller!"

For a minute, no one said anything. They thought about Carson's comments and stared at the ground in shame. Then Dave said, "Carson, I'll talk to the chief about this. We'll at least see what he has to say. Now, just get into your truck and go home. Get some sleep. Cool down a little. Can you at least do that?"

"What if we go over there with the police to look for the paint?"

Dave pointed toward the parking lot. "Carson! Go home! We'll take care of it."

Carson gathered his personal belongings from the defaced ambulance and looked over at Eric with no kindness in his face. "I'll see you tonight, Eric," he said, "and we can talk more about trophies."

Eric stared at the red graffiti on the side of the ambulance until Carson walked away. "What are we gonna do?" he asked his bosses.

"There's not much to do," Hank said. "We're just gonna have to take E60 out of service for a while."

"For how long?"

"A few days . . . a week maybe. Depends on whether we have any more decals in the garage."

"So, we're back in E35?"

"We gave E35 to Medic Three while 65 is getting a tune-up."

"Oh, crap."

"We don't have much choice. You're just gonna have to take E22 for a while."

"Are you kidding me?" Eric was deflated. "We have to use 22 as a frontline ambulance?"

"Only for a little while. Just while E60's at the dealership getting painted. Then you can have her back, even if we have to wait for decals."

"I can't tell you how much that sucks, Hank. I do not feel comfortable in that thing at all. This is the last thing we need right now."

"Eric, there's a lot that's been happening lately that we don't need, but we don't have a choice. Maybe if you guys weren't posting in front of the Fire Station, you wouldn't have to worry about it! We're gonna deal with it and march on."

"Is Carson right? Are we just getting rolled over by them?"

"No, Eric," Dave said like a concerned father. "There's plenty of fight in us, and we have things we're working on. The Millennium Plan seems to be working well. But if you guys keep doing things to antagonize them, it's just going to get uglier. You need to make Carson understand that."

"I don't know, Dave. Carson's not the reason why they want the contract." Eric gathered a few of his belongings as he made preparations to leave. "And even if he was, if *you* can't turn him off, I can't either."

———

They had all gathered at the Denton Volunteer Fire Station at the prompting of Nathan Tompkins. He was the volunteer fire chief there in addition to his job with the Lancaster County Fire Department, and it was a good, out-of-the-way place to meet. Sheila was there, still shaken up by recent events. Next to her around the small card table was Tyrone, her crewmate from Engine One. Marty and Joe, two of the men who'd been on the Adam Turner call, were there from Engine Two. All told, there were a dozen of them. They had either seen firsthand or heard through the grapevine about the reporter, Harvey Miller, and the events near Station One the week before.

The problem was, though, none of them knew exactly what those events were. Sheila and Tyrone were out on the "suicide" attempt when it happened. Neither Nathan nor the others were there, but they had heard talk, and Sheila told Nathan about her suspicions. Nathan hoped Harvey had been assaulted by one of the homeless men, but that was too coincidental. Since he'd called the meeting, as usual, he was the first to speak.

"Thanks for coming, everybody. Everyone knows why we're here. We've already talked about the Harvey Miller incident, and it seems that no one has been able to come to any definite conclusions about what happened that night, but I think you have the same guesses I have."

He looked around the table and at those standing and saw several of them give a somber nod.

"If what I suspect is true, then our fire department has sunk to an all-time low. In the sixteen years I've worked here, I would never have dreamed that things would come to this. The bottom line is that the fire department has fallen into the hands of the wrong people. They don't listen to us. They haven't even polled us to see what we think about the ambulance contract. They just drive ahead with their own plans, and it appears that they won't tolerate anyone who gets in their way.

"But we're partly to blame here," he continued. "We're the ones who have let them creep into the positions of power within the department, and we're the ones who have not raised our voices to give a dissenting opinion. That's why we're here. I know you guys, and I know that even if I hadn't called this meeting, one of you would have. What we have to do is decide what we're going to do about this situation, if anything."

Tyrone spoke up. "We definitely have to do something. The deputy chief's not right in the head, and the chief casts a blind eye to anything we bring up."

"I agree," Sheila said, speaking from experience. "I knew this before, and I definitely know it now. He's flat-out dangerous."

"Hmm," Nathan said, "maybe you're right. Does everyone else agree we have to do something?" He looked around the small room, and everyone slowly, but resolutely, again nodded their heads. "So, what do we do?" he asked. "Any suggestions?"

"Don't you think the chief will listen?" Joe asked.

"I don't know," Nathan said. "What are we gonna tell him? That we don't like the deputy chief? I tried talking to him once about some of Killion's conversations with me about my wife and Lynda's friendship. He didn't seem too concerned. Instead, he kind of sided with Killion. Now, I just feel lucky he didn't tell Killion that I had talked to him. Besides, I think there are forces over his head pulling the strings here and he's just looking forward to retirement. It's sad. He used to be a better leader, but has never been the same since his wife died."

All the firefighters knew that Chief Winkenwerder's wife died of cancer five years back, and they had noticed the change too. It was during that time that his hair turned completely gray. He had lost his ambition and zeal after that long ordeal. Nathan felt like he lost a friend, even though he still saw him on a weekly basis.

"Well," Marty said, "I don't know if we have a lot of options. I know O'Malley and Rader and them have been using the newspaper a lot to their advantage. Maybe it's time we turn it against them?"

"What do you mean?" Nathan asked.

"I don't know exactly. Maybe we should write a letter to the editor together. We could tell them about Harvey Miller and everything that's been happening."

Some of the firefighters in the room raised their eyebrows as they mulled the idea over in their heads. Others shook their heads no. One of them was Sheila.

Nathan said, "You're saying no, Sheila. Why's that?"

"Well, I mean it's a good idea in one respect. It would take courage and it would be a way for us to raise our voices like you said, but what would we write? None of us *knows* for sure what happened to Harvey Miller. Again, I think we know, but there were dangerous people around, and even the police have nothing to say about it. And none of us were there to hear Adam Turner's mom say yes or no. I mean, we all know in our heads what she said, but we weren't there."

"Yeah, but that's not everything," Nathan said. "It's not just those two incidents. We can talk about how we don't like the whole way the department's being run, and how we disagree with those running it. I've practically been threatened by the deputy chief because my wife is being a friend to Lynda."

"Okay," she said, "then maybe we just write that it's time for new leadership. We won't exactly be able to say why—"

"But," Tyrone said, "we could say that we don't necessarily support the takeover of the EMS contract."

Nathan corrected him. "Yeah, but Tyrone, there are some here who *do* like that idea. The only thing we all agree on is that our fire department has been headed in the wrong direction for years now, and we'd like to see that change."

"If that's the case," Tyrone continued, "then we should just change the leadership."

Sheila asked, "Like how?"

"If what we all agree on is that our department has the wrong leadership, then let's change it. There's a union election this month. We have a few weeks to prepare. Let's just make sure someone other than O'Malley gets elected."

Sheila nodded her head to indicate his idea had merit.

"That way," Tyrone said, "we'll at least knock one chink out of the tower of power."

"And let's get Rader outta there too," Joe said. "How can someone so young be vice-president anyway?"

"I agree," said Nathan. "I think you're on to something, Tyrone. But the thing is, we have to have people to run against them. We can't just vote them out."

Tyrone looked at Nathan and said, "Why don't you run?"

"Me? Well, I've never considered myself the political type."

"Good. That's good. That's our problem; we have people in power who are too political. And you're the only one here who's senior enough, and you're pretty much a leader in the department already. After all, you called these meetings."

"I don't know," Nathan said.

Sheila looked at him. "I think he's right, Nathan. If we're gonna do this, then you're the only person who can. Why don't you think about it?"

Nathan let out his breath and stared at his hands neatly folded on the table in front of him. "Well, I have to talk to my wife, of course. I think she'll support whatever we decide, though."

"Let's vote on it," Sheila said.

She quickly asked for a vote from those present, and they all raised their hands.

"You see, Nathan," she said. "You have at least these twelve votes, and I know we could get more. This way we can start to make the changes we want. I don't know how we'll get rid of Killion, but at least this will be a first step."

"All right. I know you're right. I'll talk to my wife. But we also need to determine who should run for vice-president. I think it should be you. You have the seniority and the respect, and we know whose side you're on. Plus, if anything, this fire department could use a woman's perspective. It might calm things down around here."

Nathan looked around at the others and used Sheila's own tactics. "Everyone in favor of Sheila running for vice-president?"

Again, all of them, glad that they themselves hadn't been tagged, raised their hands. Sheila could not argue after just having goaded Nathan to do it.

"All right then," she said reluctantly, "but if we're gonna do this, we really need to get on the ball. We need to start talking to others and gathering support now. One way or the other, it will be too late to affect the EMS plan, but maybe we can start to heal the fire department."

As quickly and unceremoniously as the meeting started, it came to an end, but this time with a real, concrete outcome: Nathan and Sheila would attempt to overthrow the entrenched powers of the fire department.

21.

After sleeping most of the day, Eric finished his late afternoon breakfast, then logged onto the *Lincoln Cowboy* website. He saw nothing new on the homepage.

He clicked the "In-Depth" link, and saw the links for "Fraud, Waste, and Abuse," and "Pork-Barrel City Park," but not "Fire Department Corruption." He questioned himself for a moment, wondering if he had forgotten where the link was, but he hadn't. He did a site search for "fire department" and "deputy chief" but nothing came up.

Eric dropped his spoon into his bowl and stared at the blank screen. Harvey had deleted everything about the fire department. Tired of thinking about it, Eric rinsed his bowl, placed it in the sink with all the other dirty dishes, and went to bed for nearly ten hours.

"Please tell me you're joking!" Carson said when he saw Eric sitting in the back of E22 with the doors open, going through the inventory of the BLS bag.

"Believe me, I wish this was a joke."

"Why do I feel like everywhere I turn, this old thing is waiting for me? I swear, this thing follows me, Eric! We have to run around in E22 tonight?!"

"Yep. And probably not just tonight."

Carson's face was white.

"Oh my God! Where are all the other trucks?"

"They're either assigned to other Medics or they're being overhauled or painted or something."

"We're going to be the laughing stock of the fire department. Or worse, an embarrassment to the city."

"Aren't we already?" Eric said.

"What do you mean?"

"I mean, look at this thing! Look at this place! We never have enough money for anything. Do we have traffic signal pre-emption? No. Do all our bags have working zippers? No. This stupid thing is held shut with medical tape!"

"That's because this is a fifteen-year-old ambulance, Eric. It's not the best of our stuff."

"I know; I'm aware of that," Eric said. He quickly shifted gears. "Did you know Harvey deleted everything about the fire department from his website?"

Carson looked up, shook his head, and turned to inventorying the ALS bag without saying a word.

When they finished going through all their equipment, Carson said, "Oh, I almost forgot." He walked over to E60 and removed the tally sheet from the sun visor. Just as before, he attached it to the sun visor in E22, only with less pomp and circumstance.

"Are you kidding me, Carson?" Eric said.

"What?"

"You can pretty much give up on that while we're in this thing."

"I don't think so," Carson said. "This doesn't mean we have to give up."

The two sat in silence for most of the next hour, parked in a downtown alley. It was growing dark, and they watched the college kids making their way to the clubs. They left the engine running for fear of shutting it down.

"I wonder what Katie's doing tonight?" Carson said as two girls strolled by.

"I don't know," Eric said.

It was nearly impossible to see Katie now that they worked the night shift. She had started doing her ride-alongs with some of the day crews.

Finally, the radio broke the stillness.

"Medic One, Engine Five, Truck One . . . Twenty-seventh and 'O' on an injury-accident."

Eric slid the transmission into gear, but inched out of the alley to avoid pedestrians. It was strange driving E22 again. He felt like he was in a pickup from the 1970s. He was used to the roar of a diesel engine, not the normal revs of gasoline. He threaded the van through stopped traffic, quickly crossed the one block to "O" Street, and turned left.

"Medic One, Engine Five, Truck One," the dispatcher called again, "be advised that bystanders report overturned vehicle with a car fire. Passengers still in the vehicle."

"Drop the hammer, Eric!" Carson grabbed the mike. "Dispatch, Medic One clear."

Eric pressed the gas pedal until he was doing seventy miles per hour down the wide, straight road. He was in serious violation of the safety parameters, but people were about to die, and the danger of them staying in a burning vehicle exceeded the danger of Eric doing seventy. They knew they were ahead of the fire department; they were already only blocks away from the scene while the fire companies were still scrambling into their gear and trucks. Street-basing worked brilliantly.

"Engine Five, clear," Mark Rader called on the radio.

"Truck One, clear," Jon Carver's voice said.

The dispatcher continued, "Bystanders report the vehicle is a silver Buick on the northwest corner of the intersection. Flames are coming out of the engine compartment. Police and media are on-scene."

"Medic One clear," Carson said before leaning over and turning the stereo from loud to very loud. "This is the big one, Eric. This is why we exist!"

It took only a minute to get to the intersection. Eric sped down the road, music blaring on the radio. Carson tapped his hands on the dashboard. Cars parted like the Red Sea.

Carson pointed out the windshield toward a black column of smoke rising in the dark sky. The music was too loud to talk. Eric looked and nodded.

Seconds later, they approached the scene. Several cars parked alongside the road, and people gathered around two damaged vehicles. One was a large SUV, its front end smashed halfway through the engine compartment. No one appeared to be inside. The other was the silver Buick. The SUV had nearly broadsided it, hitting it in the right front fender and sending it into a rollover until it came to rest on its roof. Flames rose two feet high between the front tires, a blaze that lit the entire area around the car.

A television crew was setting up equipment just outside their news van. Two men and a police officer dragged the female driver of the Buick out of her shattered window. Eric pulled up fast, keeping a safe distance from the vehicle. Carson started to tell him to pull closer, but Eric had already stopped.

"Eric, what are . . . nevermind!" Carson jumped out the door before Eric could put it in Park. Eric was caught off-guard by his emotions. He fumbled with the door handle, forgetting where it was in the new vehicle, almost exited the vehicle, then thought to call Dispatch.

"Dispatch, Medic One!" He realized he hadn't turned the music down. He reached over and turned it off. Carson was already at the woman's side, helping to stabilize her head as the men dragged her close to the ambulance.

"Go ahead, Medic One."

"Medic One on-scene!" he said, realizing he was wasting precious seconds and should have said that the first time.

"Clear."

He dropped the mike while trying to set it in its clip, replaced it, then exited the vehicle. Much of the Buick was engulfed in flames. Eric tried to think what to do first. Carson yelled something at him.

"What?" Eric yelled back as he approached the woman's side. Blood ran down the side of her motionless head. Eric realized he couldn't hear due to the siren of his own ambulance. He returned to it, opened the door, and turned it off. When he did so, he heard Carson yelling angrily at him.

"Get the cot, Eric!"

The roar of the flames and the distant approach of more sirens was deafening. Eric ran to the back of the ambulance, swung the doors open, and pulled out the cot, already loaded with bags. Since he was by himself, he had to let go of the foot and reach up to the head to disengage the safety hook.

He pulled the cot to the front of the ambulance. The fire trucks arrived. Eric saw that Carson had left the woman in the care of the police officer and bystanders, and was now running around the vehicle to the passenger side, shielding his face from the heat.

Eric's thoughts finally started to pull together. He lowered the cot to the ground, removed the bags, and placed the spine board next to the woman. He performed the tasks he had learned through so much repetition. He placed his ear over her mouth and his hand on her chest. She was breathing. He felt her carotid pulse and estimated its rate, writing the number on his latex glove.

Eric looked up for a second. The fire trucks had stopped but were unable to get as close to the burning vehicle as they wanted, and began preparing their hoses. Carson had come back around to this side of the vehicle, presumably unable to gain access on the other side as he tried retrieving another passenger. He crawled through the broken window, with his arms and upper body fully in the car. Eric wondered if Carson needed help but looked at the woman again and measured her neck with his hand. He pulled a C-collar from the bag and asked the policeman to unbutton her blouse to look for other injuries. Eric quickly applied the collar, then instructed the other two to hold the woman's head until he got back.

Eric stood halfway up, shielding his face as he walked toward the vehicle. From the corner of his eye, he saw firemen with a hose approaching the vehicle in full masks and oxygen gear. Carson was backing out of the car. He emerged with a small child limp in his arms. The firemen sprayed the flames as they approached, waiting for Carson to exit before they could apply full pressure. Eric made it within fifteen feet but felt his skin and clothes burning from the intense heat. A small explosion came from the car's engine.

He turned his head from the explosion and felt a hot blast on his back. He reopened his eyes and saw the faces of bystanders, covering their mouths in shock, and a cameraman filming everything.

The world moved slowly as seconds turned to minutes. Eric turned and looked for Carson, just a shadow in front of the intense light. Carson climbed to his feet awkwardly with the child in his arms, but just as he began to run from the vehicle, a second, larger blast erupted from the rear of the car. It knocked Carson down to his knees and elbows. Eric covered his face and backed away quickly, losing his balance. He felt as though his face were on fire. His eyes burned and filled with tears. He stumbled and looked around. The firefighters had been turned away but were quickly recovering. Eric saw Carson only a few feet away, reached and grabbed Carson's arm, helping him back to his feet. They both ran and stumbled, crouching over the child cradled in Carson's arms. Blood streamed from Carson's forearms and dripped from his elbows.

Just as soon as they had gotten away, two fire hoses poured water on the car with several hundred pounds of pressure. At a safe distance, Carson, looking exhausted, went to his knees voluntarily, gently placing the little girl on the asphalt only a short distance from the ambulance. A firefighter ran up and lifted his mask. It was Mark Rader. He removed his helmet to assist Carson and Eric as they assessed the girl's condition. Carson looked like he might faint, and Eric noticed his eyebrows and eyelashes had been singed.

"No, Mark," Carson said, placing his hand on Mark's arm. "We've got her. Go get the other patient. Get her loaded in the ambulance."

Rader looked up in anger and turned away in a huff. Carson squinted his stinging eyes, and tried desperately to open them but couldn't. Tears streamed down his face and he rubbed his eyes. Eric again let repetition kick in as he worked down the Basic Assessment Checklist without thinking.

Airway. He lifted the little girl's jaw with his fingers without moving her head and neck. Breathing. Look, listen, and feel. He placed his ear to her mouth and watched her chest, feeling for movement with his elbow on her torso.

Nothing.

He tried again. He repositioned her jaw, this time tilting her head back ever so slightly. He glanced up at Carson who was in no better condition than before. Eric listened again. No change. He pinched her nose and placed his lips around her little mouth. He held her mouth open with his other hand that easily straddled both sides of her jaw.

Breath one. Remember . . . small lungs, little breaths. Breath two. One of Eric's tears fell on her eye. Circulation. He removed his left hand from her jaw, placing it under her upper arm. Between her little bone and muscle, he inserted the tips of his fingers onto her artery. Eric's heart skipped a beat in response to the heart that was tapping through the artery back at him.

Circulation good, back to breathing. Breath one. Little breath, Eric, little breath!

"Not breathing?" Carson asked in a strained voice.

"No." Breath two. Perfect, that one was perfect.

"CPR?"

"No, she's got a weak pulse."

Carson's eyes cried a little harder, and he took a deep breath, releasing it slowly. "Let's go!" he said, holding his eyes open with a hand on his forehead.

Breathing trumped spinal precautions at this point. It was Eric's turn to cradle her in his arms. As he did so, a strange thought came to his mind. He thought he would like to have a little girl of his own someday. One just like her. He lifted her up toward his mouth, probably the same way her mom did this morning to wake her with a kiss. Breath three. Again, perfect. He knew the size of her lungs now—smaller than any he had ever felt.

He and Carson stood. Carson grabbed Eric's forearm, feigning assistance toward the ambulance. But Eric could feel that he was pulling Carson more than the other way around. Breath four. They jogged toward the ambulance. Breath Five. Rader and the others had already loaded the mother. She lay strapped on the backboard with a bandage on her head. Breath six.

"You definitely have to drive, Eric. I'm getting better, but my eyes are stinging."

"I know," Eric said. Carson jumped into the back with Rader. Eric handed the girl up to him, feeling inexplicable loss and sadness. He didn't want to give her up just yet. The doors slammed, Eric ran to the front, passed the cameras, and jumped into the cab. He placed the transmission into gear, looked into his mirrors, and pressed the gas. Nothing happened. His heart stopped. Nothing . . . the engine wasn't running. He looked at the gas gauge but saw the whole vehicle was off. He reached for the keys and turned the ignition forward. The starter turned. That was a relief. The engine didn't catch. It was a punch in his gut. His stomach was in his throat.

He tried again. It turned and turned. Damn this piece of shit, he thought.

"Let's go, Eric!" Carson yelled from the back.

What happened, Eric asked himself? Did he turn the engine off? Wait. Think for a second. Was the ignition off a few seconds ago when you first turned it? It didn't seem like it.

He tried again. He tried for a long time, trying to shut off his ears so they couldn't hear the sound of the starter whining. Closing his eyes to the people and the cameras, he turned the key again. Now it was flooded.

Rader stuck his head up front. "What's going on?" he snapped.

Eric's mouth spit out the words mechanically. "The engine won't start."

"What?"

"The engine won't start!"

"Oh my God!"

"Shut up, Mark. Help me think of something to do."

"What do you want me to do?"

"I've got to call for another ambulance," Eric said.

"Okay . . . okay . . . wait, no, I've got a better idea. We've got our new ambulance; it's closer."

Carson yelled from the back, "What's goin' on?"

"Your ambulance?" Eric asked Rader. "The M.A.V.?"

"Yeah, it's at Station One now. They can get here quick."

Eric looked out his window at all the people watching. He felt like running away. Was this a dream? He closed his eyes; he could almost feel her in his arms again. Rader was right, the other Eastern units were much further away. Be decisive.

"Okay, Rader. Call them quick!"

Mark spoke into his portable radio.

"Carson!"

"What the hell's goin' on, Eric?"

"The truck's down cold. Get ready to transfer the patients to the fire ambulance."

"To the wh—?"

"Don't ask. It'll be here in a few minutes." Carson shut up and did as he was told. The only saving grace, Eric thought, was that it was not unusual for medics to work on patients for a few minutes to stabilize them before transport.

"Carson," he said. "I'm coming back there. At least we can stabilize the girl."

Within minutes, the Medical Attack Vehicle arrived, strobe lights beaming. Eric, Rader, and the other firemen quickly made the transfer. The interior felt cavernous as they loaded the still barely-conscious mother and laid her daughter on the bench. She still wasn't breathing, but her pulse remained strong. Within seconds, the M.A.V. pulled away with another fireman at the helm.

Rader had already applied a Pediatric Bag-Valve-Mask from the other ambulance and attached it to the oxygen. Eric used it to push breaths into the girl. Carson let Rader start the IV in the little girl's arm as he tended to the mother, who was barely conscious and confused. Eric was glad to see that Carson was also recovering.

It had been a few minutes since Eric last checked, so he paused the mechanical respirations. Look, listen, and feel. Eric removed the B.V.M. and listened at her mouth again.

"I've got something!" Eric said.

"You do?" Rader asked.

Eric listened and felt again. Even Rader saw it now.

"I see it," he said. "They're shallow, but I see it." A great deal of tension in Rader's pale face vanished, and he took a deep breath himself.

"Good girl," Eric said, "that's it." He replaced the B.V.M. on her mouth and pumped another breath into her. He looked over at Carson, who cocked his head at him to say, "Good job." Never had Eric felt so terrible, then so overjoyed in such a short span of time.

The mother started to speak despite having her head taped between two cushions and a C-collar. She was coming to. "What did you say?" she asked with her eyes full of tears. "Are you talking about my baby?"

"Yes, ma'am," Carson said. "She wasn't breathing when we got there, but she's doing better now."

The mom burst into tears and could barely speak. She was also still very confused. "Is she okay? Is she gonna be okay?"

"Yes," Carson said.

"I don't know what happened," she said. "It was so quick. I remember waking up and being upside down. I was choking, and I looked over at Emily, and she was hanging from her seatbelt not moving."

She burst into deeper sobs. Carson established the IV and removed the tourniquet from her arm.

"I know, ma'am," he said reassuringly. "She might have breathed in too much smoke."

The woman continued, retelling a nightmare. "I looked over, and I thought she was dead. She was pale and didn't move and was hanging upside down. I knew she was in Death's arms, and I prayed,

'Dear God, no . . . no!' I tried to get to her, but everything started to go black. I couldn't reach her. I couldn't reach her! I . . . I don't know what happened after that, but . . . I knew . . . I knew he was taking her." Her chest convulsed deeply with sobs. Tears streamed from the corners of her tightly shut eyes.

Carson stood up and grabbed the handrail on the ceiling so the woman could see him. He rubbed her arm with the back of his fingers, then glanced over at Eric to see how the girl was doing. Eric gave a thumbs-up and a smile. "Ma'am," Carson said, "Death doesn't have her now."

"Thank you . . . thank you, Jesus." Then she asked Carson, "What did you do?"

Carson leaned across her to adjust the drip-rate on the IV bag hanging over her head. "Ma'am, we did what we always do." He finished with the slide-valve, squeezed her hand, and looked her in the eyes. "We told him to reschedule."

She smiled back and burst into a mixture of laughs and sobs. Eric could tell that they were the happy kind of tears that cleanse the soul and fill you with belief. He looked down at the girl who was beginning to breathe more strongly on her own. She would be okay. Everything would be okay.

22.

"Carson, I saw what you did last night," Dr. Windholz, the director of the M.O.A., said as he flipped through the paperwork on Adam Turner's case. But he wasn't talking about Adam Turner just yet. "That was some pretty amazing stuff."

Carson sat in a chair in front of Dr. Windholz's desk. Jeff Davidson and another M.O.A. member sat in chairs on either side of him.

"I can't say that it wasn't at all foolish," Dr. Windholz continued, "but it was admirable . . . and . . . well, heroic, I guess."

The skin on Carson's face was pink from the heat injuries, like a bad sunburn. His eyebrows and lashes were little more than stubble, but there was no serious damage to his eyes.

Dr. Windholz was a young man for a doctor. He did his residency in Emergency Medicine but had gotten burnt out in the E.R. after six years and leaped at the opportunity to work at the Medical Oversight Agency.

Carson spoke, "I don't know if I would use those words. I just did what I had to do when I got there . . . without the fire department there yet."

Dr. Windholz read an underlying meaning into Carson's statement and fired back. "But from what I hear, it was a damn good thing that the fire department did show up."

Carson glanced at the corner of the ceiling while looking for words to say. "Yeah," he said, "I didn't really mean that. I was just sayin'—"

"Oh, I know, Carson. I'm sorry." He tried to gloss over his assumption. "What was wrong with your ambulance anyway? Have they determined that yet?"

Carson let out a deep sigh. "I don't know," he said. "It's an old ambulance. We were only gonna be in it for a night or two while E60 was getting repainted."

The three auditors in the room listened intently. Adam Turner's case would have to wait for a few minutes. Their minds were already made up on that issue, anyway, and this was a more pressing quality concern.

"It has an old gas engine, too. It runs fine, it just doesn't start too well once it stops. But I guess you guys know about that now."

"Did you turn the engine off?"

"I didn't. Eric was driving, and he probably did. Or it just died."

"What does Eric say?"

"He says he doesn't know either."

"What do you mean?"

"He can't remember."

"Was it off when he got back in?"

"He said he doesn't think so."

"So it probably just died then?"

"It could have."

"Has Eastern known about this problem for long?"

"Yeah, it's like that every week."

"And?"

"And Joe, the mechanic, has worked on it several times. He replaced the starter and battery, but that didn't help." Carson sighed again. "I don't know. If you guys wanna know more about that stuff, you'll have to ask Dave or Hank. I just don't know."

"Do you feel that your company put you in an unsafe vehicle that night?" Jeff Davidson asked.

"No, it's safe. It drives well, I mean."

"I mean unsafe for the patients."

"Oh. Not really," Carson said and scratched his chin. "Well, I guess I can't really say that after what happened. But really, they had no choice. Our newer vehicles are in the shop or getting worked on, and this was only a temporary fix. It's definitely not the best vehicle, but it would've worked fine if it hadn't been turned off."

"So you think it *was* turned off?" the female auditor, Betty, asked.

Carson lifted a hand in bewilderment. "Well, no, I just meant that if that's what happened."

"Is the company still going to be using this vehicle for 911 response?"

"I don't think so. They're getting E60 repainted today. We don't have new decals yet, but the graffiti has been painted over. One side will just be blank for a while."

"That's the right thing to do," Jeff Davidson said. "Even if the ambulance doesn't look pretty, just get it on the road."

"I agree," Carson said. He was already worn out by the questions, and he hadn't even expected any about this issue.

"Well, Carson," Dr. Windholz said, "we're going to talk to Eastern management about the issues with this vehicle and make sure you're right about it not being used for emergency response anymore. What happened last night was unsatisfactory. Of course . . ." he said, pausing with a finger in the air, "by that I mean the part about the ambulance. *That* we don't blame on you or Eric. That we blame on management. Your actions last night were exemplary, and I think I can speak for all of us by saying that you probably saved at least one life."

Carson tilted his chin down. For as much as he sought it, he wasn't good at receiving praise.

"Your work last night made all of us proud to be in EMS, and I know you made your company proud. What I'm trying to say is that apart from the snafu with the vehicle, which was realistically out of your control, you did a great job."

"Thanks. I . . . I appreciate that. Believe me, no one is more frustrated with the vehicle situation than I am."

"I really do believe you, Carson." Windholz turned his attention away from Carson for a moment, looking again at the small pile of papers in his hands. "But as you well know, that's not why we're here today."

Carson felt a lump in his throat.

"We're here to talk about the call on August 27, the case of Adam Turner."

Carson took a drink of water.

"As you know," Dr. Windholz said, "there were certain allegations made against you that necessitated an investigation. The death of a child is always a serious occurrence, and we have to deal with it seriously. We've read the reports and the call sheets from that night and previous visits, and we've thoroughly reviewed your statements, those of your coworkers, and everyone else involved.

"What I'm trying to say is that the allegations are hearsay. This is not a black and white case—did he do it, or did he not do it—it's a judgment call that would require us to crawl into the minds of others and know what they were thinking. And I guess I don't need to say, we can't do that."

Carson felt the conversation going favorably, and the muscles in his neck relaxed.

"Carson," he continued, "we've worked with you a long time, and we know the kind of Paramedic you are. We know that you keep the patients' interests at heart, as exemplified by your courageous activities yesterday. Betty, Jeff, and I all agree that the statements made about Adam Turner do *not* show negligence on your part. If anything, they might have resulted from too much care—too much concern, if such a thing exists.

"We're all aware of the unfortunate antagonism between you and the fire department." Windholz ran his hand down the back of his head. "And it breaks our hearts to see the political situation result in accusations of this sort. That's all I'm going to say about the political stuff. That should all be worked out this Friday. I think you get my point."

Carson nodded his head.

"The bottom line, Carson, is that we find you in no ways negligent. There are no grounds to believe you should have reported anything."

As he concluded, Dr. Windholz folded his hands and looked at Carson. "Do you have anything to say?"

Carson rubbed his eyes with one hand, feeling the tiny stubs of his eyebrows, and he felt like his eyes might tear up again.

"No, not really. I'm just glad you saw it that way. I think what I said about Adam was just because I . . . I took his death a little hard, you know."

There was a pause.

"I'm sure you did, Carson. If it's any consolation, as an E.R. physician, I can say that I've been there many times, and I know how hard it is. You've just got to put it behind you and move on."

"I know."

"Maybe you can look at it this way: the life you saved last night might make up for Adam's life."

Carson looked up at him, feeling wishful and sad. "I wish I could, doctor. I'll try to do that."

The four in the room stood up, and Dr. Windholz placed his arm around Carson's shoulders. He honestly grieved for him, and only now fully realized the strain he had been under for the past many months.

"It will come with time, Carson. It'll come with time. Just know that you did everything right, no matter what others say."

"Thank you. I'll do that. Am I free to go now?"

"Definitely. Why don't you go home and relax a little."

Carson and the doctor walked toward the office door that led out to the lobby. Outside they found several reporters and cameramen. Katie and Eric were there, too, sitting on a lobby bench. They were there for support, and to take Carson out after the stress he'd been under. They stood when he emerged from the office.

One of reporters asked a question and thrust a microphone toward Carson. "Mr. Treffer, what were the results of your board?"

Carson did not answer. He was still stunned, and the flashes from the cameras made his eyes sting again. Dr. Windholz answered for him. "Mr. Treffer was found not negligent in any regards in the Adam Turner case."

Another reporter asked, "Was last night's case concerning the ambulance malfunction discussed?"

"Yes, it was," Dr. Windholz said, "but we have no comments at this time."

"Does that mean there is going to be an investigation?"

"No, not necessarily. There was an equipment malfunction, but it appears Eastern Ambulance has already taken steps to remedy that."

"Mr. Treffer? Mr. Treffer, how do you feel? Were you injured last night?"

"No," Carson said, "just some scrapes and bruises . . . and some missing eyebrows."

Some of the reporters laughed as they scribbled on notepads.

"What caused the vehicle to malfunction?"

"I don't know. It was old. I honestly don't know more than that."

"Mr. Treffer," the reported asked again, "do you feel last night's call with the vehicle fire will hurt Eastern Ambulance or help it in Friday night's county council vote?"

"I don't know," he said. "I like to think it won't affect it one way or the other. I'm sorry, but it's been a long day, and I need to rest."

"Mr. Treffer," a different, male reporter asked, "why did you call Child Protective Services after Turner's death?"

"I felt like . . . I wanted them to know what I knew . . . or what I felt about his mother. I mean, I thought it might help them?"

"Had you ever had to report Turner's living conditions to anyone before?"

"No . . . I didn't see anything." He rubbed his eyebrow stubble again, mostly to shield his stinging eyes. More flashes went off. "I mean, I didn't see anything that concerned me."

"But I thought you called C.P.S. because you *had* seen things that concerned you?"

"Look!" Carson said, "I assure you, if there was anything I could have done, I would have done it. I would have done anything to save him! The last thing I wanted was for Ahmadjon to die."

The reporters were silent, motionless, with various looks of consternation. Who was Ahmadjon?

"What was that last thing you said?" one of them asked, his pencil poised for clearer direction.

Carson looked at them, and noticed Eric's furrowed brow behind them, and realized what he had said. "I mean Adam. The last thing I wanted was for Adam to die. I'm sorry, I'm tired. I've got to go."

He walked away. Dr. Windholz tried to shoo the reporters away. "Okay, folks, that's enough. Carson always performed professionally in Adam Turner's care. End of story."

Carson made his way past the crowd and joined Eric and Katie. The three walked out together. As they descended the stairs outside, Eric said, "Well, that's really good news."

Carson didn't say anything. He looked down.

"But I can't say I'm surprised. Of course there wasn't a case against you."

"Yeah," Carson said, putting on a front of normalcy. "It is a relief, though."

Katie chimed in. "So, Carson, we're here to take you out. We figured you could stand to unwind a little."

He gave a weary smile. "Thanks, guys, I really appreciate that." After a few more steps, he said, "So where we goin'?"

"We thought we'd try something different," Eric said. "Something more up your alley."

Carson looked up with intrigue.

"The High Noon Saloon and Pool Bar."

"Harvey's joint?"

"Yeah, I thought we should support Harvey since you're such big fan of his."

Carson patted Eric on the back. He actually felt more upbeat and wondered why he hadn't thought of doing this himself. "That's a great idea, but what are we gonna do with Katie?"

"What do you mean," Katie said, holding up a new I.D. she acquired from a contact on campus. "I'm legal."

Climbing into Eric's car, Carson said, "We are corrupting you, aren't we, Katie."

"Just a little."

The three pulled into the gravel parking lot of the High Noon Saloon and Pool Bar on the outskirts of town. A wooden structure, it looked as though it might have been a church or a barn or something else in the past. There were no windows except in the vestibule, and those beamed with neon beer signs. A white cinderblock addition had been added to the back. It was the kitchen.

Katie, Eric, and Carson passed from the vestibule through two swinging doors into the dark, smoky building. The bar lined the back wall. A doorway entering the kitchen was cut in the wall in the far corner. A stage and small dance floor stood across from the bar. Only one couple danced to the jukebox that filled in for a band. In between stood a half-dozen pool tables, along with dining tables. The three chose one of the empty booths that lined the walls.

An older woman came over to take their order. "Can I get you guys anything?"

Carson and Eric chose their beers from a table menu, and waited for Katie.

"Budweiser, please," she said, sounding confident, but Eric sensed the slightest trepidation in her voice.

"A Bud Light?" the waitress asked.

"No, the real stuff, please," Katie said.

"No problem," the older lady said, and walked away without even asking for IDs.

Carson said, "The 'real stuff,' huh?"

"I don't like watered-down beer. I'll cut calories elsewhere if I have to."

Carson laughed and shook his head. Eric smiled.

The waitress did not return with their drinks; Harvey did. "By God, why didn't you tell me you guys were here." He didn't give them a chance to answer. "I saw you guys sittin' over here, and I said to myself, I think that's Carson Treffor, and sure enough, it was."

"Hey, Harvey," Carson said, tipping his glass toward him. "How you holdin' up."

"Not too bad . . . not too bad," he said. "Just been takin' it easy," he added as he gently touched his head. "How 'bout you guys?"

"Not too bad," Carson repeated.

"We came out to celebrate," Eric said, "Carson had a meeting today where he was cleared of any wrongdoing in the case of Adam Turner."

"Well I should say so," Harvey said. "I'm glad to hear that, Carson. I really am. And you know I probably owe you guys my life."

"That's definitely an exaggeration," Carson said. "You weren't gonna die."

"Still, I really appreciate your help that night." Harvey leaned closer to the table. "And I'd appreciate it if you don't really talk about it in front of the Mrs."

"Oh, is she here?"

"She's the one that took your order."

"All right," Carson said, "when she comes back for the bill, I'll not get into the details."

Harvey winked at him. "Thanks. And there will be no bill. You got that?"

Harvey walked away and left the group to themselves again, alone in the corner of the bar. Eric had been waiting for this. In the car on the way over, he sensed Carson was not in a mood to talk much, so they chit-chatted about what Harvey's bar would be like, and talked about what transpired with the M.O.A. But there was something burning in his mind.

"Carson," he said, "can I ask you a question?"

Carson looked up from his beer. Eric could see in the dim lights that Carson already anticipated the question. "Sure."

"What was that you called Adam in front of the reporters?"

Carson's eyes glanced toward the table again. He furrowed his brow as he thought about it. "Ahmadjon?"

"Yeah, Ahmadjon. What is that?"

Carson turned to the side and scratched his eyebrow with his thumb. He looked at Eric, then Katie. "Ahmadjon was a boy, a patient of mine in Afghanistan."

Katie and Eric sat across the table from him, listening intently.

"It's a long story."

"I'd really like to hear it," Katie said with a great deal of earnest in her eyes.

Carson sighed, looking at her, wondering if this is how he wanted to relax. It wasn't. But Katie and Eric looked so serious, and they were his friends, and maybe it was time to talk about it. It would have come up someday, anyway.

Carson started reluctantly, "I was on patrol in the mountains around Forward Operating Base Mehtar Lam." He stopped for a swig of beer. "There were eight of us out patrolling the mountains in two Humvees. We had been operating out of there for several months. It was a hotbed for insurgents around there, and we were going around trying to establish good relations with the people, trying to knock out the insurgent activity—break the will of the people to support them.

"It was a tough time for me. I knew my mom was sick. She never took care of herself after my dad died. She smoked like a chimney you know, and she had already been diagnosed with congestive heart failure before I even joined the Army. We had given up the farm, and I decided I wanted to be a medic. The only way I knew how, and the only way I knew how to get out of Nebraska was to join the Army. Most of my money went home to Broken Bow. My mom moved there after my dad died.

"Well, for the whole year I was deployed, I got word from my mom and others that she was getting sicker and sicker. I sometimes wondered if I should ask for humanitarian leave, but the doctors had no idea how long my mom had. I just knew she was getting worse. The last I heard, she had been admitted to the hospital for a few days, but was discharged. I began to dread any word from home.

"So that night—the night I'm talking about—we were up in the mountains and got word that I had to return to Mehtar Lam immediately. They said I had a message from the base commanding officer." Carson slowly exhaled, and closed his eyes for a long second. "So we struck camp as it was getting dark and started out for Mehtar Lam. It would be a several-hour trip down those winding roads, going through dangerous territory, but all the guys said they didn't mind. They did it for me.

"We drove for an hour. What a ride—we drove without headlights, winding slowly down the main road. There was a clear sky, though, and plenty of moonlight. I didn't know for sure what the message was about, but I was pretty sure it had something to do with Mom, and I was pretty sure I knew what it was, and I was so . . . sad, I guess. Yeah, I was sad, and I wanted the trip to take forever. I didn't want to hear any news.

"Well, we were all on edge, kinda jumpy, ya know, watching everywhere for movement. I was in the front Humvee, peering out the window, trying to concentrate, but thinking about Nebraska. We were in a valley leading down the mountains.

"The road had a high bank on the right," Carson said, spreading out the lay of the land with his hands, "and I concentrated on the side of the road and the bank, looking for booby traps or any sign of insurgents. We went through a small gorge where the road had been cut through a hill. On the other side, I turned around and saw high up on the bank the dark silhouette of a man with a shepherd's staff standing on a rock. I told the guys what I saw, and we stopped the caravan. We peered around for several minutes but couldn't find him and decided to go on.

"About two minutes later, a man, maybe the same man, stood on the road in front of us waving his hands. McCullough, the driver, screeched to a halt. The interpreter was in our truck and he said the man was saying, "Help! Help us, please. My nephew is hurt." We stopped to talk it over. We saw no one around, so the Staff Sergeant decided the interpreter and I could go talk to him.

"His name was Khalid. He said his nephew had fallen off a rock a few days prior and cut his leg, and was now very sick. He asked if we could help. I wanted to help; I could tell he was legitimate. So we talked to the Staff Sergeant, and since I was the medic, and I wanted to go, we decided it would be a good mission for hearts and minds.

"Khalid took us to his little village, which was not far from our road. It had only a few mud-floor buildings. He took me to his nephew, Ahmadjon. He was lying on the floor—on the dirt—with a small fire burning nearby. He had a bad fever and was only half-conscious. I unwrapped an old rag from his calf and saw a portion of his calf was missing down to the bone. The rag was soaked in pus, and his leg was badly infected. I gave him some antibiotics and cleaned and wrapped his wound but told Khalid and the boy's mother that he would have to come back to the hospital at Mehtar Lam with us. They were both very thankful and very agreeable, and we were all onboard with doing it. I thought he had a chance if we could get him to the hospital. I knew he would probably lose his leg, though."

Carson stopped for a moment. The dim light bulb high above their head cast a shadow in his eyes. Katie and Eric could barely make out the whites of his eyes, but saw they were bigger and disturbed. He took a few more gulps for strength.

"So I wrapped Ahmadjon in a blanket and held him in my lap. It was decided his uncle would come with us. We began to drive away, and the mother followed us, crying. Then some other men came up to us and demanded we stop. One man came up to the Humvee yelling something, trying to take Ahmadjon away from me. The interpreter said he was yelling, 'The boy must not go! The boy must not go!' He would not say why. Khalid tried to tell him that it was all right, and the interpreter said we were trying to help the boy. Ahmadjon's mother pleaded with the man to let us go, but he pushed her aside. Other men started to surround the vehicle, so the interpreter and I got out of the vehicle. I left Admadjon in my seat. I yelled for McCullough to get the hell out of there, and we'd be behind shortly. He took off down the road as the interpreter and I tried talking to the man, trying to buy time. But they ran after the first vehicle.

Carson's head was lowered now, his eyes fully shadowed, staring at the table. "A hundred yards away McCullough passed between two large rocks and hit an I.E.D. The vehicle exploded. We jumped in the second Humvee and rushed down there. We tried to pull them out, but they were all dead—McCullough, Khalid, and Ahmadjon. We had to leave them. The Staff Sergeant made us get out of there; there was nothing to retrieve."

Now all three stared at the table, apathetic, saying nothing for a minute. Carson looked up at Katie and said, "So, you sure you wanted to hear all that?"

She wiped tears away from the corners of her eyes. "Wow, Carson." She laughed a little. "Your stories always make me cry."

"That's pretty sad. It says something about my life. Maybe I'll tell a happy story next time." He smiled.

She laughed again. Eric said, "Wow, Carson, I never knew about all that."

"I figured I'd tell you sometime."

"I'm glad you did. So, what happened?"

"What do you mean?"

"Well . . ." Eric fumbled in his seat. "What was the message from the Commander?"

"Oh," he sighed. "Yeah, there was a Red Cross message. My mom had passed away." Carson was silent for several seconds. "My dad prayed that I would outlive my parents, and I did, but just barely. They sent me home on emergency leave."

"Man, I'm sorry to hear about all that."

"That's okay."

"I think I understand what you mean by close calls now."

Carson looked back at him, a deeper level of understanding in his eyes. "Yeah, well. Who knows? I'm probably just making stuff up in my head. But I don't feel like talking about any of it anymore. I thought we were here to celebrate."

"You're right," Eric said. "Sorry about that. Let's talk about something else."

The three of them talked a bit more. Katie even danced with each of them once, while the other sat and stared at his beer. After a while, Eric noticed it was getting late into the afternoon, and realized it was almost time to go to another Eastern meeting.

"Carson," he said, "are you going to the meeting?"

"What meeting?"

"The Eastern meeting this afternoon."

"I didn't know about it."

"Don't you ever check your messages?

"What's it about?"

"Dave said something about a backup plan for the county council meeting."

"What, are we planning on losing already?"

"I don't know, man, but one way or the other, we need to leave now."

Carson sighed deeply. "I don't think so. I'm exhausted. I didn't sleep well last night. I think I'll go home and pass out for a while. You guys can tell me about it later on."

"Are you sure, Carson?" Katie said, a sadness in her eyes. She didn't want him to be alone.

He pursed his lips, feeling a pervasive funk throughout his body. He couldn't think enough to care about anything right now. But he cared about Katie. He cared about the concern in her eyes, and that was the one thing that made him feel better. It was a thought that could put him to sleep—a sleeping aid he needed, a sleeping aid he did not have last night. He would use it to his advantage now. He would take Katie's eyes to bed with him. He was happy to have it, for that's what he needed—her eyes watching down over him as he slept, displacing his constant companion, the dark cold eyes that watched him all day long.

23.

Katie and Eric found two open seats in the classroom. Sitting down, Eric noticed more than a few people staring at them. Tim looked over and raised his eyebrows. Eric ignored them.

"Okay, folks," Dave said from the front of the room, "let's keep this short and sweet."

Some jokers started clapping. They had already died "death-by-meetings" over the past few months.

"As you all know, Friday night's the night—the big night, if you will."

Eric sang under his breath, "Waiting for tonight . . . oh-ohh . . ." and it made Katie laugh.

"I'd like to say that I know how it's gonna turn out, but I don't," Dave continued. "I know one thing—if they give the contract to the fire department, it was railroaded through the system."

Some people clapped.

"But let me cut to the chase. We've been working with an independent civic group to introduce a charter amendment to be placed on the ballot in the November election. This is a fall-back just in case we lose the vote. It's a long legal document, but what it basically says is that any decisions made by the county council will be put on hold. Then the county will appoint an Ambulance Committee to come up with ambulance requirements to start the process all over next year. If we can get the signatures we need, the county council will have no choice but to put it on the November ballot."

Dave paused while everyone mulled it over in their heads. "I'm confident we can get the signatures by October 15, and if we do, it will be on the ballot. When it's on the ballot, the people of Lincoln can vote for the amendment. If they do that, we will continue to provide service for at least another year while the city comes up with a better, fairer system."

Eric looked over at Katie and raised his eyebrows. She nodded her approval.

"Secondly," Dave continued, "I have someone to introduce. His name is John Otto. He is an attorney from Kansas City who specializes in EMS agreements. John, would you like to stand up?"

An older man with a thick walrus-like mustache stood from a front seat and waved at the crowd.

"Mr. Otto has been asked by the Lancaster County Medical Board to look over the fire department's charter and to give his expert opinion at the meeting. Mr. Otto has helped design EMS systems for more than twenty cities, and he's looking at the fire department Charter very closely. Well, I'll just let John speak for himself. You have anything you want to say, John?"

The walrus-mustached man stood up again and faced the crowd. "Hello, everyone," he said after running his hand over his facial hair and down his chin. "I'm not gonna bore you with the details right now, but I have five points of contention with the fire department's proposal. It's reckless, and in the end, it may cost lives."

Someone from the crowd asked what the five points were. Mr. Otto looked pleased to elaborate on them for some time. They were very compelling, and several people asked him questions. In the end, he concluded by saying, "As you can see, I believe we have a pretty powerful argument, so I hope to see you all there."

Dave reassumed his position at the front of the room. "On that note, I think it goes without saying that I *strongly* encourage all of you to show up on Friday. Let's make a collective statement. I'd like to see as many people as possible wearing their blue Eastern sweatshirts."

Dave made his way over to a box in the corner. "Is there anyone here who has not received a sweatshirt?" He grabbed up several.

"Joe, you didn't? Here you go. Is that the right size? Okay."

Katie raised her hand for one.

"Small?" Dave asked her.

"Medium, please." She looked at Eric.

"Go with the Small," Eric said. "It's a good look on you."

She swatted her sweatshirt against Eric's chest.

"Are you sure you want to wear that thing?" Eric asked.

"What do you mean?"

"I was just thinking that you probably didn't want to be too partisan with your family situation and all."

"I know what I'm doing, Eric. I'm a big girl now."

After only a little more rambling, the meeting concluded surprisingly soon. Eric wondered if Carson were awake now, awaiting their call—wanting to see Katie. But he looked over at Katie, stretching as she got up from her seat, and he dismissed the thought quickly.

"All right, Mr. Eric Wright," she said, "what's the plan?"

"I thought we might go out to the Hiway Diner for a hamburger and ice cream," he said.

"Whoa, Eric," she said smiling, "are you asking me out on a date?"

He thought about it a second. "Well, it depends on what you mean by a date. Obviously, this isn't an off-the-shoulder-gown kind of event," he mused.

"Oh," she said, feigning disappointment, "here I was going to wear my off-the-shoulder gown, but I guess I won't now. You missed your chance, I guess."

"Can I take a rain check on that?"

"That all depends on how the first date goes," she said, smiling.

―――

At 5:00, Carson reached over and silenced his alarm clock. It didn't wake him, because he had been awake for the last half-hour. The events of the week poured through his mind. He even wondered what Dave's backup plan was, though he tricked himself into thinking he didn't care. Behind it all, he had subconsciously listened for the phone to ring.

He propped himself up on his elbows and thought about what to do. Maybe he should have gone to the meeting after all, he thought. His sleep hadn't done him any good. He thought about getting up and making something to eat in order to stop the gnawing in his stomach, but when he thought about food, he realized he wasn't that hungry. Instead, he plopped himself back down and stared at the ceiling.

If Katie and Eric didn't call, he thought about calling one of his on-again, off-again girlfriends. Yeah, maybe that's what I'll do, he thought. He ran over a few faces in his head, then dismissed the thought altogether. It wasn't until then that he realized how substandard some of those girls were. No, only thinking about Katie put his mind at ease. He looked over at the answering machine to see if he'd slept through any messages. Unusual for that machine, there were no blinking lights.

———

"Oh my God, Eric!" Katie said after scooping another spoonful of milkshake into her mouth. "I never knew that you were such a brain."

"I wouldn't go that far," he said, using a long spoon to take a scoop from the same glass.

"I just assumed—" she said.

"Assumed what? That since I wasn't in college now that I was a bad student in high school?"

"Well, yeah, I guess," she said. "So you actually went to the university for two years?"

"Yeah."

"Why'd you quit?"

"I don't know, it was getting old, and my grades started to slip. I guess I wasn't motivated enough. I got this job and really liked it, so I went to EMT-Intermediate school at Creighton, and I just haven't gone back yet."

"What do you mean, 'yet?' Are you planning to?"

"I might."

"I would if I were you. Did you know that college grads . . ." Her voice trailed off as Eric took in the moment. He had learned early in life to appreciate good moments when they came, and this was surely a good moment. As Katie talked, the '50s-style jukebox played some old ballad that he didn't know but would never forget. The neon Diner sign cast a pink hue on Katie and her strawberry milkshake. Talking to him about school, her green eyes widened with enthusiasm, and her skin glowed with youth.

"You really like milkshakes don't you?" he asked, interrupting her.

She stopped talking and jerked her head back ever so slightly. "Where the heck did that come from?" Then she noticed she had been taking several bites of the dessert in between sentences while Eric only leaned forward and looked at her. Her face glowed redder in the neon light.

"Have you even been listening to me?" she asked.

Eric realized the foolishness of what he'd said. "I mean, you just look so happy, like you're really enjoying yourself. You're smiling ear to ear, and you're devouring that shake!"

She put the spoon down. "Yes, I *do* like milkshakes, and yes, I am happy right now." She sat back in the booth, warming her hands on her lap, and smiled at Eric.

"Well," Eric said, "the night's still young. What should we do?"

"Hmm," she said as she placed her cold hands under her thighs and leaned forward. "I hope you're not trying to get me alone, Eric. This is only our first date, you know."

Eric could have stayed in that moment for a long time, for at least a year or two, but he moved the conversation along because he had to. He looked at his watch. "It'll be getting dark soon," he said. "Do you want to drive up to Arnold Heights to view the city?"

Her chin cocked back again. "Ah-ha, you *are* trying to get me alone."

At that point, he honestly didn't know what she wanted. "No, I promise. I just thought it would be fun to go up there and talk with a blanket wrapped around our shoulders."

"Oh, and let me guess, you've got a special blanket stashed away in your car for moments like this."

"Actually, I don't. Contrary to what you might think, this isn't something I do a lot. We'll have to swing by my place or the store to get one."

"Okay," she said somewhat skeptically. "Maybe I will. The thing is, I was supposed to go to my mom's tonight for a 'stitch and bitch.'"

Eric laughed. "A what?"

She looked embarrassed. "Well, my mom calls it a knitting party, but I like to call it a 'stitch and bitch,' because that's what it really is. It's every other Wednesday with a lot of the firefighters' wives and some ladies from church and sometimes me. I haven't gone in such a long time, and I promised her I would go tonight."

"So what are you saying? That you're going to your mom's?"

She paused for a moment only. "No, what I'm saying is that I'd rather go out with you."

Katie saw a new light in Eric's eyes and felt she had said too much. She looked for a humorous way out. "On one condition though—no funny business under the blanket," she said, holding up a finger, but with a smile.

"No funny business," he promised. They got up from the table, and Eric left money to cover the bill.

Outside, in the warm evening air, Katie looked up at the sky and the trees, whose leaves glowed pink as the sun began to touch the horizon. Eric looked at her and noticed the glittering necklace nestled between her collarbones.

"That's a cute necklace," he said with curiosity in his voice.

Without looking down, she reached up and felt it with her fingers. "Thanks," she said. "My mom and dad gave it to me."

"Oh," Eric said, wishing he hadn't brought it up. No one was around as they stood next to Eric's car beneath the trees. She looked at him through the tops of her eyes. Eric thought she might be waiting for a kiss, then noticed a sadness in her eyes. She looked down at the necklace.

"Eric," she said in a low voice.

"Yeah?"

"Maybe I was wrong back there."

"About what?"

"Maybe I can't go to Arnold Heights with you tonight."

Eric felt his lungs deflate. Everything had seemed so straightforward but now was convoluted by some unknown factor. Another man? Her past? Maybe even Carson?

"Why?" he asked.

"Because it's getting dark, and I made a promise that I wouldn't go out after dark except in large groups or with my girlfriends."

"To who?"

She hesitated to say it. "To my mom and my dad."

"Really?" he said, genuinely shocked.

"Yeah. I know it's silly, but I did it, so I have to keep it."

Eric stood speechless for a moment. "Okay."

"Really?"

"What do you mean, 'really?'"

"That's cool with you?"

"Well, not really. I wanted to spend more time with you, and I promise I wasn't trying to get you to do something you don't want to do."

"I know you weren't, Eric," she said with a smile that came from realizing she fully trusted someone, "and I like that about you."

"And I have to say," he continued, "that I think it's kind of crazy that you have rules like that when you're nineteen years old and live on your own."

"You're probably right. But just because I live on my own doesn't mean I no longer have a family that I owe a lot to."

She looked at the ground, and Eric saw her family life in a new light. They *were* her family, and they were good to her, and she loved them after all.

"So, you're going to the 'stitch and bitch' then?" he said, forcing a smile that Katie always liked. "I didn't know people still did things like that."

"People like my mom do."

"When can I see you again?"

She didn't answer right away, so Eric added, "I guess when it's daylight, huh?"

"Or with a large crowd?" she said, laughing. "Unfortunately, I'm pretty busy tomorrow. I don't think I'll see you again until the county council meeting."

"Oh," he said with mock boredom, "that will be tons of fun. Very romantic too."

"I know. I'm sorry. I'm just so busy, Eric. Maybe we can do something this weekend."

"All right."

"But I should probably go now; I'm already super late."

Eric opened the passenger door. "No problem."

Before he closed the door, she stopped it with her hand. "Eric, thanks for understanding."

"No problem. I've already had a great time, anyway. Someday we'll pick up where we left off."

―

Thirty minutes later, Katie arrived at her parents' house. Her mom looked overjoyed and kissed her when she showed at the door.

"Honey!" she said, holding the door open for Katie, "I didn't think you were coming."

"Sorry I'm late, Mom."

Katie sat in one of many chairs circling Margaret O'Malley's overly decorated living room. The ladies sipped tea and gossiped while they worked their needles. They talked about Margaret's new floral arrangements, but the conversation eventually turned to their husbands and to the wives who no longer made it to knitting night. Katie could tell that if she hadn't been there, they would probably be talking about her as well. It was then that she decided she would no longer come to these parties.

"What do you think will happen at Friday's county council meeting?" one lady asked the group in general, looking at the half-finished scarf in her hands. "I hope they come to their senses and see that the wisest thing—" Her eyes met Katie's, and she obviously felt she had made a blunder. "Well, whatever they decide, I'm sure it will all work out in the end."

The others in the room felt uncomfortable, more so than they needed to, Katie thought. She looked at her mom. Margaret fiddled with the top button of her blouse. Finally, Jenny Carver, Jon's wife, and the one who had reportedly seen Katie going out that night with Carson, found a way to change the subject.

"Ladies, you wouldn't believe who called me the other day."

The women around the room gave looks that indicated they couldn't guess, so she continued.

"Lynda Killion."

"Really?" Margaret said.

"Yes, the poor thing. I understand she's had it up to here with her husband, always calling, always coming over to her parents' house to talk to her, to win her back."

"She's staying with her parents? I thought they were from New York," one lady asked.

"Yes, the Andersons. They're retired and moved out here from back East to be close to their grandchildren. They live off Seventy-first Street. She says her husband's constant visits and calls are stressing her parents, making them more worried all the time."

"Well, you can't blame him," Katie's mom said. "I would hope that any good husband would strive to get his wife back after he'd made some mistakes."

"Yes, but she sounded desperate and said she couldn't put up with it any longer. You'll never guess what she asked me."

Again, the ladies couldn't guess and waited on Jenny's every word. "She actually asked if she could stay at my place for a while so she could rest while things simmered down and the divorce finalized."

"Nooo!" several of them said quietly. Katie listened intently.

"Where are the children?" Katie's mom asked.

"They're staying with their father for now. He insists on that, but I imagine there will be a custody battle. She sees them on weekends, but she says their father is turning them against her, and they can't understand why she's left."

"What did you tell her?" Margaret asked.

"What *could* I tell her? I told her that I would help her if I could, but that it just wouldn't be right with Jon working with the deputy chief and all. It would be too complicated. She had been hanging out with Lilly Tompkins, and I don't know why she didn't ask her. So I just asked if there was some other way I could help. She was a dear, though. She said she understood and was sorry she asked. I told her not to worry about it, but to call if she needed anything."

"The whole thing's a shame," Margaret said.

Katie put her unfinished tea down on her saucer. Why hadn't she gone out with Eric, she asked herself. She couldn't stand being here anymore and felt more out of place the longer she stayed.

She leaned over to her mom. "Mom, I'm not feeling well. I think I'm going to go home now. Besides, I have a little studying to do before I go to bed."

"Well, all right, dear. Is there anything I can get you for your stomach?"

"No, I'm fine."

"Well, thanks for coming, honey. I'll see you again in two weeks?"

"Maybe, Mom." Katie grabbed her things and left. She felt claustrophobic and didn't find relief until she stepped under the stars again. She should have been up at Arnold Heights with Eric looking at those stars, she thought. That was a mistake. She went home and went to bed but tossed and turned for more than an hour before she fell asleep.

24.

It had become a regular scene now, the county council chamber filled with people wall-to-wall, Eastern Ambulance leadership with the hospital staff and members of the Lancaster County Medical Society on the front, left side, and the fire department with their proponents on the right. Behind each team—for that's what it looked like—sat the employees, family, and friends. Blue on the left, red on the right. Concerned citizens and the press sat or stood in the back.

Katie arrived earlier than last time. Though she wanted to come, she didn't want to make a scene. She wore the new Eastern Ambulance sweatshirt she'd received a few days prior, and she slipped into the seat next to Carson fifteen minutes before the meeting. Eric had not yet arrived.

"I haven't seen you in a while," Katie said to Carson.

"I know," Carson replied. "I wondered if the three of us would still go out on Wednesday, but I guess you guys went out instead."

He and Eric had worked together the day before. Eric told him that he and Katie didn't have a chance to call because they ate dinner early, and Katie left abruptly for her mom's knitting party.

"I'm sorry, Carson. I decided to go to my mom's that night." She looked for a way to explain away the situation. "Which, by the way, was a mistake. I'm never gonna do that again. Next time, I'm going out with you guys."

"Let's go out tonight."

"Tonight? After the meeting?" She felt a little uncomfortable with others sitting so close to them.

"Yeah, you said you wanted to go back to the lake sometime."

"Yeah," she said, "but, I—"

"I couldn't think of a better way to forget or celebrate the night than to have fun with you."

Katie was flattered, but she hoped her father wasn't watching from the front row. Just the sight of Carson whispering in her ear would make him blow up. She and Carson were speaking as discreetly as possible.

"But what about everyone else?" Really, she had someone specific in mind when she said, "everyone else." "Don't you think everyone will want to get together after the meeting at P.O. Pears to talk? Maybe we should just hang out with them tonight, and go out some other night?"

Carson nodded like he could see her point. "I tell you what," he said. "If we win tonight, then we should go out and celebrate with everyone."

"I agree," she said.

"But if we lose, I don't necessarily feel like moping with everyone, going over backups to backup plans. I would rather just go out with you. If we lose tonight, my job is probably over, and I'm gonna need a swim at the lake."

She felt sorry for him. He didn't smile; he just looked empty inside.

Katie let her eyes casually flit toward the front of the firefighter side of the room. Her father was leaning over talking to Deputy Chief Killion. He apparently hadn't noticed her yet. She thought about him winning the contract tonight, and how angry that would make her.

"All right, Carson," she said. "If we win tonight, we're going out to celebrate with everybody, but if we lose, I'll go to the lake with you."

"Promise?"

"Promise," she said, trying to analyze the cause of the guilt she felt inside.

Within minutes, Eric arrived and took the seat Katie had been saving for him.

"Nice sweatshirt," he said. "Did you get that from your parents?"

She laughed. That was one thing about Eric; he could always make her laugh. "Yeah, actually. My dad bought it for me last Christmas."

"Did I miss anything yet?" he asked.

"Nope," Carson said. "Pull up a seat and get ready for the action."

Not long into the meeting, several members were given opportunities to speak.

"I just want to conclude by saying," Leslie said, standing at her seat, "that this company has been a cornerstone in this community for a long time, and never, never has there been an issue with the quality of care we provide or the service we provide to the city." It looked like she had done some extra tanning and had gotten a new perm for the event. She had a knack for bringing out her worst for special occasions. "No good reason can be given for changing the perfect system we have now."

Well, I don't know about it being "perfect," Eric thought, but it was a great speech anyway.

"Thank you," Moscatelli said. "The floor is still open."

"Mr. Chairman," Dave Conrad said as he stood.

"Mr. Conrad, you've already had your chance to speak."

Dave cleared his throat. "Yes, I know, Mr. Chairman. I merely want to introduce someone who has a few things to say about the issue."

Moscatelli looked bored again, or impatient; Eric couldn't tell. "Go ahead."

As Dave introduced John Otto, Eric leaned over and whispered to Katie, "How was knitting with your mom?"

"Boring," she whispered back. "Eric, I wish I would have gone out with you instead, but at least I made my mom happy for one night."

"That's okay," he said. "You should always feel good about keeping your promises. Besides, we'll have other opportunities." Katie smiled at him.

Otto began to speak, reemphasizing a lot of the same things Dave Conrad had already brought to light. Then he plunged into the meat of his argument.

"Compared to all of the ordinances I have either seen, worked on, or helped write," he said, "this one, the ordinance that the Lancaster County has written for the fire department, has to be one of the worst. The problems are, in some cases, quite serious, and will result in a drop-off in the quality of care being provided. It's going to cost more money, and it's going to pose a danger to patients in the city."

The crowd had grown considerably quiet.

"I see five major problems with the ordinance. First, it does not specifically require all ambulances to have Paramedics on-board. The contract with Eastern *does* require at least one Paramedic to be on every ambulance. I am told that most of them have two, with the occasional ambulance having a Paramedic and an EMT-Intermediate."

"Mr. Chairman!" Deputy Chief Killion said, standing. Mr. Otto stopped abruptly, like a politician interrupted by a train whistle.

"Yes, Chief?"

"Mr. Chairman, Mr. Otto is making some very serious allegations. May I address these?"

"I don't know . . . I—"

"He can't just throw arguments out there without us being able to defend ourselves!" Lou Killion said.

Mr. Otto spoke. "Mr. Chairman, if I can just present all my thoughts first, the deputy chief can respond to them later if he so chooses."

"Now, Mr. Otto," Killion said in condescending tones, "you don't mean to tell me that as an attorney, you are afraid to openly debate these serious topics. You've accused us of hurting people!"

"I did *not* accuse you of hurting anyone. I said the ordinance that the county has written *could* cause harm to patients."

"Same thing," the deputy chief said, waving his hand dismissively. "Mr. Chairman, I would like to be able to answer Mr. Otto's points as they come."

"Mr. Otto," Moscatelli asked, "are you willing to let the chief do this?"

"Sure," he said. "If that's what he wants, let him say what he has to say."

"Very well. Go ahead, Chief."

"I think Mr. Otto's suggestion that the county should require paramedics on every ambulance is ludicrous! I mean, of course we're going to have paramedics on every ambulance. We do not intend on running an EMT-Basic service here. Paramedics on every ambulance is the plan. Writing it into the ordinance is redundant."

Mr. Otto responded. "My worry, Deputy Chief, is that in situations where the fire department is stretched thin, the department will be tempted to treat the ambulance function as a secondary service to firefighting. If you intend to have paramedics on every ambulance, what's the harm in writing it in the ordinance?"

"It's an unnecessary level of control. We can take care of that administratively."

"Very well, Chief. Then let me get to another point. The second problem I have with the county ordinance—and I have a hard time believing this after so much debate has centered around it—is that the ordinance does not require the fire department to meet a response time standard. Eastern Ambulance's current contract requires the company to respond to ninety percent of all calls within eight minutes or less. It is my understanding that the fire department has criticized Eastern Ambulance for slow response times and promises to be faster. If that is the case, why is there no response-time requirement in the county ordinance?"

"Mr. Chairman, I can address that," the deputy said. "The reason that Eastern's contract has mandated times in it, is because Eastern is a private company, a separate entity. The county controls that company through a contract, and there are penalties in that contract for not meeting those response times. Clearly, Mr. Chairman, you and everyone here realizes that when the fire department assumes EMS, we and the county are one entity. The county cannot penalize itself. It can't fine itself for not meeting a response-time standard. That is why there is no standard in the ordinance."

"My friend," Mr. Otto said, stroking his grey moustache, "that is completely beside the point. You do not have to penalize the agency monetarily to have a standard. One way or the other, it just makes common sense that the county clearly state in the ordinance what the response-time standard is. The fire department must be held accountable just like a private company. Such things have been done in cities across America. What's the problem with setting a standard?"

"We *have* set a standard, Mr. Otto. As we have mentioned throughout this campaign, the fire department plans not only to meet, but to exceed the current levels maintained by Eastern Ambulance. We intend to respond to ninety percent of all calls in six minutes compared to the current contract's eight."

"That's an admirable goal, Chief, but why not put it in writing? The way it is now, the fire department merely has to give their best effort in responding to calls."

"I believe I have already answered that question, Mr. Otto. Eastern Ambulance is a private provider, and therefore requires contractual control. We *are* the county. Any problems with response-time standards can be dealt with administratively by the commissioner or by me."

"We're not through with this issue, Mr. Chairman. Another serious flaw I find in the ordinance is that it doesn't even allow the medical director to set a response-time standard."

Mr. Otto picked up a small ream of paper and read off the page. "The ordinance specifically states, 'The Medical Director is charged with establishing medical standards . . .' but later on states, 'those standards shall not include the setting of a maximum response time for any ambulance service provider.'"

"Mr. Otto, I have made myself perfectly clear about this issue. The fire department *is* going to respond more quickly. Period."

"But you're not going to put it in writing. You're not even going to allow your own Medical Director to require that of you?"

"No."

"Why?"

"Any problem with response times will be dealt with by me! I can take care of that."

"What happens if you can't?"

"I will. If I have to take some sort of disciplinary measures, I will. If I have to reconfigure department operations, I will. If I need to move some trucks around, I will. The fire department has consistently shown that we are faster responders. As such, it doesn't have to be mandated in the ordinance!"

"Moving on then. The fourth problem I have with this document, Mr. Chairman," Otto said, waving the ordinance in the air, "is that nowhere in this document does it require the fire department to respond to all medical calls."

"Oh, c'mon!" Killion burst out. "This is absolutely ridiculous! Does the ordinance have to state the obvious?!"

"It's a legal document, Chief, and therefore, it *does* have to state the obvious."

"Of course we're going to respond to all medical calls!"

"What I am getting at, Mr. Chairman, is that even though this may appear to be obvious to some, a well-written ordinance would state it. My fear is that the fire department will prioritize firefighting over emergency medicine. What happens when there is a large fire, or two or more small fires in the city? Is the fire department going to utilize all its assets on those fires and leave a medical call hanging in the air?"

"Of course not," Deputy Chief Killion said, folding his arms across his chest. "They will carry equal weight."

"Let me guess—just because you said so." Otto said, garnering some laughs from the crowd.

"No, not just because I say so. Because that is the way the commissioner wants it, and that's the way it's going to be! That's the purpose of the EMS service! Are you almost done, Mr. Otto?"

"Almost, Chief. The fifth—and final—problem I have is the fact that the only medical oversight put in place over the fire department is a medical director hired by the fire department."

"They do that in cities across America."

"Yes, but it's a step backward for this city. Currently, both Eastern Ambulance and your own Fire Paramedics fall under the medical jurisdiction of the independent Medical Oversight Agency. Under the county ordinance—which I am increasingly suspecting has been co-written by the fire department—the fire department would *hire* a physician to serve as their oversight and do away with the M.O.A."

"As I said, that is common practice."

"But it's *bad* practice, Chief. Think about it. It's common sense. How much authority does a person have over his own boss? If you, the deputy fire chief, or the chief for that matter, hire and fire the medical director, how empowered is he to demand strict clinical accountability from you? He's not! You're his boss! If you don't like the decisions he makes, you fire him!"

"I wouldn't do that!"

"How can we be so sure? From what I hear, you already have a difficult time answering to the M.O.A.!"

Several Eastern employees started to clap, but Moscatelli tapped his gavel until they hushed.

"I'm not even responding to such accusations!" the deputy chief said.

"Chief, I'm not asking you to. I'm asking you why the county should take a step backward from a robust Medical Oversight to a hired lackey that does your beck and call!"

The crowd burst forth into more applause, even including many of the civilians in the back. Eric saw Dave smile on the front row.

Lou Killion, exasperated, made a move to sit down but decided he could not go down looking defeated. "Mr. Chairman, the arguments this man is making are nitpicking details! He has been hired by Eastern to come in here and scare the citizens of Lincoln."

"I was not hired. I came here freely," Mr. Otto said.

The deputy was taken aback for a moment, then said, "Nonetheless, he is pointing out minor details in the ordinance that our own county attorney wrote. Yes, the county is going to employ a physician as Medical Director. He is not going to become someone's 'lackey.' I hope the board members see this man's arguments for what they are—an attempt to trash the fire department! It's a last-ditch desperation move by Eastern Ambulance on their way out!"

Eric, Carson, and many others booed, hissed, or otherwise vented their disapproval. Again, Moscatelli's gavel brought them to order.

"Is that all, Mr. Otto?" Moscatelli asked.

"Just one last thing, Mr. Chairman. Medicine is a very difficult business that requires high standards. It needs to have standards that are real and enforceable and have teeth. The fire department Ordinance does not have standards that are real and enforceable, and they certainly don't have teeth. Instead, the plan relies on best efforts, genuine intent, and people's words. And that's no way to run an EMS service. That's all I have. Thank you, Mr. Chairman."

Mr. Otto sat down to a rousing applause from the left side of the room. Eric looked over at the firefighters who did not respond in kind. What's more, Eric felt something he hadn't felt in quite a while—hope. Carson looked as though he were in deep concentration. Katie leaned forward with an almost expressionless, but evident, look of anticipation.

"Are there any final thoughts on the ambulance issue?" Moscatelli said after a few moments.

"Yes, sir, I do," said a voice from the middle of the firefighter crowd. It was Mark Rader, who stood to speak.

Chairman Moscatelli looked slightly annoyed, but he knew Rader and gave him some leeway. "Okay, go ahead."

"Mr. Chairman, I just wanted to say a few things before the Board makes such an important decision." Rader scratched his head and appeared to be winging it. "I'm afraid that the Board and the citizens here might have gotten the wrong impression from what Mr. Otto said.

"He claims that it is the fire department that lacks accountability. That's not true! It's the other way around. It's Eastern Ambulance that lacks accountability. All we have to do is look at some of the cases that have recently been in the news. Just a week ago, everyone saw a situation where it would have been better if the fire department had run EMS. You know what I'm talking about. I'm talking about the situation downtown where right in the middle of an emergency, when a little girl's life was at stake, an Eastern ambulance broke down!

"You want to talk about accountability costing lives! A little girl almost died the other night because Eastern Ambulance didn't even have functioning equipment!"

Now it was the firefighters' turn to cheer, and they did. Eric felt a sharp sting of guilt, and he knew it was probably even sharper for Carson.

"I mean, that was absurd!" Rader continued. "Eastern Ambulance actually responded to that call in an ambulance built in the early 1990s. That was reckless, and it almost cost someone dearly. Luckily, the fire department, who is directly accountable to the county, was able to respond with our own equipment and save the girl's life."

Councilmember DeLong spoke, "From what I saw on TV the other night, it appeared that Carson Treffer saved that girl's life more than anyone else."

Rader was befuddled. "Sir, that's not what I'm talking about . . . I'm focusing on the incident that occurred with the ambulance."

"Are breakdowns unheard of in the fire department?" DeLong asked.

"Well, yeah . . . virtually. Our equipment is maintained to the highest standard, sir."

DeLong posed another: "Can you recall any other instances in which an Eastern ambulance broke down?"

Mark hesitated. "No, not off the top of my head. Breakdowns don't occur very often."

"I see. And it doesn't appear that they happen too often with Eastern Ambulance either. I think the real story the other night was the bravery and skill of the Eastern Medics, who I can safely say, even though I am not a medical person, saved the life of that little girl."

"Sir," Rader said, "that was . . . that was reckless endangerment of crew."

"Oh come on, Mr. Rader! You're grasping!"

Rader was on the defensive and feeling trapped. "Sir, their actions don't always save lives. If Carson Treffer is so quick to jump into fire, why is he so slow in reporting child abuse?"

The crowd booed and jeered. Leslie and several others were on their feet in outrage. Moscatelli pounded his gavel in vain. Katie looked over at Carson who looked strangely helpless. She couldn't read his thoughts, but he looked sorrowful. She thought of Ahmadjon, Adam, and the burdens Carson bore. She hated Mark Rader, Lou Killion, and her father for hurting Carson. They had no idea.

"Mr. Rader," DeLong said over the crowd. "Mr. Rader, that is not germane to our discussion. That issue was looked at and, I believe, dealt with a few days ago. That is not part of what we are discussing tonight."

"I'm only saying—"

"Well don't be 'saying' unless you have something to say about Mr. Otto's allegations."

"Councilmember DeLong," Rader said, "am I not allowed to speak at this forum, or are only pro-Eastern people allowed to speak?"

Cheers from the fire department.

"That's not what I'm saying, Mr. Rader, and you know it!"

"It sure sounds like it. That is a serious issue of accountability. How come the city employee, Mr. Murray, got fired when Adam Turner died, but the private ambulance employee did not?"

More cheers from the right, jeers from the left.

"Mr. Chairman," DeLong said to Moscatelli, "can you please clarify to Mr. Rader that that issue is *not* what we are discussing tonight? Perhaps we should remind Mr. Rader that there was an investigation into that and no fault was found!"

Moscatelli was hesitant but maintained the duty of his position. "Mark, this is indeed the case. We are discussing the merits of the two services providing EMS, not individual cases. Do you have anything else you would like to add?"

"I was discussing the case, Mr. Chairman. My only point is that the county has no accountability over Eastern. They answer only to themselves." Mark sat down, happy to get out of the discussion having saved some face.

"Thank you, Mr. Rader," Moscatelli said. "It's beginning to get late. We will proceed to the vote if no one has anything else to say."

The Chairman scanned the crowd. Eric wondered if he should say something, but he didn't know what would help. The arguments made by John Otto were better than anything he could say.

"All right then," Moscatelli continued, "anything from the board members?"

They shook their heads.

"No?" He turned to the county clerk. "Mr. Jones, can you please read the proposition."

A man stood and read the motion to not renew the current EMS contract with Eastern Ambulance, and to adopt County Ordinance number 5141, "Ordinance Governing Emergency Medical Services Provided by the County Fire Department." When he finished, he took his seat.

"Thank you, Mr. Jones. Please take the vote."

"Yes, Mr. Chairman. A simple majority of four 'yeses' will carry the vote."

The clerk called out the names of the board members one-by-one, starting on Eric's right.

"Johnson?"

"No."

"Martinez?"

"Yes."

"Mallory?"

"Yes.

"Davidson?"

"No."

"Moscatelli?"

"Yes."

"Johannsen?"

"Yes." Eric's heart sank.

"DeLong?"

His answer came more slowly than the others. His vote didn't matter by that point.

"No."

Eric didn't remember much of the next several minutes. It was too quick and uneventful. He wished he could turn back the clock. Maybe he should have said something. Maybe they'd been too sure of themselves. Moscatelli pounded his gavel. It was over. It was too late to speak. There was little left to be said in a county council meeting that had already gone very late. Eric felt hollow inside. Had they not listened to a word Mr. Otto or anyone else had said? Were the questions brought up by Mr. Jenkins, the accountant, ever addressed? It didn't matter. None of those things counted now. Somehow, the fire department and the county council had ended the game in the third quarter without anybody noticing.

The only thing left to do was to process the bitter truth and consider the options. The one consolation Eric had was that he would have time with Katie tonight, albeit in a crowd. For it was nearly certain the Eastern people would hang out at P.O. Pears for a long time. Eric didn't know Katie had prior obligations, and the night was far from over.

25.

Eric, Katie, and Carson filed out of their seats and made their way to the lobby. People gathered in small circles and talked. As much as possible, they tried to avoid eye contact with the firefighters, but Katie's father came to speak with her.

"Katie," he said, placing his hand on her shoulder, "how 'bout you come have dinner with me and your mother tonight? She promised to have something waiting for us."

Katie's heart beat rapidly, and she was fearful it might give her away. O'Malley made brief eye contact with Carson, who turned away.

"I don't think so, Dad," she said, gently removing his arm from her shoulder. "It's getting late, and I'm super tired." She wasn't good at lying, and she knew her voice trembled when she spoke.

He glanced once more at both Eric and Carson. "All right, honey. That's fine. I trust you after the agreement you made with me and your mother."

He looked down at her flower necklace. "It's dark. Do you want me to follow you home to make sure you're safe?"

"No, Dad, I'll be fine." He hesitated, and she knew he would drive by her apartment anyway.

"Okay, honey, have a safe drive home."

"I will, Dad. Good night."

O'Malley smiled at her, then turned and looked at Carson and Eric.

"Tough break, guys," he said with a grin. "I hope you're able to find some other job in some other city." He turned and walked away.

The three stood silent as they waited for O'Malley to disappear into the crowd. As soon as he had, Carson looked back at Katie. She knew what was on his mind.

"Did you drive yourself?" Carson asked.

"Yeah," she said, before glancing at Eric. He could see the awkwardness in her face but didn't know what it meant.

Carson saw it too and looked up at Eric. "Eric, you goin' over to P.O. Pears?"

"Yeah, I plan on it," he said with a curious tone. "Aren't you?"

"Actually," Carson said, "Katie and I made a deal tonight that if we won, we would go celebrate with everyone, but if we lost, we would go for another swim instead—to put it all behind us."

"Oh," Eric said. He could barely feel his face move but didn't have anything to say anyway. He had been letting Katie make the decision for herself without any undue influence on his part, and now it appeared that she had.

Katie ached inside. She so badly wanted to invite him to come, but she knew that's not what Carson wanted. She wasn't even exactly sure what she wanted, but hurting Eric was not part of it.

"Man, it's been a sucky night," Eric said, trying to change the subject. "Can you believe that crap in there?"

The other two shook their heads.

"So, you guys plan on catching up with us over at Pears?" he asked.

"I'd like to," Katie said.

"Yeah," said Carson, "it's a possibility."

"Good," Eric said, not really believing it. "Then I'll probably just catch up with you guys a little later."

Eric stared back at them for a moment, and it killed Katie.

"All right, then," Eric said. "I guess I'll be heading over there so I can drown my sorrows with everyone else." He tried to smile.

"You sure, Eric?" Katie asked.

"Yeah, it'll be fun," he said facetiously. "I don't know if I'll be there long though. You know, it's just been a sucky night. I might just go home soon and not think about it till tomorrow. But hey, if I don't see you tonight, maybe I'll see you tomorrow."

"Definitely," Katie said.

"All right, Eric," Carson said, "give me a call tomorrow."

"All right," he said. Mustering what little energy he had left, Eric walked away.

Katie and Carson made their way outdoors, trying as hard as possible to avoid firefighters and reporters. Sneaking around the crowd, Carson took Katie's hand. She felt like they were in a spy movie.

When they got outdoors, they made their way off to the side where few people would see them. Katie was a little out of breath.

"God," Carson said, "can you believe that?"

"Believe what?" So many momentous things were happening to her at once that she seriously didn't know what he referred to.

"That they actually gave the fire department the contract?"

"I know. It's crazy. To be honest, I don't even know why my dad and them wanted it so bad."

"I think there were many reasons," Carson said, "but for one thing, I think they were tired of guys like me telling them what to do."

Katie thought about it for a second, and only then fully realized the situation. Her dad, a man of many years and a lot of pride, had to take a back-seat to "punk kids" like Carson, and Carson was the epitome of them all—confident, cocky, and not afraid to speak his mind.

"That was it, wasn't it?" Katie asked, looking up at Carson. He looked slightly sad as he scanned the crowd, but still confident and strong. "My dad and them just didn't like answering to you?"

"Your dad can't stand guys like me," he said.

She looked up at him. "I can see why not."

Carson's lips turned in a devilish grin. There was that smile again. Katie was happy to make him smile.

"You ready to go?" he asked.

"Yeah."

They ducked around the edges of the crowd that lingered in large numbers. Dave, Hank, and others formed a large group, which Carson avoided. Tonight was not a night for discussion.

They made their way to the parking lot. The crisp October air was cooler than any night Katie had felt in quite a while.

"Do you want to take my truck?" Carson asked.

She glanced around, wondering if her dad had left. "I don't think so," she said. "If anyone saw me getting in that truck, I'd be dead."

He did not argue with her. He was a wanted man in her father's eyes.

"I'll follow you," she said.

When he looked at her face, his heart started to thrill. All it took was getting out of that chamber, away from those people, and alone with her. He was so depressed inside but was trying to ignore it. This was the something he needed.

"All right." Carson opened the creaky door of his truck and climbed in. He smiled at her. She was struck by how good-looking he was. She had noticed it many times before, of course, but tonight, under the streetlamps, she fully realized it. What's more, he was everything she wasn't supposed to do.

"I should probably stop by my place to get my . . ." she said but didn't finish her sentence.

"To get what?"

She wanted to say a swimsuit. "A towel, I guess."

"You really need a towel?" he said, almost laughing.

"No, I guess not." She looked worried and confused. "All right, I'll see you there."

He started the engine. She folded her arms, thankful for her new sweatshirt; it might come in handy to dry off. She nodded at him and walked to her car.

She followed his pickup out of the parking lot. The traffic backed up, and several cars separated her from the white truck with the red stripe down the side. But it was not a hard vehicle to spot. Only farmers drove trucks like that, and farmers avoided Lincoln as much as possible.

Katie thought about the night, what had happened, and what was happening. She was a confused mess—torn, angry, nervous, excited—she didn't know. Her cell phone rang.

"Yeah?"

"Katie? It's me," a voice said. It was Mike O'Malley.

"Oh . . . hi, Dad," she said, sounding startled.

"What's the matter, you sound like you thought I was someone else?"

"No . . . I didn't; I'm just tired."

"Are you on your way home now?"

Bands tightened around her heart, and she hesitated. "Yeah, but I'm caught in traffic."

"Okay."

"Did you call me just to ask that?" she said with obvious displeasure.

"No . . ." he said, stumbling, "I just wanted to talk to you to make sure you're doing all right."

"What do you mean?"

"I just wanted to make sure you know that what happened tonight happened for the best. I know you're going through a stage where you—"

"Dad! I'm not going through a stage. I work for them because it's a good job for my career."

"I know, honey. As long as that's the only reason, that's good. Because you know that they're not the greatest group of people."

"What do you mean?" she said.

"I'm just saying that they're not the type of people that really have their act together, in their lives or in their company."

"Dad, that's so not true. They are all great people, and they do well enough with their lives!"

"Then why did they lose?"

"They lost," she said, "because you guys made them lose!"

"Honey, we didn't have to do anything."

"I don't want to talk about this right now."

"Okay, that's fine."

"I'll talk to you later, Dad."

"All right. About how much longer till you get home?"

"I don't know. Are you policing me now?"

"Katie, don't get like that! I thought we had an understanding. You know as well as I do that I worry about you. I'm your father; that's my job!"

"I don't know. I might not go home right away."

His heart sank into his stomach, and she could feel it over the phone. "Katie?"

"Yes, Dad?"

"Honey, please remember what you told me and your mother. You made a promise to us."

"I know, but Dad, I can take care of myself!"

"I wouldn't be able to sleep tonight thinking you're still out with God-knows-who."

Both God and Katie knew who he was talking about.

"You don't want to keep your mother and me up all night do you?"

"No, Dad."

"We'd feel much safer if you just went home tonight. Can you do that for us?"

"Dad, I'm not going to do anything wrong."

"I know you wouldn't Katie; you're an angel. I just don't trust everyone else, especially knowing how a lot of your Eastern friends feel about me. They think of you like some kind of trophy, you know."

"Dad!"

"I know you don't want to talk about it, honey, but I have to lay it on the line. Don't do things that you'll regret later on. Don't do things that you're not certain you want to do. Think about your future. Think about where you want to be in five or ten years, and how your decisions tonight might affect that."

Katie was almost in tears. Just when she had convinced herself that her father was neurotic, why did he have to come back and say something that made sense? She thought about where she wanted to be in five years and ten years, and she hadn't necessarily seen her life unfolding like this. She liked Carson, and sometimes wanted him badly, but she couldn't see him fitting into her future. She touched her necklace and thought about the promise. It was good to keep promises, Eric had told her.

"All right, Dad! I'm going home! Are you happy?"

"Thank you, Katie. God has blessed me with you, and I knew I could trust you."

She had no response. His honey-soaked talk was grating on her nerves like never before. What he said made sense, but the decision she chose was not because of him.

"So what time do you think you'll be home?"

She hesitated, struggling inside. The white pickup with the red stripe was only two cars ahead.

"Probably ten minutes."

"Okay, honey. I hope you don't get too emotional about all this. Go home, relax, and have a good night. It'll all make much more sense in the morning."

"Good night, Dad." She hung up before he could reply.

Katie dropped the phone on her thigh in frustration, then picked it back up and dialed Carson.

"Carson?"

"Yeah?"

"I *really* hate to do this—"

"Oh, Katie, c'mon. You don't have to go skinny-dipping. You can stay on the bank, or we can both stay on the bank. We can go get your swimsuit. I'm not trying to pressure you into doing this. I didn't think it would be that big a deal."

She almost laughed at his series of offers but wasn't in a mood to. "It's not that, Carson. It's none of that. You're right, it's not that big a deal . . . well, it kinda is, but that's not the problem."

"What is it, then? Is it Eric?"

She stopped a moment. She hadn't anticipated that.

"No . . . uh . . . it's not that, or not all that, it's—"

"It is, isn't it?"

She paused again. "It's my dad," she blurted out to avoid the awkward questions.

"Your dad?"

"Yeah, I made a stupid promise that I wouldn't go out after dark."

"Oh my God! I thought Eric was making that up. Forget your dad, Katie! It's *your* life."

"I know, but I did it, and I don't like to break promises."

She glanced at her watch. It had already been two minutes. "Look, Carson, I know this sucks for you, and you're having a terrible night, but I've gotta turn around."

Carson was utterly deflated. He should have known this was going to happen. Katie was far more upright than any girl he had ever met. "Are you sure?"

"Yeah, but you can still go if you want to."

"No, I don't think so."

"I thought you enjoyed swimming by yourself."

"Not tonight."

"Oh, Carson, I'm so sorry. I know this is one of the worst nights for you, and I wanted to make it better. Can we call it a rain check?"

As she spoke, she turned off the road. She couldn't please anyone no matter what she did. Carson saw her turn around in his rear-view mirror and knew it was pointless to try to change her mind.

"That's okay, Katie," he said, "but just as a friend speaking to a friend, you need to break away from your parents someday—someday soon. At least just enough to know you're your own person."

"I know." She felt frustrated and torn. "Thanks for

understanding, Carson. There was a big part of me that really wanted to go."

"Don't say that. It just makes it harder."

"Sorry."

"It's okay."

She had two minutes left, she thought to herself, looking at the time on her cell phone. In her mind, Katie questioned whether her father would drive by her apartment.

Yeah, she thought, he was probably already there.

She needed to hurry. He would get her mom all worked up, too, but her mom wouldn't worry as much. In fact, she probably wouldn't worry much at all if he didn't make her worry. Her mom trusted her much more than her father did.

That was it, wasn't it? He didn't trust her; he just liked to say he did. She wasn't going out "fooling around." Or . . . well, was she? That was an interesting question. How would the night have ended? The thought scared her and thrilled her at the same time. One way or the other, it was nothing compared to what all her friends were doing and had been doing for a long time. And yet, she was the one who couldn't go out when she had always been the perfect one. Her dad was probably parked in his truck a few blocks from her apartment just to make sure she was home. He didn't trust her at all.

She pulled the car over again. She needed to be back at her apartment soon to keep her dad happy, and that's exactly why she decided not to do it.

Fifteen minutes later, Katie stood on the bank of the lake. No one else was there, not a soul, not even the sound of birds or frogs or . . .

Don't think about frogs, she thought.

It was downright cold. It had been a warm fall, and it had been a warm day, but the temperature dropped quickly when the sun went down. But there was a lot of moonlight, and she could see fine.

She took off her shoes and climbed down to a root lying just over the water. She sat down and dangled her toes in the water, which was surprisingly warm. Maybe she could do this after all. She crossed her arms over her chest and scrunched her shoulders as she looked around again for other people. She wanted to make sure Carson hadn't changed his mind either.

Nope, she was alone. She looked down at her sweatshirt, seeing the white Eastern Ambulance logo emblazoned over her left breast. She pulled the sweatshirt over her head.

She had better hurry, because the water might be warm, but the air wasn't. She pulled off her T-shirt, then leaned from hip-to-hip to tug off her jeans. She folded them and placed them neatly on a nearby root.

For a moment she sat there in just her bra and panties, until the openness and exposure overcame her hesitation and fear. She ran her hands through her hair, down the back of her neck, and around to the front.

Oh, she thought, she had forgotten her necklace. Her hands rested just a minute on the small diamond flower, then reached back to remove it. Her hands were cold, though, and they trembled as she struggled with the tiny clasp. After a minute of frustration, she gave up. She grasped the pendant and gave it a tug. The delicate chain snapped, and she poured it out of her hand until it all sat in a little pile on her sweatshirt.

As she reached back with both hands to unclasp her bra, she saw more of her own body below her in the moonlight and realized how pale she was. She wondered if she should start tanning, then thought that it was probably just the moonlight. She was a healthy white, a contrast to the darkness around her.

Her bra slipped onto the pile, as did her panties. She inched off the root into the water. It wasn't as warm as she had expected, but she quickly waded to the drop-off, took a deep breath, and submerged herself by buckling her knees. Without thinking, she leaned forward and swam underwater, deeper into the lake—into the darkness where she could see nothing. The black water streamed past her face and through her hair, over her shoulders and down her legs with every stroke. Finally, when her breath grew short, she lifted her chin, then her chest and her legs. She rose toward the moonlight and gasped for air at the surface.

Katie shivered from the cold, or from delight. She thought of her father waiting at her apartment, his heart breaking. But she didn't feel bad. It would be a release for him. She was here, not there, where he wanted her, and he had to get used to that fact. Even if *he* didn't get used to it, she was used to it now, and that mattered more. Carson would deal with his emotions and move on. He had plenty of ways to do that. Her father's actions toward Carson did not oblige her to make it up to him. Eric was sad, and for that she was sorry, but she tried not to think about that now.

She dove forward again, scissor-kicks driving her into the deep. What a feeling this was! Her heart overflowed with such joy that she was almost sad that the rest of her life lacked so much of it. She had been trapped—by herself, and by her friends and family. She wouldn't let that happen anymore. When she did, everyone suffered—mostly herself. She had things she wanted to do. She had dreams. She had a world to see, and she would see it with the people she chose. That would make her happy as well as the people around her. She had that power, and she didn't even know it until now.

Her new thoughts slowly led to more new thoughts. There were other things she needed to do. She needed to help others escape the traps of their own lives and become empowered—empowered to be themselves, not confined by the vagaries of men. She had come to this realization by the time she returned to the shore.

What were their names, she asked herself. I hope I can find them in the phone book. So many people would not want me to do this, but she needs help. Their names were the Andersons, and they lived on Seventy-first Street, she remembered. I'm sure they're in the phone book. When I get back, she told herself, I'm going to look them up. If Lynda needs a place to hide for a while, she can hide with me. It's my life, and that's my decision, and it will be good for both of us. Besides, what's the worst that could happen?

26.

After leaving Carson and Katie, Eric climbed into his car, but he didn't start it right away. He leaned back in his seat and absorbed the momentous events of the past half-hour. This was it. There would be no more Eastern Ambulance in a few short months. He had lost his job. He'd lost Katie too. Apparently, she had no special concern for him, or it wasn't as strong as her desire for Carson. Why do women always choose the bad boys?

Eric's thoughts were interrupted by people getting into the cars around him. He couldn't just sit in the parking lot. He actually thought about just going home, but being alone sounded too depressing, so he went to P.O. Pears. He didn't know that anyone was actually going there, but it was a safe bet. Even if most of them were still at the City-County Building, they were eventually headed there. Still, it was a depressing prospect. The disaster of the county council meeting would have been made tolerable if he'd been the one driving off with Katie. But he wasn't, and that was the worst disaster of all.

In the parking lot on the other side of the building, Mark Rader approached his own truck. He knew there was going to be a party at Fire Station One, and he looked forward to it. More than that, he wanted to talk to Eastern Medics. He came out to the parking lot early hoping he could catch Dave or Hank or Carson so that he could offer lip service to their defeat. The night would only be half as sweet if they flew off to their station or P.O. Pears, escaping before he could talk to them. He wanted to see the look on their faces. He wanted to see the defeat in their eyes.

As he made his way between the cars, he saw Carson Treffer in the distance. Perfect! He had to hurry to catch him. That was just like Carson to try and sneak away so quickly. Something else caught his eye. It was Captain O'Malley's daughter, Katie, walking with

Carson toward his pickup. Mark hid behind his own truck. His exultation quickly turned to anger.

Mark had tried to talk to Katie many times in the past. Not too long ago, she was just a fifteen-year-old girl, but even then he knew she would grow to be beautiful. Now she was a woman, and just as beautiful as he had expected. In the past, he'd been cautious in talking to her because of her dad's position. Though Mark was O'Malley's self-proclaimed protégé, O'Malley was very protective of his daughter, and Mark was smart enough to bide his time. She was almost ten years younger than he was, but in time, he knew that difference would grow small. Every time he talked to her, she showed no interest, and at times had been curt with him.

Now she worked at Eastern, hanging out with Carson, and walking alone with him to his truck. Mark stood behind his own vehicle and watched as they stood close, talking. They were too far away to see much or hear anything, but he saw her glance over her shoulder a few times, and he could easily see Carson smiling at her.

Soon she walked briskly away from Carson toward her own car. It looked like she was in a hurry, like she had a plan—like *they* had a plan. His imagination went wild, and for the first time, she looked cheap to him. How could she sink to Carson Treffer's level?

Carson pulled his truck past her car, and she followed just behind. Sure enough, he knew it! Mark climbed into his own truck and followed. The firefighter party could wait. Besides, O'Malley would want to know about this.

Several minutes later, Mark was certain—Katie was following Carson. Were they going to his apartment? He thought about her as a sweet fifteen-year-old girl again. Her father was so proud of how upright and chaste she was, but look at what she'd turned into. It was almost unbelievable! So unbelievable he knew it was Carson's fault. Rader had seen him date more women than he could remember. The same wiles he turned onto those girls, he had now turned onto Katie. What was his deal? Did he have to hoard every woman, even Katie!

The traffic through downtown was tight, and at each stoplight, Mark lost ground. He had a hard time spotting Katie's small car, and he could only see Carson's truck in the distance.

There! As Mark sat at a stoplight, he saw Carson's truck turn several blocks ahead, and Katie's car three or four spots behind. They had turned down Ninth Street. He didn't know where they were going, but Katie was definitely not heading to her aprtment. He waited for the light to turn green, a very frustrating feeling for a man used to lights turning green at his approach. When it did, it was too late, and he knew it. He sped down Ninth, but couldn't find them. After ten minutes of searching, he gave up. But he had seen enough—enough to know that Katie and Carson were up to no good.

Mark pulled off the street and wondered what to do. He was miserable, and that was so unfair! His dream of the past few years had just come true, and this was supposed to be a night to gloat. Instead, Carson made him burn yet again. Could anyone feel the way he was feeling now?

Her father? Yes, he would burn inside, but it would be different, and truthfully, Mark did not want to be the one to tell him. Oh, he hated those Eastern guys! How could they make him feel this way on this night? How did they still win? He wanted *them* to feel this way. That's why he came into the parking lot in the first place—to see *them* miserable.

Then it dawned on him. He knew that Carson and Katie were part of a trio. The third leg—*he* was probably having the most miserable night of all. That is, if he even knew about this. And even better, if he knew, he would probably put a stop to it. Yep, that was it! There was still a way Mark could achieve everything he wanted to accomplish tonight and possibly stop everything he wanted to stop.

Eric arrived at P.O. Pears sooner than the rest of the Eastern crowd. They had probably lingered in the hallway outside the county council chamber. But that was okay; they'd be here soon enough, he thought.

"I'll have another beer, Steve," he said, motioning to the bartender. Steve poured another Red from the spigot and placed the glass in front of Eric.

What a day! What a week! It had started with so much promise and hope. He had one of the most memorable afternoons in recent memory. Everything was going so well. Now what? In two-and-a-half lousy months he would be without a job. He would probably ask

Toby Dunham, the Eastern-Medic-turned-carpenter, for a job. He had never drywalled before, and he wondered if he would hate it.

How depressing—drywalling? It would be hard for Katie to respect that. What was he doing with his life anyway? It seemed like he'd had a purpose with Eastern, but drywalling or building decks or whatever it was that Toby did—that was a dead end. Working for someone else, making minimum wage with no benefits—he would not be respected. He would be someone without a future.

He had been going somewhere once, when he attended the university. But he didn't like studying. He wanted to be out there doing something, and that was why he left. That was why he took the job with Eastern, and he hadn't regretted it until now.

"Steve!" he said to the bartender.

"Yeah, man."

"I'll definitely take another one of those."

"Comin' right up," he said. "You guys must've lost the contract, huh? You usually don't drink much."

"Yep, ole buddy, we lost the contract. They had us from the beginning, ya know. The county council didn't even care what anyone had to say. Really, we lost a long time ago."

"So, where are all your friends?" he asked, and passed Eric another beer. "Where's Carson and the rest of your people?"

"Well, Steve, the rest of my people are sitting back at mighty City Hall devising ways to make themselves think they're not defeated. And Carson . . ." He took a deep breath. "He's out havin' some sort of fun."

Steve read between the lines. "Oh," he said, leaning both hands on the counter. "I tell you what. This one's on me, but it should probably be your last."

"All right. I appreciate that. You know? You're a friend I can count on, Steve. But don't worry, I can pay for it. And I'll still be able to pay for it next year, if you're wondering about that."

"I'm not wondering about it, Eric," he said before giving him a sad look. He left to tend to other customers.

Yep, Eric said to himself, if I wasn't blue-collar before, I sure am now. Steve, he thought to himself, here's three dollars I earned from half-an-hour of drywallin'. It was tough, and I'm dusty, and this cold beer will really hit the spot.

He took a deep gulp and almost didn't notice the man who slid onto the stool beside him. He swallowed and looked over.

"Holy shit, Rader!" he said. "Just when I thought my night couldn't get any worse."

Mark smiled and ordered a beer.

"So, I can't imagine what brings you here, Mark?" Eric said.

"What do you mean, Eric? It's been a long, stressful night, and I need a cold one."

Eric stared forward without looking at him. "From what I hear, Mark, you can get those down at the station."

Rader paused an imperceptible second, then reached for his beer. "That's what you hear, huh?"

"Yep, that's what I hear."

"So, Eric," he said, turning toward him, "I hope there's no hard feelings over what happened tonight."

"Ah shit, Mark. Don't start feeding me that crap! *Yes*, there are hard feelings! We didn't have a fair shot from the beginning!"

"Well, actually, I think the entire process *was* fair, but that's not what I'm talkin' about."

Eric looked at him. "What do you mean?"

"I mean, I hope there's no hard feelings between you and Carson. You know, with him and Katie hooking up tonight or whatever it is they're doing."

"How do you know about that?"

"Oh, I just saw them sneaking off together. I didn't know you knew. You know where they went?"

"That's none of your business."

"Oh, sorry." There was a pause when no one said anything, then Mark continued, "Probably doesn't matter where they went at first anyway, because we all know where they'll end up."

"And where's that?"

"At Carson's apartment, I'm sure."

Eric didn't say anything.

"Yeah, I saw them driving away together . . . sneaking away, looking over their shoulders, hoping no one would see their little affair."

Eric wished someone would turn off the jukebox. It was so cliché, he thought, but the steel guitar was making him extra sad right now.

"They're not having an affair, Mark."

Mark forced a fake laugh. "Oh, c'mon, Eric. I think we can all be grownups about this. You know how Carson is. He's probably mad and upset with the world and has only one thing on his mind."

Eric couldn't disagree.

"And poor Katie. She feels sorry for him and will probably do anything to make him feel better. The poor Eastern Ambulance hero did everything he could, but it wasn't enough in the end. Yeah, she'll do her duty for him."

Eric wanted to punch Mark but held back. He felt he was two seconds away from breaking into tears. He could feel it and had to cut it off. He wanted to think Mark was full of it but couldn't.

"That's fine," Eric said, his voice cracking a little. He held his glass up as if to drink but was trying to cover his eyes. "They're my friends, and I want them to be happy."

"Yeah," Mark returned, "I saw them heading to Carson's place. I can just about guess that they're happy all right. God, I wonder what it would be like to fuck her!"

Eric slammed his glass on the bar but took a deep breath. "Go to hell, Mark!"

"Oh, I'm sorry man. I didn't know. Were you were interested in her or anything like that?"

Eric took another swig and cleared his glass. "That's none of your business!"

"What are you talking about! Now you're making me feel like an idiot. Here I am talking about them having sex over at Carson's, and you've got feelings for her."

"They're not having sex!"

Mark looked at Eric with mock disbelief.

"Katie wouldn't do that," Eric said.

"Well, what do you think she's doing at his apartment then?"

Eric rubbed his forehead and didn't have an answer.

"C'mon, Eric," Mark continued, "grow up. You know you'd be doing the same thing if you were in his shoes."

"No, actually, I wouldn't."

"Why not?"

"Because I wouldn't want to do that to her."

"You wouldn't?"

"I mean I would, but I would wait for the right time, like when we got married, or at least after we'd been dating for a while."

Rader laughed again, but he didn't have to force it anymore. Thank God for this Eric kid. Finally, he was having fun again.

"You mean to tell me you thought you guys were getting married someday?"

"No, that's not what I meant."

"It sounded like that."

No response.

"Well, I hope you don't plan on marrying her now, buddy. It would be awfully awkward at the backyard barbeque with your wife thinking about that wonderful night she held your friend in her arms and soothed away his sadness. Isn't it crazy," Mark continued, "how someone's life can be screwed up by one night of indiscretion?"

"Mark, do you really think that's what they're doing over there?"

"Eric, you know Carson better than I do, and I know you've heard more conquest stories than I have. You tell me."

Eric dropped his forehead into his hand, and his eyes grew watery. Despite Eric's efforts to shield it, Mark saw it and was feeling better.

"Think about it, Eric. Before the night's up, Carson is going to be teaching her all he knows about sex. I mean, I don't know if they're doing it yet, but unless something happens before then, they sure as hell will be doing it before the night's over. It might take a few wine coolers first."

Eric stood abruptly. "I've gotta put a stop to this." He stumbled a little. "I've gotta stop this for Katie's sake!"

Mark nodded in affirmation.

"I kept letting this happen, thinking it was all good . . . good . . . what's the word?"

"Intentions?" Mark said.

"Yeah, intentions! But I'm not gonna let him do this!"

"You know what, Eric, you're right. Carson gets his way far too often."

Before the bartender even noticed, Eric put some money on the bar, picked up his car keys, and was gone. Mark turned back to the counter and casually sipped his beer, feeling much better than he had before. He only wished he could see how it played out.

Captain Mike O'Malley sat in his three-quarter ton truck a block away from Katie's apartment. He was parked—no headlights, no engine—just sitting, watching, and fretting. He looked at his watch again. It had been forty minutes since she said she'd be home in ten.

"Damn that girl."

He sat in the silence and watched for any sign of her car. Finally, he picked up his cell phone and pushed her speed-dial number. It rang several times before her sweet voice came on the answering service, but he didn't leave a message. Maybe she didn't hear the phone, he thought. He tried again with the same result. Again he left no message. He didn't want her to know that he had been looking for her. He wondered where she was until he couldn't think about it anymore. He started the engine and pulled away so quickly that everyone on the street was startled by the screech of tires.

Within fifteen minutes, Eric was at Carson's door. As a Medic and a self-promoted responsible person, he had never driven drunk before. But he had tonight, and was more than lucky to have made it to Carson's apartment alive and intact.

He didn't see Katie's car, but he hadn't looked around back. Besides, she might have left it someplace else. Carson's truck was there, though.

He banged on the door, and his heart raced. Oh, dear God, he thought, don't let me see something I don't want to see. He could never be Carson's friend again.

He waited a few seconds then banged again. He had to let them know that whoever was at the door was not going away.

Carson, who had only come home some thirty minutes earlier, appeared at the door after a long pause. He wore only hospital scrub-bottoms, and apparently nothing else.

"What the hell, Eric?"

"Let me in."

Carson didn't move out of the way at first, and Eric barged right through his arm. "Where is she?"

"Where is she? What the hell are you talking about?"

"You know what I'm talking about."

"Eric, you're totally drunk!"

"That's beside the point. Is she in there?" he asked, pointing toward the bedroom.

"You're being a total asshole, Eric!"

"No, Carson, I'm not. I'm trying to do the right thing!"

"The right thing? By making sure I don't corrupt Katie?"

"Exactly."

"Thanks. Thanks for thinking that all I am is a corrupter!"

"That's a very hypocritical thing to say right now. Is she here, or did she leave already?"

Carson had no patience for Eric's behavior, so he decided to feed it. "She left already."

"What did you guys do?"

"It's none of your business."

"Oh my God, Carson, please don't tell me—"

"Tell you what?"

"Rader and I pretty much know what you were up to."

"Rader! Did you say, Mark Rader? Eric, have you totally lost your mind? What? What the hell did Mark Rader tell you?"

"Mark and I know that you're only trying to bang her because she's the Captain's daughter!"

Carson's face flushed red at the mere mention of Rader's name. "Is that what you two *geniuses* figured out? I bet that was a real tough conclusion for an imbecile and a drunk!"

"No! I mean, yes! Did you or didn't you?"

"So what if I did? Is that what you want to hear, Eric? Would it be so completely unacceptable for me to say that I did?"

Eric was silent and stared at Carson with anger in his eyes.

"Yes, Eric! How does that make you feel? Yes, I had sex with her. And you know what? It was wonderful . . . for the both of us!"

Eric threw a punch toward Carson's face, but it only landed in Carson's hand. Carson tugged Eric's arm toward him. The sight of Carson's fist was the last thing Eric could remember from that terrible night.

27.

"Hi, this is Katie O'Malley." It was early the next morning. "Is Lynda there?"

"Why yes," an older lady said. "Who did you say this was?"

"It's Katie O'Malley. I know Lynda because my dad works with Lou." In truth, Katie had only talked to Lynda a handful of times, but she figured that was enough to say she knew her.

"Oh, okay," the lady, presumably Lynda's mom, said. "Let me go get her."

A moment later, Lynda was on the phone. "Hello, Katie?"

"Yeah. Hi, Lynda." Katie was suddenly more nervous than she'd expected.

"How are you doing Katie? Is everything okay?"

"Actually, yeah, everything is okay. Things are going well in school and everything."

"I'm glad to hear that. I always knew what a bright girl you were, and that you would go far."

"Thanks, that means a lot."

There was an uncomfortable pause.

"So, Katie, what's up?"

"Well, actually, I'm calling to see how everything is for you?"

There was silence on the other end of the phone before Lynda said, "Well, I'm guessing you've heard that Lou and I are getting a divorce."

"Yes, I have, and I'm so sorry to hear about that."

"Well, you know . . . that's the way life goes sometimes."

Katie tried to think of what to say. "I heard—and I don't know how true this is, but I believe it's true—that Lou has been bothering you and your family a lot over at your parents' place."

Another pause.

"Where did you hear that?"

"I heard it from Jenny Carver at one of my mom's knitting parties."

"Hmm," Lynda said, "I knew I shouldn't have done that. I don't know what I was thinking. And I certainly didn't expect it to become common knowledge."

"Well, what can you expect from that group?" Katie said.

Lynda laughed. It made her realize that Katie wasn't the little girl she used to know. "Yeah, you're right, Katie. I should have known better."

"Lynda," Katie said.

"Yeah."

"The reason I called is that I . . . well, I wanted to see if you . . . I mean, what I mean to say is that I want to invite you to stay at my place if that's true."

"Oh, Katie," Lynda said, feeling her heart break again, as it had done time and time again throughout this ordeal, "I can't—"

"No, let me finish. I have an apartment that no one lives in but me. No one ever comes over here, including my dad or my mom. It's just my place, and if I ever see anybody, I usually go out to see them. If you wanted some place to get away for a while, but still be in town, I would love it if you stayed with me."

Katie heard nothing on the line for several seconds. Then she detected a sigh and quiet sniffling.

"Are you okay, Lynda?"

Lynda pulled herself together. "Yes, I'm fine. I just . . . I just thought that's really nice of you."

"Can I ask you a serious question?"

Another sigh. "Sure."

"Does he abuse you?"

"Wow," Lynda said. "I never dreamed I'd have conversations like this with little Katie O'Malley, but I guess you're not so little anymore, are you."

"No."

"To answer your question—not really. He doesn't really abuse me in the way you're thinking. Only on a few occasions has he become physical during our fights." Her voice grew quieter. "He's grabbed me and choked me a few times for just a little while. But it's verbal and emotional mainly, and that hasn't stopped. He calls me eight, ten times a day. I try to keep it from the kids, but we can't even go anywhere without him calling and bothering . . ." Her sentence broke off with a sigh of exasperation.

"He *does* abuse you, Lynda. If he grabs you and chokes you, that's abuse! That's why I want you to come stay with me. You need to get away from all that crap. He doesn't know my phone number—he wouldn't even know you're here. You could relax awhile without him pestering you."

"Katie," she said, a mother's concern in her voice, "I couldn't ask you to do that."

"Why? There's nothing to ask really. I don't have the nicest of luxuries, but I have a couch and a warm, quiet place to stay that no one would know about. That way you could relieve some of the pressure off your parents for a while."

"Oh, Katie, I really do appreciate it. I just don't know."

"What's there to know, Lynda? You can come for a while, then leave for a while if you want. You won't be disrupting my life at all. Like I said, I don't have people over, and all I do is study when I'm here. If anything, it might be kind of boring for you, but no one will know, and you can relax. Please say you'll do it."

Katie could tell that Lynda's mom was asking her something in the background.

"Hold on a second, Katie," she said, then covered the phone, and all Katie could hear was muffled, incomprehensible talk between the two women.

Lynda got back on the phone. "My mom seems very encouraged by your offer."

"Does she? Good. I just want to help. Will you do it?"

"I tell you what, Katie. I'll think seriously about it, but only if you promise that I won't be disrupting your life at all."

"You won't."

"If I did it, it would only be for short periods, just to rest. Are you sure that wouldn't be a drag on your life?"

"Are you kidding me? It would be fun to have a roommate. Maybe sometime we can rent movies and have a girls' night in."

Lynda laughed at the thought of having fun. She hadn't had that feeling for quite some time, and it surprised her in its novelty.

"So, it's a done deal?" Katie asked.

"I . . . I don't know," Lynda said. "I guess I could come over for just a few days. Maybe you and I can have a little bit of fun, but then

I'll get outta your hair."

"Good," Katie said, genuinely pleased. "I'll give you my address, and sometime when you feel it's appropriate, tell Lou you're going out of town and give me a call. And don't back down. Promise me that. This will be good for you *and* me."

Eric woke with a throbbing headache. He wanted to sleep for several hours more, but the bright light streaming through the windows prevented it. He massaged his head and noticed the swelling around his left eye. He gingerly palmed it with his hand and remembered the events that led to the injury.

He thought about his conversation with Carson, or at least the parts he could remember, and felt saddened deep inside. His mouth was extremely dry; he felt thirst more than he felt pain. He turned his head and a pulsing ache pressed outward from his brain. He was lying on Carson's couch, a blanket over him, and a pillow under his head. Carson had left a glass of water on the coffee table. Eric drank half of it immediately, then noticed a note and a newspaper when he replaced the glass on the table.

He picked up the note. It was from Carson and was straight to the point. "Eric, sorry about last night. What I said wasn't true. Check out the paper. We lost Station Three."

Eric couldn't think about the paper for a moment. Carson's simple revelation—what I said wasn't true—was momentous and had to be processed. He felt immediate relief, and the sunlight bothered him less. Everything was always much better in the morning, he thought. Then remorse sank in. He remembered more and felt like an ass.

To take his mind off the subject, he reached for the paper, and saw the article Carson had circled.

"Landlord Cancels Lease on Eastern Ambulance Station. Fred McCaffrey, the owner of the McCaffrey Business Center and the small garage behind it, has announced that a contract with Eastern Ambulance for the garage will terminate at the end of the month. Eastern's lease on the building expired in July. Rather than renewing

the lease, McCaffrey had offered extensions on a month-by-month basis pending the outcome of Eastern's long political battle to retain control of the County's Emergency Medical Services contract. Last night, the Lancaster County Council voted to terminate the contract and to provide EMS service through the Lancaster County Fire Department. (See EMS, Page A1)

"McCaffrey announced that he had a new tenant for the building who was interested in moving in as soon as possible. Eastern manager, Dave Conrad, expressed disappointment at McCaffrey's actions in a phone call this morning. 'It was never my understanding that Fred would terminate our lease before the end of the year. He basically pulled the rug right out from under our feet.'

"According to Mr. Conrad, McCaffrey asked Eastern to vacate the building by the end of the month. Such a prospect leaves Eastern without the strategically important station for two months, which provides coverage for the southeastern portion of the city. On January 1, the fire department will assume all Emergency Medical Services. 'Certainly,' Conrad continued, 'this puts us in a very difficult position and seriously comprises healthcare coverage in the county.'"

Eric dropped the newspaper on the table and finished his glass of water. He closed his eyes a brief span, hoping to go back to sleep, but he thought about work, and about work without Station Three, and how bitterly cruel the city seemed at the moment.

What time is it, he wondered. He looked for a clock. Damn, it's already past three! He had to work again tonight.

———

"Where's Carson and Eric?" Hank asked Katie that afternoon as they milled around the back of the classroom. It was half past five, and they had just concluded a relatively long meeting. Dave had announced the charter amendment and kicked off the signature drive. The first petition hung on the back wall, and everyone lined up to be among the first of the 10,000 signatures to get the amendment placed on the ballot for the November election. The election was only three weeks away, and the petition was due two weeks before that.

"I don't know. I've been wondering the same thing," Katie said. "Did they know about the meeting?"

"I left messages on both their phones, but I didn't talk to either one. Eric should've been here. He, at least, checks his messages."

"Yeah, I'm surprised."

"They're working tonight," Hank said, "and probably just don't want to come in early."

"I know. I plan on working with them," she said. "I haven't worked with them since they've been on the night shift . . . I mean, if that's okay with you."

"Absolutely," Hank said. "How many ride-alongs you got left?"

"Four, if you include tonight. And I'm real sorry about that, Hank. I know I should be done by now, and that's partly why I'm doing this tonight. I've got to get these knocked out because I know you need me to do some real work on the transfer car."

"It's no problem. You'll get it done soon enough. But you're right—we're hurting on the transfers."

She looked at her watch. "They should be here any minute, I'd think."

"They'd better be."

Katie and Hank got through the line and placed their signatures on the petition. Katie was number thirty-two. She wrote in purposeful, legible script that anyone could read. It was time for her dad and the deputy chief and the county council to stop making all the decisions. It was time for the people to decide, she thought.

She and Hank went down to the garage. They found Carson and Eric already there talking with Tim and Lisa and several others. Carson leaned against the side of E60. It had been repainted, but the new decals had not yet come. The side was stark white. Eric sat in the open rear doors on the patient gurney with the Airway Bag on his lap. He had paused from his inventory and focused on the conversation. He had a swollen, purple eye.

Katie was taken aback by his appearance but didn't want to interrupt Tim who was speaking. She scrunched her eyebrows at Eric in an obvious expression of wonder as to his condition. Though he was happy to see her, he was not happy to have her see him. He turned away, shaking his head as if to say it was nothing.

Tim was talking about their situation in pessimistic terms. "You see, I knew this would happen. That's why I already talked to Toby about work."

"It's not over, Tim," Leslie said.

"Oh, c'mon, Leslie. Can't you read the writing on the wall! We just keep prolonging the inevitable. The County has this thing fixed."

"Hello!" she said sarcastically. "Tim, weren't you just at the same meeting I was at? That's why we're taking the decision out of the County's hands. We'll get the signatures for the amendment, and the citizens will choose."

Tim shook his head. "Les, they're going to win. They'll fight this just as hard as they did with the county council."

"I disagree," Leslie said.

"Carson agrees with me," Tim said, matter-of-factly.

Carson, standing with his arms folded across his chest and the heel of his cowboy boot propped up on a tire, looked up at the others. "Yeah, I agree with Tim. We shouldn't prolong this any more."

"Now, wait a minute!" Hank said, entering the conversation. "What are you guys saying?"

"Oh, c'mon, Hank," Carson said, dropping his boot to the ground. "You really mean to tell me you intend to keep on fighting this? A decision has already been made. There's not even three months left in the year. We're out of arguments, and we're out of time."

"Carson, c'mon, you don't normally talk like this! You mean to tell me that you're done. That's it? The fire department has won? You're gonna let Killion and O'Malley and Rader and all the rest of them have their way after that spectacle last night?"

Carson looked down at his boots, which angered Hank all the more.

"Carson, don't be like this! Don't you think we've got to do it for the people . . . for the patients?"

"What do you mean, Hank?!" Carson said with intensity. "What do you mean? You mean to tell me that this fight is all about the patients? It's not about our jobs? It's not about you guys preserving a company you've had for thirty-five years? What you're telling me is that you sincerely believe the fire department is going to take over, and the people of the city, the *patients* of the city, are going to suffer?"

"Yes, I do. Don't you?"

Carson shook his head. "I used to think that, but not anymore. If that were true, then why are so many patients and concerned parents standing up and voicing their support for the fire department?"

"We've had all those kinds of people stand up for us too, Carson!"

"I know, Hank, but that's my point! It's not black and white! They have their supporters, and we have ours. It all depends on what kind of experience they've had with us. And it depends on their political views."

"Oh, c'mon Carson! You mean to tell me that you . . . *you* of all people, think that the citizens would be better off with the fire department!"

"I don't know, Hank! You tell me! I mean, look at this place. *Look* at this place! We're driving around in piece-of-shit ambulances that don't even run when you need them to. I mean, that fucking thing over there is over fifteen years old! It's a freakin' embarrassment!

"How about this thing?" he said, taking the bag from Eric's lap. "You can't even zip it closed. Hank, we've got bed sheets hung over windows upstairs to block out the light. I'm just saying that sometimes all I have to do is look around to see that we might not have what it takes to do our jobs the right way. We don't even have *three* stations anymore!"

At first, Hank had no reply. He shook his head. "Carson, you're right. We don't have the best equipment. I'll give you that. But we've got the best people, and that's far more important."

This made Carson stop and frown. "I know we do, Hank. I'm not arguing with that. I'm just saying that a little girl might have died a week ago if someone with better equipment wasn't there to bail us out."

"I know, Carson," Hank said, "but that little girl would have been dead already if two people hadn't saved her life first."

Eric looked over at Katie during the pause and saw that her eyes were tearful. He thought about that night and the little girl in his arms, and welled up with emotion. He looked away.

Neither Carson nor anyone else responded.

"Carson, are you saying that you won't sign the petition?" Hank asked.

"Hank, I want to, but I'm not getting my hopes up anymore. Like Tim said, we're just prolonging the inevitable." He looked over at

Tim, then Eric and Katie. "I'm tired of fighting. And after what happened at Twenty-seventh and "O" last week, we're running out of arguments. Everyone saw that on TV, and if we choose to keep fighting, the County is going to make sure they see it even more. It's one thing to be turned down by the commissioners, it's another thing to be shot down by the people."

After a long pause, Hank looked around the room, and said, "All right, Carson. I can understand how you feel. Just know that the majority of us are gonna push on, and we're gonna do what it takes to get those signatures. We've formed a citizen's group, and they're running the whole campaign. What about you, Eric, and what the hell happened to your eye?"

"I had a little too much to drink last night."

"Hmm." Hank grimaced. "And what about the amendment?"

Eric didn't look at Katie but felt her presence anyway. "Yeah, I'll sign it."

"Good, I'm glad to hear that. We can still win this thing, you know."

Eric, feeling not too convinced, said, "Yeah, I know."

Hank turned away and left the garage.

While Tim and the others finished the tail end of their conversation with Carson, Katie approached Eric.

"Eric, what happened?"

"Nothing glamorous," he said. "Like I said, I had a little too much to drink last night and slipped on my way to my apartment."

"You slipped . . . onto what?"

"The railing or something I guess."

"Let me see it."

Eric cocked his head to one side. "Does it hurt?" Katie reached to touch his eye. Several feet away, Carson noticed the gesture.

"It throbs a little," Eric said, "but not bad."

She looked in both his eyes now with a soft expression. "Why did you drink so much?"

"Why? I don't know. I was just feeling . . . it was just a terrible night, ya know."

"Just because of the vote?"

"Yeah, what else could there be?"

"I don't know; I'm just making sure."

The others had left, and Carson joined Katie and Eric. "Haven't seen much of you lately, Kate" he said. "How many more ride-alongs you have left?"

"Just three, after tonight."

"After tonight?" Eric asked.

"Yeah, I thought I'd do a night shift tonight."

"Good," Carson said. "That's the first good news I've heard in several days."

"Same here," Eric said. "It hasn't been the same without you."

She smiled at them, feeling that she had missed them too.

Carson stepped forward and draped his arm around her shoulders. "Welcome to the night shift. It's about time you see the seedier side of Lincoln."

28.

Eric wondered if he was getting old fast. He found himself saying that he couldn't do this for long; he was losing his edge. It was nearly seven o'clock the next morning, and he, Carson, and Katie were on their sixth call, and this one would likely postpone their turnover. There had been a car accident—a DUI, of course—a heart attack at a party, an alcohol poisoning at a fraternity, a battered wife case, and even a prostitute cut by a bottle. On the surface, Eric thought, Lincoln shined like a pearl in the heart of America, and well she deserved that reputation. But as the majority of people lay their heads to rest, this city, just like every city, wakes up to a new world, like the giant pearl picked off the ground and found to be corroded and decayed on the bottom. Eric pictured himself replacing the pearl in the ground so that it could shine again. He loved Lincoln, but if he did the night shift much longer, he was afraid the pearl would forever lose its luster. They were on their way to a potential suicide.

No matter how much Eric tried to reverse his days, it wouldn't work. He was so tired. He looked over at Carson to see if he was similarly affected. No, he drove with as much concentration as ever. Eric felt his eye throb as his heart worked hard to wake him up. Neither Eric nor Carson talked about what had happened between them the previous night, other than one comment by Eric, who had said, "Thanks for the note. I'm sorry I was such an ass." Carson waved at Eric like it was nothing, and from then on, that's what it was—nothing.

Katie leaned her head and shoulder through the space into the cab, watching the houses go by as Carson drove. It was growing light. According to the 911 call, there was a body hanging in the living room of a small ranch home in one of the older neighborhoods. A child had seen it while cutting through the backyard after spending the night at a friend's. A terrible thing for a child to see, Eric thought. Carson cut the siren as they approached the small, white home—a shoebox with two windows on either side of small porch—a house with a nose and eyes.

Adjacent to the nose, Carson threw the transmission into Park and flipped the engine to high idle, a small intrusion into the life of this sleepy neighborhood. He had been successful again, and placed a check on the tally sheet. Even the police had not yet arrived. Carson debated a moment while Eric and Katie removed the equipment from the back. In the twilight, Carson saw a man standing in his yard several houses away. He could barely make him out but could see he had a large black dog on a leash, the two of them standing and staring at the ambulance. Carson thought about the police again. This could turn out to be nothing, just a kid with an overactive imagination or a cruel sense of humor. But if it was true, it was a just a suicide, their work would be done quickly, and the police would take care of the rest.

Carson thought about whether he should go in alone. It wasn't necessary for everyone to view a thing like this. Some memories don't go away. But Katie and Eric, each carrying a bag as they followed Carson onto the porch, would not be turned away, and he knew it.

Carson knocked. No response. He tested the doorknob and found it open. He cracked the door and yelled inside. "Eastern Ambulance! We're coming in!"

The door opened on a morbid scene—into the kitchen, which ran both left and right. A bar separated the kitchen from the living room except for an opening in the middle. On the other side of that bar, framed perfectly between two pillars on the counter, hung a body—a shirtless man, perhaps in his mid-twenties, his head and neck contorted by a belt that hung from a bicycle hook in the ceiling. A large window opened onto the backyard behind him, a tepid light pouring through it as the twilight intensified.

Carson closed his eyes in a moment of quiet sadness for the deceased, then opened the door more fully. He, Katie, and Eric stepped into the dimly lit kitchen. Standing to the left of Carson, Katie followed Eric's cue and let her bag slide off her shoulder to the floor. Eric glanced at her and saw a blank, shocked countenance that made him even sadder. He looked back at the man, who had clearly been dead for some time.

Eric's eyes adjusted to the darkness inside, and he saw what the others saw—a legible script made with a black marker covered the man's bare skin. Upon his chest and belly were the words, "Sara, you did this to me." His right arm was more difficult to read. "How could you do this to me, Sara?" it said. His left arm: "I know where you were last night . . ." And written in smaller letters under that, "and all the other nights." Finally, above his bulging eyeballs, written on his purple face, were the words, "I hate you."

The hatred, the despondency, the acidic, cruel emotion was palpable. A freight train called the real world slammed Katie in the face. Katie could feel death in her stomach, making her want to vomit, but she held on, tried to put on a brave face, tried to look past the man. Looking out the window, she was again horrified. Behind the hedges at the back of the yard crouched several terrified children, trying hard not to be seen, staring at the ghastly sight inside. They wore book bags and were dressed for school, but had evidently been diverted from the bus stop by the rumors. The expressions on their faces said they were too shocked to leave or move or go to school.

"Carson," Katie said. She found it difficult to say, so merely pointed out the window.

"I know," Carson said. "We have to close the blinds."

Katie, anxious to confront her fear and to spare the children her own sickening grief, took a few steps toward the opening in the bar.

"I'll do it," Carson barked. As Katie stepped into the living room, Carson lurched forward to pass her. Unbeknownst to the two of them, there was a taut string running an inch above the floor between the two cabinets and crossing the floor at the seam between the old linoleum and the stained carpet. Fixed to a nail on the right side, it ran through several eyehooks and wound like a snake around the room until it reached the back left corner. Passing through the last eyehook behind the loveseat, it ended under a blanket, tied to the trigger of a shotgun—a shotgun pointed at the opening in the bar.

Both Katie and Carson tripped the line at the same time, but the combined force of Katie's step and Carson's launch was too much for the system to handle. The string pulled the shotgun from its mount at the same time it pulled the trigger. The blast shook the house and instinctively sent all three medics to the ground. Eric saw the birdshot as it passed through the bar into the kitchen cabinets.

"Are you all right?!" Eric yelled as he scrambled toward the other two.

"I'm fine. I'm fine," Carson said, reaching out to Katie. She leaned back against the bar, her hand pressed against her left side. Carson and Eric saw the gaping shotgun hole in the bar just a little to her left. If she had been hit, it had only been by a few stray pieces of shot. Sensing there was no more danger, or perhaps ignoring it, Carson and Eric made their way to either side of her.

"Are you hurt?" Carson asked.

"Yes," she said, wincing in pain. She moved her hand, revealing a small spot of blood near her waist at the very edge of her shirt. Eric pointed at a rip in the thigh of her jeans. He gently peeled the cloth apart. "It's an even cut," he reported aloud, "half an inch deep and about three inches long. Doesn't look bad." The small shot cut the side of her leg like a knife, but this wound at least was certainly nothing serious.

Katie began to unbutton her shirt as the police entered the building. They heard the gunshot, directed the firefighters to wait outside, and came running with their weapons drawn. When the life of a firefighter or EMS worker is jeopardized, the police grow heedless and less tolerant.

"Police! We're comin' in!"

"Come in!" Carson yelled.

They entered and quickly surveyed the scene. The shotgun had been jerked and blasted out from under the blanket. The body, the shotgun, the string quickly told the story.

Carson and Katie both finished unbuttoning her uniform shirt. There was still only a small amount of blood. Carson pulled his shears from his holster and cut Katie's undershirt up to her arm. He found a small entrance wound and an exit wound an inch above her pelvis. A small trickle of blood oozed from each hole, but nothing more.

"It may have gotten a little muscle," Carson said, "but it looks mostly like adipose tissue."

"Are you saying I'm fat?" Katie said, laughing between shallow breaths of pain.

"No, just human," he said.

"How bad does it hurt, Katie," Eric asked.

"It stings bad," she said, looking down at the wound, "but I'm okay." Feeling more confident about her condition, she lifted her leg to look at the other wound. She touched it and winced, then slouched back against the bar. Looking to her left, she gasped at the large hole in the cabinet. "Oh my God!" she said. She looked up at Eric.

"You're not kidding," he said. "You're okay, though."

"Let's get you outta here," Carson said. "Eric, go get the cot."

"Right."

One of the policemen asked, "Is she gonna be okay?"

"Yeah, she's all right. There's kids out there. We were just gonna close the blinds and wait for you guys."

The policeman looked outside and nodded his head. He pointed for the other guy to take care of it. Then he looked at Katie. "You're very lucky."

"I know."

"We'll get statements from you later."

"Okay."

Eric returned in a minute with the cot. He had easily ignored the firefighters' questions. It was Engine Seven, guys he didn't know very well anyway. He lowered the cot halfway to the ground, and he and Carson helped Katie onto it. She was probably capable of walking, but that was beside the point. They strapped her in and wheeled her toward the ambulance. A faded blue car had just parked on the other side of the street, and a distressed young woman hurried feverishly up the sidewalk.

Holding an IV bag over his head, Carson looked up at the woman and saw the many questions on her face, the panicky fear filling her eyes. "Are you Sara?" he asked.

"Yes." She grew more panicky at the notion that he knew her.

"Don't go in there," Carson said, looking away in contempt as he wheeled past her with the cot. A policeman came behind her to block her path to the house.

The firefighters gathered round. Carson took ten seconds to tell them what happened and to describe Katie's minor flesh wounds while he and Eric slid the cot into E60. Carson stepped inside while Eric paused at the door. He looked at Katie and started to close the doors.

"Wait, Eric!" Katie said. Eric froze and Carson stopped to look at her.

275

"Carson," Katie said, turning toward him. "Do you mind if I ride with Eric?"

Carson looked out at Eric somewhat dazed. "Oh . . ."

Katie felt awkward. "It's nothing against your patient care or anything. I mean, it doesn't really matter, I guess."

"No . . ." Carson said. "That's fine, I can drive." Standing motionless for a second more, he exited and handed Eric the clipboard. "Yeah, that's no problem." Eric felt like he should say something, but didn't know what it would be.

On the way to the hospital, Carson wrestled with his internal demons. He glanced up at the rearview mirror and saw Eric holding Katie's hand, which was ninety percent of the care she needed anyway. He didn't drive with lights and sirens, but he drove fast. He wanted to put distance between them and that putrid house. The house reeked of death.

Death, himself, had been there, had committed a crime, but didn't leave. He was still there when Carson, Eric, and Katie arrived—standing down the street, or crouching in the bushes next to the children—watching, waiting, just like the dark person standing in the corner near his deathbed as a child, just like the shadow with a shepherd's staff in Afghanistan. Carson shuddered at the thought of him squatting next to the innocent children. But He wasn't after them, was he. He wasn't even after Sara. He was—Stop! Carson grew terrified at his own thoughts, scared of the notion he was losing it.

At the hospital, he grabbed a cup of coffee and walked out of the garage into the sunlight. He calmed down, but the bright sun did nothing but further open his mind to the grim reality.

Inside, Eric sat with Katie in her emergency room. Her leg had already been stitched up by a doctor, and a portable X-ray was shot of her side. The doctor was gone for now, waiting for the X-rays to come back, but he knew he would find no birdshot in her. He would release her to go home shortly with instructions to change the dressings on her side. She was lucky.

Katie lay on her pillow, still holding Eric's hand.

"Thank you, Eric."

"For what?"

"For being there for me."

"I didn't do anything."

"You didn't have to do anything. I'm just glad you were there . . . and that you're here with me. I don't miss anyone else right now, and I don't feel alone."

"I'll always be there for you, Katie, if you want me to, no matter what we do, or where our lives may take us."

She turned her head and smiled at him. After a minute or two, she said, "Eric, I have to tell you something."

Eric was curious, pensive when he looked at her. "All right."

She then proceeded to tell him about Lynda. She had been meaning to tell him anyway, but she really wanted to tell him now. Besides, she needed an ally. She knew her parents would rush to her apartment as soon as she called them, or sooner, once they received word she was released from the hospital, and she had to ensure Lynda was not there.

Eric used Katie's cell phone to call her apartment. He talked to Lynda, told her what happened, and assured her over and over that "little Katie" was going to be all right. Katie then got on the phone and explained that she had to go back to her parents' for a few days, but that it was only temporary. It would be best if Lynda was not at her apartment for a while, but that she would be terribly saddened if she didn't come back once things blew over.

29.

As the weeks of October passed by, Eric and Carson continued to plug away at their jobs. They had no more shifts with Katie, though she did ride with Leslie during the day. Her father and mother were of course thrown into a tizzy about her injuries, and there was a small newspaper article dedicated to that morning's events. Yet the doctor's prognosis was correct—they were only mild flesh wounds that mostly healed in a matter of days. She was back to work in a week.

Work was a great juxtaposition for Eric—Carson's continued cynicism conflicting with the enthusiasm of the Amendment activities. Carson did start a new fire department kill sheet in E60 because he had accidentally left the old one in E22. That ambulance went to the shop for scrap, and Joe, the mechanic, bought the past-its-prime ambulance from the company to turn it into a camping van. Meanwhile, Dave Conrad, Hank, and the Public Affairs Officer worked diligently with the citizens' group to garner support. They set up a stand at a city festival to solicit signatures.

The citizens' group was called C.E.A.S.—Citizens for Equitable Ambulance Selection. Under the C.E.A.S. banner, volunteers—some of them Eastern employees and others, concerned citizens—manned the booth, asking passersby if they would like to sign the petition for the Charter Amendment.

"We're not asking you to choose an ambulance provider," they argued. "We want to create a non-partisan body of doctors and government officials to reevaluate the whole process next year. With your signature, we will get a referendum placed on the ballot in next month's election, and that referendum will determine whether or not we postpone the county council's decision and create the Ambulance Selection Committee."

It was not difficult to get signatures. Most people didn't have a stake one way or the other but signed the form because it was noncommittal in nature.

Eric worked the booth on one of his days off. He had promised

Hank that he would support the Amendment, and Katie asked if he would pull a four-hour shift with her. All Eric had to do was sit back and keep the paperwork straight while Katie brought in the signatures—especially from the men.

"Why sure, honey," one old man said. "You look like you should be out here selling lemonade, not doing something as serious as this."

"Well, sir, I don't like lemonade." Katie smiled, not caring how she got the signatures. She casually rebuffed the men as soon as they signed, looking for the next passerby to reel in. "Excuse me! Excuse me, sir, can I talk to you a minute?"

Eric had fun watching her. The advantage he had over all the other men was that he didn't have to leave her. After a while, he became more comfortable soliciting people himself. Before the four hours were over, there was an almost implicit understanding between the two that Eric concentrated on the women, and Katie on the men. It was one of the most productive four-hour stretches that C.E.A.S. ever had.

———

Without Katie, work turned into drudgery. Medic One now had to share the station with Medic Three. The firefighters were exuberant in their county board victory and showed only the slightest worry about the Charter Amendment. Carson put on an outward show of determination by beating the fire department to the scene and by keeping his tally sheets religiously, but after Katie was injured he merely went through the motions. His anger was no longer directed at the fire department only, but at the county, the drunk drivers, the demanding, manipulative patients, and the violent families.

Despite his mood, Carson did sign the petition after only a few days. A lot of people asked him to, including Katie, and he knew they needed him to be a team player. Yet, his cynical predictions did not fall short of the mark. Just as soon as C.E.A.S. unfurled its banner, another citizens' group sprang from the ranks of firefighters' wives and disgruntled patients. They called themselves S.A.A.F.E—Securing an Appropriate Ambulance Future for Everyone. They posted signs in yards with the words, "Everyone wins with the fire department—Better, Faster, Cheaper." A half-page ad in the newspaper broke it down this way:

> "BETTER – Better equipment. Vehicle failures should not be a reason for the death of a loved one.
> FASTER – Faster Response. No more waiting for an ambulance to come to your door.
> CHEAPER – Cheaper costs. No one should worry about an expensive bill when calling 911.
> Vote "NO" on the Charter Amendment. The Lancaster County Fire Department IS the Answer."

Carson was livid when he read the ad. It was a targeted attack and blatantly misleading, he argued. He knew the fire department planned on having no more ambulances than did Eastern, and he knew they would not be street-basing.

Slapping the paper with the back of his hand, he said "Read this! 'No one should worry about an expensive bill when they call 911!' That's ridiculous! They make it sound like they won't send *any* bill, which most people probably think anyway since they're the fire department. They're only promising forty dollars cheaper than us!"

But the most galling aspect of all was the first point: "Vehicle failures should not be a reason for the death of a loved one." It was clear that was a direct reference, and the city news stations kept that event fresh in people's minds. When covering the ambulance campaign and reporting the fire department's three planks, they added, "This is a clear reference by S.A.A.F.E. to the incident last month when an Eastern ambulance failed to start during an emergency." And truest of all to Carson's predictions, the television flashed the scene of Eric and Carson offloading the little girl and her mom from E22 and wheeling her into the fire department ambulance—from a small, worn-out van to a large, beautiful, red ambulance. Either the TV station was complicit in the department's campaign, or the planners at S.A.A.F.E just knew how to get the press they wanted.

The reminders rekindled old emotions.

"I am so tired of them making such a big deal of that," Eric said one night when they posted downtown.

"I told you, Hank, and everybody that would happen," Carson said.

"I know."

For a moment Carson was silent. "They wouldn't be able to show anything if we hadn't turned the damned vehicle off."

Eric looked over at him. "What's that supposed to mean?"

"What do you mean, 'what's that supposed to mean?' It's pretty straightforward."

"You're saying I turned it off?"

"You never denied that you did, Eric. We all know how jumpy you can get in an emergency."

"What?"

"Well, did you turn it off or didn't you?"

"We've been over this a thousand times. I don't know."

Carson shook his head in frustration. Eric could tell his mind was made up.

"If I did, Carson, I'm sorry. You're right, I can get a little flighty sometimes. I'm not a veteran like you—literally."

"Don't worry about it, Eric. The bottom line is we shouldn't have been out there in that piece of shit anyway."

"Yeah, maybe that's one of the fire department's points that actually *is* legitimate."

"Maybe so." Carson paused in thought. "You know what, Eric?"

"What?"

"They say the average Paramedic burns out after only eight years."

"Yeah?"

"Counting my Army time, I've done it for almost ten, and I'm finally burned out."

Eric stared out the windshield. "Really?"

"Yeah, I think so."

"Have you felt this way for a while?"

"Mmm, not too long, but I really feel it now. Obviously a lot of it has to do with the fire department and all."

"Obviously."

"But I'm just tired of it in general."

"Yeah, I'm kind of the same way, I guess."

"Are you?"

"Yeah, I feel like I'm growing old fast in this job."

"Try doing it for ten years, Eric. I used to love it, but now it's just wearing me down."

"You didn't seem too worn down a year ago?"

Carson rested his right hand on top of the steering wheel and placed his chin in the other. "No, I wasn't . . . a year ago. What a difference a year can make, huh?"

"No kidding. A year ago, we had no doubts. Now we're two months away from drywalling." Eric paused a second. "Do you think the Charter Amendment has a chance?"

"Not really."

"But you have to admit there's a chance?"

"There's a chance, but even if we did win, we'll get beat up again next year, and maybe lose again. The County won't create a fair, independent board. The Fire Union pulls too many strings."

Carson's pessimistic attitude was, as usual, starting to sound wise to Eric. Carson looked in the long term; it wasn't about this month or this vote. It was an ongoing struggle, and it wasn't going away.

"So," Eric asked, "if we lose, are you through being a Paramedic?"

"Yeah, maybe even if we win."

"Even if we win? That's a bummer. Have you told anyone else?"

"No."

"They can probably tell, though."

"Yeah, they probably can."

"What will you do?"

"I don't know for sure."

"Have you started looking at other jobs?"

"Yeah."

Eric was surprised. Carson said, "I've been looking at stuff in Oklahoma and Texas."

"Like what?"

"Just . . . all kinds of stuff. Construction mostly."

"Construction?"

"Yeah, I've already been offered a job in Tulsa."

"Really? But you're gonna wait till January, right?"

"Yeah, I'll wait. I won't bail, but I've started packing."

"Wow." Eric grew sadder by the minute. "I guess I might be doing construction for a while too."

"What, with Toby?"

"Yeah."

"You shouldn't do that."

"What do you mean?"

"You shouldn't work for him. You're still young. Go back to college and make something of yourself."

Eric reflected a moment. "Yeah, I guess that would be the smart thing to do."

"What do you mean, 'you guess?' Of course it would be the smart thing to do, you idiot."

"But," Eric said, "I'm already older, and I've been out of it for a few years."

Carson shook his head. "Eric, don't be ridiculous. You're only twenty-two."

"Yeah, but I didn't do all that well the first time."

"Why? I thought you did really well in high school, and you kicked butt in EMT-I school?"

"Yeah, I can do well when I want to, if it's something I enjoy."

"Eric, I have no doubt that you can go back to the University and kick ass if you put your mind to it. In fact, you have to do that. It would be totally absurd for someone as smart as you, and as young as you, to go work for Toby."

Eric leaned back and thought a moment. He realized Carson was right, and it all seemed so foolishly simple. He didn't quite know what he would study yet, but it didn't matter. Going to school and doing the minimum work necessary to get passing grades had been a lot less stressful than his job. With a little more work, he would do much better. He was already thinking about registering for Spring classes when his mind turned back to Carson.

"You could probably do the same thing, Carson."

"No, it's not for me. Two years of medic school almost killed me. Besides, there's really nothing else I'd rather do. I was never the college type, not even in high school. I wasn't Mr. Valedictorian like you."

"I was only Salutatorian."

"Whatever you were, you know what I mean. That's just not me. You should've never left college in the first place. When this is all said and done, you need to go back to school. You and Katie need to be wasting less of your time out here, and spending more time in school and with each other."

Eric was surprised by Carson's comment. It was the first time they had spoken of Katie being in a relationship with Eric, but Carson was right. At times, Carson could see right through life; he had lucid foresight that made others listen. In only a few minutes, he made Eric view his own life in entirely new, hopeful terms. But the lucidity with which he gleaned Eric's future was never usefully applied to his own. Perhaps that was one of the curses of being Carson.

"Maybe you'd still like being a Paramedic, just in a different city?" Eric ventured.

"Maybe later, but not now. I'm gonna try something else."

"It'll be sad to see you go, Carson."

"Yeah, thanks."

The two Medics sat in their ambulance and watched and listened to the rain sprinkling on the windshield. It spoke to them about their lives, turning points, and the future. Eric's future was filled with hope, but he couldn't rejoice in that now. Instead, he only heard the sound of points-of-no-return. As much promise as the future might hold, change marks the end of a time, and that in itself is a reminder of the brevity of life. Even though the future looked good, the future meant the disbanding of a friendship, of many friendships, and a memory-filled life he had lived for two years. He wanted life to pause. He wanted to have the past, the present, and the future, but life is a river we float in, and there is no turning the tide.

Katie had grown increasingly busy during the run-up to the election. As Katie had planned, Lynda moved back in once they were certain there would be no more visitors, and Katie grew accustomed to having her around. For brief periods Lynda would leave to stay with her parents, where she would take the kids for the weekend. Then she told her parents and Lou that she was going out of town again. She never even hinted where "out of town" was, and no one asked except her husband. Of course, she never told him.

On her latest return, she began to feel like she had a new home. Not only was Katie's apartment a refuge from visits by her increasingly unreasonable and unstable husband, but she and Katie developed a friendship. A difference of twenty years separated them, but being with Katie made Lynda remember the joys of being young and single. It made her remember what life was like before Lou. After years of darkness, she allowed herself increasing degrees of hope.

When she returned the previous Sunday night, Lynda relayed how great her weekend had been with the children. They were the light of her life, she would say. She told Katie that her parents gave her money to buy the kids presents, and how excited they had been. It dawned on Katie that Lynda had practically no money of her own, and she thought about how she never did anything for herself.

"Lynda," she said, "I've been thinking. You know that girls'-night-in we talked about?"

"Yeah?"

"We haven't done that yet, and we should. You know, we'll go out, buy some ice cream, rent a movie—a romantic one of course—and just have fun."

Lynda's face was almost expressionless for a moment. "That . . . that would be really nice."

"All right, but I'm sorry I can't do it till the end of the week. I'm so busy!"

"That's fine. Like when?"

"I've got a test on Wednesday and a study group Thursday night for a midterm Friday, but I'm free Friday night."

"Friday night then?"

"It's settled. We'll stay up late Friday night and have fun before the election. We can think about something other than Saturday for a while. I'm sick of talking about politics."

―

Normally, the Firefighter Union elections were uneventful. Generally, they were uncontested. But in the past four weeks, the election committee had received the names of two new candidates for President and Vice-President—a great surprise to everyone, but not to the incumbents. Before putting their names in the hat, Nathan Tompkins and Sheila Olson both sat down and told O'Malley what they were planning to do.

It was not an antagonistic meeting. Nathan and Sheila told

O'Malley they had nothing against him or Mark Rader, but that these were just personal goals. Of course, O'Malley believed very little of this, but at least they talked to him first. After that, there were a lot of backroom talks at the fire stations, at neighborhood barbeques, and over the phones. Nathan and Sheila divulged a great deal to those they felt they could trust and little to all the others, merely stating that it was healthy for the department to experience an occasional turnover in leadership.

But at the same time, O'Malley and Rader did not sit idle. They used their pull as much as possible. The deputy chief did the best he could to let others know whom he supported. Of course, that was bending the rules, but the attempted usurpation of power rattled him, and he couldn't let the power structures that he had taken so long to build change at this critical juncture. What rattled him the most, however, was the fact that word got back to him that the real chief had said many favorable things about Nathan to several firefighters. Apparently, this was one round in which he chose not to sit it out.

There was a great deal of mumbling as the firefighters fumbled in their seats at the Union Hall waiting for the election chairman to announce the results. When Jon Carver went to the podium, the room silenced.

"All right, everyone," he said. "Great turnout this year. Let me start with the results for Treasurer."

There were no contests at Treasurer, Secretary, or Master-at-Arms. The incumbents were merely voted back in.

"Now, for the position of Vice-President, the candidates were Sheila Olson and Mark Rader. The results are: Sheila Olson – 51 and Mark Rader – 37. We have a new Vice President."

No one clapped or cheered. That would defeat the spirit of harmony the union was meant to foster.

"And now, the results for President. The candidates were Mike O'Malley and Nathan Tompkins. The results are: Mike O'Malley – 56 and Nathan Tompkins – 32. Mike O'Malley will retain his post as Union President."

Nathan felt a mix of emotions inside. He felt dejected, somewhat relieved, and perhaps most of all, somewhat regretful. His relationships with O'Malley and the deputy chief were irreparably damaged, but Sheila's victory was something—one small chink removed. However, her victory was perhaps best an indication of the firefighters' general dislike of Rader. Whatever the cause, he thought, it was at least a change, but the fire department still rolled ahead like a steam engine with the wrong engineers at the throttle. After O'Malley's significant win, neither Nathan nor Sheila nor any of their supporters knew of anyone who could knock the barreling engine off its track.

30.

The days passed rapidly for Eric. After a year of drama, it almost seemed anticlimactic. While the ambulance issue was talked about over and over on the radio, on TV, and in the newspaper, Eric thought even more should be happening. That *he* should be doing more. It hadn't taken long to gather the petition signatures, and as soon as that was done, the petition was sent to the county and they entered a period of inactivity. It was announced that the Charter Amendment, as written, would appear on everyone's ballot on Saturday. All Eric could do was hope that it would be enough.

He and Carson didn't have work scheduled for Friday or Saturday, and that was just as well for him. He would rather be free all day to watch every return and every update on TV.

However, late Friday morning, Hank called. He said he had a BLS transport halfway across the state, and both the BLS crews were already out on long runs. The transport was for a psychiatric patient transfer to Mary Lanning Memorial in Hastings. Eric didn't want to go; he worked enough. Carson had made him realize that just the other night.

"Have you asked Katie?" he asked, not knowing what her schedule entailed that day. He hadn't seen much of her lately since she was now a full-fledged worker on the transfer cars. Besides that, she had tests and papers, and was busy some nights with Lynda.

"No, but I probably will," Hank said. "She did have the day off, but I thought I'd offer it to you and Carson, too, in case you wanted the hours."

Eric wondered how he could say, "I'll go if Katie goes," but knew he couldn't. "Sure, I'll do it."

"Great. He needs to be picked up from St. E's at noon. He's ambulatory but has chronic back pain and suicidal ideation."

"So? So do I."

"Don't even joke like that, Eric," Hank said. "I'm going to call Katie and Carson. It's better to have three for something like this."

Hank did call them both. Katie decided she would go since she had just finished her morning midterm, and it worked out well because she wanted to spend time with Eric. She only asked what time they would return. She had Friday night plans with a girlfriend, she said. Hank promised seven or eight at the latest, and she said that'd be fine.

Hank called Carson and told him Katie and Eric were doing an over-the-road transfer, and asked if he could go too.

"Katie and Eric are going? Why do you need me?"

"Because it's a psych transfer, it's a long haul, and I don't want those two young kids on it alone. I'd just feel more comfortable with you there."

"Really?"

"Yeah, you know the drill. I don't want to endanger crew more than I have to."

"All right, I'll go," Carson said, thinking it might be like old times, but this would be the last time. From here on out, it would be Katie and Eric alone.

———

"You don't have to lie on the cot," Carson said, helping the patient step into the ambulance. "If you feel better sitting up, you can do that too."

"No," the man said through gritted teeth, holding his back as he slowly lowered himself onto the cot, "I'd rather lay down."

"No problem. Do you want your head up?"

"Yeah, thanks so much, Carson."

Carson raised the head of the cot forty-five degrees and handed the man a pillow. "How did you know my name?"

"Oh, you're one of the only Eastern Ambulance drivers that I do know—you and Eric and just a few others. You've helped me and my family out before."

This was one of many times when Carson couldn't remember a patient's face. "Oh, I'm glad to hear that. Hopefully, it's all been good."

"Yeah, it has. I'm a big supporter of Eastern, and I want to thank you for all you done for me, but I'm real sorry about you having to do this," the man said.

He was quite a tall man with a thick torso and long limbs. He was roughly Carson's age, but his face showed the wear and tear of stressful years.

"There's nothing to be sorry about," Carson said. "This is my job."

Eric came to the back, got the thumbs-up from Carson, and closed the doors. He joined Katie in the cab. Carson insisted on that, at least.

"I'm really sorry about you guys having to do this," the man said again. "I just can't sit up in a car no more."

"Again, don't worry about it. I get paid by the hour," Carson said with a smile.

"Yep, sometimes that's the only way to go."

"So, George, what do you do for a living?"

"I work in a warehouse."

"Oh, yeah? Forklift operator?"

"Sometimes. We use forklifts and pallet jacks, and sometimes just our hands."

"Is that what you did to your back?"

"Yeah, I went to lift a coupling, and I got it up, but I was on the ice and I fell backwards. When I fell, I jerked and busted something in my back."

Carson winced in sympathetic pain. "Aghh! Were they able to do anything for you?"

"No, but I've been to a lot of doctors. I had surgery, but I think it's almost worse off now."

Carson, who had been writing in the man's chart, stopped and looked at him. "Do the pain meds help?"

"Only a little." George was holding his body stiff to avoid movement.

"Why are you going to Hastings?"

"I have to see the shrink there."

Eric pulled the ambulance out of the garage. Carson realized the patient had misunderstood the question. "Oh, I mean, why are you going there versus staying here, for example?"

"Oh, I'm sorry; I see what you mean. That's where I'm originally from, and I don't have my job out here no more. The doctors say I need to go to the mental health ward for a while, and I'll be close to my mom out there, ya know."

"Oh. So, you lost your job, huh?"

"Yeah, I can't do that no more."

"Do you have Disability or anything?"

"I don't, but the doctors keep tellin' me I should get it."

"Why don't you?"

"I don't want to be on Disability. My dad always said that was the wrong way to live. He said that Nebraskans don't live like that. In Nebraska, there's always a job a man can do."

"I admire your dad's attitude, but sometimes you don't have a choice, George."

"I don't know. My dad was a tough old man."

"Was he?"

"Yeah, one time he was sittin' in a diner with his friends, and a lady fell asleep at the wheel of her car and came barreling through the restaurant. She hit the corner of the restaurant where my dad was sittin' with his friend. His friend died, and they thought my dad would die, too 'cause he got knocked clear across the diner. He went to the hospital for a few days, but he pulled through. They put some casts on his arms, but he couldn't work too well with them, so he cut 'em off after a few weeks."

"By himself?"

"Yeah, he cut 'em off himself. Well, I helped him, I guess."

"Wow, he does sound tough, but that doesn't mean it was the smart thing to do."

"Yeah, he was *real* tough. He healed right up, though. And he kept on workin.'"

"Hmm," Carson said. "Yeah, my dad was like that, too. His tractor rolled over on him, broke about half the bones in his body, and when I found him, I thought he was dead. He was a bloody mess, but he wasn't dead, and the ambulance came and picked him up. He went to surgery, but the doctor said that there was nothing they could do and that he would die in a few hours, so they left my mom and me alone in the room with him. But he didn't die in a few hours. In fact, he even talked to me. The doctors' never believed me, but he told me to be a good boy." Carson wiped a tear from his eye. He almost heard his father's words now. He thought of them every day, but he could almost hear them now.

"His body fought hard, and every day the doctor was dumbstruck that he was still hanging on. After four days, he finally passed away, a lot later than they thought he would."

George looked at Carson in total awe. "That's what I'm talking about. That's exactly what I'm talking about! Those old guys were tough."

Carson could tell this man put the older generation of Midwest stock on a pedestal. They were no different from George, but he wasn't wrong about them. "Yes, they were."

"I wish I could be more like them."

"It sounds to me like you are," Carson said. "You're dealing with some very tough issues—issues that I, myself, might not be able to handle."

"Yeah, but I can't go back to work."

"That doesn't mean anything. What it means is that you've got a worse condition than your dad had."

The man looked down at himself strapped in the gurney. "I don't think so. I didn't even break anything."

"That's not true. From what I've read in your chart, you've got some herniated discs and a pinched nerve. That's some serious stuff, ya know. Your dad may have broken his arms, but that's not near as bad as hurting your back. Unfortunately, back injuries are some of the worst injuries for pain, and they're the hardest to fix."

"Are they?"

"Definitely," Carson said, speaking slowly. "Unfortunately, it might take you a long, long time to heal."

"I can't do that."

"Why?"

"I don't have the money."

"That's why you need to take Disability."

"I really don't want to do that, Carson."

"I think you should, though."

"That's what the nurses back there were just telling me. They even filled out the paperwork for me. I got it right here with my other paperwork." He pointed at his backpack sitting at the foot of the cot.

"Listen to me," Carson said, taking a serious tone. "Taking Disability does not mean that you're not tough. What it is," he said, laying the chart down, "is a temporary fix for people who need it until they can heal. Promise me that when you get to Mary Lanning you're gonna sign that paperwork."

"I'll think about it."

"No, George, you've got to do more than just think about it; you've got to do it."

"All right," the man said, looking down again at his pain-filled body.

"Do you have health insurance?"

This question got George animated, and he reached for his wallet as he looked at Carson with a worried expression. "Oh, uh . . . I don't have no health insurance no more."

Carson realized his error. "No, no, I'm not asking for my company. I was just wondering out of curiosity . . . like I was hoping you were still taken care of by your company."

George was still in a bothered state, still reaching for his wallet, though it caused him obvious discomfort.

"Yeah, I . . . I don't have insurance with my company or anything, but I'm an Eastern Ambulance subscriber."

"Oh, you are?" Carson said. The man pulled out a card with the familiar Eastern Ambulance logo on it and showed it to him. "I'm glad to see that," Carson said.

Carson took the card and saw that the man was true to his word. He handed the card back and said, "This one's on us, then."

"Yeah, I'm tellin' you, that member card's a lifesaver."

"It's a big help for a lot of people. I'm glad it's helped you."

"I'm tellin' you, it really has helped me. I've got a lot of medical bills. Thousands and thousands of dollars, ya' know, and I get all kinds of bills in the mail and people calling me about them. It just makes me *sick* to think of all those bills. I ain't never gonna be able to pay them, and it really does make me feel sick. It makes me wish I didn't ever go to the doctor. Sometimes, I think it would be easier for me and my family if I could just go away and make all the bills go away with me."

Carson grew profoundly sad for the man. He had always been keenly distressed by the unbearable costs that the healthcare system placed on the uninsured. It was a plague of its own, slowly growing in the lives of the poor until the mountain of debt killed any hope for the future. A man making ten dollars an hour would never be able to pay off fifty thousand or more.

"But I tell you what," George continued, "I don't get any bills in the mail from Eastern except once a year. That's why I'm a member. I'm a member for my whole family and have been for years."

"Yeah, it was a good service we provided," Carson said. "It was one of the things I liked most about our company, that we were able to help people who couldn't afford a lot."

"What do you mean, 'provided?' You talk like you're going to lose."

"You're right. We might not, and if we win, we'll keep providing it."

"I'm real worried 'bout if the fire department takes over," George said. "I guess they're not havin' a member program for people who need an ambulance a lot."

"No, they haven't talked about one yet."

"'Course, I don't need it so much now."

"What do you mean?"

"I mainly had it for my son, ya know."

"What do you mean?"

"He's dead, of course."

"Really?" Carson said, thinking he couldn't imagine this guy's life being any worse than it was. It was hard to fault him for being hopeless. "What happened to him?"

George looked at Carson with a quizzical expression. "He was burnt in his house, of course."

Carson's heart froze. He looked at the run-sheet where he had just written the man's name: "Turner, George." He leaned his head against the ambulance wall. He was Adam's father. Of course! What was he thinking? He had seen him once before when he was at the trailer. He couldn't think of anything to say. In his head, he relived his memories of Adam and felt like he wanted to go back in time. "Oh, my God, George," Carson said, "I'm so sorry, I forgot that you were . . . that you're Adam's dad."

George said, "That's okay. I know you see a whole lotta people. He was a real nice boy, though, wasn't he?"

"Yes, he was."

George sat in silence. Carson was overcome by emotion and

disbelief, then questions. "So, you know that I knew Adam, right?"

"Yes."

"I guess you know that I was the Paramedic there on the night he passed away?"

"Yeah, I know that."

"George, I just want to say that I'm sorry about . . ." He involuntarily took a gasp of air, but suppressed the sob. "About what happened to Adam that night."

"I know you are, and I know it's not your fault. It was all his mother. She's in jail now."

"Yeah, I heard that," Carson said. "That must be awfully hard for you to deal with. I can't imagine—"

"She was goin' crazy, I think." George wiped a tear from his eye.

"Yeah," Carson said, "she had a lot of stress, I guess."

"Yeah, it got to her, but she wasn't always like that, ya know."

"Like what?"

"Crazy and mean."

"She used to be pretty nice, huh?"

George nodded and looked up at the ceiling of the ambulance. "Yeah, she used to be a real nice girl . . . back when I met her. We got married when we were eighteen. We were young, ya know, and didn't have no babies yet, and we were both from the same town.

"One reason we got married, though, was 'cause she got pregnant, and then we had Alice. I was working for my dad on the farm then, but he couldn't pay me no more, so we moved to Lincoln. Then we had Bobby, and she started to get *real* depressed right after that."

"Really?" Carson said, leaning his head closer. His life was so entwined with this story, and he didn't know much about it.

"I don't know why, Carson. She just got real depressed after having Bobby and just stayed that way. She said she didn't love me no more, and we were real poor too."

"That can make it very tough."

"Yeah, it was real tough. I took her to the doctor, and he put her on pills, but they didn't help too much. They just created more bills, and that made things worse. Then she got pregnant with Adam. I think she was happier for a bit, but then Adam was born, and they told us . . . well, you know about Adam. He was born sick, with the cerebral palsy."

"Yeah, I know that," Carson said, wanting to hear this story but not the end.

"Adam was such a good little boy, too, one of the nicest boys ever," George said. "Don't you think?"

"Oh, yeah," Carson said, briefly wiping his own eye and looking out the back window over the flat prairie landscape. This call was tough. He felt like his emotions were riding the hilliest road in the country. "He was always a real polite kid to me. He always said thank you and said sorry . . . well, I guess he was a lot like you now that I think about it—always saying sorry."

George looked over at Carson with a proud expression. "Yep, you're right." He smiled. "I'm glad you could see that too, Carson. He *was* a lot like me." George turned away from Carson and stared at the ceiling. He pursed his lips as he reflected on Carson's comment.

Eric and Katie had been listening, and Eric turned and looked back at them for a brief second. The large man was too long for the cot. The back of his head protruded over the top, and his feet hung off the end. Carson propped his boots on the wheel-rail of the cot and stared at the clipboard across his lap. He didn't write anything; he just sat and listened, and talked and cried.

Carson asked, "Why didn't you live with them, George?"

"We got separated two years ago. She didn't want to see me no more, but I stayed in Lincoln and kept working and paying the money and the bills. I mean, the house bills and stuff, not the medical bills."

"George," Carson said and laid his hand on George's forearm, "you're a *much* tougher man than you realize. I think you might be tougher than your dad and my dad—maybe even combined. I don't know if they could have stood up and done some of the things you've done and dealt with the things you've dealt with. You kept plowing ahead with life even when life dealt you the roughest cards. If that's not tough, I don't what is. I know I couldn't have done it."

"You could, Carson, because you wouldn't have no choice."

"I don't know."

"I can't do that now, anyway. I can't even work or send them money, and my kids are in foster homes."

George looked like he was about to break down, so Carson nudged the story along. "Did you hurt your back before Adam was . . . before he was injured in the fire?"

"Yeah, it happened just before that. I had to tell all this stuff in court not too long ago."

Carson realized that George had been through a lot with the police and the law, and he could sense he didn't want to go over it all again.

"Hey, George, I just want you to know that on that night . . ."

George tried adjusting his body on the cot and winced in pain.

"I just want you to know that we did everything we could for Adam, but we couldn't—"

"I know you did, Carson. Like I said, I know you did. I know you're the best Paramedic in the city, and I was glad you were there."

"Well, I'm definitely not the best Para—"

"He always thought real highly of you," George interrupted.

Carson looked up. "He what?"

"Yeah, Adam did. He felt real highly of you . . . and Eric," he said, pointing toward the cab.

"How do you know that?"

"Because he told me about you, and how you would come and talk to him and fly him to the hospital when he was sick."

"Fly him?"

"Yeah, it's kind of a funny story, really. He once heard somebody talkin' about an air ambulance and so he thought that all ambulances could fly."

Carson smiled, relishing the thought.

"What with all the radios and stuff," George said, "I think he thought you were in an airplane."

"I guess I could see that coming from an eight-year-old."

"He talked about you a lot when I saw him."

"He did?" Carson said, holding back the tears.

"Yeah, I thought about asking you sometime if you might want to be a Big Brother for him."

A few tears finally escaped down Carson's cheek. He quickly wiped them away. "Wow, George. I don't know what to say. I really liked him. I should have taken him out to the park or something."

"I did that, ya know, when I could. But I think you did enough. You talked to him and made him feel good and always treated him real well."

George shifted again in the cot, though it hurt him to do so, then reached for his backpack. Carson handed it to him instead.

"There's something in here I think you might like."

Carson watched as George shuffled through the medical records, the disability papers, and a large stack of letters and drawings from little kids. He pulled out a worn piece of paper, folded in half, and handed it to Carson.

"What's this?"

"It's a picture Adam drew. I want you to have it."

Carson unfolded the paper. It was unmistakably the work of an eight-year-old with crayons, and with Adam's condition, was even more difficult to make out. But Carson saw an ambulance with people in it and wings on the side.

"Wow, that's a . . ." His voice started to crack. "That's a great picture," he said, feeling overwhelmed, "but I don't need to have this, George. You should keep it."

"No, I have hundreds of his pictures." George patted his backpack. "I want you to have that one."

"Thank you. It means a lot to me."

Carson scanned the picture, slowly picking out more detail. The ambulance zoomed away from a house. In a box there was a small stick figure in a wheelchair. In another box, in front of the wings, three people sat crammed together with a steering wheel, headlights, and red emergency lights.

"I have a question," Carson said. "Who are the three people up front?"

"That's you, Eric, and Adam."

"Adam?" Carson said, confused. "Then who's the boy in the back—in the wheelchair?"

"That's just some other boy, I guess."

Carson looked at him skeptically.

"That's what Adam said. That's another boy. You see, this is a picture for when Adam grows up. He asked me if people in wheelchairs could be Paramedics. I told him yes. I didn't know what else to say, ya know. From then on, he always said he was gonna be a Paramedic when he grows up. That picture is you, Eric, and Adam working together when he's grown up, and you're flying a boy to the hospital."

Carson's emotions flooded to the surface, and he began to sob gently. He cradled his head in his hand and wept. He wished it was later in the day, and the ambulance was filled with darkness, but he sobbed openly in the daylight. It felt strange, but not wrong, to expose himself so openly to the world. As the radio played quietly in the background, George cried with him. Eric looked over at Katie, who had been looking down, trying hard to listen to the conversation in the back. As he did so, she looked up at him with tearful eyes, and it was the dearest sight Eric ever saw. It was an hour of time that would be forever imprinted in Eric's mind.

No one talked much for the rest of the trip. George asked if they could turn the radio up when it played one of his favorite songs. Eric did so. The four sat in thought and listened to old country songs until all the miles passed beneath them. When they arrived at Mary Lanning Memorial, they turned George over to the nurses' care. Carson told George that he admired him and thanked him for the picture, and then they said good-bye.

On the road back to Lincoln, Carson lay on the freshly made cot by himself in the back of the ambulance. It grew dark, and neither Eric nor Katie knew if he was sleeping. They thought he probably was. They talked a little bit, listened to the radio together, and sometimes sang along. Eric did some of his best country music impersonations and made Katie laugh. As the evening wore on, the stars grew brighter over the wide Nebraska landscape, and Katie reached over and took Eric's hand. She held it for a hundred miles.

Hours later, Carson pulled into his drive. After his nap in the ambulance, he felt refreshed, not ready for bed. He grabbed a Coke from the fridge and went to the corner of his living room where there was a pile of cardboard boxes. He picked up the first one, unsealed the tape, and unpacked until everything was back in its proper place.

Only a few miles away, two women perused the ice cream in a downtown grocery store. They had already picked out a romantic movie, but this part—the ice cream part—was the more important selection of the night. As they meandered through the rows of flavors, they joked, talked about men, and laughed like they were in high school. One of them was in high school only a year before. For the other, it was a dimming memory only recently reawakened.

They didn't have a care in the world other than their ice cream choice, but their excitement would have diminished quickly had they noticed Manny Alvarez standing in civilian clothes at the end of the aisle. Yet, even if they had seen him, they probably would not have recognized him. He certainly knew them, though, and that was the problem. Deputy Chief Killion had been wondering where his wife had been staying for quite some time. Alvarez pondered what he should do. In the parking lot he finally concluded that it was awfully late, so he would tell O'Malley tomorrow at the election party. O'Malley could deal with the situation himself, or decide whether they should tell the deputy chief.

31.

The weather on the prairie is highly unpredictable. For four hundred miles in any direction around Lincoln there are no obstacles—no bodies of water, forests, hills or mountains—to moderate the weather. No one knows, really, what October is like, or how the weather will be in November, or next week, or even tomorrow. It just blows in from hundreds of miles away, and it blows in fast.

The first week of November was a week like that. It had been cold. Some people wondered if snow would soon arrive. Yet, as Carson, Eric, and Katie drove across the prairie on their way back from Hastings, they were outrunning a storm that followed not far behind. It was the result of a warm front coming in from the south that collided with the cold air hovering over Lincoln. Though the temperature was rising, it was a bad day to hold an election.

While voters formed lines outside their polling stations, some of them lost their newspapers to the wind, which carried the tumbling papers across the parking lots to unknown resting places. But the weather did not stop the people from coming. It was a big election—president, congressmen, city chair, board seats, and more than a few referenda. As is typical for Nebraska, there was little contest over the federal seats. The real battleground involved the local seats and the local issues.

The plan for Eastern Ambulance folks was to wake up early, go vote, trickle into P.O. Pears for drinks, and perhaps a late night of watching election results. Eric woke up with his alarm, ate breakfast, and drove to his polling station. He checked the boxes down the line for representatives, but took his time on some of the referenda—the tougher social issues, things affecting the farmers, and the future of all Cornhuskers. Of course, he checked "yes" on the "EMS Referendum."

Katie had planned on doing the same, but atypical for her, she turned off her alarm after staying up so late watching movies with

Lynda. She heard the wind howling outside, realized there was nothing that *had* to be done right away, and closed her eyes on a day she was not particularly fond of anyway. Why start watching election results so early, she asked herself. The earliest anyone would know anything was this afternoon. For the first time in several weeks, she experienced the joy of turning her back on the world and going back to sleep.

Carson, on the other hand, never planned on waking up early—he didn't plan on anything. Because of his nap in the ambulance, he had stayed up even later than usual unpacking boxes. As he did, his progress had been slowed by the distractions in them. He read old notes and letters, looked at the pictures of himself as a boy and a young man—from Boy Scouts to the golf team in high school to his time on the rural EMS squad. It was amazing how his mom got him to all those activities by herself. Even in the pictures, though, he noticed that his Boy Scout uniform was old and used and didn't quite look like the others. He remembered how embarrassed he was about stuff like that but now realized she had done the best she could. He wished he had never complained. When he finally fell asleep on the couch, he dreamed of his childhood. No, there was no alarm clock going off at Carson's place. He would get up when he felt like it and play it by ear from there.

By the time Eric had finished voting, the weather was markedly different. Leaving his apartment in the morning, he thought he didn't have on enough layers of clothes, but now he removed some. The sun was shining, and the warm front the weatherman had been talking about had arrived. Eric took off his sweater and threw it in the back seat next to a coat and a pair of shorts. He thought about how mad he got trying to plan on Nebraska weather. Every time he watched the news, Carson laughed at him when he talked about what he should wear. Eric, he would say, you've got problems.

It was past 11:00 A.M. by the time Eric got to P.O. Pears. Hank, Dave, Leslie, and several others were already there eating, drinking, and watching TV. Without even saying hello, Eric asked Hank if any results had yet come in.

"They're starting to," Hank said, "but it's way too early to tell. About fifty-fifty so far."

Eric felt both relieved and nervous. If the early results showed an eighty percent favor one way or the other, he would already have a good idea as to what the outcome would be.

"It might be a late night then, huh?" Eric asked.

"It could be, Eric. I hope not. I hope we win decisively enough to call it early."

"It could still happen," Eric said without much conviction.

An hour and a half passed. More Eastern people trickled in the door, and every time the election ticker on the bottom of the screen cycled through the issues, people stopped what they were doing. When the ticker flashed, "EMS Referendum: Yes 48%, No 52%," they fell silent. When it came back, "Yes 51%, No 49%," they cheered and high-fived one another. The whole event felt too much like a football game. They watched the TV just as excited or crushed as they did when touchdowns were scored.

For all the nerve-wracking tension, it was fun at the same time. Eric looked around at the faces he had grown to know and love. Leslie was there with her boyfriend, Lance. Tim came, but without his wife. That was a little sad, but he sat at the bar, beer in hand, talking to Leslie and Lance. Even Toby came. It had been a while since he'd left Eastern for his construction job, but he came today as if he were still part of the company. Eric was actually joyful to see him, not because he was so fond of Toby, but because it made him appreciate his decision to go back to college.

Dave had invited most anyone remotely connected to the company. Some of the owners were there. Jim Homestead was there representing his hospital as part-owner, and doctors from the Lancaster County Medical Society had joined the group. Some emergency room nurses from Lincoln General were there, most likely looking for Carson. After a while, the place became so packed with Eastern people that Eric thought they would run out of room before the end of the night.

Still, there was no sign of Katie or Carson. There was a void without them, and many people asked where they were. Eric was used to being asked where Carson was. He had become his brother's keeper. He considered calling the two but realized Carson was probably just sleeping, and . . . well, he'd wait a while to call Katie. He was always conscious of acting too dependent on her and scaring her off. Instead, he just told people, "Oh, they'll be here a little later."

By midafternoon the weather turned almost hot. People who arrived in the afternoon wore only T-shirts, and if it weren't for the wind, the sun outside the windows would have made Eric feel like it was summer again. However, the weatherman occasionally cut into the election coverage to warn people not to start making plans for the lake. The Doppler radar showed a large thunderstorm coming in from the west. "While the temperature might continue to rise," he said, "expect thundershowers later in the evening."

As strange as the weather was, though, a more ominous trend began by about two o'clock. The election ticker had flashed by nearly a dozen times since the last Eastern advantage was seen. The "Noes" were not running away with the result, but a continuous trend of being in the minority was developing. Increasingly, the "Yeses" hovered around forty-seven to forty-eight percent.

No one voiced their concern out loud, but the collective mood changed noticeably. After the last display, Leslie yelled out, "C'mon! We're almost there!"

Toby said, "Maybe this is good, though. Let them have the lead now, before we take it back when it counts."

Eric was less optimistic. He knew that it was easy for leads to change early in the game of numbers, but that as more votes were counted, the new votes lost their ability to sway the outcome.

Around two-thirty, Eric was surprised to see Harvey Miller arrive. Eric was glad to see that he had healed well. Really, it had only been a large bump on his head, but Eric had to laugh. By showing up here, he thought, Harvey must no longer care about appearing unbiased. Maybe that was because he had given up on reporting the ambulance issue altogether. Then Eric realized he was reporting after all when Harvey said that he had just been over at Fire Station One. That took courage.

In fact, it wasn't long before other reporters arrived. A man from the newspaper—the real newspaper—showed up, and both he and a TV crew began to take pictures of the crowd as they waited intently for the referendum results to show. It wasn't long before the crowd began seeing themselves and the firefighters on TV.

The firefighters were all at Fire Station One. In typical fashion, they had lit the barrel-grill and were having a barbeque. Even though their party had just begun, they had a crowd as large, if not larger, than Eastern's. Eric had to admit it did look fun. For as much as the weatherman promised death and destruction, the scene on the TV looked like a perfect picnic.

While the mood at P.O. Pears had grown somewhat somber, there was no sign of the same at Fire Station One. A big-screen TV stood in the corner of the garage, while a stereo played music outside, where the firefighters had set up picnic tables. A huge S.A.A.F.E. banner hung over the garage doors proclaiming the now-famous slogan, "Better, Faster, Cheaper."

Finally, Eric decided to call Carson. It was past three o'clock in the afternoon.

"Carson!" he said, "Where the hell are you?"

Carson sounded sleepy, but not like he had been sleeping. "What do you mean? You just called my house, and I picked up the phone, didn't I?"

"You know what I mean, smart-ass. Why haven't you come down to P.O. Pears?"

"I'm going to, Eric. Nobody told me I had to be there at a certain time. Besides, why go down there when I can just watch all of you on TV?" He laughed.

Eric laughed in return. "I guess that's a good point."

"What do you think, Eric?"

"About what?"

"What do you think of the results?"

"I think it's a *little* too early to tell, but—"

"But you don't think it looks good."

"No, it's not real promising."

"That's what I was thinking."

"Still, that's no reason to stay home."

"I know, Eric. I just stayed up way too late."

"I understand."

"I've got some things to take care of. I'm not even dressed yet. I don't think they'll announce anything till at least seven o'clock or so. I'll make sure I'm there before then."

"All right," Eric said, "just come as soon as you can. A lot of people are asking about you."

Eric returned to the crowd. It was an amusing scene now. A mass of a hundred people crammed into a barroom staring at a TV screen like they were all at a movie. The football cues were there as well. "C'mon, c'mon . . ." someone said under his breath.

There were other races they eyed with great interest. Of course, there was the presidential election, and one TV in the room was muted on the national news to watch that coverage. Interest was growing in another race that was being discussed on the local news, however. As the hours marched by, it appeared both Commissioner McDaniels and Chairman Moscatelli were in danger of losing reelection. McDaniels' opponent was now holding a four point advantage, and Moscatelli was even further behind. Everytime those results appeared on the bottom of the screen, it gave the crowd reason to cheer. They needed it because now the EMS Referendum started showing a consistent "Yes 47%, No 53%."

As Hank and the others lowered their eyes from the screen after the most recent report, Hank looked around to comment to Eric. He didn't see him, and asked Tim where Eric was.

"I don't know," Tim said. "Someone said he had a phone call a few minutes ago, then he just disappeared."

32.

Carson finally got off the couch and dressed. He had nearly determined what others had not—Eastern had lost the election. They had finally lost it all. In less than two months time, they would cease to exist—for real this time—and the Lancaster County Fire Department would be running all the ambulances in the city. After all they had done, after all they had been through, it came down to that.

Without taking the time to shave, Carson climbed into his pickup and headed downtown. He flipped the radio on to catch more coverage. They said the EMS Referendum was too close to call, but they did interview Mike O'Malley at Fire Station One. Carson turned the radio up.

"I can safely say that the citizens of Lincoln have determined that the county council made the right choice in selecting the Lancaster County Fire Department. We take this to be an affirmation of the great job our people do. Citizens were fed up with the way things were being handled, and they wanted change. They wanted professionals on the job. Honestly, I think the only reason we didn't see more of a spread in the numbers was the fact that the referendum was so poorly written it created a lot of confusion. Some of our supporters said they may have accidentally voted for the referendum when they didn't mean to. It just wasn't worded right."

Carson turned the radio off; anger would not help at this point. He wondered why they interviewed O'Malley instead of the chief or Killion, but figured he had been designated the spokesman. Thinking about the future, Carson grew saddened about leaving all those years at Eastern. He decided to park at Eastern Station One and walk over to P.O. Pears. He still needed time alone, time to think about the past, and time to think about his future, and whether that could possibly involve the Lancaster County Fire Department, though the idea sickened him after listening to O'Malley.

He parked in the lot below the station and made his way to the ambulance garage. He had spent countless hours here. What he remembered most were the conversations, those times when he stood around the rigs with his coworkers, his friends, and just talked. He wondered what this building would become once the company disbanded.

It grieved him to think about that—about the end. It grieved him all the more to think about O'Malley's comments about the city wanting professionals, and that the vote was close only because people were confused. He couldn't help it; he was angry, and there was no use suppressing it.

In reality, it was close. So close that Carson had to think that it might have been different. Perhaps Eastern management had been too self-confident. What if Harvey's article about the drinking had gotten out? What if they had printed more ads explaining to the people that they would wait just as long for a Fire ambulance, and that they would still be billed for it? And what if that terrible call in E22 had never happened? Then again, perhaps the good in that call outweighed the bad—he didn't know.

Carson thought of that incident as he looked at E22. Joe parked it at Station One for a while while he converted it into his own personal camping van. All of these ambulances will be camping vans soon, thought Carson. For as much as he hated that old thing, it was the only vehicle still at Eastern that had been there when Carson started his career. Now it looked more like an old friend than the nemesis it had become.

Outside, Carson heard the first claps of rumbling thunder. The weatherman had been right. Within minutes, it started raining—not a downpour, just a steady rain. He put his hand on the old thumb-button door handle of E22 and pulled. He climbed into the seat. Not much had changed on the inside yet. He knew that Joe had removed the old engine and replaced it with an engine from an old police car. He heard him start it the other day; it had sounded more like a hot rod than an ambulance. But it did start, and that was saying a lot. Too bad Joe didn't do that when it still belonged to the company.

Carson thought about the night that it didn't start. Of all the times for her to let him down. What were the chances of TV crews being there that night? Though everything was off, he flipped the archaic switches and knobs, wishing things could have been different. Maybe Eric didn't turn it off. Maybe it just died on its own. He stopped fumbling with the switches and dropped his head back onto the headrest. He looked up at the ceiling and saw the rubber bands from his original tally sheet. He flipped the visor down. Sure enough, the tally sheet was still there.

Carson's eyes froze on something. Beneath the long rows of his poorly drawn fire engines, there was a symbol he did not recognize, something he had not drawn. Yet, it was unmistakable. Someone had drawn an ambulance—a sign of a kill—on his own sheet. It suddenly became clear. Now he remembered telling Rader to go back to the ambulance to get the cot. Rader had turned it off, and he wanted Carson to know it. All the suppressed anger of the past months boiled to the surface. "What a bastard!" Carson said aloud. Then he thought that a girl might have died because of him! Oh, but he knew she wouldn't. He knew the Medical Attack Vehicle was close! It was becoming clearer and uglier. That's why Rader had looked so relieved when her condition improved; he knew how close he had come to killing somebody. If only . . . if only the people knew about this, how different things would have been. How different they still could be!

He had an idea. He would go to P.O. Pears where the reporters had gathered and show them the evidence. There might be enough time; at the very least, it might postpone things and spark an investigation.

He reached over and slapped the garage door button. The garage door issued a metallic whine as the motor tugged and pulled the door against its will. Carson found the keys in the ignition and cranked the new engine to life with a roar unlike any ambulance he had ever driven. Outside, it was growing dark, and a steady rain pounded the pavement. He pulled out at a speed surpassed only by the thoughts in his mind.

How could he do it? Was it really Mark? Had he seen the tally sheet before? Had he meant for Carson to see it earlier? He flipped the visor down again and glanced at the crude ambulance drawing. No, he didn't dream it. It had to have been him! No one else was low enough to do something like that. But now his own trick would be his undoing! The whole city would know, and they would see who the real professionals were.

It was, of course, not a long way to P.O. Pears, as it was just across the one-way street, but it took a drive around the block to get there. Parking would have been an issue, but Carson pulled up on the sidewalk by the front door. He turned off the camping-wagon, grabbed the sheet, and marched inside. It was crowded, more than he had ever seen. Some people looked startled to see him and acted as though they wanted to talk, but he marched right past them to the nexus of people.

He shoved his way through many people all focused on the same spot. He saw Hank and Dave in the center looking down at someone on a barstool. Carson pushed the last person aside, holding his evidence in the air. Then he froze. Eric sat on the barstool with a gash on his head and a bloody nose. He tilted his head back, resting in Katie's arms, and pressed a bloody rag against the nosebleed.

"Eric!" Carson said, still frozen in place.

"Carson," Eric said, muffled by the rag, "nice of you to show."

"Eric, what happened?"

"I got punched in the nose and shoved against a picture frame."

"What!"

"Yep, that's pretty much it."

"Cut the shit, Eric. What happened?"

"Shoot! I have to go through the whole story again?"

"Yes."

Eric pulled the rag up and folded it into a different position. "Katie has had Chief Killion's wife staying with her off and on over the past few weeks, and it was totally a secret. Today the firefighters found out."

Carson looked at Katie. "You were doing what!"

She didn't answer. Instead, she frowned to indicate that, right or wrong, it was true.

"Are you going to let me finish my story?" Eric asked in a nasal tone, the rag pressed against his nose. "Today he found out somehow."

"Who did? Killion or O'Malley?"

"Both. O'Malley called Katie to ask if it was true, and she told him it was, and he said she had to make Lynda leave immediately. She said she wouldn't. He said Killion was coming over there to get Lynda. Katie got worried and called me, and I went over there right away."

"Why didn't O'Malley go?" Carson asked.

Katie chimed in, "He said Lou made him stay to cover the election. I wish he would've come. I don't think he would have let this happen."

Eric continued, "So Chief Killion went over there with Rader and some others. When I got there, Killion, Rader, Alvarez and Johnson were all there. The chief was making Lynda pack her stuff and was pushing her to make her go faster. He and the others were in the back bedroom, and Rader was in the kitchen with Katie. She was yelling at him to leave. I heard Lynda and Lou arguing in the back room. He said she was coming home with him. She said she wouldn't, that she wouldn't argue in front of the kids—they had been through enough already. He said, you're coming with me whether you like it or not, so he said they would go talk in his office instead, away from the kids. I saw Mark yelling at Katie, after she had called him an asshole and a few other things. I rushed in, and Mark and I started fighting in the kitchen. Katie was trying to break us apart.

Throughout the story, Katie cradled Eric in her arms so naturally that it looked like she had done it so many times before. She was proud of Eric. Eric took a deep sigh, swallowed some blood, and continued. "We exchanged some blows. Phil and Manny heard us and came out of the back room. Manny grabbed my arm right when I was about to punch Rader in the face. They pushed me against the wall—against the picture frame, Manny hit me in the nose, and I went to the floor.

"Then the deputy chief came out of the back with Lynda and asked me what the fuck I was doing there. I told him he couldn't take Lynda away if she didn't want to go. The other guys picked me up, and he put his hand on my shoulder. He told me to stay the fuck outta his business. I told him that if he took her, we would just go get her back. He said if I did he would kill me, and that he meant it, and I almost believed him. Then he punched me in the eye, and they left. Then Katie and I came here to get help."

Throughout Eric's story, Carson's face showed nothing but concentration. He stood taut and riveted, every muscle in his body poised for action, listening to every word. Eric finished his last sentence waiting to hear what Carson had to say, but there was no response. Instead, Carson crumpled the paper in his hand, did an abrupt about-face, and marched toward the door. The crowd parted for him.

"Carson!" Eric said, trying to get up, but his muffled voice was lost in the din of the crowd.

Dave sped after Carson while Hank followed close behind. "Carson!" Dave yelled. Carson didn't stop. "Carson!" he yelled even louder, "where are you going!"

"Fire Station One!"

Carson made it outside where the storm was now descending full force. He strode toward the half-torn-up camping ambulance, and people spilled out of P.O. Pears into the rain to watch. He placed his hand on the door handle just as Dave and Hank made their way outside.

"Carson!" Dave yelled again with as much force as he could muster over the sound of the storm.

Carson opened the door and turned to face Dave.

"Carson! What the hell do you think you're doing!"

Carson only replied, "I've got something to take care of." He climbed into E22 and drove off in the storm.

33.

The crowd was abuzz with action. Leslie turned to her boyfriend. "Honey?" was all she had to say, and he immediately went to his truck. Toby threw on his work coat and ran toward the parking garage. Harvey Miller grabbed his bag and sped toward his car, as did all the other reporters who were salivating at the mouth. Other members of the crowd talked and debated, but most of them raced to their cars.

Due to the rain, the traffic was bad, but for the first time in his life, Carson used the emergency lights for personal gain. People pulled over, and he fought his way through the downtown traffic and the storm to Fire Station One.

Only one streetlight stood at the corner of the fire station parking lot. The area around the Soup Kitchen had no streetlights. Instead, the corner contained the shrubbery and dumpsters that Harvey Miller had tried to hide in and a lone cottonwood tree. As Carson passed the tree he was nearly startled by the sight of Samuel Spirit Dog sitting with his back to the trunk, crouched over in apparent sleep or drunkenness. When E22 approached, however, he methodically raised his head and opened his eyes. They were clearly visible in the halogen light beaming across the street, and the blank expression and lifeless eyes followed Carson for several seconds as he passed. He had never seen that look on Samuel's face before.

The station's four garage doors were open. Yellow lights glowed from the back of the garage, outlining three fire engines in black silhouette. They glared ominously at the street, ready for action. One of the central garages was left empty for the picnic, and Carson saw several people milling about inside.

As he approached the drive, Carson held the crumpled tally sheet in his hand. Squeezing it like a stress ball, he pictured his best friends being attacked by Killion, Rader, Johnson, and Alvarez. What had the chief said? "If you come to get her, I'll kill you. I mean it." Carson pulled the ambulance straight into the open bay, its bright lights and loud engine destroying the calm.

In front of the ambulance, O'Malley leaned back against a table with a beer in his hand. Mark Rader stood to his left, and a dozen firefighters milled around. When the storm hit, the picnic had faded quickly. Only the core of the department lingered on. There's no way Chief Winkenwerder would stay there to celebrate. Carson imagined that O'Malley and Rader had been going over the afternoon's events. As he pulled inside, they squinted their eyes in the headlights. After a second of confusion, O'Malley casually placed his drink on the table behind him.

E22 had old-fashioned emergency lights. It had no strobes, no light strips, just a standard light bar and large red "pancakes" on the corners of the box. Carson turned the headlights and ignition off but didn't take the time to cut the pancakes. The engine died, and in the silence, the slow, gentle "tick, tick" of the pancake relays counted off the seconds.

He climbed out, slammed the door behind him, and walked to the front corner of the rig.

O'Malley spoke first. "I *know* you didn't just pull that ice cream truck into my fire station."

"Yeah, I did," Carson said, the red lights beaming intermittently into various corners of the garage. He jerked his thumb toward Rader and said, "I thought you might want to buy something for the little boy."

Mark thrust his jaw forward. "What the hell are you doing here, Carson?"

"Funny you should ask, Mark. You see, we've been having engine problems with our ice cream truck lately, and judging by this piece of paper," Carson uncrumpled the tally sheet in front of them, "I think you guys might know a thing or two about what's causing it."

Carson directed his comment at Mark. O'Malley glanced over at his young protégé. Mark Rader looked down for a second then back at Carson. "I don't know what the hell you're talking about, Carson."

"You never seem to know what the hell I'm talking about, Mark!"

"Hey, I don't see what the problem is, Carson. There are far more fire engines on that piece of paper than there are ambulances."

"You're a real asshole, Mark," Carson said. "You could have killed that girl."

"No, we saved her—remember?"

Carson could tell that O'Malley was genuinely in the dark, and he decided to bring him further into the light. "O'Malley, did you know Mark called your daughter some pretty bad names today?"

Rader's eyes grew wide in fear and anger.

O'Malley's face darted in Mark's direction. "What really happened over there, Mark?"

"He's exaggerating. We were just arguing, that's all."

"You might want to check into that, O'Malley," Carson said. "That's not how Katie tells it."

Carson stood in front of the door that opened into the hallway leading to the deputy chief's office. Through the glass pane, he saw the lights go out inside the office and the chief's shadow emerge in the corridor. The silhouette of a figure turned to lock the office door, then strode toward Carson, his bald head and eyes lit only by the occasional red flash of the pancakes. There was anger there that bordered on rage.

Just as O'Malley turned to have a serious conversation with Rader, Deputy Chief Killion stepped into the garage, closed the door behind him, and faced Carson. When not illuminated by the red lights, his face was dark. The orange tip of a cigarette moved faintly as he spoke.

"Carson Treffer," he said in a cool, callous voice. He made no effort to hide his accent now, pronouncing Carson's name like "Treffa."

The orange glow of the cigarette grew brighter as he inhaled. Carson did not respond.

"Mr. Treffer, it's good to see you on this wonderful day. Please don't tell me you've come here looking for a job." He chuckled, as did several others.

"Actually, Lou," Carson emphasized his first name, "at one point, I had planned on doing that very thing."

A red flash illuminated the deputy's face, and Carson saw his eyes narrow.

"But that's the thing, Lou, I don't feel like I can do that now. I don't think I could ever work for you, or O'Malley or with any of your thugs like Rader or Alvarez or Johnson."

"Well, Mr. Treffer, I don't think you have to worry about that. I wouldn't offer you a job if my life depended—"

"Let me finish," Carson interrupted. "I could *never* work for you after you and your co-conspirators went into my friend's apartment and assaulted two of my best friends when they never did *anything* to you!"

For a few seconds, the only sound in the garage was the "click, click" of E22's lights. Killion crossed his arms, his face growing angrier in the flashes. "You say they never did anything to me, Treffer? Oh, I think they did. Like you and all your Eastern buddies, they had a tendency to stick their noses into other people's business, always twisting their way into other lives just to make themselves look good. There is *nothing,* and I mean *nothing,* that I hate more than people who vilify others to make themselves look good. Your little weasel of a friend had *no* business sticking his nose in *my* life!"

"That's the thing, chief," Carson said, "people do have that right when people are getting hurt."

The chief's hand shot up to point at Carson. "Don't *tell* me about hurting others, Treffer! She's my wife, and she's mine to protect! Not yours, and sure as hell not your friend's!"

"That's where we have a problem, Lou," Carson said. "I'm making it my business, and if I get nothing else accomplished this night, I'm taking Lynda outta here and I'm going to tell the whole world how you treat her."

Quietly, in the background, other cars began to arrive. Carson looked around the cavernous engine bay to size up who was there. Of course there was Killion, O'Malley, and Rader. On an engine to his right sat Manny Alvarez, Jeff Petrolak, Tyrone, and his former pupil, Brent. At the table in the back corner sat Sheila, Nathan Tompkins, and their friends from Engine Two, Marty and Joe. Phil Johnson, from Truck One, the one most suspected of hitting Harvey Miller, sat on top of the truck to his left and looked down on Carson with a sinister smile. A few others mingled around just outside in the dark or behind Carson, but he couldn't discern who they were.

The deputy chief took two more steps toward Carson, his face emerging into the light, and began to yell. "Don't you fuckin' talk to me about what's mine! I take care of what's mine! Haven't you noticed that? Look around you, Treffer! Who took care of his people tonight?"

"These aren't your people, Lou. They're just a means to an end for you. All you want is power and a department of your own. They really belong to the chief, and one of the most despicable things you've done is take advantage of that poor man."

"Shut the fuck up, Carson! You don't know what you're talking about. This place is my home now and these are my people, and I do more to take care of them than the chief ever did."

Carson stared at him, saying nothing more. The deputy chief moved slowly in his direction.

"Yeah! That's what I said. *I* took care of *my* people!"

Carson glowered at Killion, his chin cocked low, his arms in taut, curved arcs.

"Maybe that's the difference between me and people like you," the deputy said, pointing straight at Carson's neck. "I'm willing to fight for my people! Don't you see that? That's all I'm doing here. I've got my fire department, and I've got my family, my house, my friends, and everything I love because I *fight* for them! And yes, that means if somebody gets in the way, they're probably gonna get hurt."

Killion was only a few feet from Carson, and Carson spoke for the first time in a minute. "Lou, that's the thing. I'm willing to fight for what's mine too, and I would have fought more if I had been allowed. But there's a difference between me and you. I don't use crooked politics to get my way. I don't attack innocent reporters when they're taking pictures. You may feel like you've won, but you haven't. When I look back at everything I've done, I don't regret one thing.

"You see, Lou, I feel like I have won because I can look back at all this and know that, unlike you, I always did the right thing. The one consolation I have right now is the knowledge that when I take Lynda outta here, you'll be lying in your bed alone tonight, wracked by guilt and insecurity, knowing that you didn't win one damn thing."

Chief Killion cocked his right arm and let it fly straight into Carson's face. Carson didn't duck and took the blow squarely on the jaw. He took one step back and gently touched the blood forming on his lip. He looked up at the deputy chief and said, "Is that what you do to your wife every time she leaves you?"

Killion was a ball of rage, rushing headlong into Carson's abdomen, driving him several steps back before crushing him against the ambulance. He pelted Carson in the stomach and once more in the face. Then Carson struck back. He kneed the chief in the stomach and pushed him away. He brought his own elbow and forearm far over his head before crashing his fist down on the deputy's face. Within seconds, the room was a tangled fight.

O'Malley and Rader came toward Carson, but Carson used Killion's body as a shield, shoving him toward the onrushers, which slammed O'Malley and Rader against E22.

O'Malley grabbed one of the wooden chairs from the table and swung at Carson. Rather than hitting Carson, its force was broken up by Tyrone, who had come from behind Truck One to intervene. The chair broke on Tyrone's back as he tried to protect Carson. Tyrone turned around to face O'Malley's fury as other firefighters appeared from all sides, giving little sign as to who they were coming after. Leslie's boyfriend, Lance, appeared from outside, and Nathan, Joe and Marty ran into the fray in the center of the garage, where punches were being thrown in close proximity, and allies were inadvertently struck because no one was sure who their allies were.

After being crushed by the chief, Mark Rader followed O'Malley's lead and picked up chairs to strike unsuspecting heads from the periphery of the fray. Carson fought with nearly nameless faces, trying to make his way toward the deputy chief. Joe wrestled with Killion, trying to calm him down, but all he did was make the man more furious. Nathan entered and wrapped his arms around Killion in a futile attempt to de-escalate the fight.

"Everyone stop!" Nathan yelled, but he was barely heard, and no one paid attention.

Without warning, Phil Johnson wrapped Carson from behind. He pinned Carson's arms behind him while Manny Alvarez punched Carson in the face. Carson pushed back with one of his boots on Manny's chest, and Marty stepped in with a blow to the side of Alvarez's face. More bodies joined the fight until Carson could barely move or see what he was doing. The brawl resembled a stationary human stampede, where one ran a greater risk of being crushed than battered.

Suddenly free because of Marty's intervention, Carson pressed toward Lou Killion, who had nearly freed himself from his own firemen. But Alvarez and Johnson fought Marty off and came at Carson again. The two grabbed him from the sides and pinned his arms so tight, his elbows touched. Rader realized a golden opportunity, and lacking any more chairs, he jabbed Carson in the stomach.

Carson doubled over in pain, still gripped by Johnson and Alvarez on either side, then made a quick effort to stand. As he did, Mark Rader placed his left hand on Carson's chest and cocked his arm back to throw a punch. Before he could release, however, a chair appeared over his head and crashed down on him, knocking him to the floor. There stood Katie with the chair still in her hands. A blow landed on Alvarez from the side, and Carson saw Eric shaking his hand in pain.

Phil Johnson grabbed Eric with his right arm, still holding Carson with his left. With both of Phil's arms occupied, Katie reared back and landed a fist in his face so hard that Carson and Eric stood shocked for more than a second. Manny's head whipped backward, a small gash opened over his eye.

"That one's for Harvey Miller," Katie said.

Johnson didn't know what to do with Katie at first, so he released Carson to push her away. Both Eric and Carson were free, however, and Eric got him with a left jab and a solid back-swing with the right.

Carson, now in a lot of pain, looked down and saw blood on his shirt and jeans. Once he saw that Eric and Katie were fine, he desperately tried to find the deputy chief, who had disappeared. Carson spied him closing the door behind him as he went down the passageway toward his office. Killion clearly recognized the need to extricate both himself and Lynda from the situation before things got more out of hand. By now, he had seen the bystanders, some of them reporters.

Carson pressed between two bodies, keeping his eyes focused on the ground while elbows struck him forcefully upside the head. His nose bled. Finding himself on the edge of the melee, he stood up just in time to face Rader poised with another chair over his shoulder. Rader brought the chair down with all his might before it stopped motionless in Carson's grip. For a brief second their eyes met. Then Carson reared back and landed a haymaker on Rader's face. His head snapped back like an antenna hitting a sign. Carson forced Mark to his knees by leveraging his wrist. He considered giving him the one-two, but Mark's nose was bleeding and Carson saw that he'd been beat. He let him go.

As the others continued to struggle, Carson slipped unnoticed into the passageway leading to the deputy chief's office. It was dark, darker than normal as all the lights in the chief's office were out save for a reading lamp on the desk. Carson sensed the danger, knew that the office was unsafe, but advanced purposefully despite the quivering sensation in his heart.

He reached the door and saw in the light of the desk lamp the lower half of Killion's body speed toward his desk. Carson tested the knob. It was locked. Without hesitation, he placed his hand in one of the rubber boots lining the passageway and smashed the glass out of the window. He reached in, turned the handle and opened the door.

"You're breaking and entering, Carson," the deputy chief said, leaning on his desk, the lamp showing only his body below the chest. He reached down and opened a drawer, then placed a bloody hand back on the desk. "People get hurt doing stuff like that."

Carson's eyes adjusted to the darkness. He saw Lynda sitting on a couch to his left. She sat with her face in her hands, quietly sobbing. Then he looked back at Killion. Now he could see faint patches of light reflecting off the beads of sweat on his smooth, bare head, but his eyes were dark.

"I'm not here to hurt anybody, Lou," Carson said. "I'm here to get Lynda and leave, and that's it."

"You know I won't let you do that."

"I know."

"Then what are you really here for, Carson?"

Carson mulled the question over in his mind, and a feeling of profound sadness came over him. "It's complicated, Lou. It's just something I have to do, and I if I can help someone in the process, then so much the better."

The chief was silent. Carson turned to Lynda and reached out to her. "Lynda," he said. She looked up for the first time. "Let's leave."

Carson could see how the day's events had worn her to a semi-catatonic state. She moved like a compliant robot. She looked at Carson with desperate eyes, an appearance of humanity on an otherwise lifeless face. Carson felt he was moving in slow motion.

Like Lynda, he had succumbed to the dictates of another; he went through the motions fate asked of him.

"Leave her here, Treffer," the deputy chief said. "She doesn't want to leave me; she said so herself."

Lynda took Carson's hand, holding it tightly, and the two stepped toward the door.

"Lynda, don't leave," the deputy said, his voice tense with desperation.

Opening the door, Carson looked at Lynda and said, "You're all right now. It'll all be over soon. Just keep walking. This will all be a bad dream soon."

"Carson," Lou Killion said. For the first time it sounded like the chief was pleading with him. "You know I can't let you do this."

Lynda and Carson passed through the shattered door, closing it behind them. Carson heard the chief fumbling in his desk, then the sound of a drawer closing. He suddenly remembered a time when he was a boy, running through the forest to get home because he imagined he was followed by a wolf. The faster he ran, the more real the wolf became in his mind. He thought he heard twigs snapping behind him. He focused on the porch light and ran and ran until he reached the light, never once turning to see if the wolf really existed.

The wolf was here again. Carson remembered to focus on the light ahead of him—this time, the garage—where he could see the faces of friends and foes who were now breaking off from the fight. Police had arrived. The combatants leaned against trucks and nursed their wounds. Carson saw Eric and Katie, and he wanted to talk to them one more time. He found himself wishing, praying earnestly, to talk to them one more time. Just a few more steps.

It was not meant to be.

"Carson." Killion's voice came from very close behind. The wolf was real. So was the distinct double click of a cocking revolver.

"Carson!"

He would not see his friends again, and that saddened him more than anything.

The blast was louder and more horrifying than he had expected. Before he felt any pain, he saw the faces in the garage turn toward him. He saw the gloom in their faces, the guilt from the sudden realization that their petty little war had gotten out of hand, the fear in their faces, the hope that the gunshot was a warning. It wasn't. A piercing sensation radiated from his abdomen. Carson went down on one knee as the pain overwhelmed his entire body. Lynda screamed and crouched over him. Carson rolled forward onto his shoulder. A small army of legs rushed in from the garage. There was a great deal of yelling, some talking, and a struggle. Then Eric's voice: "Carson! Carson!" Eric yelled to someone else, "Get the medical bags!"

The piercing was supplanted by a burning, like a hot coal had been sewn into Carson's abdomen. He instinctively held his palm over the hole on the right side of his stomach. The chief was yelling, fighting. "Lynda! Lynda! I never want to lose you; can't you see that?" His voiced trailed off as others dragged him away. Carson felt he couldn't take the burning much longer. He grew acutely dizzy. He thought of his dad. Darkness closed in like a tunnel. The concrete floor felt cool on his cheek, then everything went dark.

34.

Eric was right. At the end of the day, there were not enough votes to sway the referendum. Only 46 percent of voters supported it. One thing Eric never predicted, however, was the fact that the referendum itself was only a footnote in the headlines.

As predicted, both Commissioner McDaniels and Chairman Moscatelli were ousted. Some editorials ascribed it to the "city hall attitude" that had gripped county politics over the past few years. They had gotten their way with the ambulance issue, but in the end, it cost them their careers. Instead, a crippled fire department, newly on the front pages of scandal, was left to sort through its mess and prepare itself to provide Emergency Medical Services to an entire county in less than two months.

The morning after, people in Nebraska woke up to the following front page banner: "Eastern Medic Shot by Deputy Fire Chief While Rescuing Wife." The article described in eyewitness detail most of the events that led to the fight, the brawl itself, the actions Carson took to rescue Lynda and, of course, the shooting itself. It described how Eastern and fire department medics worked together to transport him to the hospital in the fire department's Medical Attack Vehicle, and their desperate attempts to save his life.

It was a shock to the city, and no one, including Carson, was left without blame. However, the courage showed by Carson, and his moral conviction, made him a hero in the eyes of most everyone who read the article. In fact, he became a legend that night. Within days, reporters had researched the details of his life. Articles sharing his biography told of his honorable military career, his attempts to run the farm after the death of his father, and his distinguished service as a Lincoln paramedic, and the lives he had saved. The call with the girl and her mother on Twenty-seventh and "O" was rehashed again, but this time they focused on the selfless bravery of Carson, and the fact that Emily was alive and healthy and doing well in school, none of which would have happened without Carson. It was, the newspapers said, only one of many instances in which Carson had saved a life.

Another man whose life was forever changed by November 7 was Deputy Chief Lou Killion. Not only had he shot Carson, but the act also broke open the story about him forcefully entering the home of a young lady who was trying to protect a battered wife. That information alone would have ended his career, but that was the least of his worries. Chief Lou Killion was in jail awaiting trial for several very serious charges.

As is often the case, unfortunate events lead to fortunate effects. Lynda Killion and her parents moved back to New York without having to keep her whereabouts unknown. An even greater blessing, however, was the fact that she immediately took custody of the children with no resistance from the legal system. She would safely retain custody forever.

Chief Jack Winkenwerder probably advanced another year in age when he received several calls in the middle of the night. He went to the hospital to see what had become of Carson, then was admitted for chest pain. He was diagnosed with anxiety only and the first thing he did the next day was submit his resignation to the county commissioner who accepted it as one of his last acts in office.

Jon Carver, the Truck One Captain, became interim chief, and the first thing he did to rescue his public relations nightmare was to fire Mark Rader. His head rolled in the growing line of scapegoats. Unlike Rader, O'Malley did not go to Katie's apartment and his name therefore escaped the news.

Eric read all the newspaper articles the next morning while waiting in Lincoln General Hospital. It had been a long, emotional night to say the least. Awake all night, he watched and waited, gave reports to the police, and took calls from Dave, Hank and other Eastern folks. Many of them had come to the hospital. Some had left, but the majority remained in the waiting room just down the hall. Eric had half-expected someone from Carson's family to call, but no one ever did. Even now, Carson's history remained somewhat hidden in the mists of time and it was clear that it would always be that way. Finally, well into morning, Eric had fallen asleep in the unbearably uncomfortable visitor chair at the foot of the bed.

He didn't know how long he'd been asleep when he heard his name.

"Eric." It was little more than a whisper. "Eric." It was a little louder now. "Are you awake?"

Eric opened his eyes and raised his head from the wall where it had been resting. He looked at the hospital bed in front of him. There was Carson reclining in the bed, his head leaning gently on the pillow, the newspaper laid out on his lap.

"Carson, did you say something?" he whispered.

"Can I have some water?"

Eric chuckled quietly to himself. "I don't think you're allowed to yet. Do you want me to get the nurse?"

"Cut the shit, Eric; I'm parched."

Eric looked around, got a plastic cup of water and a straw from the sink, and held it to Carson's mouth. After several sips, Carson sighed and closed his eyes.

"Eric, talk to me," Carson said. "What's my prognosis?"

"It's good." Eric was glad he didn't have to lie. "You have no major vascular injury, thank God. But I have to tell you that you lost your right kidney. You have a closed drain in your liver, and they're watching that, but they haven't removed any of it yet."

Carson delicately lifted his head from the pillow and looked down at the newspaper. He sighed deeply.

"Eric, that was an amazing thing you did."

"What's that?"

"You and Katie both. Katie took Lynda in and helped her all that time when she had nothing to gain from it. You helped her do that, and you tried to protect them."

Of all the amazing heroics reported in the newspaper spread before him, Eric was amazed that Carson focused on this. He said nothing about the fight, about the good firefighters stopping the deputy chief, of Katie joining the fight, of the large group working to save Carson's life, or even Carson's own actions. Just this.

"To the day I die," Carson said, "I'll always remember what you guys did for Lynda. You're a very selfless person, Eric—you and Katie both."

Eric turned and looked out the window at the beautiful view from the eleventh floor. He could see for miles, all the way to downtown and the capital building. The leaves that remained on the trees were of various colors, and Lincoln looked like the wonderful town Eric knew her to be. He had looked out this same window the night before and wondered if Carson would die. But his surgery went well. He would live to fight another day.

"Carson," Eric said, "you don't understand."

"What's that?"

"We've learned to be selfless by watching you every day on every single call."

Carson's eyebrows furrowed in deep thought. After a minute, he leaned his head back and relaxed. Eric wondered what he was thinking, but Carson was silent, and soon Eric could tell he was asleep.

Two weeks passed quickly for Eric. Every day was a new saga, a new newspaper article, a new editorial, a new hire, and a new resignation. The fact that Eric knew these were his last days at Eastern Ambulance only served to accelerate the end.

The fire department scrambled to organize. Several Eastern Ambulance paramedics were hired. It was only logical since they had the experience. As he had originally planned, Carson decided to place an application with the fire department once he had recovered. Nathan Tompkins had been made Deputy Chief of EMS and did not hesitate to bring him onboard. He also hired Leslie, Tim, and eleven others. These individuals were sent to intensive firefighter training because even the paramedics had to be ready to fight fires. Carson actually enjoyed the training and wondered why he had not done something like that sooner.

*   *   *

Soon, that year and everything else about Eastern Ambulance faded away. One day, Eric woke up, and it was gone. He did not apply to work for the fire department. The spring semester started on the tenth, and he enrolled full-time. He had catching up to do, but it would not take long. The volume of studies occupied his mind quickly, but in the morning when he drove to class, he occasionally pulled over for a fire engine or a bright new ambulance. He glanced into the cabs, looking for people he knew. He often recognized them, but they never saw him. He was just another car trying to get out of their way.

Carson became a cornerstone in the fire department, and his reputation never died. The new guys knew who he was. They gave him space in the hallways and the locker room. He never became a Union President (Sheila did), but anything Carson said was taken as law. Most of the older guys, some of whom still hated him, and all of the newer ones understood that Carson was the stone upon which the old fire department had fallen. From those ruins, a new Lancaster County Fire Department had risen and fulfilled its role as the bulwark of integrity in the city.

Occasionally, Carson envied Eric. While Eric moved onward with Katie and his medical career, Carson plugged on in his role as a glorified taxi driver, but they all remained close friends. Eventually, both Eric and Katie became doctors, both called Dr. Wright. Carson never forgot what they did for Lynda, nor what Eric said to him that day in the hospital. Carson's thoughts about people had changed, but his general outlook on his own life had not, and his newest partner, Chris, didn't quite understand those feelings.

This night, they rescued a woman in full cardiac arrest in front of her family on the living room floor. It was another code-save for the year, but it was too early to tell how much brain damage she had suffered. Finishing up the call sheet, Carson prayed that she would fully recover, but he didn't have a lot of faith. He returned to the garage where he found Chris placing new sheets on the cot.

"Chris," Carson said, "you think she'll turn out all right?"

"I don't know, Carson. No one was doing CPR when we got there. It's hard to say."

"Yeah, I just like to think we did the right thing."

"Carson, you worry about that stuff too much. You've got to do what I do. Remember that it's just a job, and this is how we get paid."

Carson climbed into the driver seat of the large, powerful ambulance. Chris jumped in the other side and slammed his door.

"Chris, I've got a question for you?"

"Oh, great."

"Just be honest with me. Did you see a man smoking in the corner of the garage when I first came out?"

Chris, his face pale, looked at Carson. "You're scaring me again,

Carson."

"Just answer the question."

Chris looked in the mirror. "No, I didn't see anyone."

"That's all I wanted to know," Carson said. Chris raised his eyebrows and shook his head.

The emergency tones sounded, and the dispatcher's voice rang out, "Medic One, Engine One. Zone Sixty-one. Memorial Drive near Everett Street. Antelope Park. A man passed out on a park bench."

"Oh my God," Chris said, "another drunk. Why can't people learn to take care of themselves?" He pounded the armrest. "I'm never gonna get lunch."

Carson sighed and pursed his lips. He found himself nearly agreeing with Chris but held his thoughts in check. He performed a small ritual he always resorted to when he felt calluses growing around his heart. At those times, Carson remembered a piece of paper attached to his sun visor. On the surface, the city of Lincoln glistened like a pearl in the heart of America, but as in every city, there is a dark underbelly seen only by an unlucky few—the social workers, the firemen, the police, and the medics. Carson observed that far too often children suffered in a world with parents who didn't care for them. His heart broke at the sadness, at the constant sufferers he saw over and over, beaten by their husbands, ravaged by disease, or enslaved by addiction.

Today, he flipped the visor down and looked at the piece of paper—a faded drawing. There, in crayon, were three medics, a boy in a wheelchair and an ambulance with wings. It made him quietly close his eyes and focus. When he opened them again, he looked in the mirror toward the dark corner of the garage. The smoking man was gone, but Carson knew that he would be back. Rather than waiting for him to return, Carson decided that today, like everyday, he would go looking for him. Then he cranked the engine to a loud roar, switched on the lights and sirens, and flew off into the darkness of the city.

CPSIA information can be obtained
at www.ICGtesting.com
Printed in the USA
LVOW04s0816271116
514619LV00023B/1819/P